The Demi-heir took two more steps toward the brok [barcode obscures text] clearly the thing [barcode obscures text] at too closely. [barcode obscures text] ft-hand steering [barcode obscures text] otected, had been [barcode obscures text] e other sledge's drag. A drag-brake weighed almost a ton, it had to be that heavy to hold the massive sledge. . . . Rohin gave a choked cry and turned away, retching. Ixora wailed aloud.

The beat of rotors was much louder now, and the powerful headlights of the ambulances were already on us.

A young man in racing clothes was struggling across the track toward us, the tattered remains of a Brandr scarf fluttering from his shoulder. He didn't seem to be much hurt, and I saw Anath scowl.

"The draglines broke," the young man said, and I realized he must be Fen Erling, driver of the other team. "I couldn't do anything."

Anath's scowl deepened, but then Ixora exploded in my arms, fighting to get at the other driver. Off-worlder or not, it took all my strength to hold her.

"Liar!" she shrieked. "You did it on purpose, you did it on purpose, you killed my people!"

THE KINDLY ONES

MELISSA SCOTT

BAEN BOOKS

THE KINDLY ONES

Copyright © 1987 by Melissa Scott

A Baen Books Original

Baen Publishing Enterprises
260 Fifth Avenue
New York, N.Y. 10001

Quotations from *The Eumenides* derive from Aeschylus, *The Oresteia*, translated by Richmond Lathmore, University of Chicago Press, 1953.

First printing, September 1987

ISBN: 0-671-65351-2

Cover art by Gary Ruddell

Printed in the United States of America

Distributed by
SIMON & SCHUSTER
1230 Avenue of the Americas
New York, N.Y. 10020

THE KINDLY ONES

MELISSA SCOTT

Excerpted from the Standard Planetary Register, *20th edition revised, pub/protect date CS 1425.201 PoDr. Used by the kind permission of the Conglomerate Records Office, Baldur.*

ORESTES (Oresteian, Oresteians): SEE ALSO ELECTRA, Iphigenia. Larger of two inhabited moons of Agamemnon, planet of Atreus, Rimsector Catalogue listing 47001.q. CPC # 7E7/H9SX3/EE3B(2)*. Surface gravity = 0.81 Earth. Astronomical year = 27 standard years; local year = (Conglomerate) standard year. Astronomical day = 142.32 standard hours; local day = 24 local hours/ 23.72 standard hours. Chronometric correction (standard) ATS.993/02. Volcanically active on 24-day cycle; travellers are advised to heed local Geo/Met bulletins. Climate: Orestes is officially classified as a cold planet, with average temperatures from 5 to 10 degrees Celsius.

Settled 41 AnDr by G/SS *Home Rule*, originally intended for Agni (qv); first Conglomerate contact 993 PoDr, full Conglomerate membership 1001 PoDr. No indigenous intelligent life. Primary cities: Destiny (dos 41 AnDr, starport, riverport); Madelgar (dos 38 AnDr, starport, riverport). Primary export products: minerals (industrials, gems); woolens (luxury yarns, luxury fabrics, hand-worked clothing); furs (atossa); fish products (leva, boi-boi). Government: Orestes and Electra are governed through five overarching Kinships (Axtell, Brandr, Fyfe, Halex, and Orillon) through the Kinship Council and the Ship's Council, which supervise city, town, guild/ factory, and farmstead government. Each Kinship is responsible for one Mandate, a geographical as well as governmental unit. Language Group: Ortho-urban (index of variation RS6.0095).

Orestes/Electra are most noted for the extremely strict code of honor that defines all social relations on both worlds. Breaches of code are punished by "social death"—the offender is declared legally dead and is allowed no further contact with (legally) living beings. This code is most strictly enforced in the non-urban areas; visitors are advised that the non-urban Mandates (Axtell, Fyfe) have been declared yellow travel zones by the Travellers' Advisory Council, and should consult the appropriate TAC publications.

For more detailed descriptions of Orestes and Electra, please consult CRO publications: RSD993.501.F22, *Descriptive Index Six: Worlds of Rimsector Seven;* PDP 168847.228.V5, *Planetary Survey Pamphlets, Third Series: Orestes/Electra;* and TAC publication RS4. 7001.7E7, *City and Necropolis.*

ELECTRA (Electran, Electrans; also Oresteian, Oresteians): SEE ALSO ORESTES. Smaller of two inhabited moons of Agamemnon, planet of Atreus, Rimsector Catalogue listing 47001.q. CPC # 7E7/T8VX3/EF3B (2/2)*. Surface gravity = 0.78 Earth. Astronomical year = 27 standard years; local year = (Conglomerate) standard year. Astronomical day = 285.04 standard hours; local day = 24 local hours/ 23.75 standard hours. Chronometric correction (standard) ATS.993/021. Marginal volcanic activity on 24-day cycle; travellers are advised to be aware of local Geo/Met bulletins. Climate: Electra is officially classified as a cold planet, with average temperatures from −5 to 1 degrees Celsius. Travellers are strongly advised to heed local Geo/Met Office's weather bulletins.

Settled 2 AnDr by Orillon Kinship of Orestes (qv), as part of a feud settlement. First Conglomerate contact 993 PoDr, full Conglomerate membership 1001 PoDr, with Orestes. Electra is considered a province of Orestes (qv). No indigenous animal life above class III. Primary city: Glittermark (dos 2 AnDr, starport, iceport). Primary export products: minerals (industrials); service personnel. Government: Electra is considered a part of the Oresteian Kinship system (SEE ALSO ORESTES), and the moon in its entirety is the Orillon Mandate. Language Group: Ortho-urban (index of variation RS6.0095).

Electra is a part of the Oresteian culture, and therefore, its people follow the extremely strict Oresteian code of honor. Breaches of code are punished by "social death"—the offender is declared legally dead and is allowed no further contact with any "living" being. Though this code is not as strictly enforced as it is in the rural Mandates of Orestes, travellers are still advised to familiarize themselves with the conventions of the code before arrival.

For more detailed descriptions of Orestes and Electra, please consult CRO publications: RSD993.501.F22, *Descriptive Index Six; Worlds of Rimsector Seven;* and PDP 168847. 228.V5, *Planetary Survey Pamphlets, Third Series: Orestes/Electra.*

We hold we are straight and just. If a man
can spread his hands and show they are clean,
no wrath of ours shall lurk for him.
Unscathed he walks through his life time.
—Aeschylus, *The Eumenides*, 312–315

Prologue: Captain Leith Moraghan (Peacekeeper Drone Command, retired)

Moraghan dreamed she had two good arms again, and the bunk beneath her was the couch of a SuperWasp fighter, the latest in a long series of in-atmosphere workhorses. She was too old to fly the tricky little ships—too old at twenty to handle the demanding link of computer, ship, and pilot—but nevertheless, there she was, strapped into the crowded cockpit. She brought it down easy, holding her breath, jockeying the machine through the thickening air toward the desert field. Then, out of nowhere, came a gust of wind, tilting the unstable ship. She froze for an instant, and the ship spun out of control, computers no longer able to compensate. She fought it, cursing at the top of her lungs, wrestling the stubborn controls as the world spiraled around her, and pulled it out too late. As always, she woke before the crash.

She lay there for an instant, breathing heavily, staring up through the darkness at the bulkhead above her. Gradually, her heartbeat slowed, and she reached deliberately for her numb left arm, running the fingers of her right hand along the glove that hid the ugly scars. The doctors had done their best, but they had not been able to compensate for all the nerve damage. They had told her instead that she was lucky to have gotten off so lightly, and released her from the Drone Command. The Peacekeepers took care of their own, of course, as she'd known they would. Still, there was no place for her in active service, and she did not want a desk job with one of the auxiliary forces, Customs, or the Trade Board. That left only the mailships: undemanding, unrewarding work, but the closest approximation of Peacekeeper service she could hope to find. In the eight years since the accident, she had worked her way up to command of one of the smaller mailships on a six-week loop run of moderate importance, but she'd found nothing to replace the satisfaction of her six years in the Drone Command. Annoyed now, she swung herself out of the bunk, shaking away the sense of futility. She was doing something useful, at least; she couldn't ask for more.

After she'd showered, washing away the last residue of the dream, and dressed, she was able to switch on her console and study the figures in the work screen with a certain satisfaction. Her senior pilot, Darah Sabas, had flipped the mailship out of Drive with .5 *li* of the system buoy, for once putting them on the right side of the system for their approach. A single microjump had brought *Pipe Major* up to the buoy, in position for the five-day, no-drive run to the second buoy that marked the edge of the Oresteian rings. Or should that be the Agamemnonian rings? Moraghan wondered idly. They belonged to the planet, properly speaking, not to the inhabited moons. Whatever you called them, though, they were a nuisance, and she was grateful she did not have to navigate their complexities on her own.

A yellow light flashed on the intercom panel. Sighing, Moraghan hit the freeze button and folded back the workscreen, then touched the answer key.

"Captain here." She kept her voice even, trying not to anticipate the worst. Mailships' crews were always an iffy lot, chosen as they were from Peacekeeper pensioners either too old or too badly damaged for more active service, but the junior pilot, who had the watch, was worse than most. He had been shot up in the fighting off Thetis/Arreaias, and no matter what the psych docs said, Moraghan, thought it was far too soon to let the kid handle a ship again. Of course, she added with a bitter grin, eight years ago I might've had the patience to work through it with him, too, but not now.

"B-bridge." Tham's slight stammer was unmistakable. "D-do you want me to bounce-cast through the b-buoy, sir, or shall I use our own set?"

"Are we still in range?" Moraghan asked, as patiently as she could.

There was a moment's pause—Moraghan could almost see the boy checking his figures for the hundredth time— and then Tham answered, "Yes, s-sir."

"Bounce it, then, and keep Askel happy," Moraghan answered. Routing the D-com signal through the buoy's repeaters would significantly reduce the wear on *Pipe Major's* own crystals, and the mailship's engineer was a notorious crystal miser, but Tham hardly seemed to notice the pleasantry.

"Yes, s-sir. Shall I p-patch it into your cabin when I've m-made the connection?"

"Do that," Moraghan said, and watched the lights flicker busily across the communications pad. At least he was quick enough to obey commands, even if he didn't seem capable of independent action yet. The last light flashed yellow and the air filled with the hollow hiss of the channel search. Moraghan winced, and hastily turned down the volume. It would take a few minutes for Tham to find the buoy and slave its powerful transmitter to the ship's system. The captain turned her mind away, staring at the viewscreen that filled a third of the status board backing the console. It showed the view from one of the bow cameras, real-light, unenhanced: a starfield, no different from a hundred others, millions of brilliant lights against a velvet background, without even a nebula to give it color. One blue-white light showed brighter and fractionally larger than the rest: Atreus, the system primary. The planets were indistinguishable at this distance.

Idly, Moraghan hit a function switch at the top of her keyboard, shifting from the workscreen's limited system to the main computer, then typed in the string of commands that searched the memory banks for one particular picture. The item appeared almost at once, fading into coherence on the main screen. This was her favorite view of

Orestes, a picture of the system taken just outside the orbit of the inner buoy. Agamemnon was three-quarters full, its blue-white bulk, banded here and there with pale greys and greener blues, dominating the screen. Two of the three moons were clearly visible, Orestes itself dark against the planet's brilliance, while frozen Electra showed a distinct white disk against the dim stars. Iphigenia, the third and smallest moon, was out of sight behind Agamemnon. The planet's rings—not true rings, either, but an unstable, shifting mass of sub-planetary debris—lay invisible between the inner moons.

Moraghan sighed. Before the accident—unconsciously, almost, she rubbed at the thickened wrist beneath the disguising, shoulder-length glove, avoiding the clumsy, crooked fingers—she would have welcomed the challenge of taking a ship as large and as slow as *Pipe Major* into the rings. Now it was physically impossible, and she did not know if she was entirely sorry to be freed of the compulsion to prove herself to herself. It was enough to watch and admire—and cringe, occasionally—while the Oresteian Port Authority pilots brought the ship into the system.

A chime sounded softly in the communications pad, and the warning light turned green. Tham had linked ship's systems to the buoy, and a channel was open. The Port Authority in Destiny, Orestes' largest city and principal spaceport, should answer momentarily. Moraghan eased up the volume on the D-com channel just as Tham announced, "C-captain, the Destiny harbormaster's on line."

"Thank you, Idris, that'll be all." Moraghan switched off the in-ships channel. "Greetings, Harbormaster Rhawn."

"Greetings to you, *Pipe Major*. You're ahead of schedule." Oslac Rhawn's voice was as deep and jovial as ever, the singing Oresteian accent subdued through long contact with the off-worlders who passed through Destiny. "What can we do for you?"

"We'll need a pilot to bring us in-system, and that's about all," Moraghan answered.

"You'll be landing here at Destiny, then?" The harbormaster sounded more than a little bored by the routine question. There was another starport on Orestes—at Madelgar in the Brandr Mandate—and a third on Electra. Occasionally, the vagaries of *Pipe Major*'s cargo made it expedient to land at one of them rather than at Destiny, but that was a rare event.

"That's right," Moraghan answered. "You might want to warn the people in Madelgar to send a lighter, and the same for Glittermark, but I don't carry much for either."

"I'll pass that on," the harbormaster answered, with patent insincerity.

Moraghan sighed—she knew there was a long-standing hostility between Madelgar and Destiny, though she neither knew nor cared to know its cause—and said, more sharply than was entirely polite, "I'd appreciate it, if you would."

Oslac grunted. "What's your ETA?"

Moraghan glanced at her workscreen, confirming the figures. "We expect to reach the inner buoy in 118 standard hours. You'll have a pilot waiting?"

The harbormaster chuckled. "Wouldn't let you into the system without one, captain." Before Moraghan could decide if he was being malicious, Oslac continued, "And you're in luck, captain. The regular duty pilot's got Dark-leave, so you get your favorite *para*."

"Guil Tam'ne—ex-Tam'ne?" Moraghan asked, keeping her voice as pleasant as she could. She was not fluent in all the nuances of the Ortho-Urban dialect that was Orestes' common language, but she knew the difference between *para* and *para'*. Both could be contractions of *para'an*, outsider, but the first was bitter insult. "That'd be nice—she's the best pilot I've seen out of your office."

There was a momentary hesitation, and when Oslac answered, his tone was conciliatory. "That's right, captain. She'll be glad to hear your recommendation."

Moraghan grunted, annoyed with Oslac and with herself. Guil was hardly a part of *Pipe Major*'s crew. It wasn't Moraghan's job to protect her against groundside troubles, nor would Guil be likely to need her protection. "Thanks for the help, harbormaster."

"See you in 190 hours, with a customs team," Oslac retorted, and cut the connection.

Moraghan flicked the intercom key again. "Finished with the transmitter," she snapped, and switched off her circuit before Tham could acknowledge the order. She leaned back in her comfortable chair, watching the lights flicker from green to orange to standby blue as Tham shut down the transmitter. Guil Tam'ne—Guil ex-Tam'ne, Moraghan corrected herself, bitterly recalling the full formal phrase, *para'an* of Tam'ne in Electra—was the best of the Port Authority's pilots. It was perhaps a pity she was *para'an*—by her own choice, no longer a part of the bizarre Oresteian honor code—but it certainly made it easier to deal with Guil than with the other pilots, for whom the necessity of obeying the code outweighed all other considerations, including the sanity of the incoming ships' captains. . . .

Moraghan sighed again, the Peacekeeper training taking over. She was being unfair, and knew it. The Oresteian code had had a solid purpose—had probably saved the colonists, who had never intended to settle frigid Orestes. It had certainly meant the difference between life and death in the first forty years after the mutiny—the mutiny that must never be mentioned—that damaged the guidance computers and brought them not to Agni but to Agamemnon. But now, over fourteen hundred years after the Encounter and development of a human FTL drive, the code was clearly obsolete, and still fully enforced. I suppose, Moraghan thought, I should be grateful they've substituted "social death" for the real thing. I wonder if the ghosts are grateful?

She shook herself, refusing to consider it any further. Oslac Rhawn was a typical Port Authority bureaucrat, to be used and ignored. What really mattered was that Guil would be piloting *Pipe Major* through the rings, and that meant not only that Moraghan could relax during transit, but that she could probably persuade the pilot to join her in making the rounds of the Necropolis, Destiny's entertainment district. Like most worlds, Orestes—or at least Destiny and its Necropolis, the only part of Orestes Moraghan knew at all well—was much more fun in the company of a native guide. Guil had acted as escort for her half a dozen times before, and those were the visits Moraghan remembered best. She smiled to herself. Now, the only problem would be figuring out how to phrase the invitation. For some reason, it was always hardest asking: Guil offered no openings, no easy ways to bridge the silences. But once you'd managed it, Moraghan thought, it was always worth the effort.

She frowned then. It was surprising to realize how little she really knew about Guil, and how little of that knowledge had been give by direct statement. The pilot seemed to preserve a core of secrecy, an inner self that she revealed to no one. Maybe it was just part of being *para'an*, Moraghan thought. If you cut yourself off from all your kin, does it make it even harder to deal with total strangers? But no, Guil's occasional remarks about Electra made it clear she hadn't given up all contact with her relatives there. In fact. . . . Moraghan's frown deepened. She had asked, once, why Guil had chosen to become *para'an*. They had both been a little drunk, and for once, Guil had answered freely. She liked working as a tug pilot, she said, was better at that than at anything else, and there just weren't enough piloting jobs on Electra. Because of the union rules, the senior pilots took what jobs there were out of Glittermark, Electra's only port. On Orestes, members of the local Kinships took precedence at Destiny and at Madelgar, but there was enough traffic, especially at Destiny, to create a demand for pilots who could be available at any time. And that meant *para'anin*, who weren't bound by any Familial obligations. Becoming *para'an* had just been the easiest way to get a job, Guil had said, shrugging. Since then, she'd been good enough to work her way into the regular rotation, and still made extra money as a substitute.

Moraghan shook her head slowly. She did not for one moment believe it had been that simple a decision for Guil—if nothing else, the pilot had once said something about sending money home, and Moraghan knew how poor a world Electra was. Guil's relatives probably needed the income the pilot could provide. And even if it had been purely a matter of choosing the best way of getting the work she wanted, Moraghan thought, the emotional cost must've been high. There was the ceremony *para'anin* went through, *parachor*. Guil had never spoken of it, of course, but Moraghan had read about it in the Survey pamphlets that dealt with Orestes. To become *para'an*, you had to kill three of your own blood kin, to demonstrate the sincerity of your intentions. These days, the *parachor* was—mostly—ritual, the ceremonial beheading of three straw dummies. It was strange, though, Moraghan thought. She could not quite picture Guil swinging the great axe shown in the Survey pamphlet's photos, chopping up a gaudily dressed bundle of straw. But she had no trouble at all believing that the pilot could have killed her siblings.

She shook herself hard, and reached for the workscreen. She had been on the six-week mail run, Pippa to Orestes to Althjof, for four years now, and of all those worlds, only Orestes still held anything to intrigue her. There was something about the rigid honor code that touched a sympathetic chord in a woman who had been under military discipline since she was fourteen. Its customs were not always pleasant ones, but there was . . . something.

Chapter 1: Trey Maturin

It began, I suppose, at Per Tamarisk, toward the end of the calendar-summer. I had spent the last two calendar-weeks in the Tamar Range, a spur of the Prosperities, escorting the Patroclan survey team on a tour of the mining district, and now we were returning to the Halex Tower to report their preliminary findings to the Matriarch. The Patroclans, Dario Yan and Slade Orteja, of the engineering firm of Kassan and Cho, seemed pleased enough with their work: they huddled together in the back of the snow car, fingers busy on the keys of their lapboards as they cheerfully discussed possible solutions to the problems facing the Halex mines. I had stopped listening even before we left the mine hostel. The Patroclans habitually spoke in ellipses. Now, when they added their technical jargon to the half-sentences, it was as if they spoke another, foreign language. I looked away, staring out the small side window at the mountains around us.

For a small world—a large moon, really—Orestes had some fairly spectacular mountains—not merely the Prosperities here in the Halex Mandate, but the Greater Tolands and the Toland Hills in the Brandr Mandate, and the Spiderlegs on the unclaimed Far Continent. The Tamar

11

Range towered behind us, the rock showing reddish grey where the slope was too steep to hold the snows, but the central spine of the Prosperities shouldered up behind them, its peaks rising another three hundred meters above the tallest of the Tamars. Plumes of steam were visible against the dark blue of the sky, a massive cloud sitting above the Heartlight, a thinner feather drifting away from the Old Forge. Both volcanos seemed fairly quiet now, even though the moons would be in syzygy in four days, and the Geo/Met office in Destiny had already issued its standard "tremors and volcanic activity" warning. The miners at Tamar One, where we had spent the night—and at all the mines throughout the Prosperities, and across Orestes—had been working hard to bring out a last load of ore before the danger of earthquake closed the mines.

The snow car jerked as we reached the snowline, and the driver put down the little wheels. We bounced heavily across the rutted ground for a hundred meters, and then the car reached the metalled road, and settled to a steady swaying. The gleaming roofs of Per Tamarisk were already visible over the driver's shoulder. As the car negotiated the next switchback, still more of the town came into view. It was a typical railhead settlement, a collection of narrow two- and three-story towers clustered on the down side of the gentler slope that characterized the foothills. The steeply pitched roofs were covered with solar panels that reflected Orestes' dark sky and the hair-thin sliver of Agamemnon. The few windows were barely more than slits cut into the downwind sides of the buildings, but they, too, were covered in solar film to extract every calorie of heat from Atreus's thin sunlight. Only two buildings broke that pattern: the barnlike Guildhall, banners waving from the triple staff above its door, and the rail station. It was a long, low building, with a sharply pointed roof capped by the massive dish antenna that was Per Tamarisk's primary link with the rest of Orestes. Beyond the station house lay the silver tracery of the rail yard, and the bulky roundhouse. A small work engine was moving in the yard, shunting boxy ore carriers from track to track, and a passenger train—the train we would take back to the Tower—was drawn up to the station's main platform. At the intersection of two streets, a mixed group of laborers was digging an apparently purposeless ditch, but not much else was moving in the narrow streets. Of course, the Eclipse had ended less than an hour before, but I would have expected a little more traffic.

As we traversed the final sharp bend and turned onto the main street, I leaned forward to touch the driver's shoulder. "Is it always this quiet here?"

Corol Ingvarr shrugged. "It's a small town, Medium. And most of the people're probably up at the mines. There's extra work, this time of the calendar-month."

I nodded, leaning back in my seat. That was true enough, with the more fragile equipment to recover and the delvings to secure as much as possible, but boarded-up windows in perhaps a third of the dwelling towers told another story. Like all too many of the Halex mines, Tamar One and Two had had to lay off workers as the seams were played out. Having worked for the Halex Family for nearly eight calendar-months, I was fairly certain that the Matriarch had done her best to provide jobs or at least food and shelter for the various Kinship members thrown out of work, but I was equally sure she had found it hard to find suitable jobs for all the miners. The ditch back at the intersection had a definite air of make-work about it.

Corol glanced quickly at me, and his rather grim expression eased slightly. "And things haven't been going well," he admitted. He gave the Patroclans, still chattering over their lapboards, a quick look. "Though maybe now. . . ." He didn't finish the sentence—he didn't have to. Most Branches of the Halex Kinship, with the exception of the code-bound Rhawn, had pinned their hopes on the Patroclan survey, if only because most of the other Kinships strongly disapproved of it. Officially, the Brandr and the Fyfe and the Axtell didn't like the idea of bringing in off-worlders to solve Oresteian problems; more likely, I thought, they were envious of the hoarded wealth that enabled the Halex to afford off-world advice.

"They sound pretty optimistic," I said.

Corol grunted—he was Oresteian enough to be deeply suspicious of experts as young as the two Patroclans—and turned his attention to negotiating the turn into the narrow drop-off lane. He brought the car up to the edge of the station steps, then set the brakes and locked the engine at idle before he popped the side doors. The Patroclans, still talking, collected lapboards and their carryalls, and stepped out into the watery sunshine. They were conspicuously off-world, short and stocky by Oresteian standards, their quilted parkas showing the unmistakable sheen of off-world materials, and the adolescent who came running out to take the car checked abruptly, staring.

"Manners!" Corol growled, and the youth shook himself.

"Sorry, sor. For the train, sors?" The singsong accent was very strong in his voice. Looking at him, I guessed he had never been more than a few hundred kilometers from Per Tamarisk in his life. He wore his hair long, bound up in the old-fashioned topknot that had gone out of style in Destiny twenty years earlier. His clothes, the usual felty trousers, knitted jumper and overvest, had an indefinable something to their shape that practically shouted "country." Then he looked full at me, and I saw the tattoo on his cheek. It was the Ansson ringed mountain, but the exact branch of the Kinship was less important than the fact that he had been marked. Only the most conservative of the families still tattooed their adolescents; in the cities, it had been out of fashion for even longer than the topknot.

"That's right," Corol was saying, impassive as always. "The car goes back to the pool, with Herself's thanks to the baillie for its use. We'll handle our own baggage."

"Yes, sor, at once." Despite that assurance, the boy dawdled, spending an unnecessary length of time brushing imaginary dirt from the car's windscreen, until Corol snapped something at him in a dialect too broad for me to follow. The boy flushed, and ducked at once into the car, gunning its motor angrily.

"Idiot boy," Corol growled, hoisting his own bag to his shoulder. "Let's go."

Without waiting for an answer, he stalked off down the long platform toward the entrance. We followed, the Patroclans still murmuring to each other, apparently impervious to the boy's stares. As we came closer to the double doors, I caught sight of a woman sitting in a patch of sunlight, her legs folded gracefully beneath her thick skirts. A wooden tray full of michi—handmade tree-sugar candies—was set in front of her, a saucer full of change beside it. Seeing that, I looked again, and saw the ghostmark splashed on her forehead. Her eyes were closed, and she leaned against the wall of the station as though she were asleep.

When the left-hand door slammed, she opened her eyes for an instant, but closed them again as soon as she saw the figures that emerged from the lobby. They were all three young, two men who looked to be in their early twenties, and a woman who might have been a year younger, and all three were dressed in the height of city fashion. All were scowling, and the woman, at least, seemed to be continuing some argument with the darker of the men. He shrugged her off, but did not continue toward us down the platform. The other man, a tall blond, paused to contemplate the tray of michi, then angrily snatched up half a dozen of the candies and turned away without paying. The ghost's eyes flew open, her mouth rounding into a shocked "o," but there was nothing she could do to protest. By the Oresteian honor code, she was dead. Those who left money on her tray did so not out of obligation to her, but out of their own charity. The young woman broke off her argument to glare at the blond, but he gave her a blank look. She subsided, unable to complain without acknowledging the ghost's presence, which would in turn offend against the code. Living beings do not see the dead.

Corol stiffened in outrage, but he was as bound by the code as any other Oresteian. Orteja said, "Trey, he can't—"

"Hush," I said, cutting off Yan's protest as well, and stepped forward to confront the thief. I was angry—the ghosts have few enough rights in the cities, but the ones trapped in the rural settlements, where mediums are few and far between, are subject to everyone's petty spites, and this ghost-woman had no other way of supplementing the Kinship's meager charity. It took a real effort to keep my tone within the bounds of courtesy.

"You, boy."

The blond turned to confront me, his face setting into an expression of defiance. I touched the medium's black-hand badge that was pinned to the collar of my tunic, and his eyes wavered. As a medium, I was entitled not only to speak to the "dead," but to speak for them. I could denounce him as a thief—a mortal offense—and he knew it.

Out of the corner of my eye, I saw Corol Ingvarr give a wolfish grin. That, and the blond's fear, steadied me.

"Bad move," I said. "You owe the dead."

The blond stared at me for a moment longer, half resentful, half still afraid. "I didn't see anyone," he said at last.

"But I do." I waited, but the blond didn't answer. He was not of the Halex Kinship, of that I felt sure, but I couldn't tell which of the other Kinships he belonged to. The Brandrs ran to blonds, especially in the mainline family, but so did branches of both Axtell and Fyfe. Then I saw the design painted on the back of his thin leather gloves, three moons in the curve of crescent Agamemnon: Fira Branch of the Brandr Kinship.

"Live Halex are no concern of mine. Why should the dead ones get anything from me?" the blond burst out suddenly, with an air of grievance.

"Lael!" That was the young woman. She caught at the blond man's sleeve, stopping the angry words, and faced me with what dignity she could muster. There was a tattoo scar on her cheek, but the dermatologists had removed enough of the pigment to make the family symbol illegible. "Your pardon, Medium, we could not see." She glanced at the blond, who still looked mutinous, and added with emphasis, "Of course we will pay what's owed, won't we?"

The darker man was already fumbling in his pockets, flushed with embarrassment. He drew out a handful of money, change and notes mixed, and threw it into the saucer without bothering to check the amount. It was twice, maybe three times what the candies were worth, but I did not bother to point that out.

"Charity is always rewarded," I said, quoting one of Chan Charlot's maxims, and capped it with another. "But to pay one's debts is merely right."

The blond gave me a fulminating look, but he knew he was in the wrong. If I chose to press the matter, I could have him condemned to social death—further than I would have liked to take the matter, but he could not have known that. The woman tugged at his sleeve, and, still glaring, the blond let himself be drawn away, back toward the station. As the door closed behind them, I took a deep breath, trying to calm down. The blond hadn't hurt her, or

spoiled her stock—both tricks young bloods were known
to play when no one was on hand to stop them. It was
hardly a serious matter.

"What a bastard," Yan said, and Orteja echoed him.
Corol made a noise deep in his throat that might have
been agreement or disgust or both.

I ignored them all and went to crouch beside the ghost.
"Are you all right?"

"Yes, thank you, Medium." The ghost's voice was hoarse,
as though she did not often speak.

"Is there anything I can do?" As so often, my words
were totally inadequate. What I wanted to do was tell her
to get out of Per Tamarisk, to move to Destiny, where
there were thousands of ghosts and *para'anin*, and where
she would not be alone, but I had learned that such
advice was useless. If a ghost wanted to go to Destiny,
he/she would go there. All too often, the ghosts chose to
remain where they had lived, preferring a half-life among
familiar things and people to the strangeness of the Necropolis in Destiny.

The ghost shook her head, a half smile on her lips. "No,
Medium, though I thank you."

"If you're certain," I said, but rose to my feet. The
others were at the door now, waiting for me. The ghost
nodded. "Then good day." Corol pushed open the door for
me. I didn't look back, but stepped past him into the
warmth of the station.

To my relief, the three troublemakers were nowhere to
be seen. We walked the length of the empty lobby, past
rows of warmly polished benches, and paused at the ticket
counter only long enough for Corol to show the Matriarch's pass to the sleepy-looking attendant. The sight of
Herself's signature was enough to jolt even the attendant
awake, and he hurried to unlock the turnstiles. At his
shout, another gawky adolescent, a girl this time, just as
old-fashioned in her dress as the boy who had taken the
snow car, scurried out of the dispatcher's booth to escort
us ceremoniously to the train. There were only two cars
hooked up to the engine—others would be added as we
moved north toward the Tower—but she led us aboard
anyway and brought us to a comfortable four-seat compartment in the leading car. Once there, she unbent enough

to stow our bags in the side racks, and ask if there was anything we needed. Corol, with true Oresteian instinct, asked if there was anyplace we could buy snackboxes. The girl, motivated, I guessed, as much by the likelihood of a good tip as by the magic of the Matriarch's pass, promptly offered to fetch us four. The Patroclans, who had not yet acquired the Oresteian habit of eating at every possible opportunity, said they'd share one, but Corol told her to bring four anyway. The girl accepted his four-kip note with a grin, and vanished. She returned within a quarter-hour, carrying four foamform boxes and a large thermos. Corol nodded his acceptance, and waved away the girl's perfunctory offer of his change.

"Thank you, sor," she said, and started to back out of the compartment. The sound of voices in the corridor made her pause. It was the trio from the platform, the blond's voice rising in indistinct complaint. The girl gave us a speaking glance, and shouted, "Coming, sors, coming."

As she ducked back into the corridor, Yan said, "Damn shame those shestu are on the train."

Corol, already rummaging in his box, grunted agreement, but said, "Still, I bet I can guess the story, eh, Medium? Fira's part of Brandr Kinship, and none of the Halex kin are likely to be eager to let their girls marry into that Kinship."

I nodded, remembering the blond man's words. *Live Halex are no concern of mine. . . .* Yes, that had the sound of an unsuccessful suitor, but that was no excuse for what he'd done.

"I thought the Brandr/Halex feud was over," Orteja said, frowning.

Corol grinned, and said, through a mouthful of sausage pastry, "Officially."

Yan said, "Officially?"

"The feud was settled by the Ship's Council—that's the main governing body—about six years ago," I said patiently, "but that doesn't mean that everybody on both sides agreed with the decision."

Yan still looked puzzled, but at that moment the warning horn sounded and the train began to move out of the station. The Patroclans grabbed hastily at their lapboards, bracing themselves as the engine picked up speed. After a moment, Orteja began typing again, and Yan's attention was drawn by the figures. I settled back in my own padded chair, composing myself for the long ride north.

Even at the UHST train's top speed, it was a six-standard-hour ride from Per Tamarisk to the Halex Tower. The steady whine of the engine and the Patroclans' single-mindedness did much to discourage conversation. Of course, they did have to give a preliminary report to the Matriarch tonight, but I would have given a great deal for some distraction. Corol finished the contents of his snackbox, stowed the trash tidily under his feet, and promptly went to sleep. I tried to follow his example, I finished my food, but the encounter with the Fira youth had left me wakeful. I stared out the train's window, watching the foot-hills and then the scrubby forests of the Blackwine Valley flash past, and wished I had something to read. Overhead, Agamemnon showed its thin, new crescent, a gleaming, blue-green bow that spanned nearly eighteen degrees of sky. The clouds that had partially obscured the Noon eclipse—clock-morning eclipse, actually, lasting from seven hours to twelve, but Noon by Orestes' grand-day—had burned off, leaving the sky darkly clear. Agamemnon was very bright against that lapis background, only the lower limb of the crescent fading a little against the lighter blue of the horizon. Atreus, the system primary, was a little past the zenith, invisible overhead; true Sunset was a day and a half away.

After a while, I dozed off, to wake briefly when more cars were coupled to the engine during the quarter-hour stop at Millrace. The Blackwine River flowed fast here, frothing past the tracks to power the mills that gave the settlement its name, and I watched its hypnotic water until the train picked up speed again and the waves merged into an indeterminate blur. I fell asleep again almost at once, and did not stir until Corol shook me awake at the Tower station. Stumbling and sleepy, I gathered my belongings and followed the others off the train and through the little station to the waiting car.

By the time we reached the Tower, however, I had recovered a little. The Halex Tower was not just a tower, of course, though it had begun as one. After nearly fourteen hundred standard years of settlement, a cluster of

buildings had grown up around the original stubby, five-
story tower, and the pentagonal tower itself had been
rebuilt several times. But as the car negotiated the turn
through the carefully cultivated windbreak, there was an
instant in which you could see the Tower as it had been
when the first Halex built it. Stocky, square, unyielding, it
turned a blind facade to the constant northerly wind, and
the flanged archway that protected the entrance gave the
whole building a look of frowning stupidity. The steep,
conical roof, glittering with solar panels, looked enough
like a gaudy fool's cap to confirm the impression. Then the
car had passed between the banks of thickly intertwined
sugar-trees, and the moment passed. There was a garden
under that roof, where off-world delicacies were carefully
nurtured, supplementing the greenhouses just inside the
windbreak. The windowless front and the protected doorway were necessities on a world as cold as Orestes.

The driver turned into the main courtyard, passing between the hangars and the end of the mews, and pulsed
sedately to a stop inside the flange of the arch. One of the
Tower's human servants—the Matriarch considered me-
chanicals a waste of money when a Family member could
do the job for less—was waiting to receive us. At his
signal, a couple of the job-boys came to take our luggage,
and he himself came forward, bowing.

"Herself's compliments, Medium, and she'll expect you
and the off-world gentlemen at dinner."

I glanced quickly at the nearest clock, set deep in the
keystone above the door. It showed nineteen-thirty hours,
less than thirty minutes to the formal evening meal, and I
suppressed a curse. The Patroclans were looking at each
other in horror, and Orteja said, "Trey. . . ."

I shook my head quickly. "There's no refusing. You'll
have time to dress if you hurry." I turned back to the
waiting servant, who didn't bother to conceal a lopsided
grin at the foolishness of all off-worlders. "Tell Herself
we'll be there." My voice was grimmer than I'd intended,
and Corol gave a grunt of laughter. I ignored him, and
walked with dignity past the bowing doorman into the
Tower's shallow lobby.

It and the main corridor were only dimly lit, a conces-
sion to the fact that it was clock-evening. Shadowy figures

scurried from one pool of light to the next—mostly servants and employees, but also a few mainline Family members intent on finishing some last piece of business before the evening meal. I hurried past them myself, careful not to catch anyone's eye for fear of starting an unwanted and delaying conversation, and emerged into the lobby at the base of the main stairs. The treads spiraled slowly upward, clicking softly. I stepped onto the first platform, and let it carry me up. I could hear the Patroclans behind me, still talking, but did not look back. I liked them, but two weeks spent in close quarters with them was quite enough. I would be glad to have some time to myself again.

I had been given two rooms on the fourth floor, with the Kinship's other out-world employees. This was luxury in comparison with the housing given some of the Kin, who had single rooms on the windowless southern side of the Tower, though hardly lavish by off-world standards. Still, I had a window, and a separate bedroom rather than just a curtained stove-bed, so I could not complain. In fact, as I pushed open the door, I felt almost as though I were coming home.

One of the house servants—I did not have, and did not want, a body servant—had set out dinner clothes and a flask of Oresteian coffee, and for once I was grateful for the intrusion. I poured myself a cup of the sweet, oily liquid, and drank it while I changed into clean trousers and the woven jacket the house servant had considered appropriate. By then, the painted clock above the door showed only five minutes before the twentieth hour. The "Essentials" —flat metal card case, a handful of Oresteian coins, and the gilded formal gorget marked with a medium's black hand— were already laid out on the table beside the door. Hastily, I recovered my ID disk from the pocket of my other trousers—not that I needed it, here at the Tower, but I felt naked without it—and stuffed it, the card case, and the coins into my jacket's pockets. I clipped the gorget around my neck, adjusting its position by touch rather than pausing to glance in a mirror, and hurried back down the stairs toward the dining hall.

Despite my efforts, I was late, but not disgracefully so. There were Family members behind me as I took my place at the serving hatch. The woman on duty there gave me a conspiratorial wink, and said, "Better watch yourself, Medium. Herself's been in a mood today."

"Good or bad?" I asked, and was rewarded with a choked snort of laughter.

"Has Herself anything but bad ones?" A senior server, greying and aristocratic, gave her a disapproving stare, and she sobered quickly. "Wet or dry, Medium?"

"Dry, please," I answered, and the chance for further conversation vanished. The server deftly collected the correct set of lacquered containers, built them into a neatly interlocked stack, and pushed it across the counter toward me. I thanked her, but received only the ghost of a grin before she turned to serve the next latecomer.

As a member of the immediate household, I was entitled to a place at the high table with the Matriarch herself. I had always felt that this was an unnecessary honor, and never more so than now, as I edged my way between the crowded tables of the lower hall. The dull roar of conversation did not falter, a minor grace, but I could feel the Matriarch's eyes on me as I made my way onto the dais. To my relief, though, she merely gave me a sardonic smile as I took my place between the Demi-heir and the Ingvarr cousin who managed the home farms. Eldrede Halex, of Halex in Halex, Matriarch of the Kinship, took a certain pleasure in her deserved reputation for a sharp tongue, but she was not one to attack without reason. Besides, the Patroclans had already begun a somewhat disjointed account of their survey, and the Matriarch never neglected business for pleasure.

The Demi-heir, Rohin, eldest child of the Matriarch's eldest child, elbowed me, offering the pitcher of rikiya. I took it and poured myself a cupful, then began opening the stacked containers that held my dinner. I had asked for a dry meal, with a minimum number of sauces and condiments. As usual, that meant four different types of pastry, one sweet and three salt, and a quick-fried hash of vegetables and smoked meats, each in its own special lacquered container. There was also a small, flat dish of boi-boi, the dark red game fish of the Grand Shallows— four paper-thin slices garnished with a blob of redich paste: luxury, indeed, for a non-holiday meal. I glanced quickly at Rohin's array of dishes. The Demi-heir, too, had been given a share of the fish, though I doubted if any of the people dining in the lower hall would taste boi-boi, except on calendar holidays.

"Pass the pitcher, Medium, if you please." That was Gazel Ingvarr, the home farm's manager. I handed her the heavy jug, glancing at her dishes as I did so. Sure enough, the flat boi-boi dish was there, empty except for a little of the paste.

"What's the occasion?" I asked, and pointed to my own plate.

Gazel finished filling her cup, and took a careful sip of the hot liquor before she answered. She was older than most of the Halex kindred employed in running the Mandate, and had risen high for someone not of the mainline Family. Maybe because of that, she had a maddening habit of wrapping every word in meaningless irony, but at least she was willing to answer my questions. She set her cup aside now and laughed softly, saying, "What, you didn't notice?"

I shook my head. "I've been away," I said, patiently. "Tell me."

Gazel nodded discreetly toward the foot of the table. "Between Jesma and Fres Ansson. That's Coronis."

The name was familiar, but not as instantly recognizable as Gazel seemed to think. I frowned, and Gazel said, "Coronis who married Eyre Brandr."

That was all the clue I needed. I couldn't stop myself from raising an eyebrow, and Gazel laughed again. "I see you remember," she said.

I did. The story was a popular one, was even the subject of a holoplay down in Destiny. Eyre Brandr, grandnephew of the Brandr Patriarch, had met and fallen in love with Coronis Halex, close cousin to the Halex Matriarch, and she had fallen in love with him. The two Kindreds were nominally at feud, though there had been no active provocation for some years. When the young couple finally announced their intention to marry—either with their Families' blessings or without it, as *para'anin*—cooler heads among the Kindreds had seen it as a chance to end the feud, and had prevailed on the more conservative to allow the marriage. A few years later, as I'd told the

Patroclans, the Ship's Council had ended the feud, though only after prolonged negotiations. Despite this grudged approval, however, the marriage had reportedly not been an easy one—which one would hardly expect, I thought, given that a large proportion of the relatives on both sides still disapproved of the relationship, and would be glad to see it end.

I knew I was staring, and tried to turn my attention back to my food, but I could not help sneaking an occasional glance toward the foot of the table. Coronis Halex did not look in any way remarkable—just another of the tall, light-boned, dark-haired people who filled the dining hall. Perhaps there was something in the set of her full mouth that hinted at strength as well as stubbornness, but little more. Her husband was nowhere to be seen.

"Where's Eyre Brandr?" I asked.

Gazel gave a twisted smile. "In Madelgar, I imagine. He doesn't come to the Tower except on formal matters, any more than she goes to theirs."

"I don't envy either one of them," I said.

"Coronis?" Rohin leaned past me to reach the spice tray, and added another heaping spoonful of saur to his stew. "I don't know, she got what she wanted—though why she wanted Eyre Brandr I don't see!—and she's not dead or *para'an*. What's to feel sorry for?"

Gazel managed a significant laugh, and the Demi-heir flushed. Before he could say anything, however, the Matriarch's voice rang out through the buzz of conversation. "An excellent meal. Halena, would you do me the favor of fetching me another dish of *chee*?"

There was a stirring at the children's table to our left, and a girl of thirteen or so wormed free of the others. She bobbed a sort of curtsey, and started down the hall to the serving hatch, her blond braids bouncing with every defiant step. Clearly, she didn't take the request as a compliment, though I was sure the Matriarch had meant it so.

"Coronis's daughter," Rohin said, unnecessarily.

The girl Halena returned quickly enough, the bright blue dish cradled in both hands. She set it in front of the Matriarch, serving from the left as she had been taught, and stood back, waiting.

"Thank you, Halena, that was well done." The Matriarch gave her a thin smile, and opened the dish, dismissing Halena. The girl did not move, and the Matriarch frowned slightly, glancing up at the child without speaking.

"If you please, ama." Halena had a carrying voice, and her behavior had already attracted the attention of most of the diners on the dais. Her words rang loudly in the sudden quiet. She looked startled, but went on with determination. "May I ask a question?"

Coronis fixed her daughter with a reproving stare, but the girl ignored her. The Matriarch said, not encouragingly, "You may ask."

Halena took a deep breath. "Uncle Brandr has robots to wait on table. Why don't you?"

"Halena." Coronis did not need to raise her voice, still staring at her daughter.

"Be silent, girl," the Matriarch snapped. She turned slowly to subject the children's table to her icy stare. I leaned sideways in my own chair to see what had attracted her attention, and saw the half dozen boys and girls who were Halena's agemates sitting frozen, the picture of guilt. The Matriarch snorted softly, and turned her attention back to Halena.

"What Brandr does is no concern of mine," she said. "I do not choose to waste money that could be spent on the Kinship and the Mandate on frivolities." Her face softened slightly, and she flicked a glance toward Coronis, before looking at Halena again. "It's a fair question, miss, and I trust there's no one so foolish as to think I'd be offended by it." That was for the children's table. I saw Halena's agemates shift and whisper unhappily.

"Are you answered?" the Matriarch continued.

Halena nodded. "Yes, ama."

The Matriarch waited, and after an instant, Halena added, "Thank you."

The Matriarch smiled, and nodded dismissal. Halena backed gratefully away, and returned to her place at the children's table. Her agemates edged away from her a little, but Halena seemed to accept it stolidly enough.

"What was that all about, I wonder?" Gazel said softly, as conversation slowly resumed along the length of our table.

I shrugged, and Rohin made a face. "I bet one of the

brats put her up to asking. If it was Rosser, I'll tan his hide myself—if Father doesn't beat me to it."

"Which I expect he will," Gazel said, and reached again for the rikiya. Rohin flushed again, but his mouth was too full for him to answer. Rosser was the Demi-heir's younger sibling.

Before Rohin could say anything else, the Matriarch pushed back her chair. All conversation ceased as we scrambled to our feet, and the oldest of the group at the children's table made haste to fetch her silver-headed cane. The Matriarch eyed him without approval, sending the boy scurrying back to his place, then swept the main tables with an imperious glance.

"Magan, Rohin, Jesma, Coronis," she began, touching each of them with a look. "Ixora, Master Orteja, Master Yan, and yourself, Medium. It would please me if you'd take coffee with me in the solar this clock-evening." There were nods of agreement, but the Matriarch went on without heeding them. "Kindred, gentlefolk, good night."

The diners responded with a ragged chorus of "good nights" and good wishes. The Matriarch inclined her head in regal acknowledgement, and made her way down from the dais, leaning heavily on her cane. She was not a young woman, and, like many Oresteians, suffered from a form of arthritis. Her progress down the hall was slow, but not a person moved or spoke until she had left the room. Conversation resumed, more loudly now that Herself had left, and several parents left their places to reprimand their offspring at the children's table.

Under normal circumstances, we would have been free to sit for another hour or two, drinking coffee or hot wine, but the Matriarch's invitation was tantamount to a command. At my left, Rohin made a face, and drained his cup of rikiya.

"Will you walk with me, Medium? Herself doesn't like latecomers."

"I will, thank you," I said. The others the Matriarch had summoned were pushing back their chairs, too, hastily collecting shawls and jackets and workbags. The Patroclans, in particular, looked nervous. I gave them what I hoped was an encouraging smile, but got nothing in return.

"I don't understand them," Rohin said, involuntarily, as

we followed them down the length of the dining hall. His father, hurrying past us, shot him a reproving glance, and the Demi-heir shrugged uncomfortably. "Well, I don't. Are all the Urban Worlders like them?"

"No!" I said quickly, and Rohin grinned at the unfortunate emphasis. I had to smile back, reluctantly, and said, "Patroclus is the exception. It's in the trade ring, but it's not really part of the Urban culture. I'm an Urban Worlder myself, you know."

Rohin nodded. "You're not like them," he agreed. "Why—what makes them so strange?"

As a trained Mediator, representative of Conglomerate and Urban society, I knew I should respond with some platitude about no human society being truly strange. But the Patroclans were unique among the Conglomerate worlds, and no one except natives or a few specialists made any pretense of understanding them. "I don't know," I said. "Patroclus is a hard world; there was a lot of trouble settling it. And then almost everything on the planet, plant or animal, has a symbiotic partner of some kind. But anyway, for whatever reason, they developed a culture based on pairs, and that's the standard social unit, not the individual."

Rohin nodded again, and said, with surprising insight, "But then, I suppose most of the Urban Worlds think our society's a bit odd."

That was very true, though I was not about to say it, or to admit that I agreed with that opinion. However, the lag between the first colonial ships—massive generation ships, all of them—and the development of a true FTL drive, had let a lot of peculiar cultures flourish, especially on the more distant planets. Only on the Urban Worlds, close enough to make interplanetary trade feasible from the first year of FTL travel, had any more universal culture developed. The Conglomerate itself existed only to enforce a semi-uniform commercial code, not to provide a cultural base. Orestes was not so different from other worlds of the Rim, or the Farside. . . . I couldn't go that far. Orestes was different, very different, from worlds like Herne or Bastet. On those planets, the long separation from other human cultures had produced intricate and apparently anomalous societies, but none of their customs had the deadly strength of Orestes' honor. I had been an actor, before I realized I would make a better Mediator, and I had been in enough tragedies to lose patience with honor as a cause.

Rohin was looking at me rather oddly, and I brought myself back to the conversation with an effort. "Probably. And you'd probably find any of the Urban Worlds pretty peculiar yourself."

"I suppose," Rohin said, without conviction, and then we had reached the solar.

I had never suspected that Rohin harbored an interest in the Urban Worlds, or in anything off-planet. There was a rather wistful expression on his face as he tapped on the door of the solar, and well there might be. As a Halex not merely of mainline Family but in the direct line for the genarchy, it was highly unlikely that he would ever have the opportunity to go off-world.

Then the door opened, breaking my train of thought, and we went in. The Matriarch's solar was a low-ceilinged, almost triangular room at the point of the pentagonal Tower. The heavy shutters were pushed back to make the most of the sunlight, and the holdstone floor was percepti-bly warm underfoot. The Matriarch herself sat with her back to the windows, her heavy, hooded armchair drawn close to a small table. Her face was invisible in its shadow. She was busy with some piece of handwork, which she released long enough to gesture toward the chest that held the coffee service.

"Welcome, Rohin, Medium. Serve yourself, if you please. We are as Family here."

"Thank you, ama," I said, and crossed to the chest. I took my time, choosing spices and sugar and a shot of the local whiskey to help offset the taste of the coffee, survey-ing the assembled group. Rohin and I had been the last to arrive; the other Family members had been quick to choose chairs standing either in the wedge of sunlight or beneath the slender pole lights, and most were busy with some handicraft. The Patroclans, looking more ill at ease than ever, were perched on matching drumseats by the short inside wall. Moved by some obscure, defensive instinct—after all, I had been the one who had suggested Patroclus; despite their peculiarities, they were among the best engi-

THE KINDLY ONES   29

neers in the Conglomerate—I settled myself in an armchair next to them, facing the Matriarch. She leaned forward, reaching for a tiny pair of scissors, and I saw her smile.

"Well, Medium, I have a verbal report from these, and I'm promised a written one by Sunset. What did you think of the situation in the hills?"

I took a sip of the scalding coffee, trying to buy time. "I'm not an engineer, ama. I don't know what I can add to their report."

"I didn't expect you to answer engineer's questions," Herself shot back. "What about the people?"

"In brief, ama—" I began, and the Matriarch said sharply, "Not necessarily."

Magan, the balding Heir, sighed deeply, and gave me a sympathetic look. I said, as though she hadn't spoken, "In brief, ama, I found the area still much depressed. The retraining has helped, and the subsidies for the factories outside the mine towns, but not everyone's willing to leave. The public works have helped, too, but there's only so much you can do." I took a deep breath. "There were some other matters I wanted to take up with you—a 'death,' and some troubles with *para'anin*—but I'd prefer to follow Slade's example and give you a written report. Will you allow me the same deadline?"

Magan nodded thoughtfully and, when his mother did not answer, said, "Ama, I would appreciate seeing a written account."

The Matriarch ignored him. "A 'death,' Medium?"

"Yes." I took another sip of coffee, marshalling my thoughts. The case had not been pretty, a girl—a seventeen-year-old girl of beauty and talent—accused of a seemingly trivial breach of code that the settlement council had insisted on viewing as mortal. I said, carefully, "There was a case at Feibourg, four calendar-months ago. The council insisted on the strict construction of the code, though the accused was very young and there were both mitigating circumstances and some evidence of malice. I have copies of the documents. With your permission and consent, I'd like to press for a review."

The Matriarch leaned forward again into the light, the corners of her mouth turned down in disapproval. "A review?" She glanced down at the heap of yarn, took two quick stitches. "I'll see your report first, Medium."

"Of course." Any review of that sort of judgment would not be undertaken lightly, and I had not expected that it would be.

"And the *para'anin*?" the Matriarch went on, still stabbing at her knitting.

"Ama." Magan set aside his own work, a rounded, competently abstract animal shape of seastone that he was polishing, and glanced quickly in Coronis's direction. "Surely we could leave that for tomorrow's cabinet? This is a social occasion, after all."

Coronis flushed, but bent over her workbox without a word. After a moment, she retrieved a child's wool jacket and unfolded it on her lap, fumbling in the box for needle and thread. Her hands were trembling. I couldn't help but feel sorry for her, set apart from her own family and from her husband's kin, but didn't know how to turn the conversation.

It was Rohin, to my surprise, who leaped into the breach. "If all these reports'll be due by Sunset," he said, "maybe we could make an expedition into Destiny after Dark. I don't think the guildmasters have seen any of the sights."

Ixora, one of Rohin's agemates, a wild-haired, high-tempered hellion who belonged to one of the Halex cousin-lines, looked up from the underboot she was laboriously knitting. "You'll be going into the Necropolis, then." It was not a question, nor did her tone seem malicious, but Rohin scowled.

"That's the best part of the city, in the Dark." He met his grandmother's stern gaze, and said defiantly, "And the theater's worth seeing."

The Matriarch snorted. "They say the plays are worth seeing. However, the company you have to keep to see them. . . . Ghosts and *para'anin*, all of them, and most of them more whore than actor. Though how you can tell the difference, I don't know."

The Patroclans exchanged an embarrassed glance. I took a deep breath, controlling an old, instinctive anger, and Jesma said quietly, from her place by the window, "I think you exaggerate, ama. Certainly customs differ—as I'm sure Trey would tell you."

It was neatly done, reprimand and reminder all in one. A spasm, as much of pain as of embarrassment, flashed across the Matriarch's face, and she said, stiffly, "I had forgotten your former profession, Medium. No offense was intended."

I knew that this was not the time or the place to champion actors, or to justify the popular conception of their morals. Even so, it was hard to give the right answer, and I could hear how stiff I sounded. "And none taken."

The Matriarch swivelled her attention back to Rohin, her frown deepening. "If you intend to go into Destiny during the Dark, I expect you to behave properly—no, carefully. I don't want anyone to be able to say anything against you."

"Have I ever given cause?" Rohin asked, fairly reasonably.

The Matriarch glared at him. "That's not the point. There are—" She checked abruptly, reminded of Coronis's presence by the younger woman's sudden movement, and continued, in a more subdued voice. "There are enough people who would like to see our Kinship discredited, for whatever reason. I don't want the Demi-heir to give them fuel."

Rohin took a deep breath, and said, "I'll continue to set a shining example, ama."

Ixora laughed, and was silenced by a look from Herself. She bent hastily over the underboot, concentrating on the complex pattern of its cuff, but her sidelong glances betrayed her amusement. Coronis's lips were white-edged, pinched tight with anger. She continued to set small, precise stitches, jabbing vindictively at the jacket's torn hem. Jesma gave her a compassionate glance, and said, "Have you been to the new mills in Destiny yet, Coronis?"

"No."

Jesma ignored the curt monosyllable, talking gently on about the yarns she had seen there. She was working with half a dozen different yarns herself—subtle gradations of color and texture that showed to advantage in the strong light from the window. After a moment, almost in spite of herself, Coronis began to respond, and Magan put aside his polishing cloth to examine Jesma's delicate work. Even

Ixora added a comment or two, though she was known for her lack of interest in the usual Oresteian crafts. She only made what she could not afford to buy. I knew that underboots with patterned cuffs that showed above short bootshanks were very popular with the sporting set, and guessed that they were correspondingly expensive. But Ixora was part of the sporting crowd, who raced teams of the immense, ox-like hoobeys across the frozen Little Steppes, in the north of the Axtell Mandate. She would hardly allow herself to go without the latest fashion, even if she had to do the tedious work herself.

I leaned back in my chair and took a swallow of my cooling coffee, wishing I had put more whiskey in it. I was getting tired of the constant crosscurrents within the Halex Tower, the obsessive analysis of every word and glance. I was not cut out for court life, no matter how you defined it. . . .

I shook myself then, and sat up straighter in the chair, taking another sip of the laced coffee. I was tired indeed if I was seeing scheming courtiers in this company. I needed a break—perhaps I should go into Destiny myself, during the three-day Dark. I had a few friends in the city, mostly off-worlders, and Moraghan, captain of the six-week mailship, should have landed by then. I could at least have dinner with her, maybe sample some of the delights of the Necropolis, and get my mind off the Halex Kinship for a while. I nodded to myself as I finished my coffee. I would ask for a few days' leave when I turned in my report.

Secure in that decision, I set the cup aside. The conversation ebbed slowly, and the Matriarch's needles moved more stiffly. At last, with a sigh, she bundled the fabric together and tucked it into her battered workbox. The others, recognizing the signal, began putting away their own work. With Magan's discreet help, the old woman hauled herself to her feet, leaned heavily on her cane for a few moments, and dismissed us. I, for one, was not sorry to make my escape.

As I headed up the stairs, however, I heard Rohin call my name. I was tempted for a moment to play deaf, but then the Demi-heir was clattering up the stairs behind me.

"I'm sorry for what happened," he said. "It's just—Herself has a thing about actors."

"I gathered," I said, rather sourly. I could feel that it was getting late, despite the unchanging sunlight outside, and wanted very much to go to bed. Rohin grimaced, and I shook myself, trying to be polite. "Look, it doesn't matter. I'm not an actor anymore."

"No, but—I think I owe you an explanation," Rohin said. He grinned suddenly, almost sheepishly. "And there was a favor I wanted to ask you, but I'm not sure this is the time. Could I come in?"

We were at my door already. I hesitated for an instant, then shrugged and twisted the old-fashioned handlock, motioning him inside. Rohin slipped past me with a murmur of thanks, and there was something in his eyes that made me glad I had said yes.

Sunlight was streaming in through the open thermal blinds, warming the outer room nicely. I waved Rohin to the nearest seat, and said, "Coffee?"

The Demi-heir shook his head, stretching his feet into the triangle of sun, but pulled himself up abruptly. "Thank you, no."

"Esco?" That was the liqueur I had brought with me from Athene. It was expensive even there, and I was a little relieved when Rohin shook his head again.

"Nothing, thanks."

"As you wish." I settled myself in the hooded chair opposite him, turning it slightly so that my feet were in the sun, and waited for him to say something. "You really don't owe me any explanations, you know," I said, after a moment, and the Demi-heir cut in.

"But I do. Herself may be unreasonable—" He paused, then grimaced. "All right, she is unreasonable, but it's not the way you think." He paused again, searching for the right words. I waited, and realized after a moment that I was folding my hands, acting the psychiatrist waiting for a confession. Deliberately, I moved my fingers apart, resting each hand on its armchair.

"You know my sib, Rosser," Rohin said at last. I didn't see quite what that had to do with anything, but I made an affirmative noise. I knew him, all right. Rosser was thirteen, almost old enough for the Choice—the ritual acceptance of the code's strictures—and eager for it.

"There's also Rehur," the Demi-heir went on. "My twin. He's dead."

He had used the common form, not the inflected word that meant true-dead: so one of the mainline Halex was a ghost, and not just any mainline kinsman, but the son of the Heir himself. I didn't say anything, however, and Rohin seemed to relax a little.

"He didn't do anything, really. It's what he didn't do. . . . Rehur went off to Destiny, spent a lot of time in the Necropolis, in the theaters—with actors," he conceded, with an odd little smile, at once protective and worldly, and I had no trouble translating what he meant by the cautious phrase. "And instead of getting himself declared *para'an*, he just ignored everything, the whole family, so Herself had no choice but to declare him dead—and she's never forgiven him for it."

Privately, I had to admit I could see her position, and it did go a long way toward explaining her attitude. It seemed the height of irresponsibility to allow yourself to be declared a ghost, with all the restrictions that entailed, when you could become *para'an* by fulfilling the ritual obligations. A *para'an* was at least visible, could speak and be spoken to. . . . I pulled myself together, and asked, "He's an actor, your twin?"

"Yes, in the puppet theater. He's with a company now."

There was a strong note of defiance in Rohin's voice, and I could understand why. "Real" actors generally looked down on the holopuppet theater, though many of them had gotten their start there, claiming that puppet theater required no talent except a good body—some said the less talent the better. It was at least partly true, but the new-style companies, the ones that mixed live actors and holopuppets, needed actors with a good deal of talent. And the new style was very popular on Orestes. Dimly, I remembered reading about an Oresteian company winning one of the Dionysian competitions, to a great deal of critical acclaim. That had been while I was on Delilah, though, mediating a particularly complicated trade-rights dispute, and I hadn't paid much attention to the details. I'd been to the theater often enough since coming to

Orestes, though, to see that the puppeteers were doing something new and exciting, and said as much.

Rohin grinned at that, relieved. "I'm glad you said that, you know, since that gives me the excuse I needed."

"Oh?" I waited. You never knew if you were going to regret it when a Halex asked a favor.

"You remember I said tonight that I wanted to go into Destiny at Dark?" the Demi-heir began. "Well, Herself's right when she says we have to be careful these days, even if she couldn't speak plainly in front of Coronis. The Brandr are just itching for a chance to put one of us in front of the Council. That way," he added, seeing my confused expression, "they could also bitch about us bringing in off-worlders, whether it's an act of cowardice or not."

It was on the tip of my tongue to say that I didn't see how even the Ship's Council could call it that, but I was on Orestes, and I stopped.

"But no one could object," Rohin went on, "if I were accompanied by the family medium. Would you come with me, act as medium for a few calendar-days?"

I had been looking forward to a little time away from Orestes and my responsibilities, but then I saw the look in Rohin's eyes. "I take it your twin's performing?" I asked.

"Yes," Rohin said, rather defiantly. Then, as I said nothing, his pose crumbled a little. "His company, Witchwood, was invited to take part in a *khy sonon-na*, and I really want to see it."

I hesitated. I really didn't want to work while I was in Destiny, during what I'd already half-decided would be a three-day vacation, but if one of the theaters was holding a *khy sonon-na*, I would want to see it anyway. It hardly seemed fair to let Rohin invite trouble by going into the Necropolis unaccompanied, when it would cost me nothing to let him come with me. I hadn't seen a *khy sonon-na* yet—the cabaret theaters held the shows, a competition among several holo-companies to see who could perform the best version of a set scene, at irregular and inconvenient intervals—and I had always wanted to see one.

Rohin took my hesitation for refusal. "Look, I promise you won't have to keep me company. I just need your sanction when I go to the theaters, that's all."

I hesitated a second longer, but I really couldn't say no.

Besides, I owed the Matriarch one for her remark about actors. "There are some people I want to see," I said slowly, "but I'll at least go with you to the *khy sonon-na*."

"Thank you," Rohin said. "I do appreciate it—and I'm sorry Herself said what she did." He rose politely, with an apologetic glance at the clock. "I'm sorry to have stayed so late, especially with you just back from the Prosperities. . . ."

"It's all right," I said, and let him bow himself out. When he had gone, I closed the blinds and turned up the lights, and began to get ready for bed. As I crawled into the stove-bed, drawing the curtains and pulling the down-filled blankets close around my ears, it occurred to me that I might be letting myself in for more than I intended. It was not a pleasant thought. I pushed the idea away and wriggled my feet closer to the bed's heating unit, giving myself up to sleep.

Chapter 2: Guil ex-Tam'ne, para'an of Tam'ne in Orillon

Pipe Major settled gently onto the landing pad, and there was a sudden silence as the last of the jets cut out. Guil, who had ridden out the landing at the back-up pilot's station, nodded grudging approval, and then wished she hadn't as *Pipe Major's* senior pilot swung to face her, a cocky grin on his handsome face. Light glinted from the plate-and-sensor rosette of his artificial eye.

"Pretty good, huh? If I do say so myself."

Guil eyed him warily—he was new to *Pipe Major* this trip, but she knew his type, the sort who made up for perceived loss of beauty with an aggressive sexiness—but had to admit Sabas had done well. A lot of off-worlders failed to compensate properly for Orestes' relatively low gravity; Sabas had balanced it perfectly.

"It'll do," Moraghan said, forestalling the Oresteian woman's response. "Idris, get a line to the pad-captain, and let's get inside. Askel, we're finished with the main generator."

"Finished with main generator, acknowledged." The chief engineer's voice sounded almost human in the speakers, the distortion of the artificial larynx obscured by the intercom mechanism. "Shutting down main generator. Port generator engaged at one-half power."

Guil sighed softly as the unnatural gravity faded—*Pipe Major*, like most Conglomerate ships, ran at a full one G—and glanced quickly toward the door of the pilot's cabin. Elam Fyfe, her apprentice for this trip, had spent most of the run flat on his back, unable to handle the unfamiliar weight. Which wasn't too surprising, Guil thought, considering he's really Dessick Jan's apprentice. But that was typical of Dessick: not only did he do his best to avoid his own responsibilities, but in doing so he bred up another generation of inadequate pilots. Elam had been next to useless on the run in through the rings, able to take the controls for only a few hours at a time. The bulk of the burden had fallen on Guil—as usual, she thought sourly. Hell, I shouldn't even be on back-up duty now. I brought that Athenan ship in less than three weeks ago, and that was from Iphigenia's orbit, not just through the rings. But Dessick had pleaded Family business, and Oslac, as always, had picked her as the substitute. It wasn't so much that she minded the work—one of the reasons she had chosen to become *para'an* was so that she could work out of Orestes' busier ports—but the fact that Dessick and the rest were so confident they could always call on her. And they could: *para'an* as she was, she had none of the overriding Familial responsibilities the others could use to evade their professional duties. Personal wishes counted for little in Oslac's eyes—unless they happened to coincide with some Family rite. It was just a good thing that Conglomerate regulations that governed the amount of time a pilot could spend on duty left a generous safety margin.

Guil shook herself hard. She had handled the ring passage easily—the duty regs were overcautious—and could've handled the entire transit even without Elam. For once, Dessick's shirking had worked out to her advantage. Moraghan was a good friend, and it was a pleasure to work with her. Besides, the Peacekeepers—even the ex-Peacekeepers who crewed the mailships—were different, both from Oresteians and from other off-worlders. Among other things, they neither pitied her nor blamed her for being *para'an*, and their training stopped them from passing any judgment on the Oresteian code. Moraghan asked only that a pilot do her job to perfection, and nothing more. Unlike some people.

Guil glanced again at the pilot's cabin, just in time to see the door slide back. Elam appeared in the hatchway, bracing himself against the bulkhead. He was a handsome boy, tall and golden-haired, the shadowy Fyfe linked-stars tattoo half hidden beneath beard stubble, but at the moment he looked as though he had aged twenty years in the thirty-six-hour ring transit. Guil's instinctive reproof faded as she looked at him, and she said only, "Next time you'd do better not to skimp weight training."

Elam nodded miserably, but said, "Dessick always said we didn't need it."

Yeah, because Dessick doesn't take high-G ships, Guil thought. Oh, well, if this kills some of the kid's hero worship, it'll've been worthwhile. She shrugged, and said, "That's his choice, of course."

Elam looked quickly around the control room. "Aren't we going now?"

Guil gave him a puzzled glance. "Customs hasn't come aboard yet," she said. "I still have to hand over my log. . . ." Her voice faded as she saw Elam blush, and realized that this was another of the pilot's responsibilities that Dessick ignored. To calm herself, she stared at the main viewscreen, now displaying a bow-camera view of Destiny's landing field. The fused-earth apron gleamed faintly in the light from waxing Agamemnon, color fading as it merged with the Sunset sky. It was Dark in Destiny now, the best time. She would not spoil that with anger. "You can go on, if you want."

Elam shook his head, though the effort was clearly painful. "I'll wait."

Guil raised an eyebrow—she had not expected that answer—but nodded. "You can get my bag, then, if you would."

Elam nodded back, and vanished again into the pilot's cabin. Guil leaned back in her chair by the back-up console, knowing she would be least in the way if she remained there. While she had been talking to Elam, the control room had emptied, Sabas and the junior pilot heading down to the cargo hatches, the junior engineer gone below to help Askel shut down the main system, until only Moraghan was left, slouched in the high-backed captain's chair, the fingers of her good hand playing across the intercom buttons. She looked exactly the same as she always had—a little tired, brown smudges under her grey eyes, a half-smile on her wide mouth—and Guil could not repress an answering grin. Moraghan was dressed the same as always, too, in what passed for shipboard uniform: sleeveless vest colored the same faded black as her hair, and crumpled, multi-pocketed ship's trousers. Her left hand and most of her left arm were encased in a black glove that reached almost to her shoulder. It would have seemed like an affectation, if a centimeter or so of reddened scar tissue had not been visible above the cuff, and if the glove had had five fingers instead of three. Not for the first time, Guil wondered just what sort of an accident had ended the other woman's military career.

Moraghan looked up, as though aware of the other's scrutiny, and her smile widened. She pressed a final sequence of buttons, and stood, stretching. "I need some information from you, Guil, now that Darah's off the bridge."

"Whatever I can do," the pilot answered, with an involuntary glance toward the pilot's cabin.

Moraghan snorted softly. "If it offends him, screw it. This is ship's business." She paused, gathering her thoughts. "This is planetary night—the Dark, right?"

Guil nodded, looking at the screen visible over the captain's shoulder. "Just past Sunset."

"How're things in Destiny these days?" the captain asked bluntly. "Can my people fool around if they want, or do they have to watch their step?"

Guil looked away, knowing what had prompted that question. Elam was trying to make himself invisible in the doorway of the pilot's cabin, and Guil frowned, hoping he would go back inside. For once, the apprentice took the hint, closing the door behind him. "The Necropolis is just like it's always been, they shouldn't have any trouble there. You know how things work."

"I've got new people aboard," Moraghan said. Her smile vanished, making her seem suddenly years older. "And I heard about the *Tallyrand*."

"Oh." Guil looked down at the back-up console, won-

dering what she should say. *Tallyrand* was one of the
tramp merchantmen that landed semi-regularly at Destiny. Her owner-captain was well-regarded—Guil had pi-
loted for him more than once, and liked him—but, like all
the tramp-captains, he had trouble keeping a crew for any
length of time. The last time *Tallyrand* had come through
Destiny, part of her crew—new men who'd never been on
Orestes—had gotten into a brawl at a private party, and
somehow a mainline Axtell had ended up a ghost. Exactly
what had happened remained an Axtell secret—the matter
had been decided by a Family court—but it was common
knowledge that *Tallyrand*'s captain had been given the
choice of paying a bloodfine or losing his Oresteian business. It was said the price had been high enough to ruin
him, and Guil could well believe it. Bloodfines had ruined
richer men than a mere tramp-captain. She could hardly
blame *Pipe Major*'s captain for being a little nervous. She
shrugged. "It was a freak thing, Leith—Captain. They
were outside the Necropolis. It wouldn't've happened if
they'd stayed inside the greengates. Tell your people to
stick to the Necropolis—stick to pros and ghosts." She
touched her forehead. "Tell them to look for the ghostmark,
that's sure."

Moraghan made an odd face, but nodded. "Sounds like
a right mess," she said. "Poor Jens."

Guil gave her a sidelong glance, wanting to ask what
Tallyrand's captain had told her, but unable to bring herself to pry. *Para'anin* did not get involved in any Family's
business. Instead, she said, "You'll be on-planet four calendar days?"

Moraghan nodded, but her answer was cut off by the
opening of the control room hatch. "Yeah, Darah?"

"Customs team's aboard, Captain. They want the log-
tapes," Sabas answered. His good eye swiveled toward
Guil, then back toward his captain. Moraghan nodded,
and reached to touch a button on the main navigation
board. A chime sounded, and a slot opened in the board,
ejecting a plastic square about the size of a woman's hand.
Moraghan handed it to the pilot, and glanced at Guil. "Is
yours ready, Guil?"

"Yeah, thanks," Guil answered, and fumbled in the

pockets of her coveralls for the hard plastic square. Sabas took them both, and vanished from the bridge.

"Let's hope they don't take too long about it," Moraghan muttered, only half to herself. "Though why they need to check their own damn mail so carefully. . . ."

Guil gave her a sympathetic smile, and pushed herself up out of the chair. Elam was still in the pilot's cabin, obeying her frown; it was time she let him out. She hit the door control, and motioned for the apprentice to come out, taking her bag from his hand as she did so. As she returned to her place in front of the back-up console, she saw with some annoyance that Moraghan was struggling to suppress a laugh.

For once, the Customs team finished its work in record time. Sabas appeared on the bridge to return the log-tapes and to get Moraghan's initials on the main manifest, then vanished again into the lower levels of the ship to supervise the longshoremen. Moraghan sighed noisily, stretched again, and reached for the microphone that dangled beside the captain's chair. Guil paused in spite of herself. The captain's landing speeches were usually worth hearing, if only because she never seemed to edit them for Oresteian ears.

"All right, people, listen up." Moraghan's voice echoed oddly, amplified by the ship's systems. "This is Orestes, first off. Read the *Register* and the Survey pamphlets— that's an order, people. This is a weird world, and you want to know the rules. Second thing—and this is also an order—you will stay in the port city, Destiny. You're not to leave Destiny without my personal permission." There was a pause, and when the captain spoke again, her tone was almost conversational. "Those of you who've been here before know there's no need to leave Destiny; you can get just about anything you want right here. The entertainment district is called the Necropolis—read the *Register* if you want to know why it's called that—" She paused again, as though collecting her thoughts. "You all heard about *Tallyrand*, I'm sure. I don't want to see any of my people involved in any kind of incident. Stick to professionals or ghosts—you can tell a ghost by the white dot painted on his/her forehead, and I'm sure you don't need me to tell you how to find a pro."

Guil grinned at that, and Moraghan gave her a conspiratorial wink before continuing. "For the rest: this is a cold planet, people, and a light one. We've arrived at Sunset, and we'll be staying through the planetary night, which lasts about three standard days. All right, read the *Register*, stay out of trouble, and be aboard by 0800 s-day 248." She set the microphone back on its hook, and Guil stepped forward, holding out her hand.

"We'll be going planetside now, Captain Moraghan."

Moraghan accepted the other woman's handshake. "As always, an easy trip. Can I buy you dinner on the strength of it?"

Guil smiled. "My pleasure, Captain."

"Leith," Moraghan corrected, with a smile of her own. "We're down-side now. Tonight?"

"Tonight," Guil agreed. "I'll meet you on the other side of the Customs barrier?"

"I'll be there as soon as I've filed my papers," Moraghan answered. She gave an eloquent grimace. "You know how long that can take." A light flashed on the communications console, and she turned away to answer it, muttering under her breath.

Guil nodded sympathetically, and motioned for Elam to follow her from the bridge. The ship's lower levels were already crowded with longshoremen and their equipment, but *Pipe Major*'s junior engineer steered them quickly through the crush to the lower hatch. Guil nodded thanks—words would have been inaudible above the noise of unloading—and stepped through onto the field's fused earth.

It was cold out, doubly so after the unnatural warmth of *Pipe Major*. Guil threw back her head, watching her breath smoke in the still air. The combination of the cold and the light gravity was surprisingly invigorating, driving away some of the weariness of the ring passage. Elam seemed to feel it, too, cautiously straightening his spine and moving with a little more certainty.

"What do we do now?" he asked, his tone more tentative than his words. The absence of any title was very noticeable.

Guil bit back a reprimand. It was her own fault that he didn't address her by any title—the apprentice came from a conservative Branch of his Kinship, and had never worked with *para'anin* before. She had not chosen to make it easier by telling him her preference, and therefore, she told herself firmly, could not be angry. "We sign in," she said. "Then you can do what you like."

"Thank you," Elam said meekly, but Guil was not listening. As they rounded the corner of the last machinists' shack, she could see straight down the three kilometers of the main taxiway to Destiny itself. It was not a city of tall buildings—it could not be, on a seismically active world—but each building was brightly lit, so that Destiny stretched like a jeweled band along the horizon. Agamemnon, half full, was poised like a cloudstone statue on that glittering base. Its light drowned any sight of stars in the cloudless sky. Guil drew a shaky breath, and turned away. Elam followed silently.

Only a single door opened into the administrative complex from the landing field, and it gave onto a stairway that brought newcomers directly into the Customs cage. Guil found the line for Port Authority personnel and flashed her ID disk at one bored attendant while holding out her open carryall for the other man's perfunctory inspection. They nodded her through the barriers, and she lifted a hand in polite farewell to them and to Elam before turning toward the narrow waiting area. She settled herself in the most secluded chair, propped her feet on her carryall, and leaned back to think. Moraghan would be on-planet through the Dark—until a little after Sunrise, in fact. That was good: there would be time to do things without having to worry about Sunrise closing down the Necropolis. Guil frowned to herself, calculating. Dinner tonight, yes. . . . And maybe she could persuade Moraghan to stay with her, the way she had the last time. Smiling at the memory, Guil began to run down the stocks of food in her larder.

A movement on the other side of the Customs barrier caught her attention, and she looked up quickly. *Pipe Major*'s crew had emerged from the stairway and was spreading out among the multiple inspection stations. Guil watched, idly curious. Aboard *Pipe Major*, she had felt alien, set apart by her unmarred body. No, that wasn't entirely it, she decided. It wasn't just that she was unscarred—the junior pilot, Tham, his name was, showed no visible marks—but that she was in other ways so physically different. She had felt spindly, almost—too tall and thin and not strong enough, all the legacy of Electra's and Orestes' low gravities. Now, for all that there were nearly as many ex-Peacekeepers as Oresteians in the Customs lobby, it was *Pipe Major's* people who looked wrong. Guil nodded to herself, watching. It really wasn't just the scars that made them look out of place—between the mines and the mills, prostheses were common enough on Orestes— but the body types. *Pipe Major's* crew seemed collectively short and stocky, and they moved clumsily, as though it was hard to keep from breaking things.

Guil shook herself then, annoyed with the irrelevance of her own thoughts, and sat up, reaching for her carryall. The nearest agent was almost finished with Moraghan and, even as Guil thought that, the captain was waved on through the barrier. Stretching, Guil moved to meet her.

"Damn, this is a cold planet," Moraghan said. "I always forget."

"How the hell do you people stand it?" That was Sabas, grinning as he shoved through the last of the barriers. He balanced a huge travel bag on one shoulder, handling its weight with ease.

Guil shrugged. "We're used to it, I guess," she said, in a deliberately colorless voice.

Sabas eyed her speculatively, and Moraghan said, "Darah, behave." To Guil, she said, "We're still on for dinner, I hope?"

"Of course," Guil answered. Before she could say anything else, Askel had joined them, one hand at the collar of his heavy jacket.

"Where can we reach you if we need you, Captain?" he asked, the artificial voice sounding doubly harsh without the blurring hum of his engines in the background.

"I hadn't really made any plans yet," Moraghan answered.

Guil took a deep breath. "If you want," she said, "you're welcome to stay with me." Sabas raised an eyebrow, and Guil added defensively, "It'll save you some money, and I've a place right in the center of things."

Moraghan nodded. "Thanks. I'll take you up on that. You're on the service, right?" Guil nodded, and the captain looked back at Askel. "And you know Guil. So if any of you need me, I can be reached through her number, all right?"

There was a muttered chorus of agreement, and Moraghan nodded again. "Right, then. Have fun, people, and for Christ's sake, stay out of trouble."

Guil hid a smile. It was a clear dismissal—so clear that even Sabas, who seemed inclined to linger, was forced to back away. Moraghan waited until the last of her crew was out of earshot, then said, "Look, I hope I didn't force your hand."

Guil shook her head quickly. "Not at all. I was sort of hoping you'd stay over—" Someone called her name, and she broke off, stiffening.

Moraghan frowned. "Was that . . . ?"

"Oslac," Guil answered, and looked hastily for an escape.

"Guil!"

The voice was closer now, too close to ignore. Moraghan muttered a curse, dropping her carryall with a thud. Guil turned to face the newcomer, schooling her face to its most impassive mask. "Harbormaster?"

"I'm glad I caught you," Oslac said. He was a bulky man for an Oresteian, but he carried the fat lightly enough. Guil eyed him with growing suspicion.

"What's up, Oslac?"

"Well, now," the harbormaster began. "Well, now. It's a chance for you to earn a little extra, Guil, and I know how you need that—"

"Oslac," Guil interrupted firmly. "I've just come off duty as a substitute. If you want me to fly again, I've got to quote union rules at you."

"No, no, no," Oslac protested, waving his hands for emphasis. "Not flying at all, I know the regs—I'm your foreman, remember? It's just that I need an on-call pilot—Edlyn's out sick, and it's hard to find people in the Dark. It's double pay."

"Covell's always bitching about not getting his share of the extra work," Guil said. "Call him." Oslac started to say something more, but Guil held up her hand. "Covell or Martets. Not me."

The harbormaster hesitated, and Guil's hand slowly tightened on the strap of her carryall. She fought down her anger and, as always, it was Oslac who looked away first.

"All right, Guil. Just thought I'd give you the chance at the money, that's all."

"Thank you, Oslac," Guil answered, silkily. "But no thanks." Without waiting for his answer, she stalked away. Moraghan followed, grinning openly, but she did not speak until they reached the main entrance.

"He wasn't serious, was he? About putting you on duty?"

Guil lifted a hand to signal a passing tram. As the machine slid to a stop, grounding gently against its single rail, she said, "Of course he was." Try as she might, she couldn't keep the anger from her voice.

Moraghan whistled. "Regulations. . . ."

Guil nodded, and pulled herself up into the tram, running her access card through the sensor. Moraghan fumbled in her pocket for a handful of Oresteian coin, and awkwardly dropped the proper fare into the box. Guil moved down the almost-empty car. She had her choice of seats. She chose two together on the left-hand side of the car, where they would have a good view crossing the Ostlaer River. Moraghan joined her a few seconds later, and the tram jerked into motion.

"Guil," the captain said, after a moment, raising her voice slightly to be heard over the hum of the tram's motor. "What do you mean, he was serious about letting you take the on-call slot?"

Guil shrugged, wishing Moraghan would drop the subject. "If I'd said yes, he'd've put me on. You know what space is like around here—nobody comes into this volume without us knowing about it. You go anywhere else in an emergency, not Orestes. The on-call pilot's a joke."

Moraghan raised an eyebrow. "I grant you, it's not likely to happen, but suppose you get catastrophic Drive failure, and somebody gets thrown out into this sphere? Then what?"

"Come on, Leith, no one survives a catastrophic failure," Guil said, more roughly than she'd intended. She controlled her temper with an effort, said, "Besides, I didn't do it—I wouldn't. So it doesn't matter."

Moraghan looked dubious, but said nothing for a few minutes. The tram had left the port complex and was halfway to the Ostlaer Bridge before she said, "Look, Guil, if you let me, I'll file a complaint—"

"I fight my own battles, Leith."

Moraghan was silent, and after a moment, Guil glanced apologetically at her. The captain gave her a rather taut half-smile, but said nothing. Guil looked away again, out the window at her elbow. The tram was curving up the slight incline that led to the bridge, heading into the city. The buildings glowed and flashed, Agamemnon rising behind them, but Guil was looking at the river itself. The dark waters seemed almost still, not a ripple marring the glassy surface, but Guil knew that was deceptive. The Ostlaer's current was deadly, especially here in the city. As if to confirm that, the tram slowed for the barrier wall, hanging back while a gate creaked open. Then the tram slid slowly onto the bridge, picking up speed again. Guil stared out into the twilight, looking upstream toward the Prosperities. I'm not your crewman, Leith, she thought. Why don't you see that? It's not your business.

Guil took a deep breath, trying to relax. Moraghan meant well; there was no reason to blame her for Oslac's idiocies. She leaned forward again, touched the captain's knee. "Leith, I'm sorry."

"It's okay."

Moraghan's response seemed a little too quick. Guil made a face, hoping she hadn't spoiled another off-world friendship. "No, I mean it."

Moraghan turned to face her, smiling. "So did I, honest." She looked past Guil, toward the city and the planet looming behind it, and her smile widened. "God, that's spectacular."

Guil smiled back, feeling the tension ease between them. Dinner tonight, she thought, then the puppet shows tomorrow, and maybe the next day—and I think there's a *khy sonon-na* at the Blackbird the day after. We'll have enough to keep us busy until she has to leave.

Chapter 3: Trey Maturin

I finished my written report on the things I had seen at the mines six hours before Sunset began, and left it and a formal request for three days' leave in the Matriarch's mailbox. Her equally formal permission was flashing on my workscreen before I had finished packing. I hit the key that acknowledged my receipt of the message, jammed a final hoobey-wool overtunic into my carryall—I was always cold during the Dark, no matter what I did—and headed for the main door. The shuttle that would take us to the train station was already drawn up under the overhanging entrance, a massive eight-wheeler that would carry two dozen people in comfort. There were more than that milling around by the cargo door and the steps leading up to the cab, and I wondered for a moment if we would all fit inside. Then I realized that at least a quarter of the crowd were just helping with the baggage or saying their good-byes, and threaded my way through the mob toward the steps.

"Trey!"

I looked up to see Rohin leaning out one of the eight-wheeler's windows. I waved back, then nodded when he gestured for me to join him, and pushed my way through the crowd to the front of the car. Rohin was dressed for exploring the Necropolis, all right, a loose black coat thrown over tunic and trousers, the wide hood folded back on his shoulders. A thin scarf was wound around his neck, ready to double as a mask should he choose to venture into a theater or a brothel. The codes decreed that such a disguise was discretion enough—if one stayed away from ghosts. For that, he would need a medium. Rohin gestured to the seat beside him, and I nodded, tossing my carryall into the rack above.

"Where will you be staying?" he asked.

I settled myself as comfortably as I could on the thin padding. "At an inn called Colonel Grete's."

Rohin grinned. "Not our townhouse?"

"Are you?" I asked in return. The Halex Family, like most Families, owned a house in the most respectable section of Destiny for use of Family members visiting the city on business. I had stayed there once, when I first arrived, and had avoided it ever since. I went to Destiny to get away from the codes, not to follow them.

Rohin shook his head. "I'm staying at Hills', by the greengates."

That was a popular private club that catered to the sporting crowd. "I didn't know you were a member," I said.

"I'm not. Ixora sponsored me." Rohin grinned again. "She still thinks she can get me to crew for her in the Garnocks, and I'm going to take full advantage."

"The Garnocks?" I asked idly.

"It's a sledge meet," Rohin answered. "Over in the Axtell Mandate. I crewed for Ixora once—drag-brake man—a couple of years ago. Never again."

The eight-wheeler's engine started with a coughing roar, cutting off all further conversation. I nodded—sympathetically, I hoped—and braced myself as the eight-wheeler lurched away from the Tower door. Sledge racing—teams of hoobeys pulling a heavy sled—was probably the most popular sport on the planet; it was, not surprisingly, correspondingly dangerous. Hoobeys, while generally even-tempered—they were large enough, the biggest mammals on Orestes, not to need a hair-trigger defense—could be roused to frenzy during the rut. And the only way you could get a team to pull at a racing pace was to put a jill in first flush of rut at the head of the line. The trick was to control the resulting frenzy. I had seen the spiked bits, the weighted collars, the iron-woven traces, and knew that teams still broke loose, overturning their sledges and killing their crews. It took seven people to handle a four-jack team, four for the sledge itself and its complicated brake system, two for the team's side-lines, a driver, and a post-rider to control the jill. I didn't blame Rohin in the least for staying away from that game.

On the other hand, I had to admit that a sledge race was something I would like to see. Partly, it was the fact that the races were a strong part of Oresteian culture—a whole literary genre, and a subclass of holoplays, centered around the races—but mostly. . . . I had seen hoobeys often enough, grazing placidly across the plains of the Halex Mandate, or penned comfortably in a feeding corral before the shearing. I could not imagine the great, shaggy beasts—animals that towered over even the tallest Oresteians, with legs nearly as thick as a man's body and grey-white belly fur falling in hanks almost to the ground—aroused enough to run. Hell, even flagtails, the pack-hunting carnivores of the equatorial plains, were supposed to think twice before taking on a hoobey herd.

The eight-wheeler lurched again, and I looked up to see that we were already at the train station. I fumbled beneath my seat for my carryall, wondering idly if I could get leave to see the Garnocks. "When is this meet, Rohin?" I asked as we filed off the eight-wheeler and made our way into the station.

He gave me a rather puzzled look, but answered, "About three grand-days from now." The code kept him from asking the next question, but I answered it anyway.

"I've never seen a race before. I'm sort of curious."

"A lot of off-worlders don't like it," Rohin said. "It can get—well, pretty brutal."

I shrugged. The Demi-heir was looking genuinely concerned, though, so I said, "Thanks for the warning." I didn't add that I found a lot of things on Orestes to be pretty brutal. Three grand-days. . . . I made the calculations while the porters examined tickets and baggage, and led us to one of the train's forward carriages. That worked out to about seventeen calendar-days. I just might be able to arrange that.

The short ride into Destiny was uneventful. The Sunset line had slipped three-quarters of the way down the sky, and faded from the blue of Day to a rich purple-black. Only the horizon still glowed red-orange, like embers in a furnace. On the opposite horizon, Agamemnon rose like a gleaming shield. This was my favorite time of the grand-day, the hours of Sunset. I found myself craning my neck to see through the tram windows as I rode into the city, and searching avidly between the roofs of the low buildings as I walked the final blocks to Colonel Grete's.

By the time I reached the inn, though, I was glad to get inside. The chill of the Dark was beginning to settle on the city, and I was shivering. Colonel Grete's proprietor, a slim, grey-bearded man, came forward to greet me, gesturing at the same time for one of the attendants to take my quilted coat.

"Good afternoon, Medium Maturin," he exclaimed. "Or would you prefer Mediator?"

He had asked me that question perhaps half a dozen times already. "Medium is fine, Lingard, thank you." I let the attendant, a silent, steel-eyed woman, peel the coat from my shoulders. "How's business?"

Lingard—I could not remember which Branch of the Halex Kinship he belonged to—gave an eloquent shrug. "In the Dark, wonderful. In the Day. . . ." He let his voice trail off, then brightened. "But everyone suffers that."

I nodded.

"However," Lingard continued. "I have the room you asked for, Medium, with the balcony." He frowned again. "I'm afraid there will be an extra charge. . . ."

He had told me that before, too. "That's fine," I said.

"Excellent." Lingard nodded to the silent woman. "Escort the Medium to the Gold Balcony room, Huldah."

The woman nodded, and turned to me. "If you'll follow me, Medium?" Her voice was as metallic as her eyes.

To reach the main staircase, we had to pass through the inn's main room. A bar heater glowed in each wall, and a dozen chairs, each with its own low table, were drawn up in a semi-circle around the heaters. Only one of the chairs was occupied, however, drawn out of the circle so that it stood beneath the mural of Colonel Grete at the gates of hell. As we passed, the man looked up from his newssheet, and I recognized one of the inn's two mediums. He raised a hand in silent greeting, and returned to his reading.

My own room was on the top floor, on the side of the building that faced the Necropolis. Huldah unlocked the room's door and followed me inside, setting my bag at the foot of the stove-bed. I gave her her tip, and received the room key in exchange. She bowed herself out, and I turned to explore the room, wondering again about the differences between Orestes and most of the other Conglomerate worlds. On most of them—certainly on all of the Urban Worlds—her job would be performed by a robot, not because robots were cheaper or necessarily more efficient, but because on most other worlds human beings had other, better jobs to do. Not on Orestes, however. I shook my head again, and went to open the thermal shutters.

The padded screen folded back along its channel, and I took a deep breath. I had never had one of the balcony rooms before—they were usually full during the Dark, and it was only because of a cancellation that I had been able to get one this time. Lingard had said that the rooms on this side faced the Necropolis; he had understated the case. I could easily see over the wall that surrounded the Necropolis and down into the great square backing the main greengate. It was beginning to fill with people, ghosts and *para'anin* and the living crossing the metalled square, or milling around the lighted kiosks that advertised the bars and puppet theaters and brothels. Seen from above, the square had a fairy tale quality, a gorgeous unreality: from here, every person was dressed like an actor or a king; they were draped in flashing jewels, and every stone was real. Enchanted, I reached for my coat, and the intercom buzzed.

I swore, and reached for the answer switch. "Maturin."

"Trey." It was Rohin. "I was wondering. . . ." His voice trailed off nervously, and he tried again. "I bought a bottle of tsaak, and I wondered if you'd want to share it with me."

I wondered what he really wanted. My eyes strayed to

the window again. With Rohin present, I couldn't really watch the passing crowd, would have to pay attention to my guest. . . . Unless what he wanted was my view of the square, I thought suddenly. And I bet it is, too. I smiled, and said, "You're welcome, Rohin, as long as you don't mind an open window."

"Not at all," the Demi-heir answered fervently. "I'm on my way up."

I took my finger off the switch, still smiling. Until that moment, I had forgotten that this was the hour of the Promenade, when most of the inhabitants of the Necropolis—actors, dancers, prostitutes, and all the rest—paraded the length of Broad Street, the main street, advertising their various wares. I knew Hills' Club was too far from the wall to let its guests overlook the square, and Colonel Grete's was famous for its view. . . . I wondered if Rohin knew for certain that his twin would appear, or if he were merely hoping to catch a glimpse of him. Personally, I hoped Rehur would be among the crowds. I was curious about this ghost.

There was a knock at the door, and I opened it to let Rohin in. He gave me a rather embarrassed smile, and held out the insulated flask of tsaak. A massive, fur-lined cloak was draped over his other arm, and in spite of myself I gave it an envious glance as I accepted the tsaak. Instantly, Rohin held it out as well.

"I brought this, too. Jesma said you feel the cold."

"What will you wear?" I asked, but I took the cloak, feeling the heavy softness of the fur. It was flagtail, I thought, and the leather—the inner side of the furs that formed the outside of the cloak—had been scraped and finished until it was as flexible as velvet.

"I'm fine as I am," Rohin answered. He smiled as I set aside the tsaak, but continued stroking the magnificent fur.

"This is very kind of you," I said. "I'll return it after the promenade."

Rohin gave an odd little shrug, and looked away, embarrassed. "It's a gift, Medium. For your trouble."

I was struck speechless. Even on Orestes, such a garment was expensive, and off-world. . . . I couldn't begin to estimate what connoisseurs might pay. "Rohin, I'm the

Halex Medium. It's my job—my pleasure, too, in this case. It's too much."

Rohin shrugged again. "Please," he said. "I'd—like you to have it."

There was no refusing that—and, I realized, quite suddenly, I didn't want to refuse it. I ran my hand over the butter-soft leather, buried my fingers in the gleaming grey fur. "It's beautiful, Rohin," I said. "Thank you."

Rohin's smile widened, but he said only, "I'll pour the tsaak, then we'll go out?"

I nodded, swinging the cloak around my shoulders. It was heavy, but perfectly balanced and incredibly warm. I hugged it to myself for a moment, then slipped my hands through the red bound slits and fumbled for the clasp. It was a piece of blackamber, carved in the shape of a terrestrial rose. More magnificence, I thought, and turned to look at myself in the mirror that hung beside the stovebed. The body of the cloak was a soft, pale brown, a few shades lighter than my skin; the fur and my hair alike were grey, though the fur was much finer. The blackamber glowed darkly even in the room's dim light. I was magnificent now, clothed in an archaic beauty. The actor in me rejoiced.

"Put up the hood," Rohin said.

I did so, watching his reaction in the mirror. The hood framed my face in pale fur, throwing my features into shadow: I looked less magnificent, more mysterious— dangerous, I thought. Rohin smiled.

"Now you look like one of us," he said, and held out my gloves. I pulled them on obediently, knowing that I would want them, and noticed with a small shock that the red leather exactly matched the thread that had been used to bind the arm slits. Rohin saw the direction of my gaze, and sighed.

"I'm glad. I wasn't sure it would be a match." He fastened his own coat, a knee-length jacket of quilted windsilk, over his layered tunics, and reached for the cups of tsaak. "It's almost time."

I accepted my cup, feeling its heat through the thick china, and followed Rohin out onto the balcony. The light had dimmed—or rather, I realized, its color had changed. All the reds and yellows seemed to have been leached out of it, leaving only the light reflected from Agamemnon. It was a strange light, almost blue, luminous without warmth. I could not see my own skin, wrapped as I was in layers of leather and fur, but Rohin's face seemed even paler, all the blood gone from it. Ghostlight, the Oresteian poets called it, this not-quite-Dark.

In the square below us, lights began to come on. They were mostly blue-toned, like the natural light, and seemed only to intensify the eerie twilight. There seemed to be more people in the square, too. Then I heard Rohin draw a hissing breath, and realized the promenade had begun.

At first, there wasn't that much to see: a few women, in long coats that seemed demure until they turned quickly, opening the long slit that ran from the hem to just above the shoulder blades; a man in a short fur jacket over skin-tight trousers that showed almost indecently muscular legs. Then, at last, the first troupe of actors appeared, men and women in the heavy, stylized costumes of the puppet theater. One of them carried a banner, moving sluggishly in the still air, but I did not recognize its emblem. The group made a circuit of the square, nodding grandly to others in the crowd. As they passed along the wall on our side of the square, there was a shrill whistle. I looked up, startled, and saw that every window in the buildings that defined two sides of the square was open and crammed with spectators. One of the actors—a woman in a blue-grey tunic and a flat dark cap—looked up at the sound, and waved.

"Cashil's group," Rohin said, with audible disappointment. He had pulled a fist-sized distance glass from his pocket, and was using it to scan the crowd.

I nodded—I had heard of that puppet theater, though I hadn't seen their work—and looked back at the square. More and more people were filing in, moving slowly along our wall, then past the greengate and back along the far side of the square to the streets that led out again. Most groups carried their own lights, though there were lights on the corners of each of the buildings, adding to the fantastic tracery of light and shadow filling the square.

Rohin nudged me then, and pointed toward a couple just entering the square. "That's Javas," he said. "And his mysterious keeper."

I nodded. Even I had heard of the most famous scandal on the Oresteian stage—how the actor Javas, a ghost of Fira in Brandr, was carrying on an affair with a living woman. She had succeeded in keeping her identity strictly secret, and the affair had only increased Javas's popularity in the theaters. I leaned forward, but I couldn't make out any details.

"Let me see your glass a minute," I said, and Rohin handed it to me, grinning. I put the glass to my eye and twisted the lens experimentally. The scene wavered, the focusing fields momentarily splitting the light into a rainbow of enhanced colors, and then steadied. Javas's face seemed to leap out at me. He was not precisely a young man, as I had half expected him to be—he was perhaps even a few years older than myself, but he was still very handsome in a cynical, rakish way. It was the sort of face that made one think the lines had been gained through decadent experience rather than mere age, attractive to men and women alike. As for his companion. . . . I swung the glass to my right until I had it focused on her face. Whoever she was, she wore a full face mask, the sort hoobey drivers wore to protect their skin from flying ice, effectively concealing her identity. All I could see was a pair of brown eyes, half hidden beneath the disheveled strands of a scarlet wig that mocked the traditional topknot.

I adjusted the glass again, decreasing the magnification until I had the two of them framed in its lens. They were a handsome couple, all right, both dressed in the height of city fashion, he in short, belted jacket over felty trousers; she in an ankle-length tapestry vest thrown over tunic and trousers. A lion's-head broach clasped her vest across the breast; his wide belt was fastened with a buckle of the same design. I watched their slow progress toward the main greengate, wondering what they were thinking. How could she, especially, bring herself to show herself so publicly, when recognition would bring social death? Was it at Javas's command? To prove her love to him? I adjusted the glass again, watching the way she walked, the way she held the actor's arm, possessive and very much the master of the situation. She was flaunting him, I realized suddenly, throwing her affair into everyone's face.

I was certain this appearance at the promenade was her choice, not his, but I could not understand why.

Rohin elbowed me then, and, reluctantly, I gave the glass back to him. He scanned the crowd again, but with less enthusiasm than before. I set my empty cup aside, and leaned forward against the railing. "Who's that in the scarlet coat?" I asked, after a moment.

Rohin frowned, adjusting his glass. "That's Jahala."

"May I?" I held out my hand, and Rohin handed me the glass again, smiling tolerantly. I turned it on the tall woman. Rohin might be blasé about Orestes' most famous lead actor, but I wasn't. I had not yet seen her on stage— she performed less and less frequently these days, and rumor said she would soon go off-world to the Dionysian theaters—but her fame was considerable. In repose, her face was unremarkable, the regular features marred by makeup more suited to the stage than to the street, but then she smiled in answer to some question or comment, and her entire being seemed to take on new life. I lowered the glass, startled. I had rarely seen a human being so— compelling? virile? simply *alive*? More than ever, I wanted to see her act.

Rohin sighed, and I offered him the glass again. He shook his head. "I don't think Rehur's coming," he said.

I glanced at the streets leading into the square. It did seem as though the stream of new arrivals had slowed. "I am sorry," I said aloud. "When is the *khy sono*?"

Rohin brightened visibly. "The day after tomorrow, by the calendar. It's at the Blackbird, beginning at 2130. Can I buy you dinner at Hills' beforehand?"

I only hesitated for an instant. The cabaret theaters expect their patrons to drink while they watch the show, and offer very little to absorb the alcohol. "Thank you, that's an excellent idea."

Rohin nodded. "At the nineteenth hour?"

"That suits me," I said.

Rohin stayed until the promenade was clearly over, and the last of the performers had vanished from the square. He was going into the Necropolis with some of his agemates from Hills'. He very politely invited me to join them, but I refused with thanks. I'd be seeing enough of him over the next few days, though I didn't say that. When he had gone, I closed the window and settled myself at the room's information terminal. It was still quite cold in the room, though, and after a moment I got up again and adjusted the heating system until the bar heater beneath the window was glowing yellow-orange. I made contact with the master scheduling computer, ordered tickets for two plays I wanted to see, then contacted the Port Authority. As I'd hoped, *Pipe Major* had just landed, but when I called the hotels where the mailships' crews usually stayed, Leith wasn't listed anywhere. I asked for Minuke Ten, who had been chief pilot the last time *Pipe Major* had come through, but no one had heard of her either, and I assumed she had left the ship. Well, I told myself, if Leith really wants to see me, she'll call the Tower, and they'll tell her that I'm in Destiny and where I'm staying. For now, it's time to relax and enjoy the city.

Over the next two days, I wandered through the Necropolis, savoring the anonymity and the chance to be alone. I renewed my acquaintance with the younger of Colonel Grete's mediums, and went with her to a mediums' bar. I spent the better part of a day playing Chance with her older partner. I ate and drank, relishing the chance to taste off-world dishes again, and went to the theater. The first, *The Substitute*, one of the few comedies in the Oresteian canon, was competent, but unexciting; the second one haunted my dreams the night I saw it. It was *The Man Who Killed in His Sleep*, based on an old local story that might have been true, about a man who wants to leave his mistress to marry another woman. Under the code, she must give her permission—there is an implied contract between them—and she refuses. His honor and his duty to his Family require him to marry the second woman and, in desperation, he strangles his mistress with her own sash. He marries the second woman, but soon after the wedding, is visited by the ghost of his mistress, who urges him to strangle his wife. He fights the compulsion, but in the end, surrenders to it, and kills himself as well.

In some versions, the ghost is a true ghost, the projection of his own guilt, and I have always thought the play more powerful that way. This time, though, the puppetmasters chose to make the ghost real—the protagonist fails to kill her, and it is implied she chooses social death to achieve her revenge—and the final act became a duel between the two characters. The plot itself isn't much, has been bettered half a hundred times. The acting was good, the puppeteering excellent . . . but what frightened me was the crowd. They were mostly *para'anin* and ghosts, and it was clear that, for them, the hero was the vengeful mistress. The wife's death was done on stage, a graceful, vicious dance of murder. At its end there was a sigh, not of horror but of pleasure, and then applause. There was an anger there that frightened me, and that night I had dark dreams of riot in the streets of Destiny.

But in the morning there was a message from Leith— just a note to say that she was on-planet and wanted to see me, and giving a callcode—and I forgot my dreams in trying to reach her. The callcode she had given belonged to a private flat somewhere in Destiny. I tried calling it several times, but no one was home to answer. By the time I joined Rohin at Hills', I had almost given up on seeing her.

The Demi-heir and I ate a leisurely dinner, and then made our way through the streets to the nearest greengate. Rohin pulled up the hood of his jacket as we approached, and after a moment's thought, I did the same. I was wearing the fur cloak he had given me, and I had never felt more Oresteian as the city police on duty by the gate waved us inside.

This greengate gave onto a much smaller square, with a central fountain where the water had frozen into an exotic, abstract sculpture. The ice gleamed in Agamemnon's reflected light, casting shadows of its own. The buildings that ringed the square were dimly lit, quiet, handsome places, and I did not ask what they were for fear of finding out for certain they were brothels.

"We can walk from here," Rohin said, "or we could take the tram."

"Let's walk," I said.

Rohin led the way through the quiet streets, moving toward the center of the Necropolis where the theaters lay. As we came closer, the buildings became more brightly lit and the streets grew more crowded, until at last we

came out into the garish lights of the Broad Street itself.
Though I had seen it before, the place still dazzled. I
slowed, pretending to fumble with the clasp of my cloak.
Rohin paused with me, grinning, but I ignored the knowing smile.

To either side, Broad Street stretched toward the two
main greengates, a street three times as wide as any other
in the city. Four-story buildings, each one hung with
bright banners and banded with lights, rose up on either
side; even the tram that edged its way along the central
rail was hung with strands of lights. But most of all, the
street was filled with people. Some were ghosts, the white
ghostmark clearly visible on their foreheads; more were
para'anin, distinguishable as such by the fact that they did
not make any pretense of hiding their faces; but the vast
majority were ordinary Family members, their features
shadowed beneath hoods or hidden completely behind
scarves or painted masks. Visually, they added a strangely
sinister quality to the passing crowd, all those masked or
hidden faces, and enough of them had thrown off all the
prohibitions of the code to make them dangerous. Even as
I watched, half a dozen adolescents dressed all in red
formed a ring around another young man. He turned,
surveying them warily, and I saw the ghostmark on his
forehead. I reached for my badge, ready to display it
if I needed to intervene, and then the ghost shrugged
and held out a hand. The pack leader gave a yelp of
triumph, and pressed a handful of notes into the ghost's
hand. The ghost let himself be dragged toward the
nearest bar.

"Come on," Rohin said. "We'll be late."

I shook myself and followed him across Broad Street and
into a heated arcade. It was almost painfully warm, after
the cold outside. I threw back the hood and loosened my
cloak, just keeping my arms through the slits.

"The Blackbird's at the end of here," Rohin said.

I nodded. The arcade was crowded—it seemed to hold
mostly bars and shops that sold off-world goods—and there
was a line stretching from the Blackbird's door nearly
halfway up the arcade. I hesitated, but Rohin shoved his
way through, and I followed. Even after eight months in

Orestes' gravity, I was newly made aware of my off-world strength, and I had to be very careful not to knock people off balance as I passed them. We were almost at the Blackbird's door when someone called my name.

I turned quickly, almost knocking Rohin over. "Leith?"

"Trey!" *Pipe Major's* captain edged her way through the crowd, a tall, fair-haired Oresteian following her. "Did you get my message?"

I said, "Only that you were on-planet. I called the number you left, but I couldn't get through."

"We've been busy," Leith said, laughing. She looked very small among the Oresteians, a diminutive, alien presence in her spacer's leather. We touched hands, and she went on, "I don't know if you'll have much luck getting in. They're sold out."

"We have reservations," Rohin said.

Leith gave him a measuring look, the humor fading from her eyes, and I said, hastily, "You know the rules, Leith. He's—one of my employers, and nameless for the evening." To Rohin, I added, "This is Leith Moraghan, captain of the six-week mailship."

Leith nodded, and gestured to the blond woman at her left. As always, she used her right hand, the gloved left arm motionless at her side. "Guil, this is Trey Maturin, Mediator—Medium for the Halex Kinship here." She included Rohin in her glance as she added, "And this is my friend Guil, who's the best tug pilot in this system."

"Look, why don't you join us?" I asked. "I'm sure they can provide a couple of extra chairs." I had quite deliberately put Rohin on the spot—seeing Leith was one of the reasons I had wanted to come into Destiny in the first place—but, to give him credit, the Demi-heir seconded me without perceptible pause.

"You'd be welcome."

Leith gave him another, more favorable glance, and said, "Thanks. Guil's been telling me about the—competition, and I'd've hated to miss it after all that."

The blond woman made a noise that might have been laughter or protest, but made no further objection when Rohin resumed his slow passage toward the head of the line. At the door, the clubman made ritual denials until

Rohin passed him a two-kip note. Unsmiling, he passed us inside, and another clubman led us to a table near the edge of the huge room. Another note changed hands; the clubman nodded, and took us to a second, larger table that commanded a good view of the drumbox stage.

"Neatly done," Leith said. She seated herself, resting her gloved arm on the table and steadying it with her right hand, looking up expectantly at us.

"Thanks," Rohin said, settling himself across from her. I took the place between them, and, more slowly, Guil pulled out the remaining chair.

"What's your Family?" Rohin asked. It was a common-place, but the blond woman checked in mid-movement and fixed him with a chill stare.

"I'm *para'an*," she said, shortly. "Do I go?"

Rohin lifted both hands in surrender, eyes wide. "Not on my account, please."

There was momentarily a note of fear in the Demi-heir's voice, and I didn't entirely blame him. There was something disquieting about the tug pilot, a feral quality that was contradicted by the cold, calculating intelligence in her blue eyes. Guil held her stare for a moment longer, then, unaccountably, her expression softened. "Ex-Tam'ne," she said, and seated herself. "Of Tam'ne in Electra."

Rohin nodded, and I thought I heard, above the noise of conversation, Leith give a soft sigh of relief. Before I could be certain, however, she had said, brightly, "What'll you drink?"

"Spiked coffee, with all the trimmings," I answered. Leith, with her Annwnite metabolism, could drink tsaak all night if she wanted; I knew my limits.

Rohin said, "We could split a jug, Trey—if you'll let me get the next round, Captain, pilot."

Leith nodded. "Fair enough." She looked to Guil. "Tsaak?" The pilot nodded, and Leith punched our order into the central box. After a few moments, a clubman appeared with the heavy tray. There was the usual confusion as he tried to fit the jug and the mugs and the tray of condiments on the table's limited surface, and wedge in the double flask of tsaak as well, but at last he'd managed it, and Leith flipped him her card to settle the bill. The cabarets in the Necropolis don't run tabs. I poured myself a mug of the coffee—from the look of it, the bartender had already added a goodly quantity of the harsh local whiskey—and added spices and sugar. Rohin did the same, but added a shot of the sweetly potent cordial as well. Guil poured tsaak for herself and Leith, and leaned forward, cradling her cup in both hands.

"I hear it's *Belos Kyrle* tonight, the temptation scene."

Rohin nodded, and I said, "That should guarantee bravura performances."

Leith gave me an inquiring glance over the rim of her cup. Guil said, softly, "I told you the plot, Leith."

I said, "It's one of those scenes actors can't resist—can't leave well enough alone. It's a good play, though."

Leith nodded, satisfied, but I wasn't really paying attention. Not only did the temptation scene appeal to actors, it appealed to ex-actors, too, and I couldn't help feeling jealous of the performers. Belos Kyrle is one of those wonderful tortured villains you find only on restrictive worlds. The character is based on a real Demi-heir, a Halex, in fact, who, after a complicated series of events, found himself obliged by the code to murder his lover's blood-sib. Rather than admit what he's done, Belos conceals the murder, hoping to keep his lover, and the bulk of the play deals with the lover's search for truth and the final, bloody vengeance. I had seen the full play twice already, and while the protagonist—the lover, who can be played by actors of either sex depending on company resources and directorial whim—is a good part, I would've given my right arm to play Belos, when I was younger. The death duel, and the death speech following, are an actor's dream.

"Is it true the playwright was murdered for writing it?" Leith asked.

Guil glanced at Rohin before she answered. "It started a Fyfe-Halex feud—it was the poet Esko Fyfe who wrote it—and he did get killed by a gang of Halex."

Rohin shrugged. "Esko Fyfe was kin to Hulder Vieva, who was Shenard's lover—that's the 'real' Belos," he added, to Leith. "Shenard Halex." He looked back at Guil. "Esko took his revenge as best he could, and so did we."

Before Guil could answer, the main lights flickered,

then dimmed steadily to near-total darkness. The pilot contented herself with a rather scornful sniff, and poured more tsaak. All around us, conversation faded to anticipatory whispers. Then lights flashed on in the center of the cabaret, webbing the drumbox stage in a complex net of light and shadow. I leaned back in my chair to see more clearly, closing both hands around my drink. I was suddenly, painfully tense, knowing what this competition could mean to an up-and-coming holopuppet group—money, certainly, but more than that, enough publicity to guarantee continued employment through the next few months. I shivered, forced myself to relax, to think only of the entertainment.

A glowing sign appeared in the air above the drumbox, a starship superimposed on a crescent Agamemnon. Leith murmured something that sounded like a question, and Rohin whispered, "Goddard Studios. Shh."

The mailship captain gave him a startled glance, but seemed to recognize the intensity on the Demi-heir's face, and fell silent. Music sounded from behind the solid column of light, eerie and biting. Slowly, the first figure coalesced on the box: a holopuppet, dressed in contemporary style, moving into a strangely awkward dance even as it took shape. It was a very good figure—I could not have been certain it was a puppet if I hadn't seen it form—and I decided that the dance was meant to be awkward, not merely the work of an unskilled operator. Then another figure, a live actor this time, vaulted onto the box to confront the puppet, while someone offstage intoned the first line of the scene in a keening falsetto.

By the fifth line, it became clear that Goddard had overreached itself: even knowing the scene, it was almost impossible to figure out what was going on. I thought the puppet—which had begun to fade in and out alarmingly, showing unpleasant glints of bone and organs—was meant for Belos, and the actors for the nightmare figures who tempt him to deny the killing, but the narration was so overdubbed and mixed with lines from later in the play that it was impossible to be sure. The *sono* ended to no better than polite applause, and I saw Leith lean across to Guil. I couldn't hear what she said, but the *para'an*'s face

eased suddenly into a broad grin, transforming her completely.

It was a contagious smile. I grinned myself, and said,
low-voiced, "Don't you like experimental theater, Leith?"

Rohin shushed us both, and Leith subsided, mouthing
an obscenity at me.

"Witchwood's next," the Demi-heir whispered, and
pushed back his hood to see better. I started to say something, but Rohin's expression was so tense, willing his twin
to do well, that I couldn't bring myself to disturb him. It
was dark enough in the cabaret that no one was likely to
notice, and if anyone did, the family medium was clearly
present.

Witchwood's tree symbol was already fading, and the
familiar nightmare music rose from the array of synthesizers
behind the stage. A figure in Belos's stylized, conventionally exaggerated costume stepped through the curtain of
light, struck his pose, and began to speak. Rohin's hand
clutched my knee convulsively.

"Rehur."

I hardly needed that confirmation: the face beneath the
actor's heavy makeup was Rohin's. I braced myself, knowing the Demi-heir would ask my opinion of the performance, but after a moment I let myself relax. Rehur was
good, at least within the Oresteian tradition. His voice was
particularly attractive, light in tone, but very flexible, and
he spoke the intricate verse well. At this point in the
play, Belos has done the killing, but hesitates to claim it,
for fear of losing his lover. Figures appear to him in a
dream, tempting him to hide the body and deny what he
has done—the ultimate cowardice, in Oresteian eyes. At
the proper moment, grotesque holopuppet shapes frothed
and flowed from Belos's body to whisper-chant their se-
ductions. All four of them had Rehur's face and spoke with
his voice: an easy effect, but nicely handled. Witchwood's
director was very good at the traditional forms of *khy
sono*. It was too bad, I thought, that this competition
required something more. In a few years, though. . . .

The music changed abruptly, ranged through a quick,
discordant variation on Belos's theme, and slid into the
blatting trumpet-and-drum of a major entrance. All five
figures faded, became translucent, and there was a collec-

tive gasp of surprise: none of us had realized the central figure was a puppet. Then the curtain of light went scarlet, and a figure stepped through it onto the stage. This was unmistakably a living being; the puppets lost all vitality by comparison, the puppetmaster helping the effect by greying their colors slightly. The new Belos wore ordinary formal dress, the sort of clothes the "real" Belos would have worn, felty trousers, deep boots, snowy knitted tunic. His coarse black hair was loose, falling in ratted hanks to his shoulders; his eyes were huge and mad in a too-pale face. He lifted his long hands in a gesture of furious despair, and a trick of the puppetmaster's lights turned them bloody red. His entourage crowded onto the stage behind him. The dream-figures had almost vanished, were barely visible shadows, but "Belos" saw them, and opened his arms to them. In a sudden whirl of light and music, the holopuppets flew toward him, dissolving into his body. "Belos" closed his arms over them, embracing them, embracing himself, bowing his head over his reddened hands. I counted three before the blackout.

There was an instant of silence before the applause. Rohin was clutching my knee again, and pounding the table with his free hand—less in sober assessment of Witchwood's *sono*, I thought, than in sheer relief that his twin had done nothing foolish.

"My God," Leith said. Her left arm had slipped from the table top; she grimaced and picked it up, then reached to order another round.

Guil leaned across to tap the table in front of the Demi-heir. "Your brother?"

Rohin could not keep the pride from his voice. "My late twin."

"He's good," Leith said, dropping her voice as the applause faded and another company's symbol appeared above the drumbox. I watched Rohin instead. The Demi-heir fumbled cautiously in the inner pocket of his coat until he found his card case, then pulled it out, waiting for the music to begin before easing back the catch. He took out a blank card and a pen, scribbled a few lines across the card, signed it with a complicated squiggle, and slipped the case back into his pocket. As the *sono* ended, the clubman appeared with our drinks. Rohin caught at his sleeve, and handed him the card, folded in a twenty-five-senes note.

"Take this to the Witchwood Belos, please."

"Certainly, sor," the clubman answered with a smirk, deftly pocketing note and card. I guessed that Rehur was popular tonight. Rohin flushed, but remembered in time that he was just another anonymous patron. The clubman slipped away, and I settled back in my chair to watch the rest of the *khy sonon-na*.

Most of the interpretations were highly experimental, ranging from good to interesting to utterly awful. One, which exaggerated the traditional gestures into near-ballet, was particularly well-received, but to my mind, Witchwood's performance was clearly the best. Then again, I thought, most Oresteians had grown up on traditional *sonon*, and had a right to be tired of them. It would be interesting to see what they made of this.

The final *sono*—a dreadful, "spacer" version—ended, and the lights slowly came up in the rest of the cabaret. Rohin hastily drew his hood back up, letting it fall forward to shadow his face. Leith leaned forward, raising her voice to carry over the noise of conversation.

"Who judges this contest, anyway?"

"They do," Guil said, nodding toward a table not far from us, directly in front of the stage. "You know, other managers and critics and such."

"I thought the audience voted," I said.

Guil gave me a sort of half-smile. "Sure, Medium, we vote—we should be getting our ballots any second now— but the hired judges make the real decision."

"A popular victory means a lot, too," Rohin objected.

"Is it a money prize?" Leith asked.

"A nominal sum only," the Demi-heir answered, and leaned back to let a passing clubman slide four ballots onto the table in front of him.

"Feed it to the central box when you're done," the clubman said indifferently, and moved on to the next table.

A nominal sum, in Rohin's eyes, might well mean a week's food for a starving actor. I suppressed that thought, and reached for a ballot, blackening the circle next to

Witchwood's name. Leith leaned over my shoulder and laughed.

"Well, that's unanimous," she said.

"You have good taste," I answered, and slid my ballot into the slot beneath the order box. "How long do you think it'll take to get a decision?"

Rohin shrugged. Guil said, almost cheerfully, "About an hour, I'd guess. The popular vote'll be counted sooner, but the judges always take forever."

"Standing on their dignity?" Leith asked.

Guil ignored her, glancing at our empty glasses. "Time for another round," she said. "Medium, and you, friend, what'll you have?" There was a faint note of belligerence in her voice. Leith gave her a quick glance, but said nothing.

I said, "I think it's my round, pilot."

For a long moment, we locked stares. The *para'an's* eyes were blue, all right, but it was a very pale color, almost grey. Ice blue, I thought, and then she looked away.

"It's Guil, then."

I nodded. "And I'm Trey." I looked at the others, all of us pretending nothing had happened. "The same again?"

"We'll split a single flask," Leith said.

"I can handle another carafe if you can," Rohin said. I saw his eyes lock briefly on something across the room, but did not glance back until I had finished punching the order into the central box. The actors and musicians and puppeteers had been making their ways back into the cabaret's main room for some time. Now, Rehur was threading a path through the tables toward us, followed by a red-haired woman and a nondescript little man carrying a sketchblock. Leith glanced toward the newcomer, then back at Rohin.

"Your twin's joining us?" she said. Rohin nodded, unable to keep his eyes off his brother.

"And how long has it been since you saw him last?" Guil asked.

"A full year, *para'*, and not by my choice," Rohin snapped.

The pilot lifted a hand in uncharacteristic apology. "Sorry," she said, and sounded as though she meant it. "Pax?"

Rohin eyed her warily, but nodded. "Pax."

"Medium?" Offstage, Rehur's voice was enough like Rohin's to make me jump a little. I turned to face him, offering my hand.

"I'm the Halex Medium," I said. "Trey Maturin."

"Rehur." The actor took my hand, smiling. "I'm delighted to meet you," he said, and sounded as though he meant it. "Would you give my greetings to my brother?"

"Of course," I said, and added, "I enjoyed the *sono* very much—it was spectacular."

"Tell him the same from me," Rohin said.

"Thanks," Rehur said, ambiguously, as I repeated his greeting to Rohin. He glanced around the table, including us all in his next words. "May we join you?" He gestured to the redhead. "This is Belit, ex-Fyfe, *para'an* of Fyfe in Fyfe, and the vulture here—" He pointed to the little man with the sketchblock. "—is Cho Vieva, of the stage-door press." He put a hand to his face, still Belos's. "I can't take off my makeup until he's done."

"Not long now," Cho said, soothingly, absently, stylus flying across the block. Prints and sketches of actors in costume were extremely popular in Destiny; they were also excellent publicity for the actors and companies involved.

I repeated Rehur's request and introductions for Rohin's benefit, and the Demi-heir nodded acceptance, too excited to speak. Leith said, "Have a seat—if you can find one. I'm Leith Moraghan, captain of *Pipe Major*—the six-week mailship."

"Guil ex-Tam'ne," the tug pilot offered. "*Para'an* of Tam'ne on Electra. I work for the Port Authority."

The redhead wedged herself in between Rohin and her fellow *para'an*. "I'm Witchwood's synth man," she announced cheerfully. "All the sound effects and none of the credit."

Rehur made a rude noise, and hooked a chair from a nearby table, pushing it into place between me and Leith. Up close, he looked less like Rohin than I had thought, less a copy than a mirror image. Maybe it was just the makeup, I thought, doubly stark now without the bulky wig to balance it. His own hair, cut even shorter than Rohin's, was as black as the wig had been.

"Can I ask a stupid question?" Leith said. "The holo-puppets—do the puppeteers tape you doing the part, and play back that tape, or do they actually manipulate an image?"

"Both," Rehur answered, still smiling. He was very up from his performance, excited and confident that he had done well. Remembering the feeling from my own youth, I couldn't help smiling back.

"This time, though, the Tempters were fully pretaped," Rehur went on, "and the puppet-Belos was pretaped except for the voice. Ash—she's the main puppetmaster—wanted me to do the voice live so that there'd be a bigger surprise when it turned out to be a puppet."

"You fooled me," Leith said.

"All done, Rehur," Cho said. Light rippled across the surface of the sketchblock, fixing the image in its memory.

"Thank God, Cho-cho," Rehur said. "Send me a copy, please?"

"I won't even charge you," the artist answered, and slipped away to sketch some other actor.

"You better send Rowan a copy," the musician Belit said.

Rehur made a face, but nodded. "I will." He glanced at the rest of the table. "Rowan's the other puppetmaster. And company manager."

"Rowan and Ash," I said. "Thus Witchwood?"

Rehur gave me a look of pleased surprise. "That's right. A lot of people don't get it."

"Like me," Guil said.

"They're kinds of Terran wood," Leith said. "Used by witches, right, Trey?"

I nodded, aware of Rehur's newly interested gaze, but before I could say anything else, Rohin tugged at my sleeve. I glanced at him, and he beckoned me closer, until he could whisper in my ear.

"Transfer your sanction, Trey, please."

I hesitated. It was possible, under the code, for a medium temporarily to transfer his immunities to another person, allowing that person to see and speak with ghosts, but it was intended for emergencies, or at least for more serious things. On the other hand, it was unlikely anyone in the cabaret would even notice, much less file a formal complaint—and the brothers had not seen each other in a year. I touched the black-hand badge pinned to my collar, put my other hand across Rohin's lips, and repeated the formula. The pleasure on Rohin's face made it worth the risk.

Rehur moved abruptly, almost spilling what was left of Leith's drink, waving broadly at someone on the far side of the room. He glanced at me, and said, "Ash and Rowan. You don't mind?"

"Not at all," I said, and the others echoed me.

The puppetmasters were a magnificently mismatched pair, Ash tall, typically Oresteian; Rowan small and stocky enough to be thought an off-worlder. But it turned out, as we traded introductions, half-shouting to be heard above the other conversations, that she was originally an Orillon of Electra, and distant kin to Guil. Ash—her birth name was Nariko, she said, but she'd picked Ash to complement Rowan—turned out to be a ghost of the Elgeve Branch of the Brandr Kinship. Rohin bristled a little at that, and made some disparaging remark, but Ash agreed so fervently that the Demi-heir's suspicions were instantly disarmed. Rehur laughed softly, and Rohin answered in the broad mountain dialect. The actor looked startled for an instant, then, glancing from me to his brother, realized what I had done. He gave me a nod of thanks, and leaned back in his chair to talk directly with his twin. The rest of us ignored them, turning to our own conversation. By unspoken agreement, we didn't talk about the *sonon*: the judges' decision would be coming up very soon, and I could see that the puppetmasters were edgy beneath their congenial talk.

And then, at last, there was a blare of music from the stage, and the Blackbird's manager stepped up into the lights, holding out his hands for silence. Conversation slowed reluctantly, but at last he was able to make himself heard.

"Good people, I thank you for your patience," he began, drawing a hoot from some of the nearer tables. "After much careful consideration, our judges have come to their decision—and a very difficult one it was, too, as you could tell from the impressive performances we've seen tonight."

"Come on, get to the point," Rehur muttered. Glancing down, I saw his hands close into tight fists, nails digging painfully into his palms. Rohin clutched the table edge in an ecstasy of anticipation.

"First, however," the manager went on. He was obviously enjoying himself. "I would like to give you the results of our popular poll. By overwhelming vote—" He paused again, drawing it out. "By overwhelming vote, you selected Witchwood as your favorite."

There was a burst of applause, and Rehur gave a brief shout of triumph. The puppetmasters embraced excitedly, and Rohin pounded one hand against my shoulder.

"And now," the manager said, and the room quieted again. "The results of the judges' poll." He made a production of unrolling the meter-long scroll and scanning the results. "The winner is . . . Mirabile!"

Mirabile was the dance group. There was more applause, and that covered the silence at our table. Rowan's face fell, and Ash said quietly, "Oh, damn!"

Rehur mouthed a curse, but managed to recover enough self-possession to clap politely with the rest of the audience.

As they quieted, Ash said, "Well, it's the popular vote that convinces the houses."

Rowan nodded loyal agreement, though her disappointment still showed in her face.

Ash shook herself, managed a smile. "We did damn well—you were wonderful, Rehur, *scary*—and we deserve a celebration." She lifted a hand to wave to the last members of the company—another technician and the four actors who had formed Belos's entourage at the very end of the *sono*—and Rowan reached to key the order box. Rohin put out a hand to stop her.

"Please, let me."

Startled, but too good a company manager not to agree, Rowan nodded. Then, looking from Rehur to Rohin, she finally recognized the relationship, and smiled. The other actors crowded up, wedging themselves in around the too-small table, submerging the rest of us in a stream of theatrical gossip. The twins leaned together again, still talking, but Rehur soon broke away, easing back into the general conversation. He was good company, quick-talking

and clever without much malice; I saw Rohin watching
him rather wistfully, as though he envied his twin's quick-
silver tongue. The others, flushed with their popular victory, were as exuberantly outgoing. It was good to be
around actors again, for however long. I let myself relax as
I hadn't in months, and ended up admitting, to win an
argument, that I'd been an actor myself in the Urban
Worlds. Rehur's eyes lingered speculatively on me for a
moment too long after I'd said that, but before I could
decide if it meant anything, I'd been drawn back into a
discussion of the Urban Worlds. The Witchwood people
argued well. Leith did not excuse herself until she was
nearly asleep in her chair, and Guil, who left with her,
looked back wistfully as they went. Rohin, too, rose to
leave, and I would have followed, but Rehur caught my
wrist.

"Rohin can get home by himself, surely," the actor
said, with a smile for his twin. "Stay a while longer—
I want news of the family, if we can get a minute to
ourselves."

I let myself be persuaded, and found myself walking up
Broad Street in the early hours of the horological morning,
slightly drunk and feeling charitable toward all humanity.
We had all become good friends, in the easy way actors
have. It probably wouldn't last, but while it did it was a
warm and pleasant feeling, the more so because I had
been so long away from the profession. Agamemnon shone
brilliant blue and white overhead, almost full, its distorted
disk dominating the starless sky. I squinted up at it, looking for Orestes' shadow crossing its face, but couldn't find
it. A tram rattled toward us, and three of the entourage
flagged it down, calling farewells to Ash and Rowan. I
would have gone with them, but Rehur caught my arm
again.

"Don't go," he said. "I meant it, I want to hear the
family news—if you don't mind, of course."

He was a little drunk, too, but no more than I was. I let
him persuade me, ignoring the sneer on the face of the
last actor. Rowan, Ash, and the other technician broke
away shortly after we turned off Broad Street, heading into
a battered, once-grand building. Belit winked at Rehur,
and pulled the other actor—Solvar, his name was—on

ahead of us. By now, I had a fairly good idea of what Rehur intended, and was inclined to go along with it.

He and Belit and Solvar all had rooms in the same nondescript building. Rehur's was a single-room flat, furnished neatly but not lavishly. Most of the pieces of furniture were old and showed signs of hard use. Rehur touched a wall panel as we came in, fading on the lights but keeping them low, touched with a hint of amber. I suppressed the urge to laugh. Until then, I'd been able to forget just how young Rehur was, and I wanted to go on forgetting.

"Have a seat," Rehur said, "and let me get my makeup off." Without waiting for an answer, he disappeared into the tiny bathroom, leaving the door ajar. There were no chairs in the room, unless there were folding stools buried in the storage blocks stacked against the far wall. I sat on the stove-bed and waited. After a moment, Rehur re-emerged, still rubbing his face with a towel. He had taken off his vest and undershirt, and was barefoot. He tossed the towel aside and started to say something, then gave an urchin's grin and flipped a switch on a breadboarded control plaque instead. Music—very soft, slow music—spilled from speakers on top of the storage boxes. "Do you dance?" he asked.

"Not usually," I answered, watching him. Even without the transforming makeup, he had huge eyes, very dark in his long face. Like most holopuppet models, he shaved off his body hair, to make it easier for the puppeteers to add later detail. It was startling, but not unattractive, and there were lithe muscles beneath that hairless skin. Oddly, though, there was a band of tattooing on his left arm, encircling the bicep like a bracelet. I wanted to touch him. I let my eyes wander over his body, saw his mouth curve into a knowing smile.

"Make an exception," he said, but there was no need. We were of a height; our lips met, and we eased slowly into his bed.

We slept late the next morning, and I would've slept later, if I had not had to be back in the Halex Tower by the end of the horological day. Rehur roused himself enough to tell me where he kept his spare toothbrush and the makings for coffee, but he didn't leave the warmth of the stove-bed. I left most of the coffee in the hob for him when he was ready to get up, and let myself out into the dark streets.

Agamemnon's disk was still a hair less than full, but I could finally track Orestes' shadow on its brilliant face. I made my way through the crowds, glad to lose myself among them. I was feeling strangely guilty—mostly, I realized, for being grateful for the casual parting. I had had my fun, but I wasn't an actor any more, and there was no point in pretending to be one. And there was at least fifteen bio-years' difference in our ages—sixteen bio-years, I amended, and couldn't help laughing at myself. I knew Rohin's age, and thus Rehur's; this was one romantic fantasy that would have to face reality, and die. I turned toward the main greengate. It had been a pleasant night, a windfall night. I wouldn't ask any more of it.

A souvenir vendor had set up his stand just inside the greengate, his placard proclaiming "Theatrical Gifts Our Specialty." On a whim, I stopped to look over his stock. Like most of the vendors, he carried dozens of crudely colored prints of famous *sonon*, and smudged black-and-white stills of noted actors. I flipped through those, but Witchwood hadn't released any photos of its stock players. There were fuzzy holocubes as well—much too expensive for what they were—and glossy holoalbums from the bigger theaters, many of them featuring Jahala or Javas. I was about to turn away when I noticed the clusters of ribbon hanging from the corners of the cart. Each ribbon held a dozen or so medallions about three centimeters in diameter, each one painted with an actor's face. Some were clearly in character, others were not. I sorted through them curiously, the vendor watching me like a hawk, and one face seemed to leap out at me. It was Rehur, made up as Belos: either he had played the part before, or the little artist had worked overtime.

"Can I help you?" the vendor asked suspiciously.

"How much are these?"

"A kip." Seeing me hesitate, he added, "The one you're holding, that's Belos Kyrle—"

"I'll take it," I said, and handed him the money. The vendor detached the medallion, voluble in his thanks, and I pocketed it with only a quick glance to be sure I had the right one. I wasn't quite sure why I'd bought it—I don't often buy souvenirs of casual encounters—and I could never display it openly in the Tower without offending Herself, and maybe the rest of the Family, too. But then, I told myself, Rehur was a fine actor, and he could be a great Belos, if Ash and Rowan ever got up the capital for a full-scale production. I was entitled to a memento of the performance.

Chapter 4: Trey Maturin

I took an early train back to the Halex Tower, not wanting to see Rohin again until his twin's spell had faded a little. I called Leith from there, and left a message with the *para'an* Guil ex-Tam'ne explaining where I was and why I'd left, and inviting her to visit me at the Tower if she had the time. As I'd expected, Leith did not come, but I did get a brief note on the mailnet, thanking me again for the evening at the Blackbird. *Pipe Major* was scheduled to leave Orestes shortly after Sunrise, to return in six calendar weeks: we would try to get together then, she said.

To my secret relief, Rohin stayed longer in Destiny than he'd originally planned, not returning to the Tower until two calendar days later, just after the eclipse. By then, I was able to face the Demi-heir unblushing—which was just as well, since Rohin was visibly knowledgeable when we finally did meet again. For safety's sake, however, I pinned the medallion to the inner curtain of my stove-bed, and let the painted face—Belos's face—replace the memory of the actor's body.

As always after I took even a single day off, business was backed up in my files. Most was routine—supervising other mediums employed by the Halex Kinship; seeing that registered ghosts received their stipends from their Families; providing more detailed reports on the areas where Herself's attempt to restructure the Mandate's economy were, or weren't, working; handling the Matriarch's off-world business—but a few things required more careful attention. Chief among those was the "death" at Feibourg. The Matriarch had read my first report, and wanted more detail before sanctioning a review. I chose to take that as encouragement, and spent the next two calendar-weeks preparing a second brief, even taking a snow car up to Feibourg to interview the parties involved in the first decision. By the time I had finally finished my report, it ran to fifty close-printed pages, and I felt smugly confident that I had secured a review.

Herself turned it down, of course. To obtain a review, she told me privately, I would have to have proved fraud, or, at the very least, malice. I had proved nothing. The council had been unusually strict, but its decision was within the letter of the code. And that was that: there is no appeal from a living genarch. I told myself I should have expected it, but I still felt as though I had been betrayed—worse still, as though I had betrayed the ghost in Feibourg. And I had betrayed her, for all I had been careful to warn her that I couldn't promise anything, and that she shouldn't hope too much. I threw myself into my other work, wincing every time I had to deal with the Kinship's ghosts, trying to concentrate on the off-world business. The Halex Kinship as a whole owned both mines and woolen mills, both of which did an increasing export business. I was able to negotiate the year's agreement-to-buy with a consortium of off-world clothiers, selling them an increased weight of hoobey yarns without the Kinship's having to absorb the shipping costs.

Still, the Feibourg business left a bitter taste in my mouth, and I felt no compunction, ten calendar-days after the decision, in asking for another few days' leave to see the hoobey races. Perhaps the Matriarch was feeling guilty, too; at any rate, she granted my leave without question, and even offered a few extra days in Destiny afterward. That I refused—the Kinship needed me, and I knew it— but I took the three days' leave gladly.

Several other members of the mainline Family were going to the Garnocks, though only Ixora was actually racing a team there, and I was glad of their company. The Garnock Steppes—the race is named for the upland plain in which it takes place—is in the Axtell Mandate, on the far side of the moon from the main continent that holds the other three Mandates, and the Axtell Kinship is probably the most code-bound of all. Of late, too, the Axtell had supported the Brandr against the Halex in the Kinship Council, and I did not want to give either of them any more grounds for complaint. I would never be as aware of the code as a native-born Oresteian, but with Jesma and Rohin among the party, I did not think I would make any significant mistakes.

We took the short flight to the Axtell Mandate, east and north across the Shallow Sea, then farther north over the chain of mountains that forms the Hook to Garnock Town just south of the Axtell Tower. We landed just before Midnight on a field already crowded with heavy transport craft. I stumbled down our transport's side stairs after the others, and stopped dead, staring up at the sky. I had been in the Axtell Mandate before, of course, but never after Dark, and in the Day it had not been so noticeable. Agamemnon had vanished from the sky, invisible from this side of Orestes; instead, the scudding clouds parted to reveal a starscape even more brilliant than the skies of Athene, outshining even the field lights. Atreus was part of a particularly dense starfield, I remembered tardily, but Agamemnon's light hid that glorious spectacle from half the moon. I looked for Electra, but she had already set behind the mountains ringing the Steppes. Iphigenia, I remembered from the almanac pinned to the wall of my room, was on the far side of the system, invisible behind Agamemnon.

Someone touched my arm, and I turned to find Jesma smiling at me, her face very pale in the starlight. "Our car's ready, unless you want to stay and help Ixora unload."

I glanced over the woman's shoulder. The dockers had already opened the transport's nose, sliding back the massive doors so that a mouth seemed to gape beneath the pilots' compartment. Ixora and her team were clustered around that opening, two of the young men straining at a hoobey's lead-lines while a third struggled to fix the animal's hobble. Ixora gestured angrily, then sprang to throw her weight against the hoobey's shoulder. The animal snapped at her by reflex, but gave way, and the handler managed to snap the hobble into place. I shook my head, smelling the lemon-and-pepper scent of a rutting jill.

"Wouldn't they do better to get the jills out of scent-range?" I asked.

Jesma nodded, frowning. "Usually, they do—I don't think it's Ixora's jill, even, someone else has let their beast make its mark. . . ."

"Careless," Rohin agreed, coming up behind her. "I hope the racemaster fines them. Are you coming? We don't want to be late for the dinner."

As sponsors of the race—the meeting, in Oresteian terms—the mainline Axtell Family was obligated to hold a prerace banquet two nights before the start. We had arrived just in time for the event, and to give the Axtell credit, it was a very gracious affair. It was held at the Axtell Tower, of course, though all of the racers and most of their kin stayed in Garnock Town, in the greenhouse at the top of the Tower. We were well above the snowline, and I was glad of the warmth. From there, we had a perfect view of the racecourse, its snows gleaming in the starlight. The starting line and the turn post were marked with banners that looked almost black in the starlight, though I knew they were blood red, the Axtell color. Looking down from the Tower, warm and well-fed and flushed with ice-wine, the snow seemed beautifully serene, untouched, the post banners beckoning me on. From what Rohin had told me, and from the voices around me, with their tales of injury and death, I knew that was an illusion. Firmly, I turned my back on the pretty scene, and concentrated on the conversation.

Despite the amount of food and drink I had consumed at the banquet, I woke early the next morning, and was not surprised to find Rohin ahead of me in the inn's breakfast room. He waved for me to join him, and I did so, glad that the awkwardness had evaporated.

"Ixora's taking the team out for a trial run," he announced, as the inn servant brought the breakfast cart. "She asked me to ask you if you wanted to come along."

I hesitated over my choice of food, glancing warily up at the Demi-heir, and Rohin grinned. "Oh, it's not a racing team, Trey. She just wants to let the jacks stretch their legs."

"Are you going?" I asked, and helped myself to the better part of a sweet cake. Rohin's grin flickered.

"For penance, yes. Zimri Rhawn—he usually mans the brake for her—ate something that disagreed with him last night, and he's sick in bed. Myself, I think it's nerves."

"You encourage me," I said, dryly.

"Will you come?"

I smiled. "Of course."

The inn was only a short distance from the Halex crew's camp, along a well-trodden path. I let Rohin fit me out with a face mask and heavy, felted boots from the Halex crew's spares, then followed him between the temporary shelter-domes to the hoobey pens. The jacks were restless, milling nervously inside the electric fences. The smaller jills, penned separately, were quieter, and I could smell their rut for a hundred meters. Someone had set out a smudge pot, but it did little to disguise the jills' odor.

Most of Ixora's crew was at the entrance to the shelter-domes, hauling the sledge out onto the packed snow. Ixora herself stood to one side, the weighted tail of her whip curled neatly over her shoulder, shouting orders. Seeing us, she broke off and came to join us, scowling a little.

"Trouble?" Rohin asked.

Ixora shook her head, still frowning. "Not really. But we need the warm-up runs badly."

"I'm sorry Zimri's sick," Rohin said, and Ixora's scowl deepened.

"So am I. And so will he be, if he's not better by tomorrow." She snapped her face mask into place before I could decide if she might have intended sympathy rather than a threat, and turned back to her crew. "Right, Tabat, that's far enough. Harness up."

Rohin took two long steps backward, out of the way of the handlers, and I copied him as the first of them moved toward the pen. One energized the inner fences of the narrow harnessing pen, which opened off the main pen,

and then a second man positioned himself at the far end of
the harnessing pen, waving a stained red rag. The jacks
turned toward him, bellowing and snorting. Another handler, a woman this time, snapped her whip expertly over
the leaders' heads, driving them back, until she had made
room for the animal she wanted to enter the harnessing
pen. The chosen hoobey, a big, brindled jack, charged
toward the end of the pen, but stopped, snorting angrily,
before it hit the fences. A handler snapped on the inner
gate behind it.

Instantly, a team of handlers was swarming all over the
massive jack, some clinging to its broad undercollar, doing
their best to steady it for the others, who would fit the
harness itself into place. It took nearly fifteen minutes to
get the weighted collar over the jack's shoulders, but the
animal quieted perceptibly when it was done, and the rest
of the harness was quickly snapped into place. I recognized the webbing they used to secure the hoobey to the
sledge—it was spacer's standard emergency line, capable
of taking the full thrust of a small flyer—and wondered
again if I were doing the right thing.

Once the lead animal had been put in harness, it was
easier to get the rest of the team in place ahead of the
boat-shaped sledge. As Rohin had promised, this was not a
racing team. Ixora had four jacks, the maximum number,
put to the sledge, but instead of a jill, the jacks would be
following a scrap of scented rag expertly manipulated by a
second driver. Ixora walked along the line of hoobeys,
tugging at pieces of the complicated harness, then nodded
to her chief handler, who dragged the lead animal around
so that the sledge faced out of the camp, toward the flat
snow-plain. Another pair of crewmen, Tabat and another
man I did not know, scrambled into the sledge, throwing
their weight onto the levers of the twin steering brakes.
Ixora nodded again, still standing just out of reach of the
lead animal's teeth, then beckoned to us. I hesitated, and
Rohin grinned.

"Nervous, Medium? I didn't think you were—unadven-
turous."

That put me on my mettle. Without deigning to answer,
I stalked over to join Ixora, the dignity of my gesture
somewhat hampered by the ankle-deep snow. From less

than an arm's length away, the hoobeys seemed even more massive than they had from a distance. The lead animal shifted uneasily on its thick legs, trying to turn its maned head far enough to the side to get a good look at me, and Ixora snorted.

"Great ill-tempered brute, aren't you?"

The hoobey swung its head toward her, its garnet eyes rolling nervously, and she smacked its velvety muzzle, ignoring the spade-shaped teeth that snapped closed a scant centimeter from her hand.

"Yes, you are," Ixora crooned. "And ugly, too." Her voice seemed to steady the animal, and I saw that the rest of the team quieted with it.

"Which one's this?" Rohin asked quietly.

"Antenor, out of Nirvana," Ixora answered.

"Crossbred," Rohin observed with a grin, and Ixora frowned.

"As good as any purebred out of Axtell herds, that's for sure."

Rohin laughed aloud, and I realized he had been deliberately baiting her. Ixora realized it, too, and colored. "It's a good beast, anyway," she said. "Isn't it, Medium?"

"I'm no judge," I answered.

"Look at him," Ixora began, and there was a shout from the sledge.

"Hey, cousin! Are we ready yet?"

"Coming!" Ixora shouted back, and gave Rohin a look that promised to continue their argument later. "Get up, dragsman."

Rohin grimaced, and Ixora added, "You, too, Medium. Tabat!"

Rohin was already trudging through the disturbed snow to the side of the sledge, and I followed him. The Demiheir pulled himself easily over the polished edge, stepping over the men on the steering brakes, and then climbed into the brakesman's turret at the back of the sledge, built like the sterncastle of an ancient ship. The front of the sledge curved up, balancing the heavy turret, to support the driver's platform. I was just putting off the inevitable, I realized, and took a firm grip on the thick wall. Tabat extended both hands to balance me as I hauled myself aboard, but somewhat to my own surprise, I hardly needed his support.

The interior of the sledge was heavily padded, and there was a padded bench set into the hollow of the prow, just below the driver's platform. At Tabat's nod, I seated myself there, wrapping both hands around the padded grips, and felt the vibrations as Ixora climbed to her place above me, knocking the snow from her boots. I braced myself, looking back toward the brake turret across the bent backs of the crewmen crouched over the levers of the steering brakes. Beyond the haze of the camp lights, bright even against the starfield, I could see the lights of the Axtell Tower, crowned by the bluish glow of the brightly lit greenhouse.

"High up!" Ixora shouted, her voice fluting clear in the bitter air. "Lights!"

Tabat released his grip on the brake lever long enough to flip a switch set into the floor of the sledge. "Lights on," he reported.

"Confirmed," Ixora answered, and Tabat pulled a protective cover across the little row of buttons.

"Brakes on!" Ixora called, and the two men leaned hard against the steering brakes. There was an unpleasant crunch as Rohin threw his full weight against the drag and its teeth bit into the packed snow. "Sideboys up."

I couldn't see precisely what happened at first, but then the sledge gave a little jump, and two more people, both women who had been part of the group harnessing the hoobeys, swung aboard, trailing long lengths of the emergency line. They settled themselves into the cockpits just forward of the two brakesmen, feet braced against the bow walls, and hauled in their lines, looping them once around low bollards set into the padded floor. They were wearing heavily padded gloves that made their hands three times their normal size. Sideboys were there to control speed, not direction, I remembered belatedly, so it didn't matter that they could hardly see over the side of the sledge.

The prow shook again as the second driver climbed onto the platform, and then Ixora shouted, "Stand clear!"

The sledge rocked again as the handlers released their hold on the hoobeys, and the sideboys leaned back hard, checking the animals' desire to bolt. "Set!" one of them shouted, and a penned jill bayed back at her.

"Brakes off!"

All three brakesmen released their levers at Ixora's call, and in the same instant, the drivers' whips cracked sharply. The sledge shot forward, almost throwing me out of my seat. I tightened my hold, wincing at my wrenched shoulders, and braced my feet against a ridge I discovered in the floor of the sledge, beneath the padding. The right-hand sideboy looked up briefly, and I thought I saw an encouraging grin beneath her mask.

"Down left!" Ixora called, and Tabat leaned to his lever. In the rear turret, Rohin leaned forward a little, just letting the heavy drag touch the snow. In the same instant, the sideboys adjusted their own lines, slowing the hoobeys slightly. The sledge swung sharply around, steadying onto the rutted snow of the practice track. It was a beautiful piece of teamwork, and I caught my breath in admiration.

"Quarter out, the sides," Ixora ordered, and the two women bent forward to the bollard, letting out their lines. I could feel the hoobeys' pace quicken, and leaned forward cautiously to peer around the edge of the prow.

The force of the wind was like a blow: I hadn't realized how fast we were already going. I blinked away the tears before they could freeze, and saw the Garnock Plain stretching away ahead of us, lit up for almost a kilometer ahead by the beams from the sledge lights. There was another sledge on the horizon, visible only as a smear of light against the black outline of the mountains. I thought I caught a glimpse of a marker banner silhouetted against that light, but then the other sledge had turned, and it was gone.

The sledge bucked as the runners struck snow rutted and torn by other racers, and I felt the whole structure give a little skip sideways before the brakesmen and sideboys had it under control again.

"God damn you, who said brake?" Ixora shouted, and the sideboys exchanged glances. The right-hand brakesman gave a little shrug, both hands still on his lever.

"Easy now, Ixora," Tabat called.

"Quarter out, I said, sides," the driver shouted, giving no sign she'd heard the brakesman.

"Quarter out," one of the sideboys shouted back, and Ixora's whip cracked again, urging the hoobeys on.

I let myself fall back into my seat, a little unnerved by it all. I hadn't realized mere animals could make anything move so quickly—or maybe, I told myself, the darkness and the featureless snow made our progress seem faster than it really was. I didn't really believe that, not after the way the sledge had started to skid, and took a tighter hold on the padded grips.

"Half out," Ixora called, and the sideboys loosed another turn of line. The sledge lurched as the hoobeys took up the slack. "Full out!"

The sledge rocked and slithered again—another patch of rutted ice—but the brakesmen didn't move. Ixora's whip cracked, pointing her leaders, and the sledge steadied. She gave a shrill yelp of triumph, and I leaned forward again, clinging to the grips. We had picked up even more speed, the hoobeys running flat out in pursuit of the rut-smeared rag the second driver dangled tantalizingly just above the leader's nose. The snow flashed beneath us, ghostly white; ahead, the marker banner swelled perceptibly in the cone of light from our lamps. There was no sign of the other sledge. The rush of wind was bitter cold, and I was very glad of my fur cloak.

Ixora let us get within about two hundred meters of the marker before she ordered the sideboys to take in their lines a little, slowing the sledge for the tight turn around the banner. Rohin leaned on the drag as well, keeping the sledge from running up the heels of the hoobeys, and the thin scree of the ice beneath the drag's teeth set my teeth on edge. The sledge bucked as we hit the part of the track already pitted by other sledges' brakes, and Ixora shouted, "Down left!"

Instantly, Tabat threw his full weight against his lever. The sledge skidded a little, moving sideways across the runners, trying to fishtail, and Rohin leaned harder on the drag. The sledge steadied, and swung into the turn. As it swung, the sideboys let out their lines fractionally, easing the turn. Ixora gave the order to lift the left-hand brake, and the sledge surged forward unevenly. Rohin had waited a second too long to let up the drag, and the right-hand brakesman gave a derisive whistle. I thought Rohin shouted something, but his words were carried away by the wind.

Then we were pounding back down the long track toward the camp. As we neared the end of the practice track, I leaned around the prow again, and saw a tiny figure growing rapidly larger in our lights. Then we were past it, and I caught a brief glimpse of a timer clutched in its gloved hand.

"Down drag," Ixora shouted. "Quarter down left, half down right. Half in, the sides."

There was a flurry of movement as her crew obeyed, and the sledge swung around to the right, throwing a shower of ice and snow, but slowing as it turned. Ixora waited a few seconds longer, then shouted, "Half down left. Down all, all in, the sides."

Slowly, protesting and moaning, the hoobeys came to a stop, the sledge crew handling lines and brakes so neatly that there was never any danger of the sledge itself overrunning the animals. Handlers came running from the camp to secure the team, but Ixora kept her crew leaning on the brakes and lines until the second driver had tucked the rut-smeared rag into a plastic pouch and the handlers had slipped hobbles on the first two animals.

"All set, Ixora," the chief handler called from his place at the lead hoobey's head, and I heard the second driver give a grunt of relief.

"Thanks, Pate," Ixora shouted back, then slid down the inner edge of the prow, landing almost on top of the right-hand sideboy. I dodged back, though she hadn't really come anywhere near me, and could feel myself blushing beneath the thin face-mask. Fortunately for my ego, at least, Ixora turned toward the stern, hands on hips, glaring at Rohin. The Demi-heir rested both elbows on the edge of the brake turret and grinned down at her. Ixora's scowl deepened, and she turned her head to include the rest of her crew in her disapproval.

"Sloppy," she said, "very sloppy, all of you. Rohin, you're not crew, I'll make allowances—but the rest of you. . . . When I want brake, I'll ask for it, but until that moment, nobody touches line or lever til I've given the word. Is that clear?"

There was a rather sullen mutter of agreement, the
sideboys and brakesmen untangling themselves from their
equipment without meeting her eyes. Only Rohin seemed
unaffected by her tirade, still leaning over the edge of the
turret. Seeing my eyes on him, he slowly shook his head.
Ixora glared at her team for a moment longer, then turned
away to lean out over the left-hand brake.

"Gisala! Time?"

"Five and a half!"

The brakesmen exchanged glances and thoughtful nods
at that, and the nearer sideboy whispered a delighted
curse. Ixora nodded slowly as she turned back to her crew.
"Not bad," she said, grudgingly. "Not bad, considering we
had an inexperienced dragsman, the heavy sledge, and no
jill. But we'd've been a full second faster if you hadn't
braked without my word." She smiled slowly, studying
their faces as they pulled off the thin masks. "Trust me,
people. I know what I'm doing."

There were reluctant smiles at that, and Rohin chose
that moment to drop out of the brake turret. "Cousin,
you're a fine driver, but you're too hot-blooded. Get another dragsman, not me."

I held my breath, waiting for Ixora to lash out at him for
damaging her crew's faith in her, but the driver threw
back her head and laughed. Her crew grinned with her,
and even Rohin was smiling rather ruefully.

"So, you don't think I need a purebred team any more?"
Ixora jeered.

"I think you need a psych-doc," Rohin retorted. "You're
mad, cousin mine." He looked at me, smile fading a little.
"Are you all right, Medium?"

"The Medium's braver than you are," Ixora said.

I said, before Rohin could continue the argument, "Fine,
thanks. It was a very—exciting experience." I deliberately
gave the words a twist, and was pleased when the sledge
crew laughed. "Seriously, though—thank you, Ixora. I
appreciate the chance to ride in one of these."

Ixora gave a one-shouldered shrug, though the praise
clearly pleased her. "You should come out in a racing rig
some time, Medium. That's the real excitement. But I'm
glad you enjoyed it."

"Very much," I said again, and Rohin and I took our

leave. The Demi-heir's smile faded as we got farther away from the sledge and the busy handlers, and when we stopped in the supply hut to put away the borrowed gear, I saw that his hands were shaking.

"Are you all right?" I asked.

"Ha!" Rohin pulled himself up short, put the folded face masks back into their box with exaggerated care. "Oh, I'm fine, or I will be. I'm just sorry you had to be along. I hope it wasn't too bad."

It was beginning to be borne in on me that the sledge ride had been more dangerous than I had realized. I said, carefully, "I told you, I'm quite all right." I stopped there, not knowing what further questions to ask without admitting that I hadn't realized anything was wrong, but Rohin went on without prompting. He stuffed the last pair of felt overboots back into the storage chest, slamming the lid, and beckoned for me to follow him from the shed.

"Ixora's just crazy," he said. "I wasn't kidding when I said she ought to see the psych-docs. Nobody drives on the edge like that when they're not racing. 'Don't touch the brakes except on my order'—that's the way people get killed, for God's sake. And on a practice run, with the family medium aboard—she's crazy."

A new voice said, "And you're jealous."

Rohin swung around quickly, fists clenched. I turned more slowly, preserving a medium's dignity. The brakesman Tabat had come up behind us as we talked, and stood there grinning. He was tall even by Oresteian standards, and handsome in a dark, flashy-masculine way. Rohin's frown deepened.

"Admit it," Tabat went on, still smiling. He was maybe two or three years older than Rohin, and not likely ever to forget that fact. "Rehur was a much better dragsman than you."

"Maybe he was," Rohin answered, and managed not to sound too much like a hurt child. "But that doesn't change the fact that Ixora drives like a madman."

"Rehur didn't have any trouble keeping up with her when he was alive," Tabat answered.

"He was just as irresponsible—" Rohin broke off abruptly, his eyes fixing on something just visible over Tabat's shoulder. "Brandrs."

I glanced around, and saw a party of brightly dressed men and women emerging from behind the nearest of the camp buildings. Most of them wore the blue-and-gold-striped scarves affected by supporters of the Brandr Family's racing team. Both the Halex stiffened, their private quarrel forgotten. Elaborately casual, Tabat glanced over his shoulder, then turned away with equally ostentatious unconcern. Rohin hastily smoothed his expression into one of intense interest, and Tabat leaned forward, saying a little too loudly, "Yes, the practice run went very well, I thought. Five and a quarter's not half bad."

"I doubt anyone's bettered it," Rohin said, equally loudly.

The knot of Brandr kinsmen slowed at that, and one of them detached himself from the group and walked toward us. He was an older man, perhaps ten years older than Rohin, and seeing that, I was glad I was with the Halex to lend them countenance. By Oresteian custom, the young are at an automatic disadvantage in dealing with their elders, and the thin-faced, sneering Brandr looked like the sort to take full advantage of the custom.

"Your pardon," he said, "but I couldn't help hearing the practice time. Can you tell me what team made it?"

There was nothing objectionable in the question, although he should have known from their faces and the faded badge on Tabat's coat that they were from a Halex team. Tabat and Rohin exchanged a quick glance, and then Rohin answered coolly, "Ixora Halex, of Halex. Her team."

"I see."

One of the other Brandr had come close enough to hear Rohin's answer, and now she sneered visibly. "Well, that's what they have official timers for."

Tabat sucked in an angry breath, but Rohin touched his shoulder in warning, and the brakesman subsided, scowling. The woman saw, and smiled mockingly at him. Before she could say anything more, however, the man who had spoken first said, "I don't believe I know you. I'm Anath Brandr, of Brandr."

He was talking to me, and the look that had accompanied the words could have been insulting, if he'd known who I was. I kept my expression serene—that kind of insult can be double-edged, and I had discovered long ago that it's far more effective to underplay the response. "My name is Maturin, sor Anath. Trey Maturin, Halex Medium."

A ghost of a frown passed across Anath's face, quickly suppressed. Clearly, he'd hoped to work up a scandal about the Halex Demi-heir and an out-worlder, and now I'd turned that threat back on him. Mediums are supposed to be inviolate, privileged, kept apart from the intra-Familial bickering, and Anath had come close to involving me. It's too easy to overplay that sort of small advantage, so I kept the knowledge of it out of my expression. Rohin made a choked, triumphant noise, and turned it into a convincing cough. Anath eyed him with disfavor, but said only, "A most impressive time. One can only hope it holds up under official conditions."

He turned and walked away without waiting for an answer, his group coalescing again around him. Tabat made a face as though he wanted to spit, but restrained himself. "How dare he?" he said, but quietly.

Rohin shrugged, not lowering his voice at all. "Jealousy. Brandr hasn't done that well in years—unless their own kin timed them."

"Rohin," I said, warning, but the Brandr were out of earshot.

The Demi-heir shrugged angrily. "I don't care if they hear me, they've said worse—they just accused us of the same thing, for God's sake."

"The medium's right," Tabat said, and sounded as though he grudged it. "We can't start a fight now. After the meeting, maybe, but not now."

Rohin grunted agreement. "Ixora'll show them."

"Even if she drives like a maniac?" Tabat asked, with the ghost of his earlier malice.

Rohin scowled. "Let it go, Tabat."

There was something in his voice that silenced the brakesman. Rohin took a deep breath, and turned to me. "I am sorry you were treated in such a manner, Medium. I can't say I'm surprised, though."

I couldn't help grinning at his formality. "No harm done. And it's bound to make him more cautious next time."

"I doubt it." The Demi-heir took a deep breath, visibly

calming himself. "Still, one can hope, I suppose. Have you chosen a viewing point for tomorrow?"

He was right in changing the subject, but it took discipline to do so, and you had to respect him for it. "Not yet," I answered. "I was going to ask one of you for advice."

Rohin's face brightened. "Well, you've a choice," he began, as we started back up the path to our inn. "There're the grandstands, by the finish and by the turn—but," he added, visibly remembering my off-world susceptibility to cold, "the winds get pretty fierce there, especially the day before Sunrise. I think the Axtell are going to let people watch in the Tower, from the greenhouse. . . ." His voice trailed off, and I nodded.

"However, that might be a little uncomfortable for me," I finished for him, "unless there were other Family members there?"

"There might be," Rohin said, but his tone was doubtful. "I'll ask—that'd probably be the most comfortable for you. Damn, it's a pity I didn't think of it before, or I'd've reserved one of the flying carpets. That's the way to see a meeting."

Personally, I wasn't so sure. The flying carpets—great lumbering hovercraft about fifty years out of date on the Urban Worlds—always made me seasick. "I would've thought they kicked up too much loose snow to be allowed," I temporized.

"Well, yes, you have to stay back from the course, but not that far," Rohin answered. "You can still follow the teams, and that's the important thing."

I shook my head. "I'll pass. I'll take a place in the grandstand." And I'll freeze, I added silently, but it was better than either the flying carpets or the Axtell Tower. At the latter, the social chill would be even lower than the outdoor temperatures.

Rohin nodded. "I'll see if I can get you a heater," he promised, "and a place inside the windbreak. I'll talk to Jesma—she usually brings everything."

"Thanks," I said, and heard my words ring hollow. I was not looking forward to standing in the cold for hours, even behind a windbreak. You wanted to see a race, I reminded myself, but at the moment I would rather have watched it on a newscast. Rohin didn't seem to notice my doubts, however, and we parted at the inn door, I to my rooms and a hot bath in anticipation of the next day's race, he to find the Axtell in charge of the viewing arrangements.

I rose early the next clock-morning, planning to eat a heavy—sustaining—breakfast before I dressed for the meet. This time, the dining room was crowded with crews and spectators out to grab the best of the unreserved seats, and I resigned myself to a wait. To my surprise, however, almost at once someone touched my shoulder. I turned to find Rohin behind me. He was breathing hard, as though he'd been running, but he flashed me an urchin's grin. I had a momentary vision of Rehur, standing half naked in his room in Destiny, and suppressed it.

"I'm glad I found you, Trey," he said. "I've just got the news, there's a broomstick available after all, but can you fly one?"

I was looking at him in complete bewilderment, and Rohin frowned. "Didn't you get my message?"

I shook my head, still confused. "I'm sorry, no."

"I'm sorry." Rohin paused to collect himself, and gave me a rather wry smile. "You must think I'm crazy. But the Axtell imported a dozen broomsticks two years ago, and they're loaning them out to people who want to follow the meeting close up. I got on the list late, of course, but it's turned out that Pamarista Jan isn't licensed to fly one after all, so I'm next—if I can find someone with a proper license. I thought, since you're an off-worlder, and an Urban Worlder at that, you might have one."

He waited expectantly, looking suddenly younger than his years, and the memory of Rehur vanished. "Rohin," I said carefully, "what's a broomstick?"

"Oh, my God." He grimaced comically. "I'm sorry, a skycycle. A Skyhopper III, to be exact."

I did have a skycycle license, of course—getting one is the major rite of passage for Athenan adolescents—but it had been a very long time since I'd flown one, and I wasn't at all sure I would want to fly a strange skycycle in the cold and in the dark, over unfamiliar territory. The machines are little more than variable-pitch Tavras generators fitted out with steering bars, a throttle, and a padded seat. Some models even leave off the seat. But once again,

Rohin's eager expression overrode my better judgment. "I do have the license," I said slowly, "but it's been quite a few years since I've flown one of those machines. The Axtell may not want me handling their cycles."

Rohin made a rude noise. "They've only had broomsticks on Orestes for the past calendar-year. Half the people they're letting fly are more likely than not to crack up. Shemer Axtell will be sweating blood until they're all in safe."

Shemer was the Axtell Patriarch, a taciturn, unbending man in his fifties who had only held his post for the past three years. From what I'd seen of him, I guessed he would never refuse to let a guest ride his expensive off-world toys—which weren't cheap even on the Urban Worlds where they were made, and must have cost him close to a year's income from the Kinship, taking into account the transportation and customs fees—but Rohin was right, he would be sweating blood until each one was returned safely. And he would be the first to demand that anyone carelessly damaging his property observe the code and repay him twice over. More than ever, I wondered if I shouldn't refuse.

I shook myself. I was probably less likely to wreck a skycycle—a broomstick—than anyone else from the Halex party, and knowing Rohin, if I refused him, he'd find someone else who had a license. I smiled to myself then, and admitted my real motive. It was a challenge, a dare, just like every other time I'd ridden a skycycle, and I never turned down a dare.

"All right," I said slowly. "I take it there're thermal suits?"

Rohin nodded, grinning again. "Everything you could want."

"Then let's go see the Patriarch."

Shemer Axtell was waiting in the garages at the foot of the Tower, watching his guests loaded into hovercraft and the larger aircoaches. As we made our way up the shallow steps to the open mouth of the hangars, one of the skycycles flashed past in a great swirl of snow and displaced air, nearly knocking us off the walkway. I heard a squeal of laughter, caught a quick glimpse of the Brandr blue-and-gold before the snow blinded me. Behind me, Rohin muttered a curse. As I wiped the melting flakes from my face, I could see that the Axtell Patriarch was watching us—had been watching us for some time, probably—but he did not come forward to meet us.

I took my time, too, adjusting my fur cloak and stepping with deliberate care across the broad threshold. The hangar floor was heated, to keep it from icing over, and free-standing heating units stood in each work bay, their coils glowing red-orange, but the space was too cavernous to be warmed. For once, it was my feet that were warm, and my upper body cold: an unfamiliar feeling, on Orestes, and oddly disconcerting.

Rohin touched my shoulder unobtrusively, and I glanced again at the Axtell Patriarch. He was watching our approach with an expression so carefully neutral as to be utterly disapproving, and I couldn't repress a frown of my own. Rohin had to have spoken with him, told him that he had a friend who could fly a skycycle—which, of course, was the problem. I hid a smile, and lifted gloved hands to fold my hood back onto my shoulders. An older face could only help reassure the Patriarch, I thought, but I could see no relaxation in his rigid stance.

"Sor," Rohin said, carefully, "may I present Trey Maturin, the senior medium of our Kinship?"

Shemer nodded—it was acknowledgement of my presence and the introduction, as well as agreement—and turned his bleak eyes full on me. He was nondescript of coloring and feature, browns on sandy brown—the Axtell were blond only in the collateral branches—but there were deep, unhappy lines bracketing mouth and eyes. I remembered what I had been told of the shaky state of the Axtell finances, and guessed that much of it was true. The Axtell had gambled on the High Dariaga's mines when they took up their Mandate—there was little land suitable for commercial grazing—and it looked as though they were losing that gamble.

"Maturin," he said, and waited.

Rohin tensed, as though he were about to speak, then seemed to think better of it. We stood silent for a few seconds, and then Shemer's frown deepened even further.

"Urban." It was not a question.

"I'm an Athenan."

Shemer grunted, and glanced quickly at Rohin. "He tells me you're licensed to fly broomsticks."

"Yes, sor," I said, and smiled. "But as I told Rohin, I haven't flown one in some years."

Shemer eyed me for a moment longer, then made a sort of shrugging movement, quickly checked. "I trust you're still proficient, then, Medium."

So do I, I thought, but he wasn't really waiting for an answer. "The broomstick is over there, and the suits. There's food packed, too, if you want it. It was for Pamarista."

There was something in his tone that made me give a cautious answer. "I wouldn't want to waste your people's labors, sor, but we couldn't deprive the lady."

Rohin said, "I thank you for the offer, sor—as long as it wouldn't inconvenience Pamarista." There was the slightest of edges to his last words, and Shemer flushed angrily.

"If you want it, it's yours—by my gift. She'll have no complaint."

I remembered then that the woman's full name was Pamarista Jan—Jan was a branch of the Brandr Kinship—and was glad I'd watched my words. "Thank you, sor," I said. "We'll accept gratefully."

Shemer's face eased a little at that, and he gave me a grudging nod with the conventional answer. "May you not go hungry." He glanced at Rohin and nodded toward a door set into the far wall. "The suits and all are in the changing room. You'd better hurry."

It was a dismissal, though not quite abrupt enough to be insulting. I followed Rohin across the bays to the door Shemer had indicated, but shook my head when Rohin offered to let me change first. The skycycle was waiting in the next bay, and I wanted to take a look at it. The Demi-heir grinned, and vanished into the warmed cubicle.

I didn't wait, but stepped across the bumper strip into the bay. The mechanic who had been tending the skycycle looked up warily at my approach, and came to meet me, neatly cutting me off from the cycle.

"Can I help you, Medium?"

The accent was Urban, and I smiled. "What's the model number?"

The mechanic, small and dark and heavily muscled, did

a quick doubletake, then smiled back. "Skyhopper III. You know it?"

"I've flown the II," I answered.

The mechanic's grin widened. "Same machine, less power. You won't have any trouble." He glanced at my face again, then at my hands, the only parts not concealed by the furred cloak. "Annwnite?"

"Athenan," I said, a little sharply—Annwn, strictly speaking, isn't one of the Urban Worlds—but his response was flatteringly prompt.

"Sss, no trouble then." He turned to the cycle, and drew back the groundsheet with a gentle hand. "It's a standard configuration, but you've got a big-ear and hot glasses for the race—if you want them."

I bent over the cycle, pretending to examine the rudimentary control panel. It had been a long time—a very long time—since I'd last flown one, but it was not a skill you could easily forget. The indicators—airspeed/groundspeed, fuel, power output, altitude and attitude—showed dead, not even the flickering of warmup and standby, but my imagination supplied the right readings, filled my ears with the roar of the engine. . . . I brought myself back to reality with an effort. "Hot glasses?" I said. "What would you want IR coverage for out here? I wouldn't think you could get any sort of detail that way."

The mechanic gave a scornful grunt. "You can't. But some of them want to be sure they don't miss anything about the race." He shook his head, the smile fading. "I keep trying to get the drivers not to wear them. There's going to be a hell of a crackup one of these days."

"Well, I'm certainly not going to," I said. "Can you get me a good headset, instead?"

"That I can do." His eyes shifted, caught by a movement behind me. "I'll have one for both of you by the time you're changed."

"Thanks," I said again, and turned. Rohin had just come out of the changing room, and was making his way across the bay to join us. I nodded to him as our paths crossed, and went on into the little cubicle, shutting the door behind me.

There were wall heaters on three sides of the narrow room, warming the air just enough to allow a person to change from everyday clothes to a thermal suit without freezing in the process. I sorted through the racked suits until I found one in my size, then stripped, shivering, and pulled it on. It was a strange feeling to be wearing one of those again—a sportsuit is basically a spacesuit liner that's failed its vacuum tests—and even stranger not to put the armor and support pack on over it. The last time I had worn a spacesuit was on Andvari, a miserable time and memory if ever there was one; I hadn't worn a sportsuit since a summer on Baldur, six months before I left the theater—another unpleasant memory.

I shook myself, hard. There was no point in dwelling on those times; I had agreed to fly Rohin to watch the race, and I would keep that agreement. I would even do my best to enjoy it: after all, I was the one who had been wanting to see a hoobey race. I chose a flat six-hour power pack from the stack in the wall cabinet, and clipped it into the belt connector. After a little fumbling, I found the right switches, and the suit began to heat up, warming me from the skin in. I plugged the matching gloves into the wrist sockets, and felt that fabric begin to warm up, too. I kept my own heavy overboots, though, and after a moment's hesitation, slung the cloak over my shoulders again. In my experience, sportsuits were never very good at keeping out the wind. People told me it was purely psychological, but I was sure I'd be glad of the cloak as a windbreak. I fastened its clasps carefully, awkward even in the thin gloves, and then, as well armored as anyone could be, stepped back into the bay.

The mechanic had stripped the groundcover off the skycycle, and started the engines ticking. I could feel the vibrations in the floor of the hangar; the noise cut off all possibility of conversation.

He had put the cycle up onto a starter stand, too. I couldn't help raising an eyebrow at that—stands were for inexperienced riders—but the mechanic winked and jerked his head toward Rohin. He had a point, and I accepted my headset without complaint. The power jack was at the back of the collar, impossible to reach. The mechanic twitched the cord out of my hand and plugged it in.

"Twelve point six," he shouted, and I adjusted the dial

until I found the general control frequency. "Ultra-short's under your left thumb."

That was for talking to my passenger. I nodded and stepped up onto the stand, then swung myself onto the skycycle. The vibration from the leashed engines set my teeth rattling. I felt along the control bar until I found the switch for the ultra-short-range communicator and pressed it.

"Are you ready, Rohin?"

"Any time." The Demi-heir's voice sounded just a little uneasy, but he stepped onto the stand eagerly enough. The mechanic steadied him as he settled himself onto the padded seat behind me. I gave him time to find the hand- and footholds, then asked, "All set?"

"Yes."

I glanced down and saw his hands wrapped tight around the twin grips. Ahead and to my left, the mechanic grinned and gave me a thumbs-up signal. I wondered if he was referring to me or to Rohin. I switched to the external frequency and said, "Ready to go."

The mechanic nodded again, and stepped back another few meters, beckoning me forward. For an instant, I was tempted to try a flashy start, locking the airbrake and kicking in all the engines together, but the sight of Shemer Axtell still waiting in the center of the garage made me restrain myself. I ran the fans to full power, and waited until the cycle lifted from the stand before touching the throttle. We left the garage under a sedate quarter-power, barely disturbing the packed snow.

It was still quite dark outside, of course, but as I swung to follow the blue lights that marked the cycle path, I caught a glimpse of the dawn-line edging the mountains above the Garnock Plain. The monotonous voice of the main controller sounded in my ears, giving a mix of traffic instructions and pre-race commentary. I listened with half an ear, following the blue lights through the twisting streets of the Tower settlement. The skycycle was hard to control at such a low speed, the fans whining close to overload. There didn't seem to be much traffic out—everyone was probably already at the grandstand, or ahead of us on the track reserved for the cycles and flying carpets—so I gently increased power. The cycle steadied in the air, and at the same time, the noise of the fans decreased.

There was a click in my headset, and Rohin said, "Won't we be late?"

Not likely, I thought, but said, "How much farther do we have to go?"

"A couple of kilometers, maybe three."

We had plenty of time. What he wanted was for me to open the throttle, show him what a skycycle could do—and I had to admit I wasn't exactly averse to the idea. We were just passing the last of the hoobey pens, and there was nothing ahead but the snow of the plain. Then my headlight silhouetted a distant shape, bobbing gently in the cone of light. It was another skycycle, but I couldn't make out the passengers at this distance. Still, if it were the Brandr cycle. . . . I touched the short-range switch again.

"You took a pair of hot glasses, didn't you?"

"Yes," Rohin answered.

"Can you make out who it is on that cycle up ahead?"

There was a long silence, and I assumed he was adjusting the glasses. Then at last he said, "I think it's Katel Erling."

Erling was yet another branch of the Brandr—there were five in all, if you counted the main line. The temptation was overwhelming. "Hang on tight," I said, and hit fan and throttle switches together. The cycle leaped forward, and I heard Rohin grunt as the acceleration threw him against the holds. I kept my headlight fixed on the cycle ahead of us, still bobbing erratically as the Brandr—Katel Erling?—fought to master the trick of controlling fans and jet at the same time, and touched the throttle again, until we were overhauling at nearly twice their speed. It was a game we used to play when I was a kid, made easy by the fact that the driver ahead of me had no idea how to play. I waited until we were almost on them—I could see the Brandr blue-and-gold quite clearly, recognized them for the pair who had thrown the snow on us earlier—than slid hard to the left, and passed them. As I cut back in front of them, thirty meters ahead and still pulling away, I let the cycle drop a little, throwing a plume of snow. In the headset, Rohin gave a crow of triumph.

"That's shown them. Oh, neatly done."

"Thanks," I said, already regretting the impulse. It was not my place, as a medium, to indulge in Family quarrels. Worse than that, I'd been acting like an adolescent.

"They'll think twice before they bother any of our people again," Rohin went on, and laughed.

The Demi-heir was usually well aware of the dangers of Brandr-baiting, I told myself, so maybe I hadn't made too bad a mistake after all. "Where do you want to watch from?" I said aloud.

"I don't know," Rohin said, after a moment. "Maybe we could follow the sledges?"

"We could do that," I said. It would be difficult, controlling the cycle gracefully at that low speed, and after I had shown off so blatantly, I could hardly afford to make a mistake. Still, I told myself, I could do it—and it was a more acceptable form of self-display than playing tag. I swung the cycle in a gentle arc and cut the speed a little, heading back the way we'd come.

We passed the Brandr cycle again—it was still bobbing—and another cycle whose riders went without Kinship markings. In the distance, I could see the Axtell Tower stark against the starfield, the lights of grandstand and starting line spread out below it like a dim reflection of the sky. I had switched back to the control frequency, and now I turned my attention to the monotonous voice, timing my approach to the starting line. I didn't want to get too close—most of the other cycles and all the flying carpets would be doing exactly what I was doing—but I did want Rohin to be able to see the start. As we passed the five-hundred-meter flag, I cut power even further, and kicked the fan controls to their highest setting. In my earphones, the controller was announcing the race, the first of four. Three sledges would go in each heat, then the winners would race in pairs, and finally, the two winners of those races would compete for the grand prize.

"Slot one, team Fen Erling," the controller announced. "Slot two, team Ixora Halex. Slot three, team Tasma Fyfe." There was a moment's pause, filled with the rush of distant crowd noise, and then the short-range circuit cut in.

"Ixora was supposed to be in the third heat," Rohin said. "I wonder what's happened?"

I didn't say anything, hoping the controller would offer an explanation of the change, but she was droning through the traffic regulations for the tenth time. According to the rules, all vehicles—and especially the skycycles and flying carpets—were supposed to stay at least fifty meters away from the sunken beacons that marked the edges of the course. I intended to obey, but I knew from Rohin's and Ixora's stories that not everyone did, and that the sledge drivers treated flying objects as just another hazard of the course.

"I can see the line," Rohin cried, and leaned forward until his chin was practically resting on my shoulder. I was reminded of Rehur, and did not look back.

The starting line was brilliantly lit, bright red post lights defining the three tracks, the hoobeys heaving shadows between the sledges' own headlights. At this distance, I couldn't make out much detail, but from the commentary, it seemed as though they were about to start. I slowed the cycle even further, ignoring the stressed screeching from the fans.

"The jill-rider's up," Rohin said, and took one hand off the grips to adjust his glasses. "They'll be going soon—they're gone!"

Even as he said it, I could see the headlights dip and sway, and heard the crowd roar over the headset. I fed power to the jet, and swung the cycle in a wide turn back the way we'd come. I didn't hurry, and then had to feed more power to the cycle as the sledges caught up with me more quickly than I'd expected. The cycle swayed as Rohin shifted in his seat to watch them, and I leaned a little to my right to compensate.

Beneath and to my left, the sledges thundered through the snow. We were about nine meters up and the full fifty meters away from the course, and I throttled down to match the teams' speed. At this point, barely five hundred meters into the race, no one had the lead. First one jill, then another thrust forward a few meters, and fell back again. In the darkness, it was hard to see individual crewmen; the sledges moved so smoothly that they seemed fully automated, centrally controlled.

Other skycycles fell into step with us—the Brandr cycle was back, making wide, sweeping s-turns because the driver was afraid to cut power too far—and, when I risked a glance to my right, I could see a steady procession of flying carpets just outside the line of cycles. I felt my skin prickle, surrounded by inexperienced drivers, and turned my attention to the cycle. In the headset, I could hear the controller calling the race, first one and now another of the teams in the lead, but I kept my eyes on the other machines.

Then we were past the thousand-meter flag, a quarter of the way through the course, and Rohin shouted, "Ixora's pulling out."

I risked a glance to the left. Ixora's team, running in the center track, did seem to be pulling a little ahead of the rest. I fixed my eyes on her sledge for a long moment, letting the other cycles avoid me, and thought the gain was real. So did the controller back at the Tower—and so did the driver of the Brandr cycle. She dropped to less than three meters, and passed the rest of us on the left, a good ten meters inside the fifty-meter limit, throwing a plume of snow. Ixora's jill shied, throwing the rest of her team off stride, and the other sledges surged ahead.

The controller said, in a bored voice, "Team Ixora Halex seems to have been startled by a spectator's vehicle." Her words were swallowed in an angry roar from the grandstand.

The short-range communicator clicked, and Rohin said, "Typical. But it won't help."

You hope, I thought, but said nothing. The other flyers were crowding in around us, jostling for good viewing positions as we approached the turn, and I concentrated on keeping the skycycle airborne. The Brandr cycle tried to edge into the line ahead of me, and I took savage pleasure in cutting it off. The flying carpets slid closer, too, their heavier fans throwing up great clouds of snow. I winced as the crystals spattered against my goggles, and lifted the cycle another meter or so to try and get above the cloud. The air was rough, and it took all my strength to hold us steady.

"There they go," Rohin shouted.

In spite of the turbulence and the swirling crystals, I had to look. Far below, the sledges skidded toward the tight turn that would take them back to the starting point.

The jill-riders had already started to turn their animals, and the rest of the teams were pointing after them. I remembered Ixora clinging to her lines in the driver's turret, could almost hear the crack of her whip urging the hoobeys on again. Then a plume of snow flared from beneath the tail of the outermost sledge: team Tasma Fyfe was the first to put down brakes for the turn. A heartbeat later a similar, smaller plume showed at the tail of the inside, Brandr sledge.

"Brake, Ixora." Rohin pounded his fist against my shoulder. "Brake, damn it."

Almost before the words were out of his mouth, the plume appeared behind Ixora's sledge, and the heavy vehicles swung sharply around toward home. In the same instant, the brake plume vanished from behind the Brandr sledge. It straightened, and the tail swung sideways into Ixora's path. The raised drag slammed into the driver's turret, then swept down across the sideboy's cockpit and the steering brake. The impact threw the Halex sledge sideways without tipping it, slammed it against a pair of the Fyfe hoobeys even as their driver struggled to turn them out of the way. One went down, and was overrun by its own sledge. The left runner lifted over the massive body, and tipped the sledge sideways into the snow.

The Brandr sledge was empty now, its crew's bodies littering its path. It swung wildly, brakeless, hoobeys completely out of control. I could see Ixora struggling with her damaged sledge, saw her whip dart out to snap over the heads of her own team, over the heads of the Brandr team. The Brandr hoobeys shied away, but it was too late. Uncontrolled, the sledge smashed again into the Halex sledge, tangling their runners. Ixora fought it a moment longer, slowing the wreckage even further, and then I saw her crew leap from their places. An instant later, Ixora had jumped, too, and the sledge slid off the prepared track into the softer snow along the verges.

Rohin was shouting in my ears, had been for some time. "—*told* you it was too light, damn it. Oh, Ixora!"

All around me, flying carpets and skycycles were converging on the wreckage. Instinctively, I swung to follow them, not knowing quite what I could do to help. "Shut up, Rohin," I said, and was obeyed.

The controller's voice crackled again in my headset, the woman for once shaken out of her invincible boredom. "Red Team One, Red Team Two, priority flight, priority flight. All private flights, clear the air immediately. All private flights, ground and wait for instructions. Blue Team, Blue Team, priority."

Rohin slammed his fist against my back again, and I lifted one hand from the controls to point ahead and down, not wanting to miss anything important from the controller. The snow of the verges would be soft and deep, difficult to fly out of once we'd landed, but the ambulances would need the solidity of the track itself. I brought the skycycle down carefully, shedding height and speed until we grounded almost gently in a drift perhaps twenty meters from the wrecks. Rohin kicked himself free of the cycle even before I'd killed the fan, and fought his way through the snow toward the track. Cursing him and my own lack of medical knowledge, I followed.

Others were there before us, thank God, and I counted all seven of the crew in the crowd surrounding the Fyfe sledge. They were at least alive, and not too badly hurt, but their animals had not been so lucky. One, the one that had been struck by the sledge, was definitely dead, and at least two more lay quiet in their harness. The others, the jill and the leader, bellowed and fought the lines, and I was very grateful for the headset that cut out the worst of their shrieking.

Rohin barely gave them a glance, all his attention focused on Ixora's sledge. Other people were floundering through the snow toward it, too, and a couple who wore the Berngard crossed axes were crouched over what seemed to be a piece of the wreckage. I vaguely remembered seeing them astride a skycycle, but saw no sign of the vehicle.

"Zimri!" Rohin shouted, and threw himself down beside the pair. I lunged, caught his shoulders before he could do anything stupid. The older of the pair, a man of my own age, nodded his thanks, his hands still busy inside Zimri's heavy jacket.

"Easy, now." That was the woman who held Zimri's head and upper body in her lap. "We have it in hand."

Rohin made a noise of protest, but the cool competence

of her voice seemed to steady him a little. Zimri was unconscious—mercifully, I thought—but there was no obvious injury. Even as I thought that, the man took his hands out of the jacket and pulled it closed again, shaking his head. I opened my mouth to ask, cutting off Rohin's cry of fear, and the woman said, "Nothing obvious wrong there. A broken leg, yes—but he'll hold till the Red Team gets here."

The Red Team was the ambulance for humans; the Blue Team was for the hoobeys. "Thanks," I said. "Is there anything—?"

She shook her head, unsmiling behind the thin mask. "He'll hold. See to the others, Medium."

Rohin was already well ahead of me, and I struggled after him, the hem of my cloak dragging in the knee-deep snow. The twisted wreck of the sledges loomed ahead, brightly lit—someone had had the sense to land a pair of flying carpets so that their headlights threw the whole scene into terrible relief.

"Ixora!" Rohin shouted, and threw himself out of the deep snow onto the track itself. The driver turned slowly to face him. Blood pulsed from a cut above her left temple, staining half her face mask and covering the clear plastic that screened that eye. She wiped one gloved hand across it as if that would clear it, but couldn't seem to focus on us.

"Where is he?" Her voice had dropped, hoarsened, become an animal cry, a hawk's scream of pain and fury. "Where is he, murdering Erling bastard, where are you?"

"Ixora!" Rohin cried again, but she didn't hear.

"Erling!" Ixora lifted her whip, turning slowly, seeking her enemy.

"Medium, for the love of Christ, get her quiet." The voice was strangely familiar. I turned, to find Anath Brandr facing me. There was blood on the front of his coat. It was his kinsman who had caused all this, and I felt a killing anger rise in me.

"Don't give me orders, Brandr—" I bit off the words with an effort, remembering what I was. *I am a Mediator of the Conglomerate, sworn to keep the peace. . . .*

Anath ignored me. "I've got the rest of her crew, the ones we could move, in the carpet til the ambulance gets here." He looked up, and I could hear it, too, the heavy beat of rotors. "But get her quiet."

He was right, for once, and I turned toward her. Rohin had her by the shoulders, trying to lead her away from the wreck. She was in the grip of a hysterical anger, and fought him, struggling to bring her whip across his face. I sprinted toward them, sliding on the packed ice of the track, but before I reached them, Ixora had fought free, knocking Rohin to the ground. I caught her then, no longer daring to be gentle, and pinned her arms with my off-world strength. She stopped struggling at last, recognizing that she was beaten. Her breath still came in harsh gasps, and her eyes were wild with anger.

"Get the whip," I shouted. Rohin picked himself up off the icy track, and did it, one hand pressed to his jaw.

"Oh, God, Tabat," he said, and turned toward the wreck.

"Rohin," I called, and Anath echoed, urgently, "Don't!"

The Demi-heir took two more steps toward the broken sledge, until he could see clearly the thing I had been careful not to look at too closely. Tabat had been manning the left-hand steering brake, and his station, unprotected, had been directly in the way of the other sledge's drag. A drag-brake weighed almost a ton—it had to be that heavy to hold the massive sledge. . . . It had swept down into and across the left-hand steersman's post. Rohin gave a choked cry and turned away, retching. I felt like being sick myself, but did not dare relax my hold on Ixora.

The beat of rotors was much louder now, and the powerful headlights of the ambulances were already on us. Anath squinted up into the light, lips moving as he calculated. "Another minute, maybe," he said. His eyes shifted to Ixora, still tensely furious in my grasp. "Blue Team's just behind them."

Ixora wailed aloud, this time for her animals, and Rohin said, "They're tended to, cousin, they're tended." He had stripped off his stained face mask, heedless of the cold.

"What about her crew?" I asked.

"One dead," Anath answered, with an effort. "You saw. The dragsman, I don't know, I don't have him, but the right-hand brake and the right-hand sideboy and the jill-rider are all right, bruises and maybe cracked bones, nothing worse. The snow's deep, it helped."

"The other sideboy?" I asked, in the same instant that Rohin said, "Iossea?"

Anath shook his head. "Alive now. I don't know. . . ." His voice trailed off, but then his face sharpened, eyes fixing on something over my right shoulder. "Well, cousin?"

I glanced awkwardly back, not wanting to relax my hold on Ixora. A young man in racing clothes was struggling across the track toward us, the tattered remains of a Brandr scarf fluttering from his shoulder. He didn't seem to be much hurt, and I saw Anath scowl.

"The draglines broke," the young man said, and I realized he must be Fen Erling, driver of the third team. "I couldn't do anything."

Anath's scowl deepened, but then Ixora exploded in my arms, fighting to get at the other driver. Off-worlder or not, it took all my strength to hold her.

"Liar!" she shrieked, sounding more than ever like a hunting bird. "Fucking liar! You did it on purpose, you did it on purpose, you killed my people!" Her voice broke in a sob as she drew breath. "Liar!"

"We'll talk later," Anath snapped, eyes on his kinsman. "Get out of my sight."

Fen drew breath as though he'd protest further, but another scream from Ixora, this time of pure rage, convinced him. He backed off, and I swung Ixora bodily around away from him. Her fury was ebbing, her taut muscles weakening perceptibly, frighteningly, in my grip. She sagged suddenly, murmured something about feeling ill, and closed her eyes.

And then the ambulances were down, settling onto the cleared snow of the track. Teams of orange-suited men burst from the doors even before the machines had touched the ice, came running toward us, med-sleds floating behind them. One of them took Ixora from me—I kept an arm around her until I was sure he had taken her weight— and eased her limp form onto the sled. One of the others triggered the protective fields, and they swung away again, heading at a run for the nearer ambulance. More followed— I counted five more, the rest of Ixora's team, then a sixth, walking and towing an unlighted sled. That would be Tabat. I looked away.

Then all the injured were aboard—the operation could

not have taken more than three or four minutes—and the two ambulances lifted just as the Blue Team's vehicle touched down ahead of us. "What will happen to the hoobeys?" I asked.

Rohin shrugged, holding his face. A livid bruise was beginning to show already, where Ixora had struck him with the whip butt, and he spoke with difficulty. "Some will have to be put down. The rest they'll bring back to the Tower, treat them there."

I shook my head, exhausted and chilled through despite the heated suit. "We'd better get back. Jesma will want us."

Anath cleared his throat, sounding almost embarrassed. "You're in no shape to ride a skycycle, Medium, not after all this." He gestured to his grounded carpet. "Come back with us."

There was nothing I would have liked better—it had a closed, heated passenger compartment, and I wouldn't have to do a thing—but I made myself shake my head. "I promised—" I began, and bit off the rest of the sentence. I had promised Shemer Axtell to return his skycycle in one piece, but that was unimportant. Anath nodded as if he'd read my mind, and I said, "No, but thank you, sor Anath. But Rohin—"

"No," the Demi-heir said, flatly.

Anath shrugged. "As you wish." He hesitated a moment longer, expression unhappy and uncertain, and said at last, "The ama Ixora. She was upset."

I bristled and heard Rohin's whispered malediction before I realized what the Brandr was trying to say. Ixora had called his kinsman a liar and murderer, to his face and before witnesses. Anath was telling me he, at least, would overlook it, and he was of high standing in the mainline kin. "She is hurt," I agreed, and Anath nodded.

"Good flight," he said, and turned back to his carpet.

"Of course he tries to cover up," Rohin said fiercely, but he had the sense to keep his voice down. "It was their fault it happened."

"Then let it be decided in the Council, not by feud," I said, as fiercely. "Give Herself the chance to settle it peacefully. Now come on."

The flight back to the Axtell Tower was probably the

worst of my life. The rest of the meeting was not affected by the accident, of course, so we had to take the long route, skirting the track. My nerves were stretched to the breaking point by the time I brought the cycle into the garages at the base of the Tower. What Rohin was feeling, I could only imagine: he had not spoken a word since we left the wreck site.

Shemer himself was waiting for us, but he had no news. He waited while we changed out of the dirty sportsuits, then led us through the Tower's maze of corridors to a windowless, well-heated room. Jesma was there before us, along with several others of the Halex party. They all looked up sharply when we entered, half hopeful and half afraid.

"What in hell's name happened?" Jesma demanded— she was the senior Halex present—and in the same moment, Shemer said, "If there's anything you need, Jesma."

The Halex bit back her questions, visibly remembering courtesy and the code. "I thank you, no, sor. You've been most kind."

Shemer said, "If you think of anything, please ask." He seemed for the first time to become aware of the way the assembled Halex were looking at him, willing him to leave, and backed awkwardly away, letting the door slide closed behind him.

Jesma said again, "What the hell happened?"

Rohin said, "Fen Erling says the drag cables broke." His voice was heavy with sarcasm.

"Not likely," one of the others protested.

"It's hard to tell at this point," I said. I hesitated then, but the bad news had to be told sometime, and Jesma, at least, would know how to deal with it. "Ixora claimed it was done deliberately—that Fen caused the accident on purpose."

"I'd believe it," someone else said, and a child's voice—a girl's voice—rose above the general rumble of agreement.

"Not even a Brandr'd deliberately kill hoobeys."

Jesma was silent, her eyes fixed on my face. "Who'd she say it to?"

She had seen the implications, as I'd hoped she would. "Fen, and Anath Brandr. But—" I raised my voice a little, cutting off Jesma's angry response. "—Anath is aware that Ixora was hurt. He said as much."

I didn't dare say more, for fear that the other Halex, including Rohin, would choose to take Anath's words as insult rather than the escape clause he had intended them to be. Jesma chewed thoughtfully on her lower lip. At last she said, quite without anger, "That's good of him. Herself may be able to do something, then." She sighed, and shook her head. "We'll know more when we hear from the doctors."

The doctors' report, when it finally arrived around Sunrise, clock-midnight, was mostly good. Tabat was dead, of course. The sideboy, Iossea, was badly hurt, and would be months in healing, but there was a good chance she'd make a full recovery. The others, including Ixora, were bruised and battered—Zimri had a broken leg, the other brakesman broken ribs, the sideboy a cracked jaw—but could be taken back to the Halex Tower and the Kinship's own doctors. As for the others, the Erling team seemed to have suffered the least, a few broken bones among the lot, but Tasma Fyfe herself had died. It had been a freak thing, the doctors said. She had seemed unhurt, just bruised, had even been helping tend the other injured, when she had complained of feeling unwell. She had sat down on the sledge's splintered runner, closed her eyes, and simply died. The doctors blamed internal bleeding.

Jesma thanked the doctors as the code demanded, but as soon as the screen went blank, she drew me aside. "This changes things," she said, so softly the others couldn't hear.

"I don't understand," I said. I was bitter tired, and too upset still to think of sleep.

"Tasma Fyfe dead. . . ." Jesma's voice was a sleepwalker's, or the voice of someone talking to herself. "Now Fyfe has a grievance."

"Tabat was killed, too," I said, more harshly than I'd meant.

Jesma gave me a bitter look. "I care about him, don't worry. But Ixora's made an accusation, and none of the Fyfes did, which gives their claim precedence—even if Anath persuades Fen to keep his mouth shut," she said, overriding my next protest, "which I doubt he can. Tasma was mainline Family, and in line for the genarchy."

I bit back my first answer. It would do no good. I had known what Orestes was like when I took this job, and I was pledged to work within the system. "What do we do?" I asked.

Jesma rubbed her reddened eyes. "We inform Herself at once, I think. And then we take everyone who can be moved, and fly home." She looked up at me, and shook her head. "No matter what we do, Trey, there's going to be hell to pay."

All holds. For we are strong and skilled;
we have authority; we hold
memory of evil; we are stern
nor can man's pleadings bend us.

Aeschylus, *The Eumenides,* 381-384

Chapter 5: Rehur

Accounts of the sledge accident filled the Necropolis's newssheets for two calendar-days after it happened: that sort of scandal-in-the-making was meat and drink to them. There had been a dozen different 'sheets at rehearsal—plain-paper dailies, pink-paper evenings—and he had found time to read them all between his scenes. The news wasn't bad, but it wasn't good, either, and he knew his performance had suffered. It was annoying still to care so much, even for Ixora, which was why he was here, in the bar of the Cockaigne Theater, instead of home in bed.

He sighed, glancing across to the time display flashing above the serving hatch. Almost two in the morning, by the clock: the Eclipse would be starting soon. That was traditionally a time of license, and he wondered briefly if he should try to make it home before full Dark. Feelings were running high after the accident, and ghost or not, he had the Halex face. He shook himself then, more annoyed than ever at his own inability to break free of the Family. You came here, he told himself firmly, to read kata, and you will read this kata-book. Boldisar's waiting for your decision.

He looked down at the book, frayed pages spread open

117

in the strip of sunlight that came in through the crack in the imperfectly closed shutters. The three columns of print—action summary, dialogue, and the kata, the written description of the carefully integrated movement of live actors and holopuppets—swam in the harsh light, and he looked away again, sighing. It was a good play, *The Three Warlords*, and the part—the Third Warlord, the lead-villain—was one of the biggest he'd been offered. The problem was that Boldisar wanted a commitment to his puppet theater as well, and Rehur did not want to give it.

"Reading for a part, Rehur?"

Rehur glanced up, not sorry for the interruption. A tall, olive-skinned man, his dark hair cut very short, slid into the seat opposite, a sardonic smile on his mobile face. Rehur smiled back, but warily. Ume-Kai was an old acquaintance, if not a friend—they had flats in the same building—but Rehur found it hard to trust the other man. Ume-Kai was a minne, a male player of female roles—with one of the satirical cross-talk companies. Anything and everything was fair game to them, and Rehur had no desire to feature in any of their performances.

"Thinking about it," Rehur answered.

"Who with?" Without waiting for an answer, Ume-Kai slid the book out of the other actor's grasp and turned it so that he could read the printed symbols. "*The Three Warlords*. Boldisar's people are doing that, aren't they?"

Rehur nodded—Ume-Kai knew it already, of course; the minnen and mannen couldn't afford to miss anything that happened inside or outside the Necropolis—and waited. Ume-Kai's long mouth curved into a knowing smile.

"The Third Warlord, right, but a company contract?"

"Yes," Rehur said again, and to his horror felt himself blushing. He leaned back as casually as he could, away from the band of sunlight.

Ume-Kai's smile widened. "And we all know Boldisar's real specialty," he said. "How good are you at *nureba*, Rehur?"

Rehur bit back his first answer—like most ghosts starting out in the puppet theaters, he'd done his share of *nureba*, wet work—and then had to suppress the temptation to boast. He shrugged. "I've done it," he said, with what he hoped was convincing unconcern.

Ume-Kai nodded, the mockery draining from face and voice. "Who hasn't? It's a living. The Third Warlord's a good part, but—"

"Witchwood's a good company," Rehur finished for him. "I know. But. . . ." He let the sentence trail off unfinished. Witchwood was poor, they couldn't always afford to stage full plays, the plays that gave him the best lead-villain roles. Both he and Ume-Kai knew the situation, but he wasn't about to discuss it with the minne.

"I was sorry to hear about your Family's troubles," Ume-Kai went on. He glanced at the other man's empty glass. "Get you another?"

Rehur shook his head. "I'm stone-broke, Ume."

"I'll put it on my tab," the minne answered, and was gone before Rehur could refuse again.

The younger actor sighed, wondering what he'd gotten himself into this time. Technically, of course, the Cockaigne's bar was a private club—only private clubs could stay open during the Day—but only the members of the cross-talk companies attached to the theater had anything approaching members' privileges. Everyone else paid cash, and at the moment, Rehur had precious little of that, and none to spare for drinks. Of course, there'd be some payment for the drink—Ume-Kai wasn't noted for his altruism—but with luck, it would be a price he could afford to pay.

He watched Ume-Kai turn back from the serving hatch, a drink in each hand, and make his way back through the maze of empty tables. He half hoped the minne would ask him to sleep with him, but that would be too easy. Ume-Kai was bound to want more.

The minne set both drinks on the scarred table and slid easily into his seat. Rehur sniffed cautiously at the steaming mug, then took a careful sip. It was hot spiced wine, liberally laced with one of the fruited brandies, and he made a mental note not to drink more than one glass.

Ume-Kai said again, "I was sorry to hear about the accident—assuming it was an accident."

Rehur made a face. That was Ixora for you, always ready to jump to the attack, without thinking about the consequences. Several different versions of her accusation had made the newssheets, but all agreed that she had insulted Fen Erling to his face. "I wouldn't put it past any of the

Brandr," he said carefully, "but Ixora was hardly in any shape to be talking, if the 'sheets have it right."

Ume-Kai shrugged. "I hear she spent a night in the hospital, but she's out now, and in the Necropolis."

"Here?" Rehur interrupted. "Why?"

"Who knows?" the minne said, shrugging again. "I thought you might tell me."

Rehur shook his head automatically, but his thoughts were suddenly elsewhere. Ixora, in the Necropolis just before Eclipse, with a grudge to settle. . . . Duelling was a very new fashion on Orestes, but it was just the sort of thing she'd do. And Fen Erling was no better. He looked up, and saw Ume-Kai watching him. The minne nodded slowly.

"I was thinking along those lines myself, but you know her better. I tell you, if she does it, I'll make her—both of them—the laughingstocks of this planet."

"What the hell business is it of yours?" Rehur snapped.

"If they keep bringing their fights here, into the Necropolis, how much longer do you think they'll let us go on?" Ume-Kai's face and voice were for once completely honest in their anger. "I don't care if she is kin of yours, I—we—won't see her destroy the one safe place we have left." Then his face relaxed a little. "Well, obviously I do care, or I wouldn't've come to you."

"You want me to warn her off?" Rehur shook his head. I wonder what Ume has against the Kinships, he thought. There must be something; otherwise, he'd never've gone into a cross-talk company. He touched the ghostmark on his own forehead. "I can't, Ume. Be serious."

"What about this medium of yours, the off-worlder?"

"Maturin." The name brought with it the memory of the night after the *khy sonon-na*, and Rehur smiled in spite of himself. He still had one of the medium's cards someplace, filched from a pocket. He said the name again for the sheer pleasure of it, recognizing his own foolishness. "Trey's probably still at the Tower. That won't help if Ixora's in Destiny."

"So hire a medium," Ume-Kai said impatiently. "There are enough of them around. Hell, I thought you'd appreciate the chance to warn the woman."

"I do," Rehur said, startled out of his momentary daydream. "Really, I do, and I will warn her, honest. Thank you."

Ume-Kai nodded, mollified.

Rehur looked down again at the kata-book, not really seeing the printed columns. The bar of light had changed, its color curdling toward the Eclipse. If Ixora were really in Destiny to fight a duel, he would have to find her soon, before the five hours of darkness gave her the opportunity she'd need. Normally, Ixora stayed at Hills', he thought, but would she stay there, risk her member's rights, if she were setting up an illegal fight? "Since you know so much, Ume, where's Ixora staying?" Anger at the entire situation sharpened his voice. He had thought he would finally be free of the Kinship when he had been declared dead six years before, but now comparative strangers were making demands on him in the Family's name.

The minne looked down his long nose at the younger man. "I don't know. If you don't care—"

Rehur winced—he had not really meant to anger the other—and said, with as much sincerity as he could muster, "I'm sorry, Ume, I didn't mean that. I'm worried, that's all."

Ume-Kai's face relaxed a little, but before he could say anything, the main door slammed back against its stops, throwing a wedge of the fading light across the bar. "What the hell?" Ume-Kai began, and an unfamiliar voice cut him off.

"Bartender! Put two liters of tsaak in a hot flask, and be quick about it!"

Rehur turned, frightened by the sudden frown on Ume-Kai's face. The man in the doorway stood with his back to the light, his face in shadow, but there was no mistaking the knots of blue and gold ribbon tied to his sleeve.

"My God, it's happened." Rehur hadn't meant to speak aloud, and his words echoed in the sudden silence. The man in the doorway turned as though he would speak, saw the ghostmark, and looked away again.

"This is a private club, sor," the bartender said. At a discreet signal, the bar's bouncer slipped from the cubbyhole where he kept his pile of newssheets, and stood ready for action. "I'm sorry."

"It's all right, Ezar, I'll vouch for him." A woman wrapped

in a swirling, bright-red cape ducked under the stranger's outstretched arm and into the bar. Rehur recognized her as one of the mannen who worked for the Cockaigne. "In fact, " she went on, posing for her audience, face alive with mischief, "you can put it on my tab, if you like."

"Have you gone crazy, Aliste?" Ume-Kai demanded, not raising his voice.

"Have you gone soft, Ume-Kai?" the woman retorted. She smiled at the bartender. "Hurry, please, Ezar, we don't want to be late."

Rehur held his breath, willing the bartender to refuse her again. Ezar hesitated a moment longer, then, shaking his head, reached into his cabinets for the heated flasks. He filled them, slowly, and Aliste swaggered across the bar to collect them, still smiling.

"What the hell's going on?" That was one of the other actors who had been sitting in the bar, her voice a little blurred from the drinks she had had.

Aliste handed the bottles to the man with the Brandr ribbons and turned to face the questioner, clearly savoring her moment. "Fen Erling's fighting to clear his name, after the Halex woman called him a murderer."

"Ask where," Rehur said, to the minne. Aliste had to be *para'an*—she couldn't be an actor unless she were—but he didn't want to give her the chance to refuse him. Ume-Kai shook his head, but then someone else shouted, "Where?"

Aliste shook her head with a richly artificial laugh. Rehur's hand closed around the mug of wine, but Ume-Kai caught his wrist, pinned it to the table.

"Not while Ezar's listening, ready to call the cops on us. But come along, if you want." The stranger put his arm around her shoulders, drawing her gently out of the bar before she could say anything more. Aliste looked back over his arm, laughing again, as the door swung closed behind them.

"Damn it, Ume," Rehur began, but the minne shook his head.

"I know where it has to be, there's no other place they can fight. Do we call the cops?"

Rehur hesitated. The police force in Destiny was a minor force at best, trained to guard the greengates and to prevent burglary if they could. They had already proved their inability to handle the new street violence the year before, when a feud-related riot killed six people. More than that, most of them were Ingvarrs, of the Halex Kinship, and to call them in would only contribute to the problem. "I don't know," he began, almost in a wail, and then said, decisively, "No. No, Ume, it'd only make things worse." He pushed himself to his feet, reaching for the light overtunic slung across the back of his chair. "Just tell me where, all right?"

Ume-Kai started to protest, then shook his head. "I'll take you there."

The sunlight had faded to the unnatural twilight of first hour of Eclipse, and there was a breath of frost in the air. Rehur shivered, hugging the knitted overtunic around himself, and wondered if it was only the wind that chilled him. He was dressed only for the relative warmth of the Day, but the temperature could not have dropped that quickly. He shuddered again, and pulled thin gloves from his pockets.

"This way," Ume-Kai said. In the dead light, his grey clothes, cap, long scarf, tunic, trousers, were blurred and indistinct, rendering him almost invisible against the grey-brown walls of the surrounding buildings. Only his hands in their scarlet gloves were clearly visible, like the disembodied projections of the puppet stage. "This way," he said again, impatiently, and Rehur followed.

This was not a part of the Necropolis he knew well, a section given over to cross-talk theaters like the Cockaigne, and to small, cheap bars and blocks of cheaper flats. Belit would know it better, he thought, would have played in some of the halls, and then was annoyed at the irrelevant memory. The bars and cabaret theaters were closed, of course, their windows tightly shuttered, doors blocked by durable steel grates. The light was fading all around them; here and there, a streetlight struggled to come on.

A few minutes later, Ume-Kai turned off the main street into a maze of alleys lit only by old-fashioned ball lights set above the buildings' doors. They gave little coverage, and Rehur was careful to stay close behind the minne as they threaded their way through the unmetalled roads. The alleys were very quiet—people tended to spend the Eclipse indoors in this part of the Necropolis—but then Rehur heard a sudden rush of voices. He stopped short, listening, and the sound was cut off as abruptly as it had appeared.

"Ume?" he began, and the minne nodded.

"I heard. That's where we're going."

Ume-Kai turned a final corner and stopped short, putting out a hand to stop the younger actor. "Do you have any money?"

"Some," Rehur answered, glancing warily around. They were in a dead-end alley, unlit except for the ball light above the grated door of the building at the far end of the street. To either side, the buildings—warehouses, perhaps, or the cheapest tenements—showed windowless walls for the first two stories, and mean, grated slits for the story above that.

"Give it to me."

"Why?" Rehur asked, but reached obediently into his trousers pocket.

"We'll have to pay to get in, and probably a lot," Ume-Kai answered. "I don't have enough."

Rehur passed him the folded sheaf of banknotes, wishing it were larger. He would figure out how to pay the rent, how to eat later, he thought. Right now it was more important to find out what was happening to Ixora.

Tucking the money into the palm of his glove, Ume-Kai advanced on the end building, Rehur following close behind. As they approached the barred door, Rehur could see steps leading down to one side, to a second, sunken door. The lower door had no grate, and a modern bar light burned above it, filling the landing well with harsh brilliance. Ume-Kai stepped down into it without hesitation, and Rehur followed, blinking.

There was a knocker set above the lock-plate, and Ume-Kai pressed it. It made no sound in the stairwell, but they could hear, faintly, its chimes echoing somewhere inside the building. The door opened almost before the knocker stopped sounding, and a hairless head appeared in the opening.

"Sorry, sors, we're closed. If you're the delivery, it's upstairs."

He started to close the door, but Ume-Kai slipped the folded notes out of the palm of his glove. "We're here for the fun," he said, in an expressionless voice.

"Ah." The bald man reversed the door's swing instantly. "You're late." Ume-Kai shrugged, and held out the money. The bald man took it, and waved them both inside. He closed the door behind them just as a wave of shouting rolled along the white-painted corridor. "You know the way?"

"Yes," Ume-Kai said, in the same toneless voice.

"Right," the bald man said, and settled himself again in the battered chair that stood just inside the door.

"Come on," Ume-Kai said, and put his hand on the younger actor's shoulder.

Rehur shivered at the touch, but did as he was told. The corridors were brightly lit, freshly painted, but the air smelled damply of sweat and dirty clothes. Beneath that, he caught the sharp scent of urine. "What is this place?" he said at last, when he was sure they were out of earshot of the man guarding the door.

"Legally, it's a gym," Ume-Kai answered. The corners of his mouth drew downward in distaste. "But they hire out for a lot of things—duels, blood sport, whatever."

"How come you know so much about it?" Rehur asked, and wished he hadn't.

The minne's face contorted. Then he mastered his expression, and said coldly, "You did *nureba*. I was *minne'* from the time I turned fourteen." He gave the word the inflection that changed the meaning from a kind of actor to transvestite prostitute, and Rehur winced. With an effort, Ume-Kai managed a lopsided smile. "I was born dead, Rehur. My mother was a ghost, and a poor one. I had to do something."

Rehur groped for something to say to that, but there wasn't anything. They walked on in silence. A few meters farther on, the corridor ended in an abrupt right turn. Rehur saw the other actor square his shoulders, and braced himself to meet whatever lay around the corner.

The shouting, which had been building as they came down the corridor, rose to a sudden climax as they turned the corner. Rehur flinched, and almost stumbled into the table set to block half the corridor. A nondescript man, heavily muscled for an Oresteian, sat behind it. "Let's see your tickets, friends," he said.

Ume-Kai shook his head. "We paid at the door, friend." He gave that word a twist, too, and the muscle-man frowned.

"Too bad, friend, you pay here."

"If I pay again," Ume-Kai said deliberately, "you'll see yourself on the Cockaigne stage. Do I make myself clear?"

The muscle-man shrugged. "Can't blame me for trying," he said. "Go on in."

Ume-Kai smiled thinly, and stepped past the table. Rehur followed before the muscle-man could change his mind. They ducked through a final, low doorway into darkness. Rehur hesitated, half-blind in the sudden dark, and Ume-Kai caught his hand, drawing him away from the door. After a moment, the younger man's sight cleared.

They stood at the back of a low-ceilinged gallery, looking through a series of low arches into an orange-lit central space. Each of the arches was packed with bodies, making it impossible to see what lay beyond. The smell of urine was stronger here, and Rehur made a face, avoiding the frequent puddles.

Ume-Kai leaned close, his lips almost against the other's ear. "The fighting's in the pit," he said. "We want your Family's box—this way."

"Box?" Rehur asked, in half-hysterical disbelief, but Ume-Kai was already pulling him toward the far end of the gallery. Rehur stumbled after him, catching only the briefest glimpses of the crowd around him. Most of them seemed to be *para'anin*, or at least if they were dead, their ghostmarks were hidden beneath hoods and pulled-down caps. Most were shabbily dressed, but not all of them; he caught sight of at least one young woman wearing a pin in the shape of the Orillon seaflower, recognized another young man's five-hundred-kip coat. Then they were pushing their way through the crowd that clogged the central arch, and Rehur recognized familiar faces, Halex faces, among the crowd. They recognized him, too, but could not be seen to see a ghost.

Ume-Kai seemed to be searching for something, swearing to himself as he pushed past people. Rehur struggled after him, keeping a tight hold on the loose fabric of the minne's over-tunic. Then, at the very front of the archway, silhouetted against the orange light of the pit, he saw a cloaked figure, saw too the light reflecting from the medium's badge swinging at its collar.

"Maturin?" In the same instant, Rehur realized it was not the off-worlder, and Ume-Kai swung to face him.

"Your medium?"

"Not Trey, but yes, a medium."

"Where?"

Rehur pointed to the cloaked shape. "There."

"Thank God," Ume-Kai said, and began pushing through the crowd again.

For once, the ghostmarks worked to their advantage. Angry spectators, turning to see who was shoving, fell back at the sight of the white-marked foreheads, and let them pass. Rehur took savage pleasure in elbowing his own kinsmen and watching their faces change from annoyance to mute, wooden outrage at his presence.

And then they had reached the mouth of the archway, and Ume-Kai reached to touch the medium's shoulder. The figure turned, frowning, and Rehur recognized Emerant Ansson, who handled much of the Kinship's business in Destiny. The medium's frown deepened as she saw Ume-Kai, then eased as she saw Rehur standing behind the minne. She turned so that her back was against the side of the archway, pressing herself against the stones so that the ghosts could squeeze in beside her.

"What can I do for you?" she asked, raising her voice to be heard over the rumbling of the crowd.

Rehur barely heard the question. For the first time, he had a clear view down into the pit, and the sight held him mesmerized. The pit was just that, an oval hole perhaps thirteen or fourteen meters long and five or six meters wide. The lip of the archway was a little more than two meters from the sanded floor, dyed bright orange by the glow of the heating lamps suspended from the ceiling. In the pit itself, two knots of people clustered around a figure at each end of the oval. Each group carried a weighted driver's whip, but it was some seconds before Rehur recognized Ixora at the center of the left-hand group.

"Tell us what happened, Medium," Ume-Kai said.

"You don't know?" Emerant bit off her own question,

glancing from one to the other. Rehur dragged his eyes away from Ixora, now stripping off knitted tunic and loose shirt until she stood bare-armed, undervest defining her tiny breasts.

"No," he said.

Emerant drew a deep breath, obviously searching for the most economical way to tell the story. "Fen Erling challenged Ixora, for calling him liar and murderer," she said, after a moment's thought. "That gave her choice of weapons, which is why it's whips. She can't kill him too easily that way. So we're here."

"Why didn't she just refuse?" Rehur asked. Emerant gave him a wry half smile, and didn't answer. Swearing, Rehur turned back to the pit. Ume-Kai wrapped one long hand around the other actor's arm to steady him, but Rehur barely felt that fierce grip. They all knew why Ixora had responded to the challenge: to have refused would have been to admit a mistake, to say she had not meant her accusation, and, for better or for worse, she believed what she'd said. At least, Rehur thought, she had the sense to choose half-lethal weapons. The seconds would have to step in before someone was killed.

"Why didn't she just stay out of sight?" Ume-Kai asked. "If this Fen couldn't find her to challenge her. . . ."

Emerant sighed, working her hands inside the pockets of her long cloak. "We tried—who are you, anyway?"

"My name is Ume-Kai," the minne began, and Rehur said, "A friend of mine, Medium, with the Cockaigne Theater."

Emerant made a shrugging gesture of apology. "We tried," she said again. "Herself sent her down to Destiny, to the townhouse, thinking Fen would come to the Tower, but he came here instead. And now. . . ." Her voice trailed off, was absorbed into the sudden roar of the crowd. Rehur swung to face the pit again, the stones slick underfoot, and was grateful for Ume-Kai's hand on his arm.

In the pit, the seconds had finished their final business and retreated to the sides of the pit. Friends and kinsmen helped them climb back into the arches, leaving the combatants alone on the sanded floor. They stood apart for a long moment, Ixora watching the weighted tip of her whip write patterns in the sand, Fen slowly drawing the braided cords through his fingers, and there were catcalls from the audience. Ixora looked up then, an odd half-smile on her face, and slowly brought her whip into the fighting position. She was afraid, Rehur knew, recognizing that expression from the days when he'd manned the drag-brake for her, and clenched his own fists to stop from shaking.

"Oh, Ixora, be careful," he whispered, knowing he couldn't startle her, that his words would be lost in the noise from the crowd.

Fen had brought his whip up, too, and the two faced each other across the pit, just within reach of each other's weapon. For a long moment, neither moved. Rehur could feel the time stretching through a dozen, two dozen of his heartbeats, heard as if through batting whistles and jeering shouts from the audience. Fen's nerve broke first. With a shout, he swung his whip in a great arc, the tip cracking through the space where Ixora had stood. She moved in the same instant, swaying easily aside, brought her own whip into motion. She missed her first counter-stroke, to tangle and trap the other's whip, and her follow-up attack missed by centimeters. Fen recovered, struck again. Ixora staggered, and there was a roar from the crowd as they saw the blood on her vest. That was what they had come to see, Rehur realized, and it added immensely to the sport that it was people of Family who bled. He swallowed hard, tasting bile.

Ixora regained her balance in an instant, skipping back a few steps to buy time. Fen came after her, whip singing through the thick air. She feinted left, dodged right, and struck. The weighted tip caught Fen on the shoulder of his whip arm, drawing blood. There was more cheering at the sight.

They were both more cautious after that, moving, using the length of the pit, breaking off the attack if their feints did not bring the desired reaction. A few voices jeered at them, calling for action, for blood, but the more knowledgeable hissed them to silence. Rehur dug his nails into Ume-Kai's wrist, hardly aware of what he was doing. The whips snapped out again and again, drawing blood occasionally, more often missing their target entirely and forcing the attacker to leap back to avoid the counterstroke. Both Fen and Ixora were bleeding freely now, each with half a dozen swollen cuts from the sharp-edged weights, but none was serious enough to stop the fight. They were breathing heavily now, and the pauses between attacks were lengthening. Rehur shivered, knowing what had to happen soon. Very few body blows could do enough damage to stop the fight; only an attack on head or face would do it, though so far neither one seemed to want to take that step.

Then, quite abruptly, Fen feinted high and struck as Ixora ducked. The crowd yelled its pleasure, but Fen was tiring. The attack fell short, the weight just grazing Ixora's jaw. It drew a thin line of blood from the middle of her cheek down across her chin, and she struck back without plan, a direct blow at the Erling's face. He had not expected something so unsubtle, was tangled in a counterfeint, and the weight struck him high on the right cheek, just below his eye. Fen screamed, dropping his whip, and sank to the sanded floor, holding his face in both hands. Blood welled from between his fingers, blood and something else. The crowd exploded with delight, urging Ixora to finish him. Rehur turned his head, fighting the desire to vomit.

When he was able to look back, the seconds had reached the pit, and the crowd's cheering had died into a sort of disappointed mumbling, mixed with the shouts of bookmakers paying off their odds. Ixora leaned into a friend's arms, face distorted, her shoulders heaving with exhausted sobs. Fen was hidden by the hovering bodies of his seconds, but Rehur caught a glimpse of one kneeling beside him, capably bandaging the injured man.

"Rehur!"

The younger actor looked around with an effort. Emerant leaned close, fighting to be heard over the noise. "You've got to get word to the Tower for me, tell Maturin what's happened. Will you do that?"

"Can't one of the others do it?" Rehur asked automatically. He looked over his shoulder for the Halex he had seen before, but the familiar faces had vanished.

"They've either run, or they're busy with her," Ume-Kai said. He nodded at the medium. "You go to her, too. We'll take your message."

"Thank you," Emerant said. She dropped awkwardly off

the edge of the archway into the pit, and took Ixora gently in her arms. Ixora, still sobbing, let herself be held.

"Come on," Ume-Kai said grimly. "We've got to find a terminal."

Chapter 6: Trey Maturin

The call came in a little before five hours of the clock-morning, on my private code. The flashing light and the muted whirring of the console alarm woke me at last, but I lay for a moment beneath my blankets wondering stupidly what was happening. Then it registered that a call on that line, at this hour, meant an emergency. I levered myself out of the bed, dragging a blanket with me because I couldn't find my robe, and hit the flashing accept button on the second try. The screen flashed on, and Rehur looked out of it at me.

"Rehur?" I said, blankly, and groped for a chair. The ghost looked very white and frightened, and I could see the blurred figure of another man standing behind him. "Are you in trouble?"

Rehur laughed, a little shakily. "No, not me, Trey." He shivered convulsively, the smile vanishing, and the other man put a hand on his shoulder. I wondered a little angrily who he was, and whether Rehur would introduce him.

"Not me," Rehur said again. "It's Ixora."

Oh, my God, I thought, and instinctively keyed on the recorder. The Matriarch had sent Ixora into Destiny in the hopes of avoiding a duel. Had the idiot girl managed to fight in spite of that?

"Fen Erling hunted her out and challenged her," Rehur was saying. "They fought, and he's hurt—and shouldn't you be recording this, or something?"

His voice trembled on the edge of hysteria. I saw the stranger's hands move gently on Rehur's shoulders, and said, as soothingly as I could manage, "I've already got the tape going, Rehur. Take it slowly, start at the beginning, and tell me what's happened."

He did his best, but it was still disjointed: Rehur hadn't been in at the challenge, had seen the whole thing more or less by accident, and was still sickened by what he had seen. It seemed to calm him to talk, however, and by dint of careful questioning, I got the full story as he knew it. He was calm enough then that I didn't feel too bad about letting him go; I broke the connection and sat there for a moment, trying to think what I should do next. Herself would have to be informed, of course, but there were a few things I could—should—do first. Ixora had to be taken care of, for one. I called up the Tower's communications net, waking the sleeping duty-operator, and got control of half a dozen outside lines. That was one advantage to the code, I thought, even as I punched in the numbers that might reach Emerant Ansson, the medium the Halex employed for their business in Destiny. My position was unassailable, unquestionable—the code said I had to be obeyed.

Emerant was not at home, or at the Family townhouse. I hoped this meant she was with Ixora—I had a fairly high opinion of Emerant's common sense—and left messages both places saying she was to find Ixora if she didn't have her, and return to the Tower at once. I called up the Tower operator then, and told her to hold those lines open for me on an emergency basis. Then I braced myself, and punched the codes that would reach the Matriarch.

The light flashed for what seemed an interminable time, but then at last it steadied, though the screen remained blank. A voice said, "Yes, what is it?"

It wasn't Herself, of course. I thought I recognized the voice of the Ansson cousin-kinswoman who acted as the Matriarch's secretary, and keyed my own camera just in

case she'd set her machine to receive. "Lenor? It's Trey
Maturin."

The sleepy voice sharpened instantly. "Medium? Is there
trouble?"

The last wasn't really a question. Even as she spoke, the
picture faded into existence on my screen, showing me a
thin-faced woman in her thirties, her long hair, braided for
sleep, falling forward across her shoulder. I said, "I'm
afraid so, Lenor. You'd better wake Herself—Ixora's fought
her duel."

Lenor's mouth twitched, and the lines at the corners of
her tilted eyes tightened momentarily, but she didn't waste
time in exclamations. "I'll do that. Would you inform the
Heir, and the Branch Holders?"

"Of course," I began. There was a noise in the background, and Lenor turned to face the speaker.

"Yes, ama," she said, and turned back to the screen.
"Herself says, Medium, would you also inform the Elders,
and ask them all to meet in the Tower conference room by
the end of the Eclipse?"

"As Herself wishes," I said formally, and Lenor broke
the connection. I sat staring at the keyboard and the fuzzy
screen for a long moment. It wouldn't be easy to arrange
for the senior members of the various Branches of the
Halex Kinship to reach the Tower by seven standard hours,
and some of them would have to attend by vis-link, but at
least I could be sure of collecting the Elders—the Matriarch's personal advisors—by then. I reopened my line to
the Tower operator and began issuing orders.

To my surprise, however, only the Holder Yslin Rhawn,
caught high in the Prosperities inspecting one of his Branch's
mines, had to use the vis-link. The other two Holders,
Barthel Ansson and Asbera Ingvarr, were in Destiny already, come to confer about the accident and its implications, and the Elders all lived in or around the Tower.
They arrived by ones and by twos, in aircraft or groundcars—only one by the UHST—and were shown instantly
to the upper room that the Matriarch had designated as
her conference room. Someone, probably the secretary
Lenor, had ordered a full meal laid out on the sideboard,
but no one seemed to want it.

The Matriarch sat grim-faced at the head of the long

table, the tape of Rehur's story cued up in a reader at her left hand. She had listened to it alone, as soon as I had summoned Elders and Holders, and had not referred to it since. Only the Heir Magan, her son, Rehur's father, had dared to ask to hear it, and she had sworn at him for his presumption.

Magan refused to be deterred. "Surely we should all hear what's happened before we make any decision," he said. The words faltered into a question under his mother's stony gaze.

"We will hear that from Ixora," the Matriarch snapped. "Not from the dead."

There was nothing Magan or anyone else could say to that, though I could see that the others, Elders and Holders alike, wanted more detail than the bald summary I had given them. I stood, sighing, and crossed to the sideboard to draw myself another cup of the vile Oresteian coffee. There was a narrow slit window above the board; I glanced through it as I stirred spices into my drink. The Eclipse was ending, the light flooding back across the courtyard. In an hour or so, the first sliver of Agamemnon would be visible in the lapis sky.

The window looked out onto the rising ground to the north of the Tower, toward the windmills that drove the Tower generators and, beyond that, toward Destiny. The thin blades were turning slowly in the steady wind, responding to air movements so light as to be almost imperceptible from the ground: there would be no power to spare this calendar-day, I guessed, but enough for common work. Then, in the sky above the left-end mill, I saw a flash of light. It was a small, fast flyer, heading for the makeshift field below the Tower, the only place flat enough to take a flyer that wasn't under cultivation in what passed for Orestes' temperate zone. Ixora, I thought, but said nothing until it came close enough for me to read the Halex marking on its tail.

"Ama," I said, pitching my voice to break the nervous silence. "I believe Ixora is arriving."

In the next breath, as they broke into nervous, low-voiced speculation, I damned myself for succumbing to the actor's instinct. It might not be Ixora, could even be Yslin Rhawn, if he'd been able to find transport fast enough. . . . The Matriarch was watching me, the shadow of a mocking smile on her thin lips. Even deep in her own troubles, she could recognize and appreciate my discomfort.

But of course it was Ixora, and Emerant Ansson with her, followed by two of Ixora's agemates who'd decided they could brave Herself's anger. One, a dark girl called Dorenn, I remembered from the gang who had managed the hoobeys at the Garnocks; the other I did not know. Rehur was not with them, of course, and, though I had known better than to expect him, I felt a certain disappointment.

They came through the door in a clump, no one wanting to be first, but then Ixora stepped out from the rest and made a sketchy bow. "Ama."

She had been hurt, all right. One bandage was pasted across her face to cover a cut running from the point of her jaw to the tip of her chin; other injuries were implicit in the stiff, painful movements of her upper body. The Matriarch saw that, too, and her voice was a fraction less grim when she spoke.

"Well, girl, you've made even more trouble for yourself this time."

Ixora took a deep breath, and winced as that stirred some hidden injury. She said, her words slurred by the topical anesthetic they had used on her face, "I know, ama. But I was challenged."

That was unanswerable, and after a moment, the Matriarch's eyes slid away toward the tape beside her. "Lenor!"

The call took me by surprise—I had expected her to demand an explanation, at least—but the secretary had clearly been waiting for it.

"Ama?"

"Do your job. Get Yslin Rhawn," Herself said, and turned her attention back to Ixora. "Then we'll hear what this one has to say for herself."

"Yes, ama."

The secretary rolled a small console away from the wall, touching keys as she did so. A holophone rose from its top, and an image blossomed above it: Yslin Rhawn, short and squat for an Oresteian, scowled at us all.

"About—" His static-distorted voice broke off as he saw Ixora, and the Matriarch said, "Then we're all here."

"No fault of mine I wasn't there sooner," Yslin protested, and I saw Lenor flush.

"It was at my order you weren't called before," Herself said impatiently. "No need to trouble you until the evidence was here to be heard."

And, I thought, no need to bring a troublemaker into the council until the last minute. At least she had silenced Yslin. His console was placed so that he could observe all of us, and I hastily smoothed my expression, willing myself to be as unobtrusive as possible. Among the Halex, only the Rhawn Holder had opposed my hiring—from sheer obstinacy, it seemed, rather than any reasoned disapproval, but I didn't want to make things any more difficult for the Matriarch.

Herself shifted in her chair until she faced Ixora again, and folded her gnarled hands in front of her. Someone— Lenor again?—had brought her a cup of coffee, but it sat untouched beside her right hand. Magan leaned forward as though he would say something, but his mother lifted one finger, and he steeled back in his place.

"Now, Ixora," Herself said. "Tell us what happened, from the beginning."

Ixora took another deep breath, and winced again. There seemed to be bruised ribs under her borrowed tunic, but her voice was steady enough, blurred only by the anesthetic on her face. "Ama, as you ordered, I went from the Tower to the Family's house in Destiny. I stayed there, and did not go out, or tell anyone I was there. But someone must've told—" She broke off, tardily afraid of making another rash accusation, and continued, "Somehow Fen found out I was there, and insisted on seeing me. He told Arnvid he lied when he said I wasn't there, and Arnvid had to let him in after that."

She stopped, gathering strength. I bit back an exclamation of disgust. Arnvid Rhawn was the caretaker of the townhouse, ten years older than I was, and with the full dignity of his years to back him he should've been able to keep Fen out. But honor forbade lying, and to be caught in a direct lie was at least horribly shaming, if not mortal; I could understand how Arnvid had been bluffed into capitulating. That did raise the question Ixora had been afraid to ask: how did Fen Erling know she was there, and know it certainly enough to risk accusing a man older and higher in the social hierarchy than himself? Someone must've talked. . . . But that was a matter I could go into later.

"Fen said I had called him a murderer and a liar in front of witnesses," Ixora said, "which I had done, and that he was owed satisfaction." She pushed back her hair with one hand and fixed a suddenly defiant stare on the Matriarch. "He said that if I didn't fight him, he would take that as admission of guilt, and that the code would back him. I didn't see anything else I could do, so I agreed to meet him. Because I had choice of weapons, I picked whips, so I couldn't kill him by accident. I hurt him badly, though."

She was silent for a long moment, thinking about what she'd done, then shook herself and continued. The rest of her story was nothing more than what Rehur had told me already, and I closed my mind to it, trying to think what this would mean. Fen wasn't dead, so the matter of Ixora's accusation still had to be decided—or did it? Would this be like the very ancient days on Earth, when losing a duel meant that you were also assumed to be guilty of whatever crime had provoked the fight? Probably not: dueling wasn't part of the original code, was really only a sort of fashion among the younger bloods. Still, the whole incident, accusation and blinding, would only add to the already deep bitterness between Halex and Brandr. I couldn't see any way of stopping the old feud from being declared again. Glancing around the table, I saw the same knowledge in half a dozen other faces.

When Ixora had finished, there was a long silence, broken at last by a faint creaking as the Matriarch shifted to face the Elder who sat at her left hand. "Well, Tirey? What do you make of it?"

The man she had addressed, Tirey Ingvarr, shook his head slowly. He was a quiet, nondescript man in his late forties, and an expert on all the nuances of the code. "This creates a number of further difficulties," he said, and couldn't stop himself from a bitter glance toward Ixora. "I cannot see that this has settled anything between Halex and Brandr, and it may well cause problems between Halex and Fyfe."

I frowned, not understanding yet, and Herself said, "Explain."

"Fen Erling is hurt—blinded, probably," Tirey said. "But he owed the Fyfe something for causing the accident and killing Tasma Fyfe—especially since she's an Heir's-daughter, even if she isn't the Demi-heir. How will he pay it now, and will it be worth anything? The Fyfe quarrel had precedence, and Ixora usurped it."

"Fen Erling challenged me," Ixora protested, and the Matriarch silenced her with a look.

"That's true, though," Magan said. "She couldn't refuse." He stared at Tirey as though daring the other man to defy him.

Tirey sighed, and I saw on his face a sudden, intense exhaustion. "But she could," he said. "She could. A matter of precedence—settle her quarrel after Fen fulfilled his own obligations."

"That claim's been disallowed more than once before," another of the Elders—a youngish woman called Jannah—said sharply.

"But it would've let us avoid a quarrel with the Fyfe," Tirey said patiently. He looked around the room, and let his gaze settle on Herself. "And we can't afford extra enemies right now. Ama, I see no way to avoid feud with the Brandr. Unless, of course, they choose to put a lenient interpretation on events."

His tone betrayed how likely he thought that to be. And he was probably right, too, I thought, and shivered a little. It is a Mediator's responsibility to do everything possible to avoid open conflict. I wasn't at all sure what could be done, except to urge that this go before the Ship's Council rather than be settled in blood. I opened my mouth to say just that, but at that moment there was a sharp knocking at the door, and it opened without waiting for the Matriarch's command.

"I beg pardon, ama," said the girl who stood there, "but there's an urgent message from the operator. The Fyfe and the Brandr Kinships wish a formal meeting with you— with the Kinship—before the clock-day's over."

Whispered exclamations rustled around the table, and all heads turned toward the Matriarch. She glared at the runner in the doorway, visibly biting back her first comment. "Did they give a reason for this extraordinary summons?" she said at last.

"They said, ama, that they wanted to see if they could come to some settlement," the runner answered. There was an edge to her tone, as though she didn't believe her own words, and Herself snorted in agreement. It hardly seemed likely, I thought. More probably, this was the obligatory meeting before the Brandr declared feud—but if that were the case, why were the Fyfe included?

The Matriarch glanced toward Tirey, who shook his head worriedly. "Ama, I don't know what's in their minds."

"What do you recommend?" Magan asked softly.

Tirey sighed again. "That we be ready to answer any accusations. That's all I can say."

Herself turned back to the runner, still waiting patiently in the doorway. "You may tell the Brandr and the Fyfe that the Halex will meet with them this clock-evening."

She glanced quickly at Magan, who said, "The nineteenth hour? Can we be ready by then?"

It was Lenor who answered, standing forgotten in a corner. "I can have it arranged, yes."

Herself nodded. "At the nineteenth hour, tell them, girl. And there's no need to be too polite about it."

I winced at that, but the hard line of the Matriarch's mouth warned me against making any protest. The runner nodded again, repeating the message to herself, and slipped out of the conference room. The Matriarch swept the rest of us with an imperious stare. "Well, about it," she said at last, and pulled herself awkwardly to her feet. "There's no time to waste if we're to come out of this with the advantage."

The rest of the day was divided between helping Lenor and the Tower communications staff set up the holo-link with the two other Towers—as an off-worlder, I was presumed to know about computers and communications links, but in actuality, my role was reduced to typing commands into the test console, freeing the others for more important jobs—and acting as a sort of moderator in the discussions that followed Herself's decision to accept the meeting that evening. There was a lot to be done—everything had to be phrased with the utmost care in order to avoid admitting Ixora and the Halex had been in the wrong—

and it was well into the afternoon before we had finished. Herself dismissed us to a hasty dinner, but despite the fact I hadn't eaten more than a sandwich snatched near clock-noon, I found it impossible to stomach the heavy food. It was my job as Mediator to prevent this kind of trouble, to keep the Halex out of feud if I could, but I could see no alternative that the Matriarch—or her counterpart of Brandr—would accept. In the end, it was a relief when a runner finally appeared to tell us that it was time for the meeting.

The holo-link had been set up in a pentagonal room on the first below-ground floor of the Tower. The technicians had shifted the treated screen-walls so that the working area of the room formed a triangle, cutting out the two screens that would not be used. Old-fashioned holo-cameras hung from the ceiling, pivoting smoothly on their well-oiled tracks as the technicians ran their last-minute checks. The Matriarch gave the mechanism a final, dubious glance, and moved to take her place at the long table that formed one of the three walls. She moved slowly, and Magan was careful to walk with her, offering unobtrusive support. The Matriarch settled herself awkwardly in her place at the center of the table, and motioned impatiently for the rest of us to take our places. All around us, the light was turning blue, as though Sunset were approaching: the technicians had started the broadcast sequence. I could feel a faint vibration through the floor, as the Tower's solid-fuel generators came on line, supplementing the wind-mills. My place was behind the Matriarch and to her left, the side of death and its mysteries on this dextra-centric world. I took it, careful not to lean against the fabric wall behind me, and waited. The same group that had been at the council this clock-morning was present, arranged in careful precedence by age and place within the Family lines. Only Ixora, standing at the end of the table, was out of place—Ixora and Yslin Rhawn, I amended. The Holder was still in the Prosperities, unable to reach the Tower. His face scowled at us all impartially from the holofunnel set to the Heir's right.

"Everything's ready, ama," one of the technicians said, and I saw the Matriarch take a deep breath.

"Very well," she said. "You may begin."

The light blued further, and the walls that converged in front of us, forming the point of the triangle, took on an odd luminescence. The technicians, hidden with their instruments behind the temporary fabric wall, murmured softly to themselves, and very slowly, images began to take shape in the walls in front of us. The left side, the Fyfe transmission, cleared first, and then the Brandr came into focus. Fen Erling, his face heavily bandaged, sat at the end of the Brandr's table, near the point of the wall, and I saw Anath Brandr beside the Brandr Medium. Not a Holder, then, I thought, and not an Elder, either, so why is he here? Then a chime sounded behind the fabric wall, and a technician said, "The link's complete, ama."

"Thank you," Herself said. Her voice was without inflection, her harsh face composed as she stared at the images in the walls. "Fyfe and Brandr, welcome."

Halfrid Brandr, the Brandr Patriarch, said, his voice equally without expression, "Fyfe and Halex, welcome."

Almost before he had finished speaking, Araxie Fyfe said, "Halex and Brandr, welcome." Unlike the others, the Fyfe Matriarch's voice was hard and angry. She knotted her fingers together as though to imprison them, as though afraid of her own intentions. Trouble, I thought, and was not surprised when she cut through the Brandrs' low-voiced courtesies.

"Sor, ama, we're here on serious business." She turned then, staring directly at the Halex Matriarch. "I'm here for my kin's rights."

Herself took a deep breath, obviously controlling her own anger. "State your grievance, then," she said, and somehow managed to keep the words from sounding too offensive.

"Simple enough," the Fyfe Matriarch snapped, and paused, to continue more calmly, "Your cousin-kin fought and wounded Fen Erling. That was our right, for the death of our Heir's-daughter—my granddaughter!—Tasma. That is our grievance, ama."

"Ixora was the challenged, not the challenger," Herself said, with surprising forbearance.

"So she says," Araxie Fyfe shot back, and there was a soft, indignant hiss from the Holder to my left. Herself threw out a hand to silence him.

"Fen Erling is standing there. Ask him yourself, ama."

Halfrid Brandr said, "It is true, my cousin was the challenger, but he had been accused of lying and of murder by this person." He nodded toward Ixora. Herself stiffened slowly at the deliberate insult. "She need not have accepted."

"Yes." The Fyfe Matriarch took that up eagerly. "Our quarrel took precedence, and she knew it."

Herself took a deep breath and let it out slowly. "If Ixora had made that claim, ama, wouldn't Halfrid Brandr be standing before the Ship's Council right now claiming code breach and cowardice?"

I held my breath. That was the best argument Herself had felt she could make, appealing obliquely to the Fyfe to ally themselves with the Halex against the Brandr. The two Families had common cause, both had suffered from the accident. . . . Araxie Fyfe's stiff anger did not ease, and I felt that brief hope die.

"Fen Erling is hardly beyond your reach," Herself continued. "He can still answer for the death."

The Fyfe Matriarch shook her head. "That doesn't erase the insult you offered us. You owe us the bloodprice."

Herself shook her head sharply, and I saw Halfrid Brandr smile.

Ixora said, "Ama, that's mine to pay."

"No," Magan said, and the Halex Matriarch shook her head again.

Ixora ignored them both, fixing her eyes on Araxie Fyfe. "Ama, I don't say I was in error, because I still don't see what else I could've done, but I'll accept the responsibility for hurting Fen Erling, and pay whatever I have to for it."

It was a strangely dignified appeal, coming from one who was possibly the wildest of the Halex Family, and I saw Araxie's face soften for the first time. Then Halfrid gave a scornful laugh.

"Do you also admit you lied, calling my kinsman a liar and a murderer?"

I held my breath again, willing Ixora not to say anything stupid. I saw the muscles of her jaw tighten, saw her wince, before she answered, tonelessly, "I didn't speak to you, sor."

"The two questions are inseparable," Halfrid said.

"Sor." In the right-hand hologram, Anath Brandr leaned forward to catch his Patriarch's attention. Halfrid frowned at him, but did not rebuff him, and I made a mental note to find out exactly where Anath stood in his Kinship.

"Regarding that—incident," Anath continued, "I remind you it took place immediately after the wreck, that no one was thinking clearly at the time. Also, as their own Medium will testify, Ixora was badly hurt."

He was offering that line of retreat again—and against the wishes of the Brandr Patriarch, if I read the deepening scowl on Halfrid's face correctly. But he was also putting me on the spot. I looked down at the Halex Matriarch as if I could read the answer she wanted me to give in the elaborate coils of her braided hair.

"Well, Medium?" Araxie Fyfe demanded.

"It's true," I said slowly, "that Ixora was badly hurt when she said what she said."

"But she hasn't—doesn't—retract it," one of the other Brandr—the Erling Holder, I thought—pointed out with a sort of malicious detachment.

"That's not the issue," Herself said, before anyone could pursue the question further. "It seems to me that the point in question is whether or not you, ama, will accept the offer of bloodprice."

She was looking at Araxie, but it was the Brandr who spoke. "Forgive me, ama, but it seems to me the question is whether that bloodprice fills two obligations or only one."

"I acknowledge no obligation to you, Halfrid Brandr," Herself returned. She continued to stare at the Fyfe Matriarch. This was the last chance to avert a Fyfe/Halex feud, and I found myself holding my breath for a final time. If only Araxie would concede that Ixora's bloodprice, whatever it might be, didn't have to include admitting that she had been wrong about accusing Fen Erling, the Halex might escape one conflict. The silence stretched on until I was sure Herself would have to say something, anything, to relieve the tension. But she was silent, and finally Araxie said, "I don't see that the two questions are separate. Guilt in one implies guilt in the other."

"Nobody said anything about guilt," Magan muttered, loudly enough to be heard.

The Halex Matriarch said, "An error in one case doesn't mean an error in the other, ama."

"Is that your final answer?" the Fyfe Matriarch shot back.

"It is." Herself inclined her head toward the other woman, a nicely measured gesture of regret and respect.

"Then this becomes a matter for the Ship's Council," Halfrid Brandr said, a little too loudly.

Herself nodded, and the Fyfe Matriarch said, "So it does."

"Rest assured I'll bring it up," Halfrid continued.

"Sor," the Halex Matriarch said. From the sound of her voice, she had finally lost her patience, though I couldn't see all of her expression. "If you don't, I will. I'm tired of your petty harassment—and I'm inclined to believe Ixora, after all." She nodded again to the Fyfe Matriarch. "Ama, until the Council." Before the others could answer, she made a curt chopping gesture with one hand, and the technicians cut the link. The images in the wall froze, then slowly faded.

"This means feud—two feuds," Magan said. He rose, offering a hand to his mother. She accepted his support, grimacing, and pulled herself painfully to her feet.

"That's for the Council to decide," she said, though her tone made it clear that she had little hope of any other outcome. "Still, we'd better see to the arsenals."

The Ship's Council could not be called in the single calendar-day that remained before Sunset, and it was against tradition to meet during the Dark. We had to wait for four long days before the genarchs could assemble: not only did the Council have to wait for Sunrise, but the Orillon Patriarch's single Holder decided to make the long journey in from Electra, now on the far side of the system from Orestes. Herself tried to use this delay to advantage, gathering allies, but so did Halfrid Brandr—and the Halex had always been the envy of the other Kinships. That was the real reason the Fyfe had chosen to pursue its feud with the Halex rather than with the Brandr, I decided at some point in those long days. The Halex, richest of the Kinships, had been able to stand the economic changes better than the others had—the mine closings, the new emphasis on woollens and luxury products—and they had even profited from it. I said as much to Magan one evening after Herself had withdrawn, but he disagreed. It was the code, he said, and shrugged. Nothing more, the gesture implied, and nothing less. The finality of his acceptance left me as chilled as I had been that night in Destiny, after I'd seen *The Man Who Killed in His Sleep*.

Then, at last, it was the day of the Council. As an off-worlder, of course, I wasn't allowed to attend, but like every other human being on Orestes not in the spectators' gallery, I watched the proceedings on the comnet. Everything went as expected—accusation followed by denial and counter-accusation, Halex accusing Brandr of deliberately causing the accident and the deaths, Fyfe accusing Halex of usurping their rights, Brandr accusing Halex of lying. Testimony was given, evidence set before the genarchs and the Branch Holders—and all the while there was no attempt at mediation. The code called for black and white answers, guilty or not guilty, and left no room for the shades of grey that were closest to the truth. The ultimate decision had never been in doubt. By decree of the Ship's Council, the Halex were declared to be at feud with the Fyfe and the Brandr. The question of a Fyfe/Brandr feud was left for later.

I sat for a long time in my room after the decision was announced, staring out the narrow window across the pointed roofs of the storage silos that formed the eastern wall of the Tower compound. By the clock, it was well past the dinner hour, Orestes sliding toward the Eclipse that would come at midnight, but I was too restless even to begin to think of sleep. I had come to Orestes during a rare interval of peace: there had been no major feud since the previous Halex/Brandr feud had been settled six local years ago, and even that had been considered more of a quarrel than a feud for a dozen years before that. I found I had no clear idea what the feud—the feuds—would mean. Would there be street fighting, raids on the outlying farmsteads, murder, riots? All those things had happened before during periods of feud—but not recently, not within living memory. After all, the code had provisions to protect neutrals—members of the uninvolved Kinships, the *para'anin*, and the dead—during times of feud. More likely, I told myself, there would be an increase in the sort of petty infighting one saw at the best of times, quarreling in the various minor councils, harassment over grazing rights and import permits, maybe the occasional fistfight between the younger bloods of both Families, but nothing more serious. Serious enough, though, I reminded myself. There would be more ghosts created, more work for me, and probably *para'anin*, too, as people chose to avoid the responsibilities of the feud. At least I hoped the ones who didn't want to fight would choose that honorable option.

Outside, the light was fading again toward the eclipse. I sighed and stretched, then reached to close the thermal blinds, shutting out the rising shadows.

The next clock-morning, and for the next several calendar days after that, however, the feuds might as well never have been declared. Business went on much as usual, the only difference being that the Matriarch quietly moved to phase out any connections the Family had with Brandr- or Fyfe-owned companies. That was expensive—together, the Fyfe and Brandr Mandates controlled the northern half of the main continent—and some of the Holders, especially Yslin Rhawn, protested the decision, but Herself was adamant. The Kinship had enough capital in reserve to accept the losses, she said, and she would not do less than her duty under the code. Neither the Brandr nor the Fyfe could really afford to lose those connections, either, she added, with one of her more wicked smiles, and the Axtell, doing their best to remain neutral, could hardly expect to take up the slack.

Still, despite those changes and the occasional shouting match or fistfight in Destiny or Madelgar, the main city of the Brandr Mandate, life went on pretty much as usual for the first two grand-days after the declaration of the feuds. It wasn't until the Dark of the third grand-day that trouble broke out in the Destiny Necropolis. Apparently, the problems started when a gang of Brandr port workers sent to pick up goods that had been carried on a freighter landing in Destiny—common practice, since the Madelgar field was small, and most business was done through Destiny anyway—decided to stay over another calendar-day instead of flying back to Madelgar at once. Probably the hostility of the Halex working at the port provoked them to it, though nobody admitted it, but it hardly mattered.

Toward clock-midnight, before Sunset had even faded, a fight broke out in front of one of the cabaret theaters inside the Necropolis. The Brandr, hugely outnumbered to begin with, were pretty badly mauled before the Destiny police could rescue them. Before Sunrise, one had died, and it looked as though at least one of the others would follow her.

The Brandr retaliated, of course, with Fyfe help. The Halex, particularly the Ansson Branch, ran sheep and hoobeys on the Equatorial Plain north of the Ostlaer River. It's desolate country there, not really suited to anything but herding. I've never envied the people who eke out their living there, alone or in pairs, thick-walled dome shelters balanced on their ATVs as they follow the animals across the prescribed ranges. I think they control the wanderings with sonics and range-ware; mainly, though, they're there to protect the sheep from the flagtails. Or from raiders, in time of feud: the Halex Mandate borders the Fyfe Mandate along the Bight, the narrow waist of the figure-eight-shaped main continent, just a few kilometers south of the equator itself, in the heart of the plains.

The first raid was bad enough. A couple of heavy flyers swooped down on a flock of sheep that had strayed too near the Bight and strafed it, killing maybe a third of the animals and scattering the rest across the plains. The young woman herder prudently did not fight back—one woman, armed with a single-pulse rifle, against two flyers? —but hid until the attackers left, then gathered the surviving animals and drove them back to the herders' base town at Anamet. I thought it was a fairly impressive achievement, but the opinion of the Kinship was against me. The herder was hauled before the Kinship council, examined on the subject of her cowardice, and declared dead. I had to preside at the ceremony, and found it extremely difficult. She, along with most of the other herders, took the whole thing stoically enough, and disappeared into Destiny as soon as the ceremony ended.

Bad as that had been, though, the second raid was worse. This time, the raiders came during the Dark, when the herders had to be most active against the flagtail packs, and they made the mistake of picking the herd run by a young Ingvarr couple. With the first woman's fate fresh in their minds, the pair made a stand, and were killed. They didn't even have time to get off a signal for help to Anamet; the attack was discovered only when they failed to answer the check signal the next clock-morning. Anamet dispatched a rescue flight at once—outfitting those groups was part of what the Matriarch had meant by "checking the arsenals," I discovered—but they were, of course, too late. Both the Ingvarrs were dead, and the herd had been slaughtered.

The attacks cast a deep gloom over the Tower for some calendar-days afterwards. Herself conferred with Holders and Elders, but since it was clear these attacks had no direct sanction from the other two genarchs, they agreed she could take no direct action herself. Responsibility for carrying on the feud fell naturally on the younger members of the Kinship. For several days, the Tower was filled with young men and women, mostly of Rohin's generation. They gathered in corners or in conference rooms that had been out of use for years, talking only to each other. Rohin was very much a part of it all, and I thought once or twice that he wanted to talk to me, ask my advice or simply share a confidence, but I avoided him. My oath as a Mediator—my commitment to my work—pushed me to tell him not to act, and that, under the circumstances, was very bad advice. Better to say nothing, I thought.

Then, as suddenly as they'd arrived, the group vanished. The repeated roar of flyers' lift-offs woke me well before the usual hour, and when I went down to the hall for breakfast, a quarter of the chairs were empty. The Tower was ominously silent for the rest of the day, and even the Matriarch seemed distracted, waiting for whatever was going to happen. I did my best to concentrate on my own work, reviewing the various mediums' monthly reports on the ghosts under their charge, but the conference room we were using had a window, and my eyes were drawn to it again and again, searching for the flyers.

The first flyers did not return until after dinner that clock-evening. I heard them from my room, and put aside my glass of esco—almost the last of my last bottle—to cross to the window and look out. Orestes was heading toward Sunset, the pinpoint sun dropping toward the horizon, lightening the dark sky. Against that brilliance, an-

other light—a flyer's running lights—flashed palely, then a
second and a third. The leading ship tilted and moved out
of sight, heading for the field behind the Tower. The
others followed, but I was no longer watching. I turned
instead to my keyboard to type in the command to bring
up the Tower's general information line. Instead of the
usual half-screen heading, I got a curt error message:
everyone else was trying to get through, too. I hesitated
for an instant. Should I go down to the hall, or to the
working levels, and see what was going on? Or should I
wait here, where I could be summoned if needed? Without making a conscious decision, I stepped to my door and
opened it, leaning out into the dimly lit hall.

Other off-world employees were milling around in the
shadows, and the few Halex who shared the floor with us
looked just as confused. I didn't want to get too far from
my keyboard, and hesitated again. Then I thought I saw a
familiar face among the crowd, and shouted to him.

"Corol! What's happening, have you heard?"

At my call, the greying driver detached himself from the
others, and came to join me. "They've made a raid, Medium, but I don't know more than that."

It was hardly a surprise, but the pit of my stomach
contracted. More dead, surely—and true-dead, too, not
just ghosts. . . . "Where?" I asked, involuntarily, and Corol
shrugged.

"I told you, I don't know," he said, but he was grinning.

"There's going to be an announcement on the 'net in an
hour," someone shouted from a doorway.

"I'll have to wait to see if I'm needed," I said, half to
myself. If the raid had been successful—and surely we'd've
heard if it hadn't been—Herself wouldn't need my services at once, though she might need me later if there was
any question of anyone's behavior being mortal. It was
obviously my duty to wait by my machines until I was sent
for—but I couldn't face the prospect of waiting alone. "An
hour?" I said aloud. "Come in and wait with me, Corol,
we'll split a pot of coffee."

Corol gave me a glance full of amused understanding.
"Thank you, Medium, I'll do that."

We retreated to my rooms, though I kicked the chock
that would hold the door open about a hand's-breadth into

place. The noise in the hall was already dying down as people realized that no news was immediately forthcoming. I buzzed the kitchens and asked them to send up a full coffee service—one of the three things the kitchen would make at any hour—and set the dumbwaiter to chime when the tray arrived. When I turned back to the room, Corol was standing at the window, staring out toward the field.

"More flyers coming in," he said, without turning. "Two, three of them."

"I saw three land earlier," I said. That meant at least six ships, I thought, and more could easily have landed while we were talking in the hall. How many people had been involved in this raid, anyway? Six flyers was a major strike force—certainly a lot bigger than anything the Brandr or the Fyfe had set against us.

As if he'd read my thoughts, Corol said, "Two of the ones I saw were light jobs, two-seaters."

So it wasn't a ground attack, I thought. A raid on the Fyfe herds, maybe? Aloud, I said, "I wouldn't think they'd be much use in a raid."

"That depends," Corol said, and turned away from the window. His face was very thoughtful all of a sudden, and I wondered what he'd seen that had worried him. Before I could ask, however, the chime sounded, and I turned to take the service from the open dumbwaiter.

"Do you mind if I turn on your 'net, Medium?" Corol continued.

I shook my head, trying to balance the coffee with one hand while sweeping papers aside to make room for the tray on the room's low center table. By the time I had things arranged properly, Corol had turned away from the screen again, shaking his head.

"Nothing yet."

I looked anyway. The screen showed only a test pattern and the words "please wait" superimposed over it. "They said an hour?" I asked.

"So Embla said." Before Corol could say anything more, there was a knock at the door.

"Who is it?" I called, a little impatiently.

"Us, Dario and Slade. Can we come in?"

"Sure."

The Patroclans pushed their way in, stepping awkwardly over the chock. I hadn't seen them, except in passing, for some weeks, and I was startled by the sudden wariness in their mobile faces. To hide my own surprise, I offered them coffee, glad I'd ordered a full service.

Yan shook his head, grimacing. Orteja said, "Trey, what's going on? They're saying that a bunch of Halex kids sank a Brandr fishing fleet."

"What?" I said, in spite of myself, and Corol snapped, "Saying where?"

"Everywhere," Yan answered.

"I hadn't heard even that much," I said. Looking at their worried faces, I put aside my own desire for information and said firmly, "Sit down, get yourselves some coffee. We won't hear anything reliable until the official announcement."

Yan made another face, but settled himself in the nearest chair, then leaned forward stiffly to pour two cups of the thick coffee. Orteja lowered himself to the floor at his partner's feet.

"Sank a fishing fleet," Corol said thoughtfully. "That would explain the little flyers, at least, for strafing."

"What a mess," Orteja murmured, and Yan nodded.

Corol gave them an amused glance, and lifted an eyebrow at me, as though inviting me to share in the joke. I pretended not to see.

"Do you think it's likely, Corol?" I asked.

The driver shrugged. "It's possible. It'd make sense—and what a revenge it would be. But I don't know any more than you do, Medium."

The rest of the hour passed with excruciating slowness. At last, however, I glanced at the time display I had called onto the main console screen, to see the test pattern fading into the pale blue walls of the broadcast chamber. I fumbled hastily for the keyboard, cancelling the time display, and heard Corol make a small noise of satisfaction. The Patroclans set their cups aside almost in unison, fixing their attention on the screen.

The picture took shape slowly—all the Tower's facilities were nearly a decade out of date, by Urban standards— the Matriarch staring sternly into the camera lens. She looked better than she had over the previous days, the grim lines eased from around her mouth, and I wondered for a split second, irrationally, if there'd been no raid at all. As soon as that thought took shape, I knew it was foolish—and then Herself began to speak.

"Kinsmen, I bring you good news, after the difficulties of the past weeks. A group of our young people, the kindred of my grandson's generation, led by Jaben Ingvarr, have successfully raided the Brandr fleet in the Grand Shallows. Not only was their primary objective, the disruption of the schools of leva now running in the Shallows, achieved completely, but nearly a dozen fishing boats were capsized or otherwise damaged. I ask you to join with me in saluting these members of our Kinship."

There was more, but I wasn't really listening. The Grand Shallows lay to the east of the Bight, an immense bay silted by deposits from the Ostlaer River to the south, and the Tarentaese to the north. Most of Orestes' commercial fishing was done there, in sheltered water, rather than in the open sea, and the Brandr Kinship monopolized that trade. Once, on a flight from Destiny to Madelgar, I had seen the fleet in action, following a run of boi-boi. The blunt-nosed, broad-beamed little ships had seemed very small from the air, very fragile. I remembered, too, the Brandr pilot talking about the risks the fishermen ran—boi-boi were big fish, predators hunted with harpoon, a rare and dangerous catch. People always died during a boi-boi chase, he had said. Someone would be dragged overboard, and the thermal suits only gave you five minutes' grace before you died of the cold. Herself had bragged of capsized ships. I wondered how many of their crews had died in the frigid water, and shivered in spite of myself.

"Isn't leva the staple food in the Brandr Mandate?" Orteja asked.

Corol grinned wolfishly. "It is that."

"It's also a staple of the Destiny population," I said, rather more sharply than I'd intended. "This won't help the Necropolis at all."

Corol shrugged that off, still grinning. "Oh, we can tighten our belts quite a bit without hurting, Medium. Brandr'll starve before we do."

I wasn't entirely sure about that—the ghosts were still partly the responsibility of their original Families, and would not starve, but the poorer *para'anin*, deliberately kinless, were another matter; however, looking at the driver's triumphant face, I didn't feel like arguing the question. Maybe I should've obeyed my first impulse, I thought—encouraged Rohin to talk to me about his plans. Maybe I could've stopped this, or diverted it into other channels. But it hadn't been Rohin's plan, I told myself. I would only have made things difficult, maybe laid him open to a charge of cowardice. Still, I couldn't shake the feeling that I could've done something.

"Will this upset the schooling pattern?" That was Yan, frowning over a new problem.

"Of the fish?" I asked, and he nodded. "Probably. They're surprisingly vulnerable to environmental disturbances. The earthquakes two years ago disturbed the runs for a whole year, according to the records."

"I hope it does," Corol said, a little impatiently. "God almighty, we're at feud." He looked directly at me. "Will you be at the celebration, Medium?"

Celebration? I thought. I hadn't heard the announcement, but of course there'd be one. I couldn't muster much enthusiasm for the idea, and shook my head. "I don't think it would be appropriate," I improvised, "just in case there're mortal questions later."

Corol nodded, apparently appeased. "I doubt there will be, Medium, but I see your point. You don't mind if I take myself off, do you?"

"Not at all," I said.

"Thank you for your hospitality," the driver said, punctiliously, and let himself out. One of the Patroclans sighed audibly.

"More coffee?" I said.

"No, thank you," Yan answered, and Orteja said, with sudden decision, "Trey, we've just about completed our survey. Would you make arrangements for us to return to Patroclus?"

"Kassan and Cho were hired to do a complete analysis of the mining district," I said. "That's not done, is it?"

"The survey work is," Orteja said.

"The rest is computer work—analysis and simulations," Yan added. "That's better done on our home equipment anyway. There's nothing here with the capacity to do it."

That was certainly true, but I waited anyway.

"Besides," Orteja went on, "there's nothing in our contract that says we have to stay during a feud."

"It's a state of war," Yan said, and added, with the air of someone playing a winning card, "union rules."

Most unions did absolve their members from taking sides in planetary conflicts outside the Urban sphere. I bit back my first angry remark, recognizing the jealousy that fueled it, and said, "You're within your rights, of course. I'll speak to Herself in the morning."

"Thank you, Trey," Orteja said, and Yan echoed him.

The Matriarch accepted the Patroclans' imminent departure more calmly than I had expected, even going so far as to bestow guest-gifts. I made the arrangements as they had requested, and managed to find them a berth on a woolship leaving in eight days for Leda. From there, they would have no trouble finding a ship for Patroclus, and I found myself envying them a little. After all, they were walking away from the whole complicated situation—they were able to walk away from it, from the code, from the feud, from everything—while I was bound both by contract and by my obligation as Mediator to remain. But there was work to be done, and the feeling soon passed.

We had all expected some sort of retaliation for the raid on the fleet, and Herself ordered special patrols for all the Kinship's outlying holdings, but days passed, and nothing happened. There were other things to do, especially in Destiny, but also in outlying areas, where some arrangement had to be made to warn the dead in case of further raids. I threw myself into that work, and became so absorbed in it that I barely noticed the quiet. I wouldn't've thought that much of it if I had noticed, but the Halex did, and the Tower subsided into a nervous quiet.

Two calendar-days after the Patroclans' departure, Herself sent for me. I was up in the greenhouse at the top of the Tower, playing hookey from my work to indulge in its warmth and conversation with one of the gardeners. She was a woman who'd been off-world and travelled quite a bit before coming home to Orestes and her Kinship's Tower; we had places in common, and I was desperate for reminders of the Conglomerate as a whole. I sat on a painted bench beneath a flowering tree, listening to her talk about the various herbs that filled the raised beds to either side. Some—the majority, I think—were native to Orestes; the rest she and the other gardeners had either brought home from their travels, or had shipped to the planet from their original worlds. One or two of the flowers I recognized as common on the Urban worlds, and was surprised they'd grow here.

"Well, you have to plant them separately," Maxa said, "and feed and light them according to the original worlds. But as long as you pay attention, you can make them thrive." She pushed herself rather stiffly to her feet, brushing absently at the front of her heavy apron, and glanced over her shoulder. "I think business's caught up with you, Medium."

I looked where she pointed. A teenaged boy, one of the Tower runners, was standing uncertainly beside the kiosk that covered the stairhead and kept the heat from escaping. The brief illusion shattered, and I raised a hand to beckon to him, suddenly aware of the steam-fogged glass walls, and the Dark beyond them. Out of the corner of one eye, I could see Agamemnon's waning crescent.

The boy came over to us, breathing heavily. He was new to Tower service, probably relocated because of the feuds. His face bore the Halex tattoo, and his hair was twisted into an untidy topknot: from one of the outlying areas, I guessed, and wondered what the rest of his family was doing.

"I beg your pardon, Medium, if I've disturbed you, but Herself would like to see you right away."

Despite the boy's politeness, it was a summons that allowed no argument. I nodded, and said to Maxa, "I'd better go. Thanks for your company."

"My pleasure," the gardener answered, smiling. "Come in the clock-afternoon, next time, and share my break."

"I'll do that," I answered, and followed the boy down the long stairs into the body of the Tower. It seemed very cold there, after the warmth of the greenhouse. I shivered, pulling on the overtunic I'd discarded, and wished for a heavier wrap.

Herself was waiting in her private office, where she conducted most of the Kinship's minor business. It was a small room, furnished with an inexpensive executive's console and some heavy, well-padded chairs. Usually, she worked there alone, or with the secretary Lenor to help her; today the little room was crowded, and they'd had to bring in extra chairs from the conference room next door. I looked around once. Magan was there, and Lenor, of course, but also the Elder Tirey Ingvarr and a woman who looked familiar but whose name I could not immediately remember.

"You took your time getting here," Herself snapped as we entered.

The boy flushed, stammered something, and I said, "I'm sorry, ama, I wasn't in my office." I didn't offer any further apology, and for a moment I thought she'd pursue the matter, but then she snorted and looked away.

"All right, Aude, you may go."

The boy's flush deepened, and he backed from the room, closing the door tightly behind him.

"Well, Medium," Herself said. "We have a new problem, one you will have to help us with. Sit down."

"Oh?" I sat. There was no need, on Orestes, to assure the Matriarch of my cooperation: that had already been guaranteed, by contract and code alike.

"You remember my kinswoman Coronis," Herself continued.

I nodded, to hide the start of surprise. Of course, that was the woman sitting beside Magan, her hands folded so tightly in her lap—Coronis, who'd married Eyre Brandr. "I do, ama."

"She has brought us news." The Matriarch was silent for a long moment, so long that Coronis looked up abruptly.

"Shall I tell it, ama?" The words were a challenge, but her thin hands moved restlessly for a moment before the fingers closed again around each other.

Herself frowned. "No." She fixed her eyes on me. "Medium, it has come to our knowledge—our certain knowledge—that the Brandr Kinship is going off-world for weapons, and maybe for men to use them. We feel we must do the same."

I shifted uneasily in my chair. Before I could say anything, Coronis said, low-voiced, "It's true, I swear it. Eyre and I both heard, Eyre confirmed it." She looked quickly at the Matriarch. "You understand my situation, ama.

Eyre's dead, by law, and I've kept the code myself, so I could tell you what's happened, but not any longer. I've done my duty, and now I want the money to go off-world, to get out of this—place."

My God, poor Coronis, I thought. To have come all that way with her husband a ghost beside her. . . . I heard Tirey give a little offended gasp, but Magan leaned across to touch Coronis's shoulder lightly. "It seems only right, Mother," he said.

"It isn't proper," Tirey muttered, "to pay for information."

"Oh, be quiet," the Matriarch snapped. "Coronis is kin; she'll have whatever she needs. What matters is to arrange weapons of our own. God knows, there's nothing on Orestes to match the things they're buying."

I could feel everyone looking at me, and said quickly, "What are they buying, ama?"

Herself waved her hand impatiently. "Guns, explosives, ammunition."

Lenor leaned forward quietly, a sheet of paper in her hand. "Small arms, with incendiary and normal ammunition," she clarified. "Artillery from five-kilo mortars up to a pair of sonic field-pieces. Nothing larger than that, however."

I drew a rather shaky breath, trying to take it all in. If this were true—and there didn't seem to be much reason to doubt it—then it looked like we were in for a very bad time indeed. And my own duty was less than clear. As a Conglomerate Mediator, I was supposed to keep things from reaching this point, but Orestes' crazy social system had made that impossible from the beginning. On the other hand, I could hardly refuse to help my employers protect themselves, even if it meant that more fighting was inevitable. It was inevitable anyway, I told myself, feeling new chill settle in my bones. "How long has this been going on?"

Herself looked suddenly tired. "We don't know."

"Eyre found out two weeks ago," Coronis said, quietly. "And it had been arranged some time ago then. He tried to find out the delivery date, but he couldn't—they didn't trust him. Then he told me, and died."

"We thought about taking this to the Ship's Council," Magan said, "a breach of code, but Tirey says it's no different from our bringing in outside contractors. We can't protest."

I shook my head. There was no telling what the Brandr had planned, when the arms would land, how much trouble we were in. "What do you want me to do?"

"You're a Mediator, as well as our Medium," Herself answered. "And an off-worlder. We need arms to stop whatever it is they're planning. I want you to advise Magan in the negotiations."

"There's another possibility, ama," I said. "I'm duty-bound to mention it." That wasn't strictly true, but it would get a hearing for something she wouldn't like. "As a Conglomerate Mediator—" I stressed the words. "—I have certain powers. With your sanction, I can appeal to the Commercial Board, and possibly stop the importation of these weapons."

The Matriarch didn't say anything, watching me through narrowed eyes. Magan asked, "On what grounds?"

That was the tricky part. I chose my words very carefully indeed. "On two grounds. First, and least good, that the technology is too advanced." Magan raised an eyebrow, and I hurried on. "Second, that its import causes economic hardship."

"No." That was the Matriarch. "We won't plead charity."

"Hardship for the Brandr," I said.

"No," the Matriarch said again.

Tirey said, gently, "This is a feud; we can't consider them."

This isn't real consideration, I wanted to say, it's a weapon you can use against them, but I knew what Tirey would say to that. The code only deals with appearances— what else can a law judge, after all?—and the appearance of kindness toward the Brandr would be enough to damn Herself and her kin. I said instead, knowing I was beaten, "Buying weapons will be expensive, especially for immediate delivery."

"If Brandr can scrape together the money, so can I," the Matriarch said. "He will have mortgaged everything for this, but we can pay."

I took a deep breath, and held it for a moment, wishing I'd never taken this job. Still, I was bound by my contract, and a part of me, the actor, long suppressed, couldn't help enjoying the inevitability of it all. "Very well, ama, as you wish."

"Thank you," Magan said. The Matriarch nodded calmly: she had never considered the possibility I might refuse.

"Get on with it, then," she said. "There's no time to waste."

Magan and I spent the next few days trying to arrange a purchase. The Kinship's Master-at-arms, a grey-haired, taciturn man called Ferril Halex, acted as advisor, and drew up a list of the things he thought the Kinship needed. There are any number of reputable arms dealers in the Conglomerate, though the Halex were too poor to afford, say, the n'Thaieona or the Hephaistians. We took Ferril's list, and went shopping among them. Prices were high, counting in the charges for delivery to such an out-of-the-way world as Orestes, and there was very little I could do to talk the prices down again, especially since we needed the weapons immediately. The best price was from a company based on Fenris, which maintained a depot on nearby Pippa. It wouldn't give us a lot of choice, but at least the shipping costs would be lower. The Matriarch agreed, committing the last of her free capital and a good third of next year's income, and we submitted the order. Now there was nothing to do but wait, and hope that the Brandr's arms would arrive later than our own.

Chapter 7: Leith Moraghan

Pipe Major landed just after local noon. It took two hours for crew and cargo to clear Customs, and Moraghan made her way across the field to the main administrative building, frowning thoughtfully to herself. Something was wrong; she had known that from the minute *Pipe Major* hit the system buoy and she'd made contact with the harbormaster Oslac, but she couldn't put a name to it. The pilot—not Guil, to Moraghan's profound regret, but a man who'd never flown *Pipe Major* before—had given careful non-answers to Moraghan's oblique questions, and his reticence kept her from asking anything directly. Had the hostility between Destiny and Madelgar flared up again? the captain wondered as she climbed the stairs to the main level. Oslac had given her a harder time than usual about the shipment she carried for Madelgar.

At the final checkpoint, she swung her campaign bag onto the counter one-handed, and waited while the duty officer checked through it. The woman smiled down—she topped Moraghan by better than a head—and waved her through, saying, "Enjoy your stay, Captain."

"Thanks." Moraghan slipped her useless left hand into the belt of her coat, then slung the campaign bag back over her right shoulder. It felt very light in Orestes' low gravity, and she walked carefully, controlling her movements. Behind her, she could hear the cheerful chatter of her crew, Sabas's voice dominating the rest, but she didn't turn. A familiar figure was waiting on the far side of the barrier—a tall woman whose oval face was crowned with fine, white-blond hair.

"Guil!" Moraghan felt her own face stretch into a grin, and pushed through the gate with reckless speed. "It's good to see you."

"And you," the tug pilot answered warmly, but there was a shadow of—something—in her pale eyes. The two women embraced, awkwardly because of Moraghan's bag and the difference in their heights, and then Guil pulled away.

"I need your help," she said.

Irrationally, Moraghan felt a surge of disappointment. The two had spent the captain's last Oresteian leave together. Surely, Moraghan thought, it wasn't unreasonable to expect a warmer greeting? Then the rest of her crew swirled around them, Sabas with a knowing smirk, the engineer Askel as expressionless as ever, the juniors, Orino and Tham, still wide-eyed at the thought of exploring another new planet.

"You be staying at your usual place, Captain?" Sabas asked, and winked his good eye.

Moraghan gave him the look she'd perfected for subordinates of his type, the one intended to make him feel that she considered him an uninteresting species of insect. "I don't know yet," she said evenly. "I'll let Askel know; call him if you need me. You will be at the Asteria, right?"

Askel touched his throat and nodded.

"I'll call you in an hour," Moraghan said, dismissing them. Sabas, as usual, seemed inclined to linger, but Askel, with a mumbled phrase, got him moving. The juniors were only too eager to be gone. Moraghan watched them out of earshot, then turned back to the tug pilot.

"What's the problem?"

Guil grimaced, then shrugged one shoulder in an uncharacteristically nervous gesture. "We can't talk here. Let's try the pilots' lounge."

Almost no one used it, Moraghan knew, for all that it

boasted a cheap robo-bar and heavily cushioned couches. The port was too close to Destiny and the Necropolis to make it attractive. She nodded, and let Guil lead her down the uncrowded corridors.

The lounge was empty, as usual, the thermal blinds half closed against the sunlight. Moraghan shivered, and Guil, with an apologetic glance in her direction, crossed to the windows to open the blinds. The light that streamed in was more warming to the psyche than to the flesh, Moraghan knew, but the bright bands turned the dark carpet to rich crimson, gave the whole room new warmth. She chose a table in the sun.

"What'll you drink?" Guil called, from the bar's order board.

"Tsaak?" Moraghan called back. The local liquor had the advantages of being cheap and hot, and probably available. The *para'an* touched a button, waited, and returned to the table at last with a padded carafe and a pair of stone cups. She poured the drinks in ceremonious silence, and Moraghan took the first sip, savoring the sudden spicy warmth in the pit of her stomach.

"So what can I do for you, Guil?" she said again.

The *para'an* looked down at her half-empty cup, turning the polished stone from side to side. "Have you heard about the trouble?" she asked.

"I knew it," Moraghan exclaimed, then waved aside the other's look of inquiry. "No, I don't know what's going on at all. I just knew something was up when we got here. What is it?"

"The Halex and the Brandr are at feud. So are the Halex and the Fyfe."

Moraghan shook her head. That meant nothing to her, except that the Halex were quarrelsome, but Destiny was in the Halex Mandate, and she kept the thought to herself. "What does that mean?"

Guil gave her a rather odd look. "It gives them license to kill each other, that's what it means. And they've been doing just that."

Moraghan felt a sudden sickness in her belly, all her Peacekeeper's training rushing back. Private wars, planetary wars were *bad*—that had been the first lesson. Bad for trade, bad for civilians, and most of all bad for the

Peacekeepers, who'd be called in sooner or later to settle things. She swallowed that reaction, reminding herself that things were different on Orestes, and that she, herself, was no longer a Peacekeeper. "So what do you want me to do about it?"

Guil flushed, and Moraghan was belatedly aware of the harshness in her own voice. "I'm sorry, Guil, go on. Bad memories."

The *para'an* nodded, mollified. "It's more than just the feud, that's nothing special. But, Leith, I think the Brandr are bringing in weapons from the Urban Worlds, stuff the Halex can't match, and—hell, it's not right. You've got connections, you used to be a Peacekeeper, so I thought—" She hesitated, then took a firm breath and went on, "I thought you might know somebody who could stop it, if they knew about it."

There's more to this than meets the eye, Moraghan thought, watching the *para'an*'s mobile face set into an angry frown, but I don't know Orestes well enough to know the key. It's not like Guil to worry about politics. Usually, she's pretty cynical. The captain hesitated, trying to frame a noncommittal answer, and Guil burst out, "I know it's not my place. Hell, they're not even my kin if I weren't *para'an*, but something needs to be done. What do you think they're going to do with those weapons, Leith—hold a football match?"

Moraghan shook her head slowly, frightened in spite of herself. For Guil to step out of her place, things had to be pretty bad. "No. I'm thinking, Guil, I'm not sure who to contact."

The *para'an* nodded, mollified, and Moraghan poured herself another cup of tsaak, grateful for its warmth. "How did you find out about this, anyway?"

Guil shrugged. "I'm the substitute, remember? They needed a back-up pilot at Madelgar. They don't have much of a staff there, and of course, they couldn't hire any of the regular Destiny port workers. Because of the feud," she added, before the captain could ask. "Most of the Destiny people are Halex. Anyway, they weren't happy about getting me, but the off-world captain wouldn't make the run-in without knowing there was a back-up available, so the Madelgar harbormaster brought me in." She gave a humorless smile, just a flash of teeth in her tanned face. "They stuck me off in a little room, and kept me there, where they thought I wouldn't hear anything. And then to be doubly sure, they made me promise I wouldn't tell anybody about this." She stopped again, scowling, and Moraghan guessed it was that broken promise that galled her most. "But I'm *para'an*, I'm not expected to keep my word. And besides, I don't have proof, just that what I heard made me pretty sure that's what they're doing."

"Why haven't you told the Halex?" Moraghan asked.

Guil gave her a blank look. "They couldn't listen to me. I'm *para'an* and I'm breaking my given word."

Damn that, Moraghan thought, but bit back the words in time. All right, if that's the way the system works, that's the way it works. Is there anything I can do? She chewed thoughtfully on her lower lip, not really feeling the pain. First, I can warn Maturin—it's a Medium's business to deal with *para'anin*, if I understand the system at all. Maturin can warn the Halex. As for off-world. . . . It takes a local complaint to bring in the Peacekeepers, but maybe a word at the Trade Bureau would do some good? Then she remembered Stephan Mojag, who'd been part of her drone squadron before he cracked up a free flyer. He'd picked a post in Trade rather than a mailship position; maybe he could help her now. She put the tsaak cup aside and reached into the pocket of her coat for her chronometer, drew it out on its short chain and laid it, miniboard up, on the table top. It was hard to manipulate the stylus one-handed, and Guil leaned across to steady the machine.

"You've thought of something?"

"Yes." Moraghan used the stylus to punch the tiny buttons, then waited for the result to appear on the finger-width screen. "An old—colleague, from the Peacekeepers. He's with the Trade Board on Ganesha; he might be able to do something." The numbers appeared at last, and Moraghan muttered a curse. "Trouble is, its the middle of the night there, and I'd have to leave a message, with no guarantee he'd upload it in the morning. I think I'd better wait and call him then."

Guil nodded. "All right. Look, would you stay with me again? It's the least I can do, after all this trouble."

Moraghan smiled. "No trouble. And I'd like to stay, please, Guil."

"Good." Guil's answering smile was rather diffident. "We can head on, then, unless—"

Moraghan shook her head. "I'm done here." To prove it, she finished the last of her tsaak, then awkwardly, stuffed the chronometer and its chain back into her pocket.

"Fine." Guil nodded. "Look, I have an errand to run, on Mill Street. You're welcome to come with me, of course, but if you'd rather go on to the flat, I'll gladly give you the key."

"I'll come with you," Moraghan said. "I've never seen the mills."

"I'm just going to one of the shops," Guil warned. "And you might not want to carry your bag all that way."

"In this gravity, it hardly weighs a thing," Moraghan said, not quite truthfully. "No, I want to come with you, Guil. If you don't mind."

The *para'an* shook her head. "Glad of the company," she said. "Come on."

It was a cloudless day, the brilliant pinpoint of Atreus almost drowning the waxing blue-green crescent of Agamemnon. The wind was from the east, and cold. Moraghan was glad of her heavy spacer's coat, no matter how outlandish it made her look. Guil loosened the clasps of her outer jacket as they made their way to the tram stop, muttering something about the heat. The others waiting in the shelter, Moraghan noticed with wry amusement, had also loosened or discarded their outer layers of clothing. The captain guessed it might be as much as thirteen degrees without the cooling wind.

The first tram that passed was a local, bound for the residential precincts just across the bridge. The second car through was the one they wanted, bound for the High Street and ultimately for the UHST terminus. Moraghan followed Guil aboard—this time, she let the tug pilot pay both fares, rather than fumble for it herself—and wedged herself with the pilot against the tram's rear wall. There were no seats available. Moraghan let her bag fall from her shoulder, dropping it between her feet, and wrapped her good arm around the nearest stanchion. Guil leaned close as the tram lurched into motion.

"Sorry about this, but we've got a way to go."

"No problem," Moraghan said, and meant it. She leaned forward a little as the tram slowed for the river barriers, trying to catch a glimpse of the city proper. It looked very different in daylight, the buildings no longer shadows picked out in strings of light, but solid, sober structures, local stone and wood shaped to local needs. There had never been much attempt to copy off-world styles, and Moraghan found herself approving that integrity. If, of course, she added silently, it was integrity and not poverty that kept the builders to this style—but Destiny had always been a wealthy city.

The tram lurched as it came off the bridge, lurched again as it came up onto the turntable. With a whine of motors that sent a new vibration through the floor, the table swung slowly clockwise, until the nose of the tram was lined up along the tracks that led down a wide, shop-lined street. The sidewalks were filled with pedestrians, and there was a surprising amount of traffic, mostly sporty three-wheelers. Moraghan remembered Guil saying those were mostly used by the younger members of the rich mainline families, and leaned forward.

"What street's this?"

"This is the High Street," Guil answered, raising her voice slightly to be heard over the rattle of the tram. "It runs from the port all the way through Destiny, and then out to the Halex Tower proper." She ducked her head, trying to see out through the tram's scratched windows. "Come on, the next stop's ours."

Moraghan followed obediently as the *para'an* worked her way through the crowd to the rear door. The tram slowed even as they went; by the time they'd reached the door, it was open, and the two women clattered down the steps to the minuscule platform. Guil gauged the passing traffic—six-wheeled cargo trucks and even an occasional Landcrawler, as well as the more common three-wheelers—with a practiced eye, and whistled, beckoning for Moraghan to follow. The captain did, expecting every instant to be struck down by a passing vehicle, and was more than a little surprised when they reached the sidewalk alive.

"Couldn't we have waited?" she asked.

"For what?" Guil returned.

"A break in the traffic, I don't know," Moraghan answered.

The *para'an* shrugged, her face exhilarated. "That's Mill Street, up ahead."

And that, Moraghan thought, as they turned onto the raw-metalled road that was the beginning of Mill Street, is all the answer I'm likely to get. She glanced around, marveling at how much the narrow-windowed mills were like the factories of her own world, or any other world, for that matter.

Guil said, "They tell me only a couple of them—Red Sheep, and the Ingvarr Co-operative—were around when I was born. The rest just sort of sprang up, what with the off-worlders wanting our wool." She nodded toward a low-roofed building, where the double doors were padlocked and paint was peeling from the cheap siding. "That's the Auction Hall."

Moraghan nodded back, staring at the ugly building. She had seen its twin on a dozen other worlds, the first real sign outside the port area of a link between Orestes and the rest of the Conglomerate. "Where is it we're going?"

"Domas Rhawn's," Guil answered, and pointed toward a shack-like structure wedged against a building labeled in bright letters "Hope Lane Mill." "They say he was a miner, before he went into the wool trade, and lost an eye in a feud, too, before he started as a spinner with the Achias Mill. He makes good, cheap wool, though, and I need yarn for a heavy tunic. You know what that costs."

Moraghan nodded, though the *para'an*'s words meant little to her. She knew that Guil made most of her own clothing, and had never seen the pilot's workbasket empty of a project, but she herself had never done any sort of handwork. It was not something that fit well into the military life.

Guil quickened her pace as she approached the staircase leading to the second-floor shop, and Moraghan had to hurry to keep up, the campaign bag slapping at her hip. At the top of the stairs, Guil paused to draw a deep breath, her face flushed with an excitement Moraghan didn't recognize. Then they stepped inside.

The air smelled oddly musty—the scent of sheep's wool,

Moraghan thought, drawing on distant childhood memories. Beneath that was a pungent, pepper-and-lemon smell, and the sweet-sharp scent that filled Guil's flat. Moraghan frowned, then remembered: tanna bark, to keep out the local insect life. Faintly through all that came the hot-oil smell of the machines. One stood immediately to the right of the door, idling gently, a strand of crimson yarn zigzagging through the wheels and eyes and coils from one filled cone to a smaller, emptier one. On the walls beyond hung the finished yarn.

Moraghan smiled, impressed in spite of herself by the long skeins. The colors ranged from subtle, natural greys and browns to the muted shades that marked organic dyes, to clear and perfect primaries, with every shade and variation in between. One skein ranged through the spectrum in a length of yarn no longer than her arm; another, jet-black strand, was wound with a thinner silver thread that glittered icily when the light hit it. The riot of color was matched by the variety of textures, ranging from coarse yarns as thick as her little finger to a cloudy, fraying stuff no thicker than sewing thread. And there was even more in the room beyond. . . . It was no wonder, Moraghan thought, that off-world clothiers came here. I've never seen anything like this.

"Guil! Welcome!"

"Domas," Guil answered, with more warmth than Moraghan had ever heard her use. "How're things with you?"

The man who came out of the inner room moved like an old spider, Moraghan thought, shocked in spite of herself. He had never been tall, by Oresteian standards, but some accident had left him bent almost double, one shoulder higher than the other. His head would barely reach Moraghan's shoulder. One eye was obviously false—the colors were a bad match— and the hand he extended in greeting was missing a finger.

"Well enough, thank you." Domas made an odd, bobbing twist that let him look up into his customer's face, and seemed to like what he saw there. His own face split into a wide smile. "What can I sell you today, Guil-pilot? Cloud-mohair? Gold-spun? Shadow-light?"

Guil laughed. "Not likely, Domas. I need a new working pullover."

"For that," Domas said, drawing the pilot after him into the inner room, "for that, I have hoobey yarn, dyed and plain, and some fine chunky tweeds. Or there's sheep's wool, that's very nice . . ."

Guil gave Moraghan a quick, apologetic glance, and let herself be led away. Left to herself, the captain moved slowly along the walls, idly examining the hanks of yarn. She felt distinctly out of place here, surrounded by the materials of a craft she had never bothered to understand. She stepped up to the doorway to the inner room, hoping to find Guil, but the only person in sight was a woman with a medium's badge pinned to her dress, knitting steadily behind the counter. Moraghan backed away noiselessly, and resigned herself to wait.

It wasn't long before Guil returned, a bulging bag slung carelessly over her shoulder. Domas followed, still talking, but Moraghan felt his eyes on her, recognizing and then dismissing her as off-world, and no customer.

Guil came forward with an apologetic smile. "Sorry to keep you waiting."

"It's all right," Moraghan said. "What'd you get?" She had started to ask out of mere politeness, then realized she was genuinely curious. What had Guil chosen, out of all the yarns displayed here, and what would that choice tell her about the pilot?

Guil's face changed, crinkling into laughter. "More than I'd intended, as always." She held open her bag. "The purple tweed, that's for the pullover, but the carpet wool. . . ." She glanced mockingly at Domas, who returned an indulgent smile. "God only knows what I'll make of it, but I couldn't pass it up."

Moraghan nodded, almost understanding the other woman's fascination with the yarns. The heathery purple was nice, a plain, practical color, but the other yarn was the color of flame. She touched it gently, running her fingers along the coarse strands. No, it wouldn't make for comfortable clothing, but it was too spectacular a color to pass up.

"Maybe I'll make a throw of it," Guil was saying thoughtfully. "Or I could put it out to a weaver, but then I'd have to get more—" She shook herself again, and laughed.

"Come on, Leith, let's get out of here before I buy anything else."

She pushed through the shop's main door, still laughing, and Moraghan followed her down the narrow stairs. "We aren't that far from your flat, are we?"

Guil shook her head. "About a kilometer. Do you mind walking?"

"Anything's better than the trams," Moraghan answered.

It was not a bad walk, with the heavy coat to cut the wind and the distant sunlight to give an illusion of warmth. The streets were busy, the market squares crowded with makeshift carts and stalls, as the shopkeepers moved to take advantage of the relatively warm weather. Moraghan was almost sorry when they turned off the High Street. Ahead, a line of jade-green stone knobs stretched across the roadway, marking the boundary of the Gilbertine Precinct and closing it to vehicular traffic. Just beyond the stones, the street opened into the local market square. It was less noisy than the others had been, and there was an oddly wary note in the vendors' cries. Moraghan tensed, not quite certain what she heard, and saw Guil shift the bag of yarn to her left hand. She glanced once around the square, and saw nothing out of the ordinary. A few shoppers, mostly older men and women, moved from stall to stall, occasionally vanishing into one of the permanent stores that lined the square, only to reappear a few moments later with another packet tucked in their painted baskets. A knot of adolescents, their sleeves pinned with black and white ribbons, milled about outside the entrance to a sweetshop near the middle of the square, and Moraghan's eyes narrowed.

"Trouble?" she asked softly, and Guil shrugged.

"I doubt it," the pilot said, but her voice was grimmer than her words.

Moraghan grimaced, wishing her old service blaster weren't buried at the bottom of her bag, then, with a conscious effort, made herself relax. Guil was *para'an*, by their own rule outside the game, and she herself was obviously off-world. No one would bother them.

They were even with the sweetshop now, and it was all Moraghan could do to keep her steps even and unconcerned. Guil was scowling, her hand white-knuckled on the neck of her sack of yarn. She looked neither to the right nor the left, and Moraghan copied her, matching the taller woman's stride.

"Hey, blondie!"

The shout came from behind them, from the crowd by the shop. Guil's mouth twitched, but she didn't turn or give any other indication she had heard. Moraghan felt a tingling between her shoulder blades, the certainty that she was part of the target, but kept walking.

"Hey, blondie!"

The voice was closer now, coming up on the right— Guil's side, but there would be more behind him. Moraghan shifted her grip on the campaign bag strap, ready to sweep it off her shoulder and into an attacker's stomach. Her strength and Orestes' low gravity would make it an effective weapon.

"Blondie! Brandr bitch, what're you doing here?"

The voice was very close, and Moraghan could hear the rest of his friends behind him. She started to turn, but before she could complete the move, Guil turned on them, right hand darting out like a striking snake. She caught the nearest boy by the collar of his tunic and dragged him forward until he stumbled and almost fell. Moraghan turned then, campaign bag sweeping out in a vicious arc that caught one boy in the stomach and sent him sprawling. The rest of the boys were already backing off, eyes fixed on the tug pilot. They were none of them older than sixteen, Moraghan thought, still poised, campaign bag swinging from her hand. Easy meat.

Guil's face was a fury's mask, white-lipped and taut with anger. She shook the boy she held, then threw him bodily away from her. He staggered, but managed to stay on his feet.

"My name is Tam'ne," she said, very softly. The words carried in the sudden silence, and Moraghan saw a couple of the boys flinch. "*Para'an* of Tam'ne in Orillon. So I'm not part of your fucking game. So stay the hell away from me."

She waited, balanced on the balls of her feet, staring at the boys. Moraghan swore softly, and caught the pilot by the shoulder, using her off-world strength to turn the other woman bodily away. Guil had silenced them for the moment, but in another minute the challenge would have been too much for their self-esteem, and they would have had to attack. Guil resisted for a second longer, and then Moraghan felt the tension melt under her hand. Guil nodded sharply, and Moraghan let her hand fall away. No one followed them out of the square.

Moraghan said nothing until they reached the door of Guil's building, waiting until the rage eased from the other's face. The anger was replaced by something else, less identifiable. Guil's hand shook as she worked the lock.

"What was all that about?" Moraghan asked, less because she didn't know than to test the emotional waters.

Guil snorted, and started up the stairs toward her third-floor flat. "The Halex punks thought I was a Brandr," she called over her shoulder. Her voice wasn't quite steady. "The Brandrs run to blonds."

"I'm going to tell Trey about this," Moraghan said quietly.

Guil's face darkened, and she pushed open the flat door with unnecessary violence. "I told you, I fight my own battles—"

Moraghan held up a hand. "Let me finish, will you? It's for me—for all us off-worlders—not for you. Whether you report it, that's your business, I don't presume to know. But those kids attacked an off-worlder, or they would've, if you hadn't stopped them. The Family needs to know that." She paused, looking around the familiar, cosy main room, with its slit windows and heavy, padded furniture. "And, by the way, thanks."

Guil looked at the captain in honest confusion for a moment, then looked away, mouth twisting in an embarrassed grimace. "Thank *you*," she said, after a moment. She sighed. "I've got a bitch of a temper. I'd've done something really stupid."

Moraghan shrugged, herself embarrassed now. "So we're even, then?"

Guil nodded, and managed a real smile. "We're even, Leith." She looked away, sighing, and gestured vaguely toward the cabinet that held her comnet console. "You're welcome to use the 'net anytime."

Moraghan nodded back, and pushed aside the heavy fabric screen. Guil vanished into the flat's inner rooms, her wool in one hand and Moraghan's campaign bag slung awkwardly over her other shoulder, but the captain stood

for a long moment, staring at the blank screen. She had
never seen Guil so angry, not even with Oslac—had never
imagined that the pilot could be so angry, or could come
so close to losing control. I don't want to be there when
she does lose it, Moraghan thought, and leaned forward to
turn on the console. Guil's all right for now, she told
herself sternly. Now you need to tell Trey what's going on.
Sighing, she punched the string of numbers into the keyboard, setting herself to compose a rational report.

Chapter 8: Trey Maturin

Leith called me from Destiny at a little after nineteen hours the eighteenth day of the tenth calendar-month. She told me first about rumors her *para'an* friend had heard while acting as a substitute pilot in Madelgar—the same news we'd already heard from Coronis—and then that she and Guil had been harassed by a group of Halex adolescents. From what she said, they were certainly old enough to have already pledged to obey the code, and I got good descriptions from her, planning to hunt them down the next day. It was too bad that Guil chose not to press her complaint, but attacking an off-worlder was quite enough. I had no patience for that sort of street brawling, and to tell the truth, I was glad of an excuse to crack down on it. I crawled into my bed that night feeling smugly virtuous: for once, I could use the code to get what I wanted.

Four hours later, the Brandr attacked the Tower.

The first dull crump of the mortars woke me, sent me groping for the light switch before I'd fully realized what was happening. With the second salvo came shouts from the hall outside my room—off-world accents, mostly—and I shook myself completely awake. The clothes I'd worn the day before lay on the storage box, and I grabbed them blindly, pulling on shirt and trousers and knitted tunic. The Tower lights flickered and died as I pulled on socks and boots, and I fumbled in momentary panic before I found my handlight. The emergency lights came on almost as soon as I'd switched it on, and I breathed a sigh of relief.

My relief was short-lived, however. The next salvo struck very close to the Tower, and my window shattered. If I hadn't had the shades closed against the fading sun, the glass would have scythed through the room. I stood for a moment, staring stupidly at the thermal blinds, feeling the outside air cold on my face while the knowledge seeped slowly through me that this wasn't acting, that survival wasn't just a matter of staying on the special-effects man's marks. Then I heard, over the thump of the mortars, the whistle of blaster fire: the Halex were fighting back.

I shook myself hard, trying to make my frozen brain work. I couldn't take much, wherever I was going, but I would need my papers and bankcards. I scooped those up almost automatically, and reached for the medium's badge as well, clipping it to the neck of my tunic. It was cold outside, despite the warm spell, and it would be Dark in twenty-four hours. I picked up the cloak Rohin had given me, and wrapped it around my shoulders. Another salvo shook the floors and sent dust and insulation drifting across the room, but still I hesitated, wondering what else I could take. There was nothing much here, a few tapes, some jewelry, all tucked away in the storage cells along the walls. Nothing worth dying for, I thought, and pushed open the door into the hall.

The few off-worlders who hadn't left with the Patroclans were all out in the hall now. Family members pushed past without stopping, blasters slung over their shoulders. They would be heading up to the roof ports, I guessed, or down to the doors to try to set up a perimeter defense.

"Trey!" The voice wasn't familiar at first, despite the Urban speech. I turned, and saw Pausha Ran standing in the doorway of her suite of rooms. I hadn't had much contact with the Family's Hodurite doctor—she always seemed to be in the back country, running clinics, when I was in the Tower—but the sight of her standing there, fully dressed, clutching her emergency kit in one hand

and her ten-year-old daughter with the other, was oddly reassuring. "Where do we go?"

I spread my hands, but said, "Down, I assume—it should be safer there." I saw one of the Agnian technicians still in his nightshift, and resigned myself to taking charge. "All right, everybody, listen to me. Get some clothes on, quick, get your ID and bring an overcoat, something warm, and follow me."

The Agnian vanished back into his room, and the talk quieted abruptly as people began to move purposefully again. Dr. Ran bit at her upper lip, pulling her daughter close against her body. "I'll be needed, Trey," she said, so quietly that I almost didn't hear her over the noise of the fighting.

I nodded. "They'll be bringing the wounded to a safe place—you couldn't treat them, otherwise. We'll get Anila downstairs, then we'll see." She nodded back, obviously reassured, and I felt terribly helpless. I had no idea what the Halex planned to do—I had no business taking charge of anything.

"Medium!" That was a Halex voice, Rohin's voice, and I turned gladly, eager to hand over the responsibility. "This way!" He pointed to a side stair, a fixed stair that led down to the kitchens. I nodded, then put two fingers in my mouth and whistled.

"All right, everybody, we're going," I shouted. The last words were drowned out by an explosion that rocked the Tower on its foundations and nearly knocked me from my feet. The girl Anila shrieked once, and clutched her mother; someone shouted curses in a distant room.

Rohin made a face. "That was an outbuilding," he said. "Come on!"

"People, move it!" I shouted, and this time I was obeyed. "Follow Rohin!"

The Demi-heir started down the stairs without waiting for further word, and this time the off-worlders followed. I hung back, counting, trying to make sure no one was left behind. The four Agnians, the little visiting artist from Osiris, Dr. Ran and her daughter, the Methusalan teacher. . . . That was the last of them, and I darted after, suddenly aware that the air was full of dust and odd-tasting smoke, and that the emergency lights were fading fast. I switched on my handlight halfway down the stairs, and saw two more lights bobbing ahead of me. Rohin had one and Dr. Ran, not surprisingly, had the other.

By the time we reached the kitchen, the emergency lights were gone completely. Rohin beckoned with his light, and we groped our way through the maze of tables and equipment, to fetch up against a white-enameled door. It looked like the hatch of an ordinary cold-storage locker, but it was obvious from the way that Rohin fumbled with its latch that it was something more.

"Give me some light," he snapped, and Dr. Ran directed the beam of her handlight onto his hands. I did the same, the circles merging, and an instant later Rohin gave a grunt of satisfaction. There was a heavy click, then the groan of counterweights and pulley wheels, and the entire locker pivoted slowly, revealing a flat trapdoor. Light outlined its edges: someone was already down there. Rohin made another satisfied noise, and lifted the trap—it was lighter than it looked, and the hinges were freshly oiled— saying, "Alkres, I've brought the off-worlders."

There was a breathy exclamation, too soft to be heard, and then a boy's voice said, "All right. We're all here."

"Good." Rohin straightened, and swung his handlight, catching each of us for an instant in its beam. "This is the Tower's escape tunnel. It'll take you out to the cliffs above the Ostlaer, about a kilometer from Federston. Herself doesn't want to take any chances with people not of the Family. Please go on, now."

His words had a rehearsed ring to them, the sound of official news rather than of truth. I gave him a sharp glance, and he put a hand on my arm. "Hang back a minute, Trey," he said, very softly. "And you, too, Dr. Ran."

The others were already climbing down the steep, ladderlike stairs into the tunnel. I waited, watching Rohin. Dr. Ran sent Anila down the ladder—an Agnian steadied her from below—then straightened and turned to face the Demi-heir.

"Well?" she demanded, but softly.

Rohin took a deep breath. "Herself's sent the kids out, too," he said, and this time I knew he was telling the unshaped truth. "Alkres—he's the ult'eir—is in charge of them, but I've told him to do what you suggest, Trey. Please, both of you, Herself asks that you take care of the kids."

"But my duty to the wounded," Dr. Ran said, on a note of pain. "My duty—"

"We have doctors," Rohin said. "It's the kids who really need you."

"You can't hold the Tower?" I asked, though I already knew the answer.

Rohin shrugged, and somehow managed a ghost of his usual smile. "Anything's possible, Medium, but it doesn't look good."

The smile vanished abruptly as another explosion shook the Tower, and I said, "We'd better be going. Tell Herself we'll do as she asks."

Dr. Ran nodded, her eyes full of tears, and slid down the ladder into the tunnel. I started to follow, and Rohin said, "Trey, tell Rehur—" He stopped and shook his head, smiling again. "Never mind, go on."

There was no time to urge him. I started down the ladder, and Rohin lowered the trapdoor over me. As I reached the bottom, I heard the groan of the counterweights, and knew that the Demi-heir was moving the locker back into place over the trap.

"Medium?"

I turned my handlight on the speaker. He was a slight, dark boy of about fifteen, who wore tunic and trousers over an embroidered nightshirt: the ult'eir Alkres, who might well be the Halex Patriarch before clock-morning. There were more children, all younger than he, behind him. Fifteen counted as adult on Orestes. I wondered, irrelevantly, how he felt about being sent off like this, or if he recognized the necessity.

"Alkres?" I said, more out of politeness than because I wasn't sure, and the boy nodded.

"We'd better be going," he said, and pointed down the tunnel with his own light.

"Right," I said. "If you'll lead, I'll bring up the rear."

"All right," Alkres agreed. He glanced at the off-worlders, most of whom carried handlights of their own. "We should save the lights, though. I'll take one, and you take one, Medium, and one in the middle—"

"Dr. Ran," I said. She nodded and moved on up the tunnel, pulling Anila with her, until she was in the center of the group.

"—and everybody else turn theirs off until we say," Alkres finished. It was a good idea, something I probably wouldn't've thought of. I nodded again, and Alkres turned away, pushing past first the off-worlders and then his younger relatives, until he was at the head of the line. One by one, reluctantly, the rest of us dimmed our lights, until only three were lit. Alkres gave a soft whistle, and we started to move.

After the first twenty meters, the tunnel narrowed abruptly, becoming a rough-drilled tube barely high enough for a tall Oresteian to walk upright. I am not particularly tall, by Oresteian standards, but even so, I had to duck occasionally to avoid lumps of harder rock that the drill had left behind. The tunnel was so narrow that I couldn't hold my arms out straight from the shoulder and we had to walk single file. Even so, I swept my torch back and forth ahead of me, making sure none of the children had somehow fallen behind. Anything was better than thinking about the Tower, and the people we'd left behind. Rohin, Corol, Jesma, Ixora, even Herself—and all the parents of the children who walked so silently ahead of me. . . . If the Tower did not hold, God only knew what would happen to them. I closed my mind to those fears and kept walking, sweeping the light ahead of me.

We walked for an interminable time through the unchanging tunnel. At some point—I had somehow left my timepiece back at the Tower, and refused to ask what time it was—we rested, because the younger children were getting tired. Later still, we took turns carrying the littlest ones. Then, at long last, the tunnel twisted like a snake, doubling back on itself, and narrowed even further, so that I had to crawl and even the smallest children had to stoop, and we came out into a broader cave, with sunlight showing at the far end. One of the children gave a short whoop of delight, quickly hushed, and we all hurried for the opening. It was heavily overgrown, and most of us were marked with bleeding scratches by the time we'd fought our way through the rough-barked vines.

As Rohin had said, the tunnel mouth opened on a broad

ledge halfway up the Ostlaer cliffs. The slope down to the river itself was steep, but manageable even with the children. Almost before I'd made a conscious decision, I slid down the bank to the water's edge, looking up and down the river. The current was dangerously fast here, as it was for almost the full length of the river, but the flat ground at the base of the cliff was easily wide enough to walk on. It stayed wide as far as I could see, and I turned back to the group on the cliff.

"Which way's Federston?"

Alkres pointed downstream. His voice came back very thin and high. "About a kilometer, I think, or a little more."

It was a long way for the children to walk, especially after the interminable trip through the escape tunnel, but I didn't particularly like the idea of leaving them behind while one of the adults went ahead for transport. If the worst had happened, and the Brandr had patrols out looking for stray Halex—well, it seemed a bad risk. And if the kids walked to Federston on top of everything else they'd done, at least they'd be tired enough to sleep without worrying about their families.

"Doctor?" I called, and Dr. Ran slid down the cliff to join me. Her round face was scratched and dirty, and her waist-length braid had come loose at the tip, the coarse strands fraying. "Do you think the kids can walk to Federston from here?"

She nodded slowly, worrying at her tail of hair. "They're a tough bunch, and we can carry the little ones." She looked up then, meeting my eyes. "I think you're right, Trey."

It took us over an hour to reach Federston, arriving at just past five hours of the clock-morning, according to the Methusalan's chronometer. The town was small, barely more than support facilities for the UHST station, with only one metalled street and no airfield. There were lights on in most of the houses, but nothing moved in the single street. Still, I was aware of eyes watching us from behind slitted thermal blinds, and shifted the five-year-old I had been carrying on my hip since we left the cave. She made a noise of protest, and I soothed her, hoping she wouldn't decide to start crying. Alkres, walking on my right, gave her a look that would have melted armor plate, and I said, hastily, "Do you know the foreman here?"

The ult'eir shook his head. "No, but that's his house."

I looked in the direction he was pointing. The house stood next to the UHST station, but was separated from it by a woven fence half covered with some sort of flowering vine. It had a broader porch than the other houses, and a carved door with an imposing knocker: clearly the place belonged to someone of importance.

"He's an Ansson," Alkres went on. "Most of the UHST people are Anssons."

"Oh," I said. I could only hope that bit of knowledge would be useful someday.

Then we were at the foot of the steps that led up to the porch, and Alkres turned, holding up his hand. "All of you, please wait here. Medium, if you'd come with me?"

I heard the echo of Herself in the boy's thin voice, and had to bite back tears. "Of course," I said, and was relieved that my voice was reasonably steady. I climbed the steps behind Alkres, and put myself at his left as he pressed the elaborate knocker.

The door opened almost instantly, and I knew the foreman had been watching us since we entered the town. Alkres said, "I'm sorry to disturb you so early, sor, but I plead urgent Family business. I am Alkres Halex."

The foreman, the first really heavy man I'd seen on Orestes, threw the door open wide. "Come in, sor, come in—all of you, please. I'm Ruland Ansson, foreman of this town."

We followed Ruland into the main room of the house, and dropped onto the chairs and benches without waiting for his invitation. I was suddenly overcome with weariness, and leaned back against the wall behind the narrow bench. It seemed almost indecent to be so comfortable, and infinitely worse not to take advantage of that comfort. I closed my eyes.

The next thing I knew, the room was striped with sunlight, and Alkres was saying, "Is there any news?"

Frightened, I stole a glance at the Methusalan's timepiece: I'd only been asleep for a few minutes, but still, I didn't dare stay seated. I pulled myself to my feet and went to join Alkres, hoping no one had noticed my lapse.

Ruland shook his head, including me in the conversation with a glance. "No, sor, nothing beyond what you've told us. All we knew was, we lost the 'net link with the Tower, and then we heard the fighting." He looked deliberately at me, and added, "Someone'll have to be sent."

I grimaced, but nodded. He was right—someone would have to go and survey the damage for themselves, and I, as a medium and thus theoretically inviolate, was the logical person to send. But I didn't have to like it very much.

"I don't think you should go, Trey." That was Dr. Ran, coming up behind us with her bag slung over her shoulder. She had treated the worst of the cuts and scratches as soon as we reached the foreman's house, without the slightest break, and still didn't look tired. I thought I envied her.

Ruland raised an eyebrow at her, and Alkres said, "Why not?"

"Because Trey's not a doctor," Ran answered. "Send me; I can maybe do some good, as well as letting you know what's happened." She touched her emergency bag as though it were a talisman. "There're people up there who'll need a doctor."

Alkres said, "All right." His voice was less certain than it had been before.

Ruland nodded thoughtfully. "I can send our flyer and a portable comnet," he offered.

"I could go along, too," I said, and Alkres looked up quickly.

"No, stay here."

Ruland said, "You might be better monitoring the 'net, at that, Medium."

He gave me a speaking glance, and I understood. The code still had to be observed. If a ghost tried to contact the ult'eir, I would have to take the call. Federston was too small a place to have a medium of its own. I said, "You're right, both of you. I'll stay."

"I'll send my boy for the flyer," Ruland said. "Teacher and my wife can look after the kids."

The next hours remain a blurred memory. Dr. Ran raided the UHST station's medical kit, and then vanished. Some time later, we heard the throbbing beat of the flyer's old-fashioned rotors. The children, exhausted, slept fit-

fully, except for Alkres and one or two others old enough
to understand what might have happened. Ruland's wife,
Ulrika, and the young man who ran the town's primary
school—I never learned any name for him except "Teacher"
—moved among them, encouraging them to rest. The
off-worlders huddled together, not talking much. Anila
Ran and the Methusalan drew a patterned square on a
piece of scrap paper, and played some simple board game
over and over again. They moved the stones that served
for counters very gingerly, afraid of noise.

At some point in the interminable morning, the comnet
technician appeared in the doorway and beckoned to Ruland.
They spoke for a few moments, low-voiced so as not to
disturb the sleeping children, and then Ruland waved for
me to join them.

"The 'net's up again," the technician said, without preliminary, "but I can't raise the Tower. I thought you might
ought to listen in, Medium, just in case."

I nodded, and looked over my shoulder to find Alkres.
The ult'eir was asleep at last, curled in what was probably
Ruland's favorite chair. Ruland saw the direction of my
glance, and smiled.

"I'll tell him, Medium, when he wakes up."

"Thanks," I said, and followed the technician out of the
foreman's house and across the dusty strip of ground to the
UHST station. The comnet office was bigger than I'd
expected, but then I realized it must serve the town as
well as the UHST line. The technician led me through the
glass-walled outer office and into the smaller, warmer
room where the machines themselves were kept. Lights
glowed green and orange across the multiple consoles, and
the technician gave his boards a quick, practiced glance
before waving me to the couch that stood against the
room's third wall.

"This line's programmed to keep searching for the Tower
signal," he said, gesturing to one of the rows of lights,
"and I've kept another three open to any signals on the
emergency frequencies. I've got another five lines I can
use to call the other towns around here, and that still
leaves one line free for UHST business." He gave me a
sort of grin, but it faded quickly. "I thought I'd call Asten
and Monas Major, for starters."

"Go ahead," I said, and leaned back against the couch's cushions. I was dead tired, after only four hours' sleep and the attack; I could feel myself slipping into a doze, and was powerless to stop it. I heard the technician talking to his fellows at the other UHST stations to the south and west of the Tower, but their words registered only as vague impressions, surreal images of fear and uncertainty. No one on the UHST link knew much more than we did at Federston. Monas Major, just south of the Tower, had heard explosions and seen flames, but their foreman had forbidden anyone to investigate until she was sure the fighting was over—a sensible decision, but a frustrating one. Nansivi', on the main line to the north, had heard a lot of air traffic, but had known nothing of the fighting that followed. The Destiny station was broadcasting a garbled message about Brandrs taking over the port, but was cut off before the technician could clear the line. The Tower station did not answer our technician's calls, and there was still no word from Dr. Ran. I drifted into deeper sleep, broken only by confused dreams.

"Medium!" The technician's voice jolted me awake, and I reached instinctively for the room controls before I remembered where I was.

"I've got the doctor," the technician went on, oblivious to my confusion, and twisted a knob that sent sound pouring into the room.

"—Federston Station. Please respond."

It was unquestionably Dr. Ran's voice, driving the last vestiges of sleep from my brain.

"This is Federston Station," the technician answered smoothly. With his free hand, he gestured frantically toward a switch marked "Foreman's House." I pressed it, and he nodded, saying, "We are on-link, Doctor. What's your message?"

"Things—things are very bad here." Ran's voice was not quite steady, and I could feel my own muscles tense in answer. "The Tower is almost destroyed, and I have not found any survivors or any signs of survivors. There has been a fire; I assume there are bodies in the rubble."

The door opened then, and Ruland came in, breathing heavily. Alkres pushed past him without a word of apology, but the foreman made no complaint.

"What—?" the ult'eir began, and broke off with a visible effort, watching the technician.

"Bad news," I said, quietly. "The Tower's burned."

"Oh, my God," Ruland said. Alkres said nothing, but I saw his hands tighten slowly on the hem of his tunic.

"Doctor, can you give us a picture?" the technician was saying. "Please ask Vereck to transmit a picture."

There was a moment's silence, and then Ran said, "All right."

The technician flipped a series of switches, eyes fixed on a central screen. The display board beneath it flickered, numbers shifting, and then steadied. Slowly, an image began to take shape on the screen above. The technician made another adjustment, and the picture sharpened abruptly.

It took me a minute to recognize what was left of the Tower. The upper floors were gone, and one corner seemed to have been completely blown away, so that only a slanted stub remained of the original building. Smoke still curled from the stone, but it was clear that the fire was almost out. Alkres gave a single cry of protest, but did not look away.

The 'net crackled, and Dr. Ran said, "Federston Station, I think you should contact the neighboring towns— and the nearest Branch Holders—to see if any survivors were brought there."

Ruland leaned forward so that his voice would reach the microphones. "I'll do that, Doctor."

"There's not much I can do here, by the look of it," Ran continued. "I'm going to stop transmitting now, and make a closer search for survivors or bodies." Her voice faltered a little on the last word, and Alkres made a soft, unhappy noise of agreement.

"Very good, Doctor," the technician said, his voice professionally imperturbable. "I acknowledge end of transmission."

"Transmission ends," Ran echoed, and the dreadful picture faded from the screen.

No one said anything for a long moment. Alkres was still staring at the blank screen, his long mouth compressed into a tight, miserable line. I wanted very much to take him in my arms, to tell him everything would be all right

after all, but I knew better than to offer that false comfort.
Ruland cleared his throat, working his shoulders like a
man who's been doing heavy labor.

"Doctor's right," he said, too loudly. "Hastain, call around,
see if any of the other townships've picked up survivors."

The technician said, "Sor, nobody I've talked to so far
has."

"So try outside the UHST link," Ruland said. "Then—
The nearest Holder's Yslin Rhawn. Raise the Hold, and see
what they say."

"Yes, sor." Hastain turned back to his machines, typing
instructions into the boards.

"How could this've happened?" Alkres asked. "The Tower's supposed to be proof against attacks."

Ruland heaved a great sigh. "I don't know, sor. I'd
guess most of the damage was done after the fighting
ended—explosive charges set on the upper floors, or maybe
incendiaries."

He had spoken to Alkres as one adult to another, and
the boy knew it. I saw the ult'eir straighten his shoulders,
visibly putting aside his own fear and grief. Ruland saw it,
too, but gave no sign, continuing gruffly, "But, with all
respect, sor, I don't think it matters right now. What's
important is what's to be done with your lot."

"Yes." Alkres nodded. "That's right."

He stopped there, and I said, "The children must have
kin outside the mainline Family. It might be best to send
them to those relatives—maybe Dr. Ran could oversee
that?"

Ruland nodded thoughtfully, but he was careful to wait
until Alkres had murmured his agreement before continuing. "And then there're the off-worlders to deal with."

"I think I ought to release them from my service,"
Alkres said. His firmness surprised me, until I remembered the holoplay *Meriban*. The heroine's first act, after
she's been deprived of her station, is to release her long-
suffering servants from their contracts, though most of
them, of course, choose to remain with her. There are
several other plays that use the same motif. Alkres was
following the models he knew best. I didn't have the heart
to tell him that most of the off-worlders would be only too
grateful to be able to leave him.

"If you decide to do that, and I think it would be appropriate," I said, "I trust you'll let me stay until things are settled." After all, I could hardly leave Alkres—who was only a fifteen-year-old boy—to manage on his own; I would at least see him safely into the hands of his relatives before I decided what I would do. And I might yet be of some use: Conglomerate Mediators are trained to salvage the most unpromising situations, and in the confusion, someone might be willing to let me try.

"Thank you," Alkres said. He shivered suddenly. "Do I have to proclaim myself the Patriarch?"

That was another idea straight from the holoplays; the trouble was, those plays reflected the code. I hesitated, knowing why the boy wanted to wait. He was hoping, as we all were, that somehow someone else—Rohin, Magan, Alkres's own mother the pent'eir, Herself, anyone—had survived and would take the responsibility from him. Still, it was time we faced the possibility that Alkres was indeed the head of the Kinship. I looked at Ruland, and saw the same conflict in his face.

I said, feeling my way, "I think you have to let the Kinship know you're alive, at least. I don't know if you ought to do anything else until we know more about what's happened."

Ruland looked relieved. "That makes sense."

Alkres nodded, but before he could say anything else, the technician said, "Sors. I'm not getting any answer from the southern settlements, but I'm picking up a general broadcast from the Rhawn Hold. Shall I put it on?"

"Yes!" Alkres said, and I saw his hands close again on the hem of his tunic, twisting the fabric into a knot.

Hastain did something to his controls, and a booming voice filled the room. He winced, and adjusted the volume. Even then, I didn't recognize the voice, but the words were clear enough.

"—Kinship Tower was attacked this clock-midnight, and destroyed by Brandr raiders. As no member of the mainline Family survived, it falls to me, as senior Holder of the Kinship, to take control. In view of the statement issued by the Brandr Patriarch, I ask—I order—the Kinship to take no action until and unless I approve it." The voice, Yslin Rhawn's, faded in a hiss of static, then began again.

"Members of the Halex Kinship, our Kinship Tower was attacked. . . ."

"That's not true," Alkres shouted. "Ruland, Medium, you have to tell him I'm alive."

"Statement?" I said, in almost the same moment. "What statement?"

Hastain had slipped on a pair of headphones and was working busily at his controls. Then he stopped, shaking his head, and pushed the headphones back off his ears. "It just repeats, sors, and I can't raise anyone at the Hold. Shall I keep trying?"

"No," Ruland said, without even a glance at Alkres. "You're right, Medium, we need that statement. Do a broad-scan, Hastain, or try Destiny, but get me a hard copy of that, and of Yslin Rhawn's little speech. Bring them to me in my office. And send the doctor in as soon as she gets back." He gave Alkres a grim look. "Sors, we need to talk in private."

Alkres let himself be drawn, unresisting, back to the foreman's house. Inside, Ulrika took one look at the boy's set, white face, and insisted on bringing us a coffee service. Ruland growled at her for wasting time, but the hot drink, and the food that came with it, seemed to bring a little color back to Alkres's face. A few minutes later, Hastain appeared, carrying several sheets of green-striped paper. Ruland took it, flipped through the closely printed pages, and grunted.

"Where'd you get it?"

"The Brandr statement's coming from the Destiny main 'net station," Hastain answered. "They're overriding any private communications with it."

"Smart of them," Ruland growled. He flipped the sheets across the desk. "What do you make of it, Medium?"

I caught the papers, and turned them so that Alkres could see as well. It was a long document, two pages of close printing, but stripped of the code's elaborate phrases, the meaning was all too clear. The Brandr Patriarch freely acknowledged both that his Kinship and the Fyfe Kinship had combined to attack the Halex Tower, and that they had used off-world weaponry to do so. This was, he said, admittedly a drastic measure, but one that was made necessary by the Halex Matriarch's constant attempts to overturn the code by which Oresteians lived. He used the same argument to justify the destruction of the Tower, and then went on to say that, because the code-breakers were a minority in the Kinship, and almost exclusively of the mainline family, he was prepared to consider the feud ended, and to recognize the Rhawn as legitimate head of the Kinship. I read the statement twice, and then a third time, as though another examination might change the meaning.

"He can't do that," Alkres said. There were tears in his eyes, and he shook them angrily away. "It's not true, what he said about Herself, and even if it were, he can't do this. I'm still head of the Kinship—aren't I?"

"It's completely against the code," Ruland said.

"True enough," I said, "but it sounds like Yslin's listening. I wonder how many of the other Holders will listen, too?"

"They'd better not," Alkres muttered, then seemed to recognize the futility of his words and subsided, scowling, into his chair.

"Hastain," I said, slowly, "see if you can raise the other Holders. Let them know that the ult'eir's alive, but don't tell them where he is. If they ask how you know, say you've heard from people who've seen him, something like that, but don't let them know he's in Federston. I think it's enough to start a rumor, at this point, and a lot less risky."

"You're really expecting trouble," Ruland said.

"Aren't you?" I snapped, and was instantly sorry I'd spoken so sharply. The foreman didn't seem angry, however. He nodded slowly.

"I think you're right. The whole system's gone to hell."

More information trickled in over the next few hours. Dr. Ran returned at last, but she reported finding no survivors. There were bodies in the ruin, she said, but they were so badly charred that she couldn't identify them without special equipment. She had left them there, and come back to Federston in the hope we'd heard something from the neighboring towns.

We hadn't. Hastain spent most of the clock-morning talking to the other foremen, and then Ruland managed to contact the Ansson and Ingvarr Holders, but there were no reports of any survivors. I wondered bitterly if the Brandr had made sure there would be none, but shied away from mentioning the possibility aloud. It might not be true, after all; the code expressly forbade that kind of killing—but the Brandr had already shattered the spirit of the code, if not its letter. Why should they hesitate at wholesale slaughter? The worst thing of all, for me, was that I was sure the Brandr Patriarch believed everything he'd said in his statement, and would stand by it to the death.

As I'd suggested, Ruland passed on the word of Alkres's survival to the other Holders, couching it as a secondhand report. The response was not particularly encouraging from Asbera Ingvarr—her Hold lay closest to the Rhawns, and was not easily defensible—but Barthel Ansson expressed cautious pleasure. Over my objections, Ruland informed him of the other children waiting in Federston, and Barthel insisted on sending a flyer for them at once. I still didn't like it—after all, admitting that we had the only known group of survivors was tantamount to admitting that we had Alkres—but I had to see the force of Ruland's arguments. The children did need to be with their own families, especially now, and it would be easier to arrange that from the Ansson Hold. Dr. Ran and the Methusalan agreed to go with them, and stay at the Hold until all the children were relocated. The other off-worlders, understandably, demanded to be sent to Destiny, and Alkres agreed.

That left only the question of what was to be done with the ult'eir. Ruland thought he should proclaim himself Patriarch and see what sort of support he gathered, while Dr. Ran argued that he should go with the other children to the Ansson Hold. I couldn't feel happy about that, and even Ruland, himself an Ansson, had to admit that, with things so unsettled, it was probably unwise for Alkres to trust himself to a member of another Branch of the Family. Reports kept coming in of resistance in Destiny—the Ingvarr stadtholder simply would not acknowledge the Brandr Patriarch, while port workers refused to service Brandr ships—and I wondered if it wouldn't be best to take Alkres there. After all, the city had benefited as much as the southern Holdings from the Matriarch's reforms, and the city-dwellers weren't directly under the Branch-Holders' thumbs. Alkres might well find a core of solid support there, and, if all else failed, he would be close enough to the spaceport to get off-world. Alkres made no contribution to the discussion, sunk in understandable apathy. When we asked directly what he wanted to do, he said only that he had always liked Asbera Ingvarr, and lapsed again into silence. We were still arguing the question when one of the UHST station's runners burst into the office.

"I'm sorry, sors, ama, but Hastain says there're Brandr flyers heading this way."

Ruland shot to his feet. "What the hell do you mean?"

The runner, a girl maybe three or four years older than Alkres, caught her breath with an effort. "He's picked up their transmission, sor, on a military band, about twenty-five kilometers to the southwest."

Ruland and I exchanged glances. The Rhawn Hold lay to the southwest of Federston, but so did the Ansson holding.

"They must've picked up our transmission to the Ansson Hold," Dr. Ran said, guiltily. "You were right, Trey. We never should've told them the children were here."

"Nothing so easy," Ruland growled.

I said, "The 'net is supposed to be shielded. They couldn't've intercepted the call; someone had to tell them we were here."

"Like Barthel Ansson," Ruland said bitterly. He shook himself. "Jannah, tell Hastain to go on the 'speaker and warn the town. Tell Teacher to take all the kids into the school basement, that's the safest place I can think of. Then tell Vereck to break out the flyer again." The girl nodded and darted off. Ruland turned back to me. "Medium, we'll have to do it your way. Take the flyer; I'll tell them it's in Monas Major for repairs. You take Himself into Destiny. He should be safe there."

I nodded, and looked to Alkres. The ult'eir—the Patriarch, now—was sitting very straight in his chair, hands folded tightly in his lap. He saw me looking at him, and managed a nod. "All right, Medium, I'll do what you say." He looked at Ruland. "Thank you, foreman, for taking care of us. I just hope—" His face crumpled, but he mastered himself and went on, bravely, "I hope you don't get into trouble for what you've done. I won't forget it."

Ruland touched his forehead. "My duty, sor."

The door snapped open again, and the runner stood there. Ruland's wife stood behind her, my furred cloak and a child's coat in her arms. A battered satchel swung from one hand.

"Sor," the girl said, "the flyer's outside, and Hastain says they're coming fast."

"Right, let's go," Ruland said. He stopped abruptly, an appalled expression on his face. "Medium, you can fly—"

"I can handle a flyer," I said. "Come on."

We left the foreman's house in a clump, Ruland's wife bundling Alkres into the coat as we walked, me shrugging my cape haphazardly onto my shoulders. Ruland handed me the satchel, telling me it held food and money, and I slung it across my shoulder, muttering my thanks. I had no gloves—the scarlet gloves that matched the cloak's trim were ashes now—but at least the cabin would be heated. In the street outside, Teacher was herding a last group of children into the schoolhouse. A child was crying in the distance, the noise almost drowned by the thunder of the flyer's engine. Vereck had taxied the machine from its shed up the main street of town, and held it now directly in front of the station. He popped the canopy as we approached, and I scrambled up and into the pod, fitting myself behind the pilot's board. When he was sure I had control, Vereck levered himself out of the machine, pausing on the edge of the pod to help Alkres aboard, then dropped free.

There was no time for farewells. As the others ran for the shelter of the foreman's house, I fed power to the engine, touching the rudder pedals to swing the ship so that we faced down the metalled street. I glanced quickly across the boards, recognizing with relief the red handle of a quick-start booster, and asked, "Clear?"

"All clear," Alkres answered, twisting in his seat to survey the street around us.

I took him at his word, and cut the brakes. The flyer trundled forward, picking up speed as we went. Then I pulled the booster handle, and we shot forward, almost catapulted into the air. Sixty meters up, still well under the usual scanner canopy, I trimmed ship, and banked onto the line of the UHST tracks, heading flat out for Destiny.

The flight into Destiny was an anticlimax after all. There was no sign of pursuit, even when I lifted the flyer into a normal traffic lane, and no signs of disaster behind us. Still, I followed the UHST line north to the station town of Newforest, and left the flyer at the field there. The local trains were running again, as I'd hoped they would be. We joined a crowd of locals, mostly mill workers, at the station, and caught the next train into Destiny's south terminal.

There were guards in Brandr battledress at the station barriers, along with the usual policemen. I knew the dark-haired man at the left-hand barrier, and turned in that direction. Alkres slowed, clutching my hand, but I pulled him along bodily.

"Act natural," I whispered. "You're my son; we're off-world workers who've left Halex service." I glanced quickly over him, seeing nothing that would immediately betray us, and was glad my medium's badge was hidden beneath my cloak. Alkres was dark-haired, but at least he hadn't grown into the hawk-boned Halex face. Only the Oresteian accent would betray him, and that only if he spoke. "Let me do the talking," I said, and gave his hand what I hoped was a reassuring squeeze. Alkres returned the pressure, but his face was very pale.

We were coming up on the barrier now, and I pulled out the double ticket, holding it out for the ticket counter. She took it without a word and nodded us through, but the nearest Brandr said, "Hold it. Let's see your IDs."

I let my Urban accent thicken. "We don't have any ID, thanks to you people. I used to work for the Halex Kinship."

"Name?" Both the Brandr were watching us now, hands on the slings of their blasters.

"Mas Zeeman." I jerked my head at Alkres. "That's my son, Tannis." I had pulled the name out of nowhere, and a characterization with it. Zeeman was an engineer, irascible, bull-headed, and thoroughly fed up with the whole situation. It was an easy part, for all that it was deadly serious. I glowered at the nearer Brandr, waiting for an answer.

The dark-haired policemen eyed me impassively and

said, "I know them, they're all right. They come through all the time."

By now, there was a small crowd backed up behind us, waiting to get through the barrier, and I could hear rumblings of discontent. The Brandr heard it, too, and exchanged wary glances. One said, "All right, you can pass."

I nodded grudgingly, staying in character, and pushed through the gate, dragging Alkres with me. A murmur of satisfaction rippled through the crowd. Buoyed by the sound, I didn't start shaking until we reached the street outside. I saw Alkres looking at me, and said roughly, "I have a friend—she's captain of the six-week mailship. We'll go to her place, no one'll trace us there."

"All right," Alkres said, in a small voice. He was looking very young, and very tired, and I made myself relax a little.

"Actually, it's not her flat—it belongs to a friend of hers, a *para'an*. Don't worry, though, I know they'll help us." I knew I was babbling, but the flow of words seemed to help. "We'll have to walk, I'm afraid. I don't think we ought to risk the trams."

"I can make it," Alkres said grimly.

We reached the address Leith had given me—was it only the day before?—around the supper hour. There weren't many people on the street, and I felt very conspicuous as we made our way along Bluestar Street, glancing at building numbers as we went. I was very glad to duck into the sheltered doorway of Guil ex-Tam'ne's flat. The outer door was locked, of course, but there was a standard guardbox beside the latch. I pressed the code sequence Leith had given me, and waited. Nothing happened, and I pressed it again, hoping they had not decided to go out for the evening. It was still Light, and would be for another six hours, so the businesses in the Necropolis were closed, and I couldn't imagine Leith choosing to leave a comnet at a time like this. Unless, I thought, with a sudden rush of fear, she had already gone back to the ship? I raised my hand to press the buttons again, and the speaker crackled to life.

"Who is it?" It was the *para'an*'s wary voice, and I shaped my answer accordingly.

"Guil, it's Trey, Trey Maturin. I'm looking for Leith. May I come in?"

There was a muffled exclamation, and then Leith said, "Of course." A moment later, the door clicked open. We stepped through, and started up the stairs toward Guil's flat.

Leith was waiting in the open doorway, Guil's fair hair just visible behind her. She frowned, seeing Alkres, and I said hastily, "Let me get inside first, Leith, please."

Moraghan's frown deepened, but she stepped aside wordlessly, and let us into the flat. It was a fairly large place, with several rooms; the living room where we stood was larger than Rehur's entire flat. Then Leith had closed the door behind us, saying "What the hell's going on?"

"I know what's going on," Guil said. She fixed me with an icy stare, daring me to contradict her. "That's the Halex kid, the ult'eir they've been wondering about, what happened to him, and your medium's brought him here."

I shook my head, and managed a smile. "You're only partly right, Guil. He's not the ult'eir anymore, he's the Patriarch. And there isn't any other place for us to go."

"He's got kin," the *para'an* protested, mechanically.

I said, "They can't be trusted. Have you heard the broadcasts coming out of the Rhawn Hold?"

"Yes," Leith said. "And the Brandr's." She glared at the *para'an*, who looked away, shrugging.

"It's not my place, Leith," she muttered. Then, as Moraghan's stare did not waver, Guil said, "All right, I'm with you. But the whole thing's fucked up."

Leith said, with the quiet competence that had always drawn me to her, "What can we do, Trey?"

I paused, marshalling my thoughts. I hadn't really thought beyond the necessity of getting Alkres out of reach of the Brandr. "Mainly, we need a place to hide until things sort themselves out a little."

Leith nodded. "You got it."

Guil nodded, too, but her expression was unreadable.

"After that," I said, "we'll need to get in touch with the Family, let them know that Alkres is alive and claims the genarchy. I don't know what, then."

Leith circled her gloved wrist with the fingers of her right hand, turning the maimed arm thoughtfully in their circle. She was wearing an oversized Oresteian tunic, probably borrowed from Guil, over her usual clothes, but she stood as straight as if she still wore her Peacekeeper's uniform. "All right," she said abruptly. "You need communications. You can't use Guil's 'net except in emergencies: the link might be traced, and that would spoil the safe house. We'll go to *Pipe Major*. The stadtholder promised to open the port tomorrow."

Something Leith had said once was echoing in my mind, something about it not mattering whether an order was right or wrong as long as a decision was made. I said, "Don't play the commander with me, Leith."

She looked up, startled and angry, and then, reluctantly, her expression eased into a smile. "I wasn't, Trey, truth. If it's communications you need, *Pipe Major*'s your best bet."

"It could still be traced," Guil said.

Leith shrugged. "So what? Do you think even these Brandr are going to risk harassing a Conglomerate mailship?"

"The way things are going," Alkres said, "I wouldn't put anything past them." It was the first time he'd spoken since we'd entered the flat, and everybody jumped.

Guil was the first to recover. "You've got a point, kid," she said, and gestured to the stacked cushions that served as chairs. "Sit down, be comfortable. You, too, Medium. I'll make coffee."

"Thank you," Alkres said. He settled himself cautiously on the largest of the piles, and after a moment, I seated myself beside him. Guil vanished into the kitchen, letting its curtain-door fall shut behind her. Alkres looked far older than his years, harsh shadows beneath his eyes and hollowing his cheeks. I held out my arm, and Alkres burrowed against me, soundlessly crying. Moraghan turned her back on us, deliberately blind. I wrapped my arms around the boy, wishing there were something I could do or say to comfort him. "I'm sorry," I whispered, rocking him as if he were a much younger child. "I'm so sorry."

We stayed like that for a minute, maybe longer, and then Alkres pushed me away and sat up, scrubbing at his face. "I'm all right," he said, almost angrily.

Moraghan said, without turning, "Did I tell you, Trey, I spoke to Stephan Mojag at the Trade Board? He said there

wasn't a damn thing he could do. I bet he's sorry now."
She turned then, not waiting for my answer, and looked at
Alkres. "Stephan used to be in my squadron—I used to be
with the Peacekeepers. When I was your age, I was piloting a drone fighter. Four years later, I was commanding
the whole squadron. Don't worry, you can handle it."

Before Alkres could decide how to answer that, Guil
said, "Leith."

There was a note in the *para'an*'s voice that made us all
turn to her, and Leith said, "Trouble?"

"Maybe. I was listening to the newscast, in there. The
Brandr are looking—actively looking—for you two now."
Guil set the coffee service on the low table, and gave a
lopsided grin. "The stadtholder's threatening to file a complaint with the Ship's Council, and there's all sorts of
speculation about what the Brandr may do to retaliate."

"How can the Brandr do anything in Destiny?" Alkres
said. "It's our city."

"Reidun Brandr says," Guil began, her voice rich with
irony, "that with your Tower destroyed, there's no real
government here and they have to step in to keep the
peace."

"Who's Reidun Brandr?" Leith asked.

Guil shrugged.

Alkres frowned. "He's their Demi-heir, I think."

"Oh." Leith twisted her gloved wrist in her encircling
fingers. "I think, Trey, we'd better find you another bolt
hole, just in case."

I leaned forward and poured myself a cup of coffee that
I didn't want. I sipped the scalding liquid, trying to think.
I didn't really know anyone else in Destiny, at least no one
that I felt sure I could trust. Emerant Ansson, the Family's local medium, was a possibility—but she was an Ansson,
and we still didn't know where they stood. Most of the
Destiny people were Ingvarrs, like the stadtholder. The
only mainline Halex I knew was Rehur, and he was a
ghost.

Did that matter? I wondered suddenly. I took another
swallow of coffee, feeling the caffeine take hold. Rehur
might be dead, under the code, but I was a medium. As
long as I was present, Alkres was acting within the code—
and if the situation were bad enough to drive us into the

Necropolis, it would be bad enough for us to risk bending the code a little. There were other advantages to contacting Rehur, I realized: who better than an actor, with all his contacts in the Necropolis, to spread the news that Alkres was alive and well, and claimed his birthright? It wouldn't matter that he was a ghost—there were *para'anin* enough to hear his message and pass it along to the living.

"You're right," I said aloud. "Do you remember the puppet actor, the night of the *khy sonon-na*?"

"How could I forget him?" Leith grinned, then sobered quickly. "He was the twin to your Demi-heir, wasn't he?"

"Rehur?" Alkres looked up quickly.

I nodded. "I think—I know he'll shelter us, if we have to take refuge in the Necropolis." I paused, wondering if I should explain the other things I had in mind, then decided not to do it just yet. Alkres had enough to worry about; let him get as much rest as he could now, before I gave him something new to trouble him. "Alkres, you stay with Leith and Guil. They'll look after you while I make the arrangements."

Alkres looked as if he'd protest, but then he nodded.

Guil said, "You're going into the Necroplis now?"

"That's right," I said, and after a second, she nodded.

"They're looking for two of you, and you don't look like an off-worlder. You're right."

Leith said, "If anything goes wrong, we'll make for the ship. There're ways to get into the port."

"All right," I said, and hauled myself to my feet. The coffee had helped drive away some of the weariness, but not all. Guil said something in a low voice and vanished into one of the inner rooms. A moment later she was back, an opened bottle in her hand.

"Stinnit," she said, and held out a blue-banded capsule. "You'll need it."

I took the pill gratefully, swallowing it dry. It was too soon for the chemicals to take effect, but I could already feel the psychological lift. "Thanks," I said, and looked at Leith.

"We'll be here or at the ship," she said. Drawing my cloak around me, I let myself out into the sunlight.

Despite the fact that it was getting into the clock-evening, there were a fair number of people out on the streets, made restless by the raid and the continuing Brandr presence in the city. It was not hard to lose myself among the crowds, and I made my way to the Necropolis wall without attracting undue notice. At the greengates, I adjusted my badge so that it lay outside the hood of my cloak, and attached myself to a sober group of *para'anin*. As I'd hoped, the city policeman assumed I was with them, and waved us through together. There were no Brandr in sight, for which I was grateful.

The Necropolis looked very different in daylight. The theaters, bars, and restaurants were all closed, their windows shuttered over. The streets were quiet, and I felt as though a hundred pairs of eyes were watching me from the buildings' upper floors. It took me longer than I'd expected to find Rehur's building, but when I finally got there, the main door swung open to my touch. That was a bit of luck: I'd assumed it would be locked, and I would have to identify myself for all to hear over the building's guard system. I climbed the stairs two at a time, hoping I wouldn't meet anyone, until at last I stood outside Rehur's door. There was a piece of yellow paper stuck to the panel just above the latchplate. It took me a minute to decipher his scrawl, but at last I figured it out: "Belit—Late rehearsal tonight, the Matador, nineteen hours/whenever. See you there." It was signed with his initial.

I stood for a moment, staring at the card. There was no telling when the rehearsal would end, so there was no point in my waiting for him here. If nothing else, I would be extremely conspicuous, sitting outside his door until he got home. On the other hand, I didn't want to return to Guil's flat without having seen Rehur. . . . I frowned at the card again, and came to my decision. I knew where the Matador was—I had seen *The Man Who Killed in His Sleep* there, the last time I came to Destiny—and I doubted small theater companies had changed too much since my own days as an actor. The stinnit was taking hold now. I felt sure I could talk my way into the theater, and wait for Rehur there.

The Matador lay on the far side of Broad Street. I retraced my steps to the main tram line, and followed its tracks up Broad Street toward the northern greengate. The buildings here were shuttered, too, shorn of banners and lights. Though I knew people had to be working inside, getting ready for the coming Dark, I felt as though I were walking through an abandoned city. I was glad to make the turn into the Matador's alley.

The front of the house was shuttered and dark, of course, but I found the stage door easily enough, and pulled the door chain. After a moment, the door opened a crack, and a woman's voice said, "Yes?"

"Is Witchwood rehearsing here?" The woman frowned, and I hurried on without giving her a chance to answer. "Rehur left me a note. He said he'd be late, and that I should meet him here."

The woman's face cleared. "Yeah, they're here. They'll be a while yet—they're taping—but if you'd like, you can come in and watch."

I had hoped she would say that. "That'd be great, thank you."

She pushed the door open further, and I stepped inside. The Matador's backstage area smelled like every other holotheater I'd ever been in, a faintly dusty smell offset by the burned smell of the puppet consoles. I smiled, savoring it in spite of everything.

"This way—I didn't get your name?"

"Trey Maturin."

The woman nodded. "Have you been to a taping before?"

"Yes, quite a few," I answered, and bit back a laugh.

"Than you know the rules," the woman said, satisfied, and pushed through a heavy curtain. We were in the backstage proper now, and I was careful to stay close behind her. We passed the musicians' stand, and the doorkeeper paused to speak to the red-haired woman at the keyboard. It was the woman, Belit, whom I'd met the night of the *khy sono*. I smiled at her automatically, and she gave me a puzzled look, not quite remembering.

"How's it going?" the doorkeeper said, quietly, and Belit transferred her attention to the other woman.

"Okay. I'd say they've got another hour, at least. What's up?"

"A friend of Rehur's is here to see him," the doorkeeper answered.

Belit's eyes widened in recognition, and she raised a

hand in greeting. "He's on right now," she said, "but I'll pass the word when he's through."

"Thanks," the doorkeeper said, and beckoned for me to follow. We skirted the elaborate lighting console, the doorkeeper murmuring a greeting to the young man monitoring its dials, and pushed through another heavy curtain. It gave onto the stage itself, at extreme stage right, and I caught a quick glimpse of the group onstage before the doorkeeper led me down the short flight of steps to the seats. She pointed to a seat toward the middle of the third row, and I sat quickly. Onstage, the blond puppetmaster—Nariko-Ash—turned toward our movement, frowning, but the doorkeeper gave some sort of hand signal. The puppetmaster nodded, and turned back to her work. The doorkeeper slipped away again.

The puppetmasters had set up a portable tape rig to stage left—a small light platform surrounded by a fragile-looking scaffold studded with cameras and secondary lights. More lights and cameras were suspended from the canopy. Rehur stood in the center of the column of light, hands on his hips in a familiar, challenging pose. The dark-haired puppetmaster, Rowan, stared up at him, hugging her kata-board against her body. She shook her head, and looked at Ash.

The blond puppetmaster put a hand to her forehead. "Rehur," she said. "You are playing a demon, the incarnation of evil. Stop looking for sympathy."

Rehur threw up his hands, and I saw that he was wearing three-inch claws on his fingertips. "All right, fine," he said. I could tell it had been a long rehearsal.

"Thank you," Ash said.

Rowan said, as though there had been no disagreement, "Tenth kata, please, Rehur."

Rehur stood still for an instant longer, then shook himself, and moved fluidly into the proper stance, torso half turned away from Rowan, his left hand extended palm up, fingers bent to display the glittering claws. His right elbow was tucked close to the body, hand out, palm down, fingers spread. In the same moment, his face assumed a sullen arrogance that contrasted nicely with his delicate features.

"Good," Ash said. "Check, please."

Rowan pointed her remote-control wand at the base of the platform and pressed a button. Thin lines of ruby light lanced from the cameras, snaring Rehur in their web. He was wearing the usual taping clothes—a skintight, hooded pullover sewn with reflective points at each joint, and a pair of dun-colored trousers. Each beam centered on a reflector, confirming camera position and outlining Rehur's upper body in little explosions of light. Rowan nodded.

"All set."

"Go," Ash answered.

The other puppetmaster touched a second button on the remote, and the red beams disappeared. In the same instant, the lights intensified, and I winced, remembering the heat and the blinding glare. I had always hated puppet work.

"Rolling," Rowan said, still calmly. "Begin—now."

Rehur's left arm curled in toward his body, a slow, inhuman movement. When the claws almost touched his shoulder, he flung both arms wide, as though he'd sprouted wings, then fell to one knee, arms wrapping protectively about himself. There was nothing sympathetic, or even human, in the gesture.

Rowan said, "And, cut." She looked at Ash.

"That's more like it," the blond woman said. "How's the film?"

Rowan crossed to the platform, bent to examine the readouts along its base. Rehur, standing now, watched curiously. "All right," Rowan said at last. "It's a workable tape."

"Good," Ash said briskly. "Rehur, we're done, thank you. Ivena?"

One of the women sitting in the clump of actors at stage right looked up alertly, and began stripping off her outer clothing. Rehur jumped down from the taping platform, pushing back the hood of his shirt.

"We'll get your tape replaced," Ash continued, "and then we'll have a quick run-through with the uncut puppets. Then we can all go home."

Some of the actors raised an ironic cheer at that, and I couldn't help grinning. I remembered nights like this only too well. At Ash's nod, Ivena stepped briskly onto the platform, and held up her arms while Rowan adjusted the cameras. The actor was wearing the marked tights as well, indicating that Rowan was making a full-body puppet. I wondered just what would be added to Rehur's half-puppet to make the demon.

Ivena's taping went relatively quickly, needing only five takes to get what Ash wanted. Her movements were less dramatic than Rehur's, and I assumed that the puppetmasters would be doing a lot with that particular image. When they had finished, Rowan bent to pull the heavy tape cartridge from the base of the platform. Ash clapped her hands sharply.

"All right, we've got the puppets. Now, let's run through the second scene—just once, to get the feel of the new tapes—and then we can all go home."

The actors who had been waiting stage right pulled themselves to their feet and moved slowly toward their places, talking among themselves. Rowan fitted the two cartridges—Rehur's and Ivena's tapes—into the master control console, and began fiddling with the dials. As the actors settled into their positions, I finally recognized the play: *The Possession*, probably the oldest warhorse in the Oresteian canon. It was no wonder Rehur had looked unhappy. *The Possession*'s lead-villain is the demon, traditionally a puppet; from the look of things, Rehur's only live role was doubling as a minor courtier.

"Places, please." Ash positioned herself behind the console, hands moving surely across her controls. Rowan, at her right, barely looked up from her keyboard. Ash pushed a button, and lights sparked momentarily on Rehur's chest and Ivena's left shoulder. The puppetmaster frowned. "Mark, Ivena."

The actor shifted, and Ash said, "All right. Let's go, the soul-stealing. Take it from your line, Per—'the forces of darkness surround us.'"

Per, playing the old advisor, obediently gave his cue, and the scene began to move. Even I had seen this short play too many times, but it never seemed to lose its appeal to the Oresteians. Maybe it was because the plot was so uncomplicated in its march of crime, supernatural retribution, and cleansing: a young and foolish prince calls up a demon to rid herself of a rival, only to have the demon demand her own soul as its reward. After much repining, the prince accepts her death, because only through that sacrifice can the demon be destroyed. This was the climax of the play, when the demon appears in its most horrific aspect, and draws the prince's soul out of her body, only to be struck down by the prince's chosen heir. At the proper moment, the puppets appeared, the puppeteers matching the figures' movements to the actors' gestures. The demon beckoned and called, its taped voice a distorted version of Rehur's; the soul-puppet was drawn struggling from Ivena's body, and was consumed. In that instant, another actor—the hero, Ysaje—mimed shooting the silver arrow, and the demon writhed and fell. Falling, it was consumed in flames, to spectacular effect. It was a rather neat performance, wasted on a truly inferior play.

"Not bad," Ash said. "Not bad at all." She looked down at her board, and flipped another switch. "Hold your places just for a minute. I want to make a quick run with the full demon. No, Rowan, don't bother with the soul, I just want to put the pieces together."

Someone onstage groaned, but the actors did as they were told. Ash touched controls, bringing the demon out from around Rehur's body. This time, the human torso was attached to a pair of scaled and taloned legs, creating an image out of a conservative religious's nightmare. Ash brought the composite image across the stage at half speed, concentrating on keeping the two halves together, and finally cut the picture.

"All right," she said. "That's all, thank you for your patience. See you tomorrow evening for the final."

The group on stage broke apart instantly, voices rising in conversation. Rehur came toward the edge of the stage, pulling off the tight taping shirt. "Trey?"

I came forward to meet him, seeing again the tattooed snake that coiled around his left bicep. In the harsh light from the stage, I could see what it attempted to hide. Beneath the dyes, his skin was pocked and scarred from yearly vaccinations: actors on Orestes count as prostitutes, and with some reason. Someone called his name, and he turned just long enough to catch the thrown tunic before turning back to me.

"What's happened?"

His voice was low, controlled, but I could hear the fear

below the polished surface. "You've heard that the Tower's taken, burned?" I said. There was no time to be gentle, but still, I felt a pang of helpless guilt.

Rehur nodded, slowly crumpling his tunic into a wadded ball.

"It's bad news," I said. "I'm sorry, but there aren't many survivors. Herself sent out the children who were at the Tower, and they're with the Ansson Holder now, but I'm afraid. . . ." I faltered, seeing the color drain from his face and the rising pain in his huge eyes, and had to force myself to go on. "Those are all the survivors we know about."

Rehur's eyes flickered shut, but he forced them open again. "Rohin?"

"He got us out," I said, wondering if the knowledge that his twin had died by the code would be any comfort at all. "He got us to the escape tunnel, and then went back. I'm afraid he's dead—true-dead."

Rehur managed an oddly bitter smile. "That's Rohin," he said, and shook himself. "Who's the genarch now?"

"That's why I need your help," I said. "Alkres."

Rehur frowned. "He's only fifteen."

"And the Patriarch," I said. "Rehur, I need your help."

"But I'm dead," Rehur protested, automatically and without bitterness. Around us, the stage lights winked out, the noises of rehearsal fading, and he shook himself again. "We can't talk here," he said, pulling his tunic over bare skin. "Will you come back to my place?"

"Of course."

We crossed Broad Street in silence. Overhead, the sky was darkening toward Sunset, Agamemnon's half-disk brighter against the deepening blue. Objects cast a double shadow, shifting toward twilight.

The main door of Rehur's building was still unlocked. The actor made a face as he pushed it open, muttering something about inviting trouble. I followed him up the stairs and into the flat.

Chapter 9: Rehur

After Maturin had left, Rehur curled himself into the corner of the stove-bed, trying to think constructively. The Tower was burned—Rohin was dead—but the Family had survived, sort of, and he was still bound to do whatever he could to help. Especially for Alkres. . . . He remembered the ult'eir as a solemn boy of nine, not shy, but very conscious of the ten years between them. That was the last time he had spoken to Alkres; a year later he had been declared dead, and was happily established in the Necropolis.

He caught up his pillow and laid it across his drawn-up knees, resting his face against the cool fabric. Maturin had asked for two things, a place to hide if they were driven out of their present hiding place, and for Rehur to help spread the word among the Halex of Destiny that Alkres lived. The actor sighed, rubbing his cheek against the pillow. The second was easy enough. Lulan, owner-manager of the May-apple, was a *para'an* of Halex in Halex, and prided herself on her connections with—and her years of service to—the various Branches of the Family. Every Halex in the capital passed through at least the gaming rooms on the May-apple's lower levels, if not the rooms on the upper floors. If he passed the news to her, it would be all over Destiny within a calendar-day.

She might also be the answer to Maturin's first request, Rehur thought suddenly. After all, he himself was known to be twin brother of the Halex Demi-heir—he had never made any secret of it—so his flat would hardly be a safe refuge. But the May-apple. . . . He sat up straight, trying to find holes in the idea. Lulan catered to ghosts and *para'anin* as well as to the living, was used to handling a mixed crowd, so there would be little risk of Alkres's breaking the code. And besides, Rehur thought, he'd have a medium with him to protect him. Yes, if Maturin and the rest were driven out of their present hiding place, the May-apple would be the perfect refuge.

Fired by his idea, Rehur pushed himself out of the stove-bed, and reached for the chronograph he had discarded on the single table. It was well after clock-midnight, the hour of Sunset and the official opening of the Dark; he put the chronograph aside, sighing. There was no point in visiting the May-apple now, he thought. Lulan would be entirely too busy with her first rush of clients to see him; better to wait until clock-morning, when the rush had slacked off a bit, and she could spare him time to listen.

He shivered suddenly, and reached back into the bed to adjust its heater. The worn mechanism sighed and crackled, but a moment later he felt a new surge of warmth against his back. He knew there was nothing to do but wait, that there was nothing he could do until clock-morning. Still, he found it very hard to undress and climb into the welcoming warmth of the bed. He pulled the thermal curtains closed across the bed's open side and drew the blankets close around him, knowing he wouldn't sleep. The rehearsal, and Maturin's news on top of that, had drained him more than he had realized. He fell into an exhausted sleep almost at once.

When he finally woke, the chronograph read seven minutes after noon of the twentieth day of the tenth standard month. Rehur swore at the glowing display, then fumbled for the room controls until he found the right switch and flooded the windowless room with hard, untinted light. He had never intended to sleep so late, had hardly thought he could sleep at all. . . . He shook himself angrily, and touched another button on the room's control plaque, switching on Destiny's primary newscast as he went into the flat's tiny bathroom.

By the time he'd finished, it was clear that the newscast wasn't saying anything useful, and he switched it off, scowling. He pulled clothes from the boxes stacked along the wall, one corner of his mind mechanically matching colors, and pulled on trousers, shirt, and knitted tunic, thinking furiously. From the things the newscasters had not said, it was clear that Brandr were still in Destiny, and while they had so far stayed out of the Necropolis, there was no guarantee they'd continue to do so. And my face, Rehur thought, with a wry smile, is Halex enough to betray me, even if no one has bothered to point out my background. Someone will, too; it's been common gossip in the Necropolis for years. The idea of a disguise seemed almost too melodramatic to be taken seriously, too much like one of the popular holoplays, and his smile widened into a grin. Then he sobered. Melodramatic or not, some sort of disguise would keep the Brandr from realizing just what he was, and if he were to help Maturin, he would have to avoid that at all costs. Still, he felt distinctly foolish as he went back into his bathroom, to return a moment later with his battered makeup box.

He set the box on the table and opened it, drawing out the heavy mirror, then kicked the wheeled storage box that served as his only chair out of its place by the door and pulled it up to the table. He seated himself in front of the mirror and stared at his reflection, turning his head from side to side to study the familiar planes and angles. Then, his decisions made, he reached into the box.

Like most actors, he wore little makeup offstage; it felt strange to wear it now. He smoothed on a creamy base, deliberately obscuring the sharp lines of cheek and jaw, then added false shadows and a touch of color, subtly rounding his long face. He paused, shifting again to study the effect, and decided that any more would be too much. Then, frowning slightly, he began to reshape his eyes. They were his most conspicuous feature, as he knew well, and the most memorable. Carefully, he rubbed a lighter base across the lids, covering the natural shadows, then fumbled among the lining pencils until he found the lightest shade of brown. With it, he drew a narrow line along the base of each eyelid, and smudged it almost to invisibility. When he looked again into the mirror, his eyes seemed noticeably smaller. A darker lip color drew attention away from the eyes. At last, he leaned back from the mirror to study his handiwork. Slowly, he began to laugh. Without consciously meaning to, he'd copied most of the makeup for Niklas Castel, the troublemaking pilot who was the pivotal character in *The Wreck of Tenshi Nen*. Niklas had been his first good role with Witchwood; he hoped it was a good omen.

He sobered quickly, studying his reflection for a final time, and quickly added the ghostmark in the center of his forehead. That would protect him from unwanted advances. The fading light of Sunset would soften the theatrical lines; it would still be obvious that he was wearing makeup, but that was nothing out of the ordinary in the Necropolis. More important, he was no longer recognizable as a Halex—at least not at first sight. He stood, stretching, and crossed to the wall of boxes, searching through the ones on the bottom row until he found what he was looking for. He spread the dark crimson fabric thoughtfully across his hands, checking for muncher holes, then wound it around his head and shoulders, creating a sort of hooded cape. Throws like that had been very popular two years before, until the Street-walkers' Tong had made them the badge of their profession. Rehur had not worn this one in some time, but hadn't been able to bring himself to discard the rich fabric. Now, looking out from its concealing folds, he was very glad he'd kept it. He found the gloves he'd bought to match it, and straightened, looking at his image in the long mirror that hung beside the door. A stranger, one of the hundreds of prostitutes that worked the Necropolis, stared back at him. Rehur nodded, already creating the character to match his new shape, and pushed open the door of the flat.

No one was moving in the hall. Rehur hurried down the stairs, not wanting to have to explain himself, and reached the street without meeting anyone. The May-apple lay on the eastern edge of the Necropolis, not far from one of the smaller greengates. It was a long walk, and the Broad Street trams, running along the Necropolis's north-south axis, wouldn't shorten it. The actor sighed, still angry with himself for oversleeping, and set off for the Nezumi Square.

The streets were unusually empty for the Necropolis after Sunset. Rehur frowned, and quickened his steps a little. Broad Street was a little busier, knots of people moving along its bright length, but here and there there were gaps in the line of lights, where a building was still shuttered. That was unheard of—the Necropolis's businesses had to open every hour of every Dark, to make up for the business lost during the long Day—and Rehur found himself looking back, half expecting to see the owners appear to remove the shutters and switch on the working lights. A tram stopped outside Rita's Rest, long the most popular of the Broad Street bars, but only a few people got off.

Rehur shook his head, and looked away, glancing toward the southern end of the street. There were even fewer people moving there, but nearly all the buildings were lit. As he watched, a group emerged from one of the unlit buildings, first four people together, and then two more who lagged behind. The four watched from the center of the street while the two lowered the shutters, making no move to help. Only when the building's lights came on did they turn away. They were wearing lumpy battledress, Rehur realized belatedly: Brandr troops, making sure life went on as usual. He shivered, and hurried on across the street. At the head of the side street, he couldn't stop himself from looking back. The four were watching him, but they were too far away, in the dim light, for him to see their expressions. He turned his head away, the movement excruciatingly casual, and made himself walk three blocks before looking back again. The Brandr were nowhere to be seen.

He took the long way to the May-apple anyway, doubling back through the Fountain Square. The water was beginning to freeze around the edges of the basin, reflecting the flaming Sunset sky. He paused, pretending to stare at the famous sight, and knew miserably that he was overacting. No one was following him.

It was only two more blocks to the May-apple, down a quiet, well-lit side street. A tall woman, masked and wrapped in a slit-backed coat, was leaving the building as Rehur approached. He looked away politely as she passed, and turned into the alley that led to the ghost-entrance on the building's side. The door opened instantly to his signal, and an adolescent looked out at him. She couldn't have been older than seventeen, and Rehur's eyes went immediately to her collar. She wore a medium's badge, and he sighed, relieved.

"Can I help you?" the girl asked. Her voice was perfectly polite, but there was a hint of wariness beneath the refinement.

"I'd like to see Lulan," Rehur answered.

The girl licked her lips uneasily, and did not answer. It was no wonder the girl was nervous, Rehur thought, with everything that's happened, but I don't understand why she's on duty at all. Shoba, May-apple's regular medium, occasionally let his daughter take over when business was light, but this hardly seemed the time.

"She's engaged," the girl said at last, drawing out the words. "Can't it wait?"

Rehur shook his head, beginning to be infected by the girl's nervousness. "I'm afraid not."

The girl didn't move from where she stood, blocking the door. "Who's calling, then?"

The actor hesitated, wondering if he should lie. But Lulan wouldn't recognize a false name, and his own name would at least get him a hearing. "Tell her Rehur. I'm with Witchwood."

"Rehur," the girl repeated, and stepped back into the entranceway, pulling the heavy door with her. Rehur followed her into an empty waiting room, and stopped at her gesture.

"If you'll wait here," she said, as though repeating a lesson, "I'll tell the conciliatrix you're here."

Rehur murmured agreement, and seated himself on one of the cushioned benches. The girl slipped away, closing the painted door tightly behind her. Rehur leaned back against the silk-covered wall, resigning himself to a long wait. Very faintly, he could hear the murmur of conversation in the gaming rooms, and the clatter and ping of the various machines. The May-apple seemed to be doing a normal business, despite everything. The actor sighed, wishing there were a chronograph in the otherwise opulently furnished room. He was due back at the Matador by the eighteenth hour for the final rehearsal—not that it mattered all that much, he thought bitterly. Rowan and

Ash had already made the puppet that was the real lead villain; he was only on stage to fill up the court scene.

The painted door opened then, cutting off his train of thought. A rather harassed-looking man beckoned from the doorway. So Shoba's finally condescended to show himself, Rehur thought, but stood obediently.

"Lulan'll see you now," the medium said, with a faint, unhappy frown. "She asked me to apologize for keeping you waiting, but she had unexpected visitors."

"I'm grateful she can see me at all," Rehur said. He followed the medium up the narrow ghost-stairs, his feet sinking soundlessly in the black carpet. He could hear voices, growing louder as they neared the top, but he couldn't quite make out the words. Then they had reached the landing, and Shoba gestured politely for the ghost to precede him into the little antechamber. The door into Lulan's office was halfway open, and Rehur could see, beyond Lulan's expensively robed shoulders, the dull grey of Brandr battledress.

The actor froze for an instant, then made himself continue on into the dimly lit antechamber, trying to move with unforced ease. He seated himself on a tambour just out of the Brandr officer's line of sight, hoping the man had not noticed the sudden hesitation. Behind him, Shoba whispered a curse and moved to close the door. Lulan's shoulders twitched, but she kept talking smoothly.

"—always cooperate with the civil authority, but frankly, sor, this is a Tong house. I'm only the conciliatrix—"

"I understand," the officer interrupted. He stepped forward, reaching past the conciliatrix to catch the closing door. "And I am sorry to have interfered with your work." He was standing full in the doorway now, staring frankly at the hooded actor. Rehur hesitated, then, trusting to his makeup and the poor lighting, lifted nerveless hands to his hood, pushing it back to expose the ghostmark on his forehead. The officer lifted an eyebrow, and Rehur made himself meet that inquiring gaze with wide-eyed innocence.

Shoba said hastily, "An audition, sor, he's looking for. For the ghost-wing."

"I see." The officer's tone gave nothing away. He turned back to Lulan, still punctiliously polite. "Again, I'm sorry to have troubled you during working hours. I hope you'll think about what I said."

"Of course," Lulan answered. She walked with him to the office's other door, smiling graciously. "This is a Tong house, which means voting, but I do have some influence. I'll do what I can."

"You're most kind," the officer said, and bowed himself out. Lulan closed the door behind him, and then, with a decisive gesture, pressed the lockplate.

Shoba said quickly, "Ama, I'm sorry. I thought I'd closed that door."

Lulan glared at him. "You're a fool, Shoba, and you always have been. Get out, we'll talk about this later."

The medium bowed and backed away hurriedly. Lulan took a deep breath, visibly calming herself. Rehur said, "I hope I haven't gotten you into trouble, Lulan."

The conciliatrix shook her head, still frowning, but beckoned the actor into the room. She waved vaguely at the chairs and tambours scattered around the opulent office, and seated herself behind her executive's desk. Rehur pulled one of the leather-covered chairs a little closer to the desk, but waited until Lulan had finished punching security codes into the desk's built-in systems.

"Now we can talk," she said, finally. "What brings you here, Rehur?"

"What did they want?" the actor asked, in the same moment.

"What do you think?" the conciliatrix said, and snorted. "They know the Family comes here; they want me to be sure there's no trouble. I repeat, what can I do for you, Rehur?"

The actor took a deep breath, and launched into an explanation of Maturin's requests. Unconsciously, almost, he borrowed the idiom of the holoplays, and when Lulan responded in kind, he borrowed more freely, building on the old themes of kinship and duty. When he had finished, the conciliatrix leaned back in her chair, her broad face set into stern, severe lines.

"So," she said, after a long moment, "we still have a genarch." There was a deep satisfaction in her voice. She shook herself, and went on, almost briskly, "Of course I'll do what the medium asks—God send this Maturin's more use than Shoba is. If they need shelter, they can come here. I've rooms for them, nobody would suspect it. The

Patriarch can depend on me. I'll see that the Family knows he's claimed his place, too—I'll make sure of it." Her spate of talk dried as quickly as it had appeared. After a moment, when it seemed the conciliatrix had nothing more to say, Rehur cleared his throat, ready to take his leave. Lulan didn't seem to hear.

"Fifteen years old," she said quietly, almost to herself. "And our Patriarch." She looked directly at the actor, shaking her head. "What's the world coming to, Rehur, that all he's got to help him are a ghost and a *para'an?*"

"And Maturin," Rehur protested.

"A medium and a spacer, two off-worlders and a *para'an* not even of our kin." Lulan gave a twisted smile. "And us. What is the world coming to?"

Rehur made his way back to his flat in an unaccountable state of depression, despite Lulan's agreeing to help Alkres. The Sunset light was fading from the sky, and lay in a smoldering band along the eastern horizon; overhead, Agamemnon swelled toward full. The twilight made everything ghostly and indistinct, draining even the lighted signs of some of their vitality. The streets were even emptier than they had been, and Rehur quickened his steps, eager to be home.

A knot of people had gathered on the building's stoop, gesturing with actors' freedom as they talked. Rehur checked, then recognized them as various of his neighbors, and made himself approach. Nodding a greeting, he started up the stairs past them, but Witchwood's red-haired musician called after him.

"Have you heard the news, Rehur?"

The actor paused reluctantly, but turned back so as not to arouse suspicion. "I've heard," he said, and his voice cracked on the words. "Rohin's true-dead." It was the first time he'd said those words, and a wave of grief washed over him. Saying it aloud, he believed it, completely and fully, and the loss was even more painful than he'd feared.

"I am sorry," Belit said, and the others—all from Witchwood, except for Ume-Kai—murmured their condolences as well. The worn formulae steadied Rehur, and he managed a wry smile.

"It's just as well for you, then, that the theaters are closed." That was Solvar, who generally played second villain. The touch of malice in his voice cleared Rehur's thoughts completely.

"Closed? What do you mean?"

"Exactly that," Solvar said, easily riding over the others' confused answers. He had been a Berngard, of the Axtell Kinship, and had no particular stake in Main Continent quarrels. "The Destiny council has decided to close everything—theaters, cabarets, bars and all—for at least three calendar-days."

"As a token of mourning," the third-lead Disa interjected.

Belit snorted. "More like trying to figure out what to do. The whole council's Ingvarrs, Halex Kindred."

Solvar smiled. "Mourning, nothing. They closed because the Brandr captain told them to."

Ume-Kai turned a doll's face toward the smaller man. He was in deshabille—woman's face and man's clothes: word of the closings had caught him dressing for the promenade. "Where did you get that story, Solvar?"

"From Gilder, then, and she heard it from Halsom Ingvarr in the gatekeepers' office," Solvar retorted.

Ume-Kai made a face, silenced, and there were thoughtful nods all around the circle. That channel, from civil servant to his *para'an* cousin who ran the Old Garret Theater, was usually reliable.

Belit said, "Whatever the reason, it means we lose our contract." She glanced up at Rehur, standing on the step above her, and gave an apologetic shrug. "I know that's nothing to your loss, Rehur, but who needs more trouble on top of it? I already spoke to Rowan, though. The Matador's cancelled the contract, so there's no pay for any of us."

"And no rehearsal, of course," Disa said, with a self-mocking grin.

The Witchwood Company had always lived hand to mouth. Rehur shrugged. "We'll manage. But thanks, Belit."

"Rehur." Ume-Kai laid a hand on the younger actor's sleeve, blue eyes registering and assessing the other's unusual makeup. "I don't know if it's true, but I heard—" He hesitated briefly, to calculated effect, and Rehur saw the quick, malicious glance toward Solvar.

"I heard," Ume-Kai continued, "that the Brandr haven't accounted for all your Kindred, not everybody that should have been at the Tower. Perhaps . . ." He let his voice trail off, and Solvar made a disbelieving noise.

Rehur stood for a second, caught between laughter and tears. This was almost certainly Lulan's work, spreading the rumor as she'd promised—the conciliatrix never wasted time—but even so. . . . He shook the thought away. Rohin was dead, he had Maturin's word on it, but the minne's suggestion had been—mostly—well meant. "Thanks, Ume," he said, and to his horror his voice broke on a sob. He turned away, blinded by sudden tears, and fumbled his way into the building.

Inside his own flat, he slammed the door behind him, then stood for a long moment before switching on the lights, fighting for control. Rohin is dead, he told himself almost angrily, but Alkres is alive, and needs you. And the Brandr know he's alive—why else would they have been at the May-apple?—and that will eventually mean a search. Emotions at bay again, Rehur turned on the lights, and then the heating coil at the foot of the stove-bed. He went into the bathroom and washed away the heavy makeup, then unwound the crimson throw and put it carefully away. He settled himself against the stove-bed's pillows, feet stretched toward the slowly warming coil, and tried to think clearly. He had to get in touch with Maturin, tell the medium that Lulan was willing to help, and that the Brandr were patrolling the Necropolis—but the comnet was too easily monitored, and the Brandr were bound to be watching all traffic in and out of the Necropolis.

Rehur buried his head against his knees, wishing, not for the first time, that he were as clever at intrigue as the lead-villains he played. In another hour or three, the last of the Sunset sky would have faded—but without the crowds moving in and out of the greengates to mask him, would he dare try to reach the flat where Maturin was hiding? There was too much chance he'd be spotted, even with the makeup; he wasn't even sure if the Brandr at the May-apple had been taken in by it. There were people he would trust with the message, but he had no way of proving to Maturin that they were to be trusted. By the same token, the comnet was quick, but it was easily monitored and traced, and the Brandr would have to be stupid not to have put a watch on it. No, he thought, he would have to risk carrying the message himself.

But not just yet. He sighed, and edged closer to the glowing coil, knowing it was fear that chilled him so. The *para'an*, the tug pilot—Guil ex-Tam'ne, her name was—didn't seem to be a fool; he would have to trust her to stay put until the Dark deepened and he could slip out of the Necropolis in safety.

A knock at the door interrupted his bleak thoughts. Lifting his head, he called, "Who's there?"

"Belit." The musician's voice was hesitant. "I brought some tea?"

Rehur rose quickly to unlock the door. "Come in, and welcome."

The redhead's smile was almost apologetic as she stepped into the flat. "If you'd rather not have company, say. I won't be hurt." She lifted the insulated pot, and the box of sandwiches she held in her other hand. "But I thought, you wouldn't want to cook, and you ought to eat. . . ."

"Belit, thank you," Rehur said, with all the warmth he could muster. "This is good of you." He pulled over another of the wheeled storage boxes and rummaged in the standing cabinet for a pair of mugs, then took the sandwiches and put two of them into the cooker to toast. "Please stay. I'd rather be with someone."

"Of course," Belit said. She poured two mugs of tea while Rehur adjusted the cooker, and then the actor seated himself opposite her, resting both elbows on the scarred table top. They drank in silence, Belit's quiet presence immensely comforting.

"Thanks, Belit," Rehur said again, after a while, and then, as the cooker chimed the end of its cycle, added, "No, I'll get it." He had just opened the cooker when there was another knock at the door.

"Who's there?"

"Solvar."

Rehur sighed, and Belit rolled her eyes, but there was nothing either could do without being unreasonably rude. And that, Rehur thought, making a face, could be fatal in a small puppet company. He snapped off the lock and pulled back the door, saying, "What is it, Sol—"

The words died on his lips as he saw who else stood

there, almost hiding Solvar behind their bulk. Three big men, no, four, all in the grey Brandr battledress, flanked by a man who wore the black-hand badge of a medium.

"Rehur, I'm sorry," Solvar began, and the tallest man, who carried an officer's wand in his belt, said to the medium, "Shut him up."

The medium made a curt gesture, and Solvar slunk away. "You, woman, out," the medium went on, jerking a thumb at Belit.

"I'm *para'an* of Fyfe in Fyfe," Belit countered warily, rising to her feet. "What's your business with him?"

"No business of yours, *para'*," one of the soldiers rumbled, and the officer said, "Get out."

Belit hesitated, and Rehur said, dry-mouthed, "Go on, Belit."

The musician did as she was told, but slowly, looking back as she went. Rehur folded his arms across his chest, trying to hide his fear. "What do you want?" he asked again, looking at the medium.

"These gentlemen want to know where your cousin is," the medium answered, with a rote courtesy almost as terrifying as threats.

"My cousins are dead, true-dead," Rehur answered, with a touch of bitterness.

"The ult'eir Alkres is alive," the medium answered. "Where is he?"

"I don't know," Rehur began, and the officer cut in.

"Tell him not to lie."

"You would be advised to tell the truth," the medium said.

"I'm a dead man," Rehur protested, with all the innocence he could muster. "How could the ult'eir come to me and live?"

"Tell him," the officer said grimly, "that he'll be true-dead himself if he doesn't stop wasting my time." He held up his hand when the medium would have repeated his words. "Tell him I know he's been in contact with the ult'eir, that he's been trying to cause trouble with Lulan of the May-apple. Tell him, too, that I'm not a patient man."

Rehur waited while all that was repeated to him, hugging himself in a vain attempt to stop the shaking. It's no use, a voice was saying in his head, it's no use, they spotted you, they *know*. . . . When the medium had finished, he took a deep breath, and shook his head. "I don't know where he is," he said again. "There must be some mistake." Even to himself, the words sounded weak and unconvincing.

"Persuade him," the officer said, indifferently, and nodded at the biggest of the soldiers. The medium laid one hand on the badge at his throat, then touched the soldier's mouth and hands, ritually conveying his own power to the other. Rehur took a step backward, knowing there was nowhere to run, and the soldier moved with unexpected speed, catching the actor in a wrestler's grip. Rehur gave a gasp of pain. The soldier calmly adjusted his hold, and doubled both the actor's wrists almost to his shoulder blades, holding them there with one huge hand. He twisted the other hand in Rehur's hair and drew his head sharply back, saying, "Answer the captain's question."

"I don't know," Rehur wailed, and the soldier gave him a shake that threatened to snap his neck or pop his arms from their sockets.

"Wait," the captain said. "Medium, your sanction?"

The medium repeated the ritual gesture. When the transfer was complete, the captain stepped forward, pulling something from his pocket. He kept his hand closed around it until he stood within easy reach of Rehur, then brought his hand up in front of his prisoner's face, slowly opening his fingers. "Do you see what this is?"

Rehur's eyes were fixed on the ugly little box. The soldier hissed, "Answer the captain."

"Yes," Rehur whispered obediently. The soldier shook him again, and the actor added, "It's a laser knife." In spite of his efforts, his voice trembled.

The captain studied him dispassionately. "I understand you're an actor, a puppet actor. Listen to me, then, if you want to go on working. I will ask you again where the ult'eir's hidden, and for every lie I will mark you, face and body." He tilted his head to one side. "They can do a lot with puppets, but I don't think even the best operators can hide the marks this leaves."

Rehur could feel himself shaking in the soldier's grip, and closed his eyes as the captain placed the head of the knife against his cheek. The focus bead was very cold against his skin. It would scar, at its lowest power it would leave scars that would never fade, that could never be hidden—he would never work again. . . . The captain's voice seemed to come from a great distance.

"Where is the ult'eir?"

Rehur choked, tried to pull his head away from the gentle touch of the knife, but the soldier held him motionless.

"I will count to five," the captain said, "and then I will push the button. One."

Rehur counted a dozen of his own quick heartbeats before the Brandr captain spoke again.

"Two."

Rehur's nerve broke. "Stop," he cried, and caught his breath quickly, for fear the captain hadn't heard. "Stop. I'll take you there, you can't get in without me, but *don't.*" Miraculously, the knife lifted from his face.

"You see?" the captain said, to no one in particular, and pocketed the knife. "Bring him."

The soldier shifted his grip, keeping one of Rehur's arms doubled behind him, then shoved the actor ahead of him out of the flat. Rehur stumbled down the stairs, still breathing in painful sobs, almost too terrified to think. He couldn't lead them to Alkres, to Maturin, he couldn't—but if he didn't, the captain would make good his threat, and— He was suddenly aware that they were in the street outside the building. The soldier shook him.

"Which way?" That was the medium, resuming his proper function.

Rehur stared at him, unable to make his frozen brain work, either to tell the truth or to invent a plausible lie. Behind him, remotely, he heard scraping, as someone opened a stairwell window to see the fun.

"Which way?" the medium asked again. In the same instant, something hissed sharply, and the Brandr captain pitched backward onto the metalled street. A crossbow bolt jutted under his ribs. There was another hiss, and a second bolt grazed Rehur's arm, then lodged deep in the side of the soldier who held him. That man gave a choked cry and released his hold, sinking slowly to the ground. Rehur stared at him, unable for a moment to understand what was happening.

"Rehur, run!" That was Belit, leaning back from the window, jerking at the winch of her double-slide hunting bow. "Run, damn you!"

The other soldier had unslung his rifle, and fired by instinct at his attacker. Belit ducked back, but the bolt splattered against the window frame. The second survivor, smarter than the first, turned his rifle toward Rehur. Belit cursed him, and fired. The bolt, half-cocked and badly aimed, barely grazed his shoulder, but it spoiled his aim, and his shot crackled into the road at Rehur's feet.

"Run!" Belit shrieked again.

The last shot snapped Rehur out of his trance. He turned and fled down the long street, weaving to spoil the soldiers' aim. All along the street, windows and doors flew open, and the air filled with questions and curses. From a window below Belit's came a wordless, ululating cry: Ume-Kai, waking the dead to this infringement of their privileges, rousing them to riot against the Brandr. Rehur put his head down, and ran.

We are the Angry Ones.
—Aeschylus, *The Eumenides,* 499

Chapter 10: Trey Maturin

We kept the newscasts on all the calendar-day, listening for any hint of trouble. To me, the droning voices of the announcers, with their monotonous appeals for calm and their continuous reports of quiet throughout the Halex Mandate, conveyed nothing of any use. Guil, with long experience of the Destiny newssystems, translated freely, but her interpretation wasn't particularly encouraging. The Branch-lands offered no resistance to the continuing Brandr presence. After everything Herself had done to help them, I had expected better—but then, there was no genarch available to lead them, and the Holders refused to act. It was hard to do anything, yet, without leaders. Only in Destiny and a few of the Prosperities mining towns were there any reports of unrest. None of it was serious, just shouting and rock-throwing, but nonetheless, I was somewhat encouraged by the reports. Guil shook her head.

"They wouldn't report trouble if it wasn't under control."

"Where the hell are they getting enough men to do all this?" Leith muttered.

Guil shrugged. "Every adult's under arms-obligation, remember. And they've got the Fyfe to help."

"And our Branch Holders aren't doing anything." Alkres, who had spent most of the day sitting on Guil's couch playing with an electronic strat-game, looked up for the first time in hours. "Trey, do you think telling them I'm alive will make them fight?"

"I hope so," I said. I hoped, too, that Rehur would contact me soon, let me know if we had another refuge. It was looking as though it would be a while before we found a Holder we could trust—and I was not going to take Alkres into any of the Holds until the Holders committed themselves.

A little after the fifteenth hour, the newscast reported that Yslin Rhawn had asked for an emergency meeting of the Ship's Council. We all froze, even Alkres, and the strat-game fell silent at last. Cautiously, Guil reached to increase the volume.

"If they broadcast the tape," she whispered, "we're in trouble."

For a moment, I didn't understand what she meant, but then the tape clicked on. Shorn of the measured rhetoric, Yslin Rhawn's speech asked only for the Ship's Council to consider the Brandr Patriarch's accusations. He said nothing of their attack or the destruction of the Tower. Clearly, he was leaving his way clear to accept the Brandr offer of the genarchy, and I waited for the other Holders to register a protest. One by one, the answers trickled in: Fyfe and Axtell agreed at once to the meeting, neither genarch mentioning the attack; the Ansson Holder also consented, stiffly, but without filing a protest. Asbera Ingvarr made a veiled reference to "present difficulties," but agreed. Brandr sent a curt acknowledgement. That left only the Orillon, and given the communications lag, we couldn't expect their answer for another half hour at the earliest. The newscast burbled on, talking about issues and precedents. With a violent movement, Guil cut the volume.

"Excuse me." Alkres stood, and very carefully placed the strat-game on the table. His face was set and white, lips pinched together to hold in tears. Without waiting for any answer, he disappeared into Guil's spare bedroom. I started after him, not quite knowing what I'd do, and Leith shook her head at me.

"Let him be a little."

I hesitated, but as an adolescent, Leith had commanded other adolescents, and ought to know what she was doing. I sat down again, hoping she was right.

The Orillon answer came promptly—the first good news we'd had all day. The Orillon Patriarch agreed to the meeting, and announced his intention of filing a formal protest against the Brandr for their questionable behavior in pursuing their feud. It was the first sign of support from any quarter, and Leith sighed explosively.

"Thank God there's somebody honest in this system!"

Guil gave a curious shrug, and looked away. She was part of the Orillon Kinship, after all, and I wondered just what she meant by that gesture. Before I could ask, however, Leith pointed toward the spare bedroom.

"You might want to tell him, now."

I nodded, a little reluctantly, but had to bow to her superior knowledge. I tapped on the doorframe, and opened the door a little way without waiting for an answer. Alkres was lying face down on the narrow pallet that served both as spare bed and as a couch. He didn't move until I said, "May I come in?"

He sat up then, drawing the back of one hand angrily across his face. "All right." It wasn't a very gracious answer, but it was permission.

Guil used the room for storage and as a workroom, as well as a spare bedroom, and the shortest wall was filled with closed and open storage boxes. There were a couple of other boxes scattered across the floor, and a comfortable working chair stood in one corner beneath a powerful standing lamp. I seated myself on one of the boxes that had a padded top, and said, "We've heard from the Orillon Patriarch. He's said he's going to protest to the Council."

"Wonderful," Alkres said sarcastically. "Why aren't my people doing that?"

I wished I knew the answer to that myself. "I don't know. They've been hard hit, remember—"

"Not as hard hit as we have," Alkres said.

"Not in the same way," I said, groping for the right words, "but pretty hard, all the same. They've lost their leaders, either killed or driven underground like you, and the person who ought to step in is looking out for his own advantage. It's no wonder they don't know what to do. You can't blame them for being cautious."

"I can," Alkres said fiercely. "And after all Herself did for them, too. They're breaking the code, and I'll get them for it. Especially Yslin Rhawn."

"Alkres," I said, and put every gram of conviction I could muster into my voice. "You're the Patriarch now, you can't afford that kind of talk. You have to lead them, not blame them—not now."

"You're a mediator, you have to talk that way." Alkres glared at me, unreconciled. "They've broken the code, and they have to pay for it."

"The code was never meant to deal with anything like this. There's no precedent, is there, for a whole Branch being destroyed? Especially not the mainline Family." I took a deep breath, and finally said what had been on my mind since we left Federston. "I think this is going to have to be settled outside the code."

"The code's the law!" Alkres's voice was outraged. "How can you settle anything without law?"

"There's law," I said, slowly, "and there's justice, and then there're the human beings who have to manipulate those abstractions. Sometimes you have to compromise—and improvise—to hold things together. And that's what's really important, holding things together. Yes, I'm a mediator, yes it's my job to say that, but I mean it."

Alkres stared at me, silenced but not convinced. After a moment, he said, "I want a cup of tea."

He was the genarch, I reminded myself—in fact, as well as name, head of a substantial local-planetary government. And I was his employee. I had done what I could, for now. I nodded, and we went back into the main room.

Guil brewed tea for all of us, and brought out a tray of the salty snacks called *sannin*. I wasn't precisely hungry, but I chewed on a few of the tough strips anyway, knowing I might need the calories. Leith paced back and forth, stopping periodically to listen to the newscast. Alkres played with his strat-game until I thought the beeps and clicks would drive me crazy. I stood it for as long as I could, but after two hours I was ready to smash the stupid thing. I was about to say so when Leith said, "Listen!"

There was a note in her voice that stopped us all. She

adjusted the volume, and the newscaster's voice poured into the room. "— stadtholder has agreed to the Demi-heir's request that the Necropolis be closed until the present uncertainties are resolved. She has also agreed to consider the further requests for a clock-curfew, and that the Demi-heir's men be allowed to supplement the regular police forces in the city."

There was more, but it was drowned by Guil's feral yelp. "If that doesn't get through to them, nothing will."

Leith said, " 'Supplement the regular police,' huh? Sounds to me like they're gearing up for a search."

"To me, too," I said, and wished we would hear from Rehur. "We'd better be prepared to move fast."

"There's always the port," Leith said again. "You'd be safe there."

"I'm not running away," Alkres said.

"We don't have to go anywhere," Guil snapped. She looked at me. "The port complex will be safer than the city, though, if it comes to a search. They won't want to offend off-worlders."

"We'll wait and see what happens," I said firmly. "Keep the volume up, will you, Leith?"

Rehur arrived on the heels of the first newscasts that reported trouble in the Necropolis. He leaned against the wall as Guil closed the door behind him, breathing heavily, his eyes as huge and mad as they had been when he played Belos. There was a bloody tear in the sleeve of his tunic.

"I did what you asked, Trey," he said, between gasps, "but it won't do any good."

"What do you mean?" I said. "What's happened?"

The ghost gave me a mirthless grin, but let Guil pull him toward a seat, wincing as she touched the injured arm. With an effort, Alkres remained in his seat, looking toward the comnet and the newscaster's voice, but I could see his shoulders twitch every time his cousin spoke.

"Off with it," the *para'an* said, and touched the collar of the actor's tunic. Rehur complied, wincing, and I caught a glimpse of a nasty cut through the ripped and bloodied undershirt. Guil whistled softly to herself, and tore the sleeve away, exposing a painful-looking gash just below the tattooed band. "Crossbow?"

Rehur nodded, and she vanished into the bathroom, to emerge a moment later with a battered aidkit. As she went to work on the cut, Rehur said, "When they closed the theaters—no, I'd better start with Lulan." He caught his breath as Guil applied a disinfectant wand to the cut, and went on slowly, "I went to Lulan of the May-apple, Trey, like I told you I would. She said she'd help—I knew she would—but there were Brandr there when I got there, looking for him—" He jerked his head at Alkres, who was still struggling not to acknowledge the ghost's presence. "—and I guess they recognized me, figured out what I was there for. They came to my flat. . . ." His voice slowed then, in a way that had nothing to do with the *para'an's* deft touch with the aidkit.

I said, "They threatened you?"

Rehur nodded. There was more to it than that, I felt sure, but I would not press him. "Yeah. Belit, our synth-man, shot two of them—she keeps a hunting crossbow in her rooms—and I got away. They're fighting all over the Necropolis now."

"Can they win?" Leith said, quietly.

Rehur shrugged. "I don't know—I doubt it." He looked at me. "Trey, they'll use this as an excuse to crack down on the rest of the city, you know that."

"He's right," Guil said, adding a last piece of tape to the actor's bandage. "We can't stay here."

"We go to the port," Leith said. "And we get off-world." She met Alkres's eyes steadily, ignoring his cry of outrage. "It's your only chance, Patriarch."

"Go where, Leith?" I asked, hoping she wasn't playing the captain again.

Leith grinned suddenly, a reckless, fighting grin. "Electra. Who else has made a protest? The Orillon may not support you, but I bet they'll give you sanctuary."

She had a point, though I distrusted the expression on her face. Then I shook myself. She was right—there weren't any other alternatives any more, and the sooner we left, the better. I opened my mouth to say as much, and felt the floor quiver underfoot. The whole building seemed to stagger forward, then sway back into place, upper floors following reluctantly behind the lower.

"Hell's teeth!" Guil reached for the comnet controls,

manipulating the service channels. "I forgot the damn warning."

Enlightened and appalled, I reached for the almanac discarded among a stack of reading tapes. I flipped through the crudely printed pages until I found the day's date, and fixed my eyes on the sketch, where the moons chased each other around a set of concentric rings. Sure enough, all three were moving into syzygy, and the date was high-lighted in red, with the words "tremors and volcanic activity likely" printed to one side. It happened every twenty-four calendar days, of course, and the Geo/met office issued regular bulletins and warnings—but surely Destiny wasn't a particularly active area? The building shook again, a violent, sideways hopping, and I heard something fall and break in the kitchen.

"What's broken?" Rehur asked. I glanced at him, sur-prised he should worry about the *para'an*'s possessions, then realized he had meant something else entirely.

"The Seam's open," Guil answered, scanning the comnet's screen, "and the Heartlight. The Old Forge is quiet, and so's Big Bertha over in the Axtell Mandate. But I don't see any signs why we should be feeling it."

The Seam was the line of volcanic islands that marked a plate boundary in the middle of the Deeps, Orestes' larger ocean. It was regularly active during syzygy, I knew that much, as was the volcano known as the Heartlight. But Destiny was situated well away from all the known fault lines. . . .

Guil said, "Wait, here we go." She read from the words crawling across her screen. "The Lower Tolands fault is showing strain, and there have been several minor trem-ors with their epicenter in the Grand Shallows just south of the Toland Point. Inhabitants of the Jan and Brandr Holdings in the Brandr Mandate, the Charlot Holding in Fyfe Mandate, and Halex Holding in Halex Mandate, are advised to take yellow-warning precautions. Be sure to have drinking water on hand, et cetera, et cetera."

"It's going to be a bad close-passage," Alkres said, sound-ing subdued.

"The port, Guil," Leith said. "Is it closed?"

The *para'an* had already cleared her screen, and was typing an inquiry into the 'net. "Damn it, yes." She swung around to face us. "There's no choice—no one will be able to get off if the tremors keep up."

"If you can't," Leith said, "I can." She turned her head slowly, including all of us in her challenging stare. Pretense or not, I was very glad of her confidence. "I've done it in worse conditions," she went on. "And I can get us a ship."

Guil stirred at that. "Not *Pipe Major*—she's too big and clumsy."

"One of the tugs," Leith said. "I can do it."

"One-armed?" Guil asked, very quietly.

"If you'll copilot." Leith waited, and slowly, the *para'an* nodded. Leith swung around again, catching us all in her glance. "Who's with me, then?"

I had a sudden feeling of being caught up, not in a holoplay, but in one of the military films that were so popular on the Urban Worlds. For the first time, I understood their popularity: it was so easy to give command to the person with the superior knowledge, so natural to answer with the proper line. *I'm with you, Captain.* I realized abruptly that someone had said it. Alkres was standing now, face flushed and eager, ready to follow Leith to the end of this world.

"Good boy," Leith said, and looked at Guil. The *para'an* nodded again.

"And me."

My answer was next, according to whatever crazy script we were following, and quite suddenly I knew I didn't want to break with it. Leith *did* know what she was doing, even if she'd chosen cheap films for her model. She was giving us our only real chance to buy time and maybe escape from the trap the Brandr had set for the Halex. I said, as I must, "We'll do it your way, Leith."

That left only Rehur. I glanced at him, and saw him staring at us, half incredulous, half hysterically amused, and knew he'd recognized the scene as well. He pushed himself up out of his chair, favoring his injured arm, and said, "Sorry, people, not me."

I recognized the part, and my own laughter died. He was playing the native leader, the resistance worker, the infiltrator, the one who stays behind to fight the good fight—the second lead, always, the one who dies. He glanced at me sidelong, slow and mocking, and I knew he'd chosen it deliberately.

"Oh?" That was Leith, preternaturally calm.

"That's right." The building trembled again, less violently than either of the other tremors, but Rehur steadied himself against the nearest chair. "I'd be endangering Alkres. Look, I'm still dead, at least to him, and he can't risk breaking code. It's a thirty-six-hour flight to Electra, even at close approach, and if he's shut up all that time in a little tug with me and three other people who can see ghosts—well, how long will it be before he accidentally breaks code? We can't risk it."

He was right, and I paid him the compliment of feeding him his cue. "What will you do?"

"I'll go back to the Necropolis," he answered, steadily. "Ume-Kai'll take me in. Together we might be able to arrange some support for you, when you return." He crossed to the door, setting his hand on the controls, and his solemnity broke suddenly into an impish smile. "Thanks, Trey," he said, in an entirely new voice. "I never played second lead before." He put fingers to his lips, still smiling, and was gone.

The others were looking at me with varying degrees of confusion and annoyance. Before anyone could ask, I said, "We'd better get moving, Leith."

It didn't take long to gather our belongings: an extra tunic and undershirt for Alkres, borrowed from Guil, along with a cloth bag to put them in; a change of clothes for the tug pilot; Leith's campaign bag. I had my IDs and the clothes I stood up in, and was lucky to have that much; I would've been glad of a change of clothes, but Guil and I were not of a size.

The streets were unexpectedly crowded, the various squares in particular filled with people. In the rising light from Agamemnon, I could see that many of them carried chairs and folding lounges, or packed heated sleepsacks. Taking shelter from the earthquakes, I realized abruptly, watching a woman place a baby into a free-standing heated cradle. Despite Destiny's strict construction laws, people seemed to feel safer out from under the buildings. The tremors had brought us some good after all: it would be very hard to spot one more "family group" among the moving, nervous crowds.

Guil led us toward the port by the back streets, through the residential precincts, paralleling the High Street, but never venturing onto its dangerously well-lit width. Once, as we passed through the Loxian Market, crowded now with people from the neighboring precincts, we saw a group of Brandr soldiers, but they seemed more concerned with the trio of enterprising shopkeepers who had chosen to set up business out of pushcarts at the entrance to the square, and we slipped through without being noticed.

As we got closer to the port, Guil's pace slackened, and I saw her exchange glances with Leith. The captain nodded thoughtfully. "You're thinking of the bridges?"

"Yeah." Guil frowned, and drew us to a stop in the lee of a windowless warehouse. There hadn't been any tremors for some time now, but still I had to make a real effort to keep myself from stepping out of that looming shadow. I turned my back on the brick walls, but that was worse. I could practically feel their potential weight, a breathing, hovering menace.

"They're bound to be watching," Guil went on.

Leith rubbed her gloved wrist. "You and I both have business in the port, and we can prove it. Trey's obviously an off-worlder—or you will be, Trey, if you take off that cape of yours. You said you managed to pass Alkres off as your own son?"

"Yes, but that was before they were sure Alkres was alive," I answered. "They must've gotten a photo of him by now, sent it to all the troops."

"Not necessarily," Leith said. "They're pretty disorganized."

Alkres tugged at my sleeve. "The last formal picture I was in was taken a couple of calendar-years ago. I've grown a lot since then."

That would make a difference, I thought, and nodded. Children change quickly, especially at his age.

"I think you can pull it off, then," the captain went on. She took a step back, surveying us with narrowed eyes. "Let Guil wear your cloak, and take off those gloves."

Reluctantly, I did as I was told, handing the cloak to the

para'an and stuffing the gloves into my pocket. It was very cold without them—I had been spoiled by the heavy furs. Leith nodded to herself, still staring, then bent and rummaged one-handed through her campaign bag. At last she straightened with an exclamation of triumph, and held out a battered leather hat, brimless, with an almost unreadable unit pin clipped to one side. Alkres took it warily.

"Wear that," Leith continued, "and get rid of your gloves and belt—here, I'll take them."

Alkres complied without protest, and Leith stowed his belongings in the depths of her campaign bag. Almost as an afterthought, she pulled out her service blaster and belted it around her waist beneath her coat. She glanced again at Alkres, and tugged the hat a little lower over the boy's eyes.

"Well," she said, "you look a little more like an off-worlder now."

I studied the ult'eir with less confidence. Even in Oresteian dress, I have the bulk to make any origins pretty obvious—unless, of course, I'm wearing something as loose-fitting as my furry cloak—but Alkres was slightly built. Even letting the heavy tunic hang unbelted didn't give him the needed breadth of shoulder. Leith saw my expression and shrugged as if to say, "What else can we do?"

Guil said, "We'd better get going." Even as she spoke, the ground trembled underfoot. It was a weaker tremor than the others had been, barely strong enough to be felt, but we all stepped hurriedly out of the warehouse's shadow. Guil gave Leith another quick glance.

"Can you lift under these conditions?"

"I told you, yes," Leith answered, and smiled. "Trust me."

"I do," the *para'an* muttered, but not happily. She pointed toward the cross street ahead of us. "We'll have to take the main bridge."

The High Street was less crowded than the other streets we'd passed through: we had left the residential precincts behind. Still, there were a few people camped out on the pedestrian strip that edged the tram line. The trams themselves had stopped running. One was stopped just below the bridge turntable, and I could see people stretched out in its uncomfortable seats. The end of the bridge was bathed in the harsh light of a portable searchlight, and there were people in battledress in the shadows beyond. Fortunately, they weren't preventing traffic across the bridge—why should they, when the port itself was closed?

I caught Alkres's hand in mine, and whispered again, "Don't say anything if you can help it. Act shy."

"I will," the ult'eir whispered back, and tightened his grip on my hand.

Leith advanced on the bridge as though she hadn't seen the soldiers, and we followed, Guil hanging back a bit. As we stepped into the circle of light, a voice said, "Hold it."

The speaker stayed just out of the light herself, was little more than a long shadow distorted by the harness and power pack of an electric rifle. I paused at the edge of the circle, keeping Alkres a little behind me.

Leith said, "What's the problem now?" Her voice held just the right mix of impatience and worry.

"What's your business at the port?" the guard asked again.

"My ship's there," Leith answered. "Look, who are you to be asking?"

Alkres's hand tightened on mine, and there was an indistinct mutter from one of the other soldiers waiting in the shadows. The woman—presumably the officer in command of the detail—made a curt, chopping gesture, one hand flashing briefly in the light.

"We're supplementing the regular police force," she said smoothly. "You know the port's closed?"

Leith nodded. "My name's Moraghan. I'm captain of *Pipe Major*—the six-week mailship. We're not in our usual dock, and I'm worried about how she'll handle the shaking." Without being asked, she proffered her ID disk.

The guard officer took it, examined it for a moment, then passed it back again. The rainbow whorls of a Conglomerate-forces ID are supposed to be impossible to duplicate. She turned her attention to me. "Are you with her?"

Leith said, "They've asked for hardship passage out. I said I'd see if we had cabin space."

"Is that right?" The guard officer's eyes didn't waver from my face.

"That's right," I said. I fell back into the persona I'd used to enter Destiny, without stopping to think if it would be recognized. "My name's Mas Zeeman; this is my son Tannis."

"Your papers?"

I scowled. "I've told you people before, I don't have them any more. They burned up with the Halex Tower—no thanks to anybody we didn't burn with them."

The guard officer eyed us for a moment longer, then motioned us forward into the light. I did as I was told, drawing Alkres after me. The boy had the sense not to try to hide his face, but he shrank against me. I put my arm around his shoulders, feeling his tension, and wondered if he could hear my heartbeat. Leith had her hand very deep in the pocket of her coat—and then I realized it was no pocket, but a gun slit, and her hand was on the butt of her service blaster. It would be suicide, against half a dozen electric rifles. After a moment, Leith seemed to realize that, too, and very slowly eased her hand out of the pocket.

"Well?" The guard officer spoke without turning, but it was clear she wasn't talking to us. Another soldier leaned forward, saying something in a low voice. I caught only a couple of words—"photos," and then, "don't know"—but the officer shrugged, scowling.

"All right, all right. Much use you are." She put her hands on her hips, still frowning. "You three, you can pass. You, blondie, give me your name and business."

"Guil, ex-Tam'ne, *para'an* of Tam'ne in Orillon," the pilot answered, rather wearily. "I'm a tug pilot with the Port Authority. My instructions are to show up when we get a yellow alert from the Geo/Met Office."

It took all my strength to not look back as I followed Leith through the knot of soldiers onto the bridge itself. Guil's tone suggested she didn't particularly care whether she made it to the port or not, and I hoped the guard officer would accept her story.

"Captain!"

I was close enough to Leith to hear the sharp intake of breath. When she turned, however, face and voice were under perfect control.

"Yes?" She was polite, but there was a hint of the Peacekeeper's steel in her tone.

"Do you know her?" the guard officer asked, and jerked a thumb at Guil.

Leith gave me one sidelong glance, then took two steps back down the bridge toward the searchlight. "Yeah, I think so. Yes, she's brought *Pipe Major* in a couple of times." She waited with ostentatious patience while the guard officer gnawed her lip.

One of the soldiers muttered something, and the officer snapped to her decision. "All right, you can pass, *para'.*"

Guil gave a sigh, and hurried through the patch of light. Leith said loudly, meaning to be overheard, "If you're going to the port, Guil, why don't you walk with us?"

"Thanks, Captain," Guil said, as loudly, and we walked on.

The bridge seemed very dark after the brillance of the searchlight. Agamemnon's cold light reflected eerily from the fencing that curved up and over the walkway, closing us off from the river, and from the tramline to our left. The strip-lights that hung at intervals along the fence itself barely seemed to affect the ghostly radiance. The Ostlaer was very loud beneath us. I hoped there wouldn't be any more tremors while we were on the bridge.

Then we had passed the midpoint of the bridge, and started down the slope toward the port. Another tram was halted on the line just beyond the protective wall, its lights pointing ahead to the port's main entrance. There was no sign of any guard there, and I gave a sigh of relief.

"I didn't really think there would be," Leith said, "not with the Authority worried about off-world traffic all the time, but I'm glad to see I was right."

"You and me both," I said. We negotiated the turnstiles at the base of the bridge—the Port Authority preferred people to enter the port area by the tramlines—then followed the line toward the open gate. The tram was empty, abandoned, and the access roads and taxiways beyond were free of traffic. It was very different from the situation in the city itself, and I frowned.

"Where is everybody?"

"Inside, I hope," Leith answered.

"The port buildings are supposed to be earthquake-proof," Guil said, with only the lightest emphasis on the word "supposed." She looked at Leith. "Should we check the pilots' lounge first?"

The captain nodded. "And then transients' quarters. I want to find my crew."

The main lobby, with its uncomfortable pressed-foam chairs, was comparatively empty, occupied mostly by people waiting to use the autobank in the far corner. The upper floor, with its maze of offices, waiting rooms, and private lounges, was far more crowded. Off-world crews and off-worlders alarmed by the attack on the Tower mingled with Guil's colleagues from the tugs and the short-range lighters. Most of the crowd seemed to have resigned themselves to a long wait. The lucky ones, the ones whose guild or union maintained apartments in the complex, would be able to sleep there, in comfort if not in privacy; the rest—the vast majority, from what I could see—were considering themselves fortunate to stake a claim to one of the padded benches that dotted the corridors. I wasn't too surprised. The Oresteian trade would be very small compared to the usual Urban runs, except during the brief wool season. It wouldn't pay the smaller unions to keep quarters here.

We turned a corner, stepping around a dice game that was overflowing a cleaner's alcove, and Leith swore. "So much for getting to check the boards."

I looked over her shoulder, and ducked hastily back around the corner, almost tripping over one of the dice players. There was a crowd outside the main scheduling office, a crowd that held any number of familiar faces: the other off-worlders who'd worked for the Halex were still on-planet, stranded by the earthquakes.

Alkres said, "What's wrong?"

"People from the Tower, the other off-worlders," I said, keeping my voice low. "Leith, we can't risk being seen."

Already, a couple of the dice players were looking up at us with something more than idle curiosity. The captain nodded abruptly. "Right, this way."

We retraced our steps through the crowded corridors. When Leith hesitated, Guil took over, leading us down a flight of stairs and through a series of badly lit maintenance corridors. Finally, we emerged from that tangle at another stairway, and Guil nodded to it.

"The pilots' lounge's at the top," she said. "Just who are you looking for, Leith?"

"A man named Trivally Rhawn," the captain answered, and started up the stairs. "He's the maintenance supervisor for the tugs—"

"I know that," Guil growled.

Leith went on as if she hadn't spoken. "We're decent friends, though he's a better friend to my pilot, and he owes me a favor or two. I think I can talk him into letting me take a ship."

Alkres stirred at my side, then stopped abruptly, staring up the stairs. "He's a Rhawn," he protested.

"He's a spacer first," Leith answered, cutting off Guil's automatic answer.

Alkres looked dubiously at me, and I nodded, projecting all the confidence I could muster. "Leith knows the port. I think we should do it."

"Very well," the ult'eir said, with unconscious arrogance. Guil's lips thinned, but Leith gave a lopsided smile.

"Right, then," she said. "Let's go."

The pilots' lounge was busy, which I had gathered from Leith was an unusual state of affairs. We paused just inside the doorway, pretending to look for a table while Leith scanned the crowd. The darkly paneled room was dimly lit, shutters closed tight against the cold of the Dark. After the bright corridors, it was hard to see.

"Captain Moraghan!"

I saw Leith jump: clearly, it wasn't the voice she'd been expecting. She controlled herself instantly, and turned toward the speaker, saying, "Darah? What're you doing here?"

"Same thing you are, I bet, sir." The speaker was tall, for an off-worlder, and very dark. The plate and rosette of an artificial eye almost filled one side of his face. "I was worried about how the *Major*'d stand the shaking."

"How is it?" Leith asked.

"Pretty well. The shocks and gyros're holding nicely." He was looking us over with frank curiosity, greeting Guil with a smile and a nod, and Leith sighed.

"Darah, I want you to meet some friends of mine. Guil, you know already—"

"How could I forget her?" the stranger murmured, with a thoroughly sexy smile.

Leith ignored him. "—and this is Trey Maturin, a Conglomerate Mediator, and Alkres Halex. People, this is Darah Sabas, my chief pilot."

The smile had vanished from Sabas's face. "Alkres Ha—" He broke off abruptly, glancing over his shoulder, and lowered his voice almost to a whisper. "The kid— You haven't gotten mixed up in local politics, have you, Captain?"

Leith ignored that question, too. "Is your friend Trivally around?"

"Yeah." Sabas shook himself and tried to recover his earlier bantering style. "He's right here—at the corner table. We were hoping for some privacy."

"I want to talk to him." Leith gave Sabas a measuring look. "And I'll need your help, too, Darah."

"You got it, sir," Sabas said, for once without pretense. "Over here."

The man at the corner table looked up, frowning, at our approach, but then he saw Alkres, and his expression changed to one of appalled recognition. He started to say something, but Sabas cut him off.

"You remember my captain, Triv'—Captain Moraghan? She wants to talk to us."

Trivally glanced from Sabas to the captain, then fixed his eyes again on Alkres. "What about?" he asked warily. "The port's closed."

There was a single empty chair at the next table. Leith appropriated it with a word of apology—the couple at the other table, locked in a lingering kiss, hardly seemed to notice, but then the man gave an offhand wave and the woman broke free long enough to murmur an agreement— and swung it around to face the Oresteian. She seated herself and leaned forward, both forearms on the table, right hand pinning her left arm in place. Trivally, a brown-skinned, flat-faced man, watched her with a sort of fascination.

"I need your help," Leith said, quietly enough that her voice did not carry to the neighboring tables. Guil leaned casually against the back of the captain's chair, ice-blue eyes slitted in menace. "I want a ship."

"The port's closed," Trivally said again.

In the same instant, Sabas said, "A ship?"

"Shut up, Darah," Leith said, and was obeyed. She turned her attention back to the supervisor. "All that means to me is that you've got lots of ships on the ground, Maintenance Supervisor Rhawn. I want one of them—emergency business."

Trivally's eyes slid again to Alkres, standing now at my left hand. Leith nodded. "That's right," she said. "You know who he is."

"I can't do it," Trivally said again. "I'm sorry, Captain, it's just not possible. It's as much as my job is worth—and you're not even one of us."

Leith frowned, and I said, "Leith." The captain quieted instantly, and Guil gave me a curious look. I kept myself from smiling with an effort. This was a situation well covered by the code, and one that I could interpret to my—to Alkres's—advantage. It was a very pleasant feeling.

"Trivally Rhawn," I said, deliberately, "my name is Maturin. The Halex Medium. I call on you in the Kinship's name to help your patriarch."

Trivally looked at me with slowly widening eyes. I was implicitly threatening him with an accusation of code breaking—with death—and while there might seem to be little I could do to enforce my sanction, I was his Kinship's senior Medium, protector of his genarch. The code gave me rights and powers I didn't think he would be able to withstand. After a moment, he looked away, and I felt a surge of elation.

"The port's still closed," the supervisor protested. "I can give you a ship, sure, but you can't go anywhere."

"Oh, yes, I can," Leith said with a savage smile, and Trivally threw up his hands.

"On your head, then." He looked at me. "Medium, I—" He broke off abruptly, sighing, and bowed his head in submission. "As Himself wishes, Medium. So be it."

"Thank you," I said.

"Yes, thank you," Alkres said. "You do a lot to make up for Yslin."

"Yslin!" Trivally's mouth contorted as though he were

about to spit. "Sor, not all of us follow him, not even in the Rhawn Branch. Don't go off-world. We need you, to fight back."

"I'm not going far," Alkres answered. "Just to Electra— and I'll be back. Will you wait for me?"

"We'll wait," Trivally answered fervently.

It was another scene from the holoplays, and I cleared my throat, breaking the spell. "How soon can we leave? The Brandr were on our heels."

"At once," Trivally answered, and pushed himself to his feet.

We followed him from the bar, Sabas, in the rear, voicing some unintelligible protest. As we came out into the corridor, the words came clear.

"What about *Pipe Major*, Captain?"

Leith gave him an unloving grin. "She's all yours, Darah. To my mind, this is a class-one emergency, and I'm still under the Oath. I have to do this."

"But—"

Leith turned on him, her stare freezing him in his tracks. "Even if it wasn't a matter for the Oath, do you think I could leave them to manage? I'm needed here, a lot more than I ever was on the ship." She took a deep breath, fighting for control, and said, more calmly, "You have command of *Pipe Major*, Darah. I'll give you that in writing, if you want."

Sabas shook his head, his handsome face very sober. "That won't be necessary, sir," he said, with unexpected dignity. "I'll take over til you return. And good luck, sir."

Leith's expression eased a little, and she said, softly, "I misjudged you, Darah. Take care of things."

"I will," the pilot answered, but Leith hadn't waited for his reply. We left the pilot standing in the corridor, shaking his head.

The supervisor led us down another long staircase, and then into the maze of tunnels that connected the port buildings. We walked for some time through the white-painted halls—I had no idea where we were in relation to the main building—and then emerged, with startling suddenness, in the Port Authority hangar.

It was a huge building, the ceiling at least three stories above our heads, the far wall almost infinitely distant in the poor lighting. Six of the slim lighters stood with their noses to the dock ports, apparently just waiting to be towed onto the taxiway; a seventh ship—one of the squat, conventional tugs—stood on its massive tracked platform at the end of the row. All were attached with multiple umbilicals to installations in the walls. Trivally waved his hand resignedly at the line of ships.

"Which one do you want, Captain?" His voice echoed oddly in the vast emptiness.

Leith rubbed her wrist again, staring at the waiting ships. Before she could answer, however, there was the sound of a door opening and closing somewhere in the hangar, and a voice called, "Who's there? Is that you, Triv'?"

"One of my technicians," Trivally said hastily, in an undertone. "She's a Halex, too." He lifted his voice. "Over here, Nezera!"

A figure emerged from the shadows, tall and thin like all the Oresteians, and resolved itself into a young woman barely older than Rehur, with a mane of black hair swept up and back into an untidy topknot. There was a wildness in her face that reminded me of Ixora.

"What's up, boss?" she asked, a little warily, her eyes sweeping over us. "You probably shouldn't be bringing people here in a yellow alert—"

"Never mind that," Trivally said.

The woman shrugged, and said, with deliberate malice, "It's your funeral."

"Nezera," Trivally said firmly, "Himself has asked for my help, and I'm charging you, on guild-oath as well as the blood tie, to help me."

"Himself?" Nezera's eyes fixed on Alkres, and widened slowly. "I beg pardon, sor, I didn't know you at first. All the pictures are old—" She broke off, flushing, and looked to Trivally. "What do we do, Triv'?"

Trivally looked at Leith. "Which ship, Captain?"

Leith didn't answer at once, staring down the line of ships with narrowed eyes. "The best of the lighters, I think," she said, after a moment. "Do I see an Erzulie III in your lineup?"

Trivally shook his head, and looked for a moment almost embarrassed. "I'm afraid not, Captain."

"No fear," Nezera muttered.

"The best one's the Koniko," Trivally said.

"She's not the newest," Nezera offered, "but we've never been able to get *it* to work right."

"I'll rely on your judgment," Leith said.

"Right." Trivally rubbed his hands together thoughtfully. "Nez'a, run a pre-flight on the Koniko. Fuel her, top the air tanks if necessary, and make sure the other supplies are in order."

"Got you." Nezera gave a sketchy sort of salute, and trotted off toward the fourth lighter in the line. More than ever, she reminded me of Ixora, and I wondered if the driver had somehow survived the battle. I didn't even know if she had been at the Tower that night. . . . Trivally was talking again, and I pulled my thoughts back to reality.

"Can you do your own course plot?" the supervisor was saying. "I don't think it'd be good to go through the control tower. I've got a computer in my office, with a pretty good analog of their main program. Sometimes people like to look at it while they're deciding about repairs. . . ."

"I can take care of that, if you want," Guil offered.

Leith hesitated only for an instant. "It's your system. Thanks."

Trivally beckoned, and Guil started off with him toward the closed door of the supervisor's office. Alkres said, quite suddenly, "Can I watch?"

He sounded like a fifteen-year-old again, which was something of a relief. I nodded. "If Guil doesn't mind."

"I'll ask," Alkres promised, and darted after them. A moment later, he had caught up, and I saw Guil shake her head. The three disappeared into the office.

I took a deep breath, feeling suddenly exhausted again. By Leith's chronograph, dangling from her belt beneath the open coat, it was well past the twenty-second hour: it was no wonder I was tired. Leith looked drained, too, strong circles showing under her eyes. There was a clattering from the line of ships, and she looked up sharply, focusing on something I couldn't find, but then she relapsed into her sudden apathy.

We stood silent for a long moment. Then, glancing sideways at Leith, I said, "I know why *I'm* doing this."

The captain looked up at me, and ran her good hand through her hair. She was smiling faintly. "Oh, well. You heard what I told Darah. It's a matter of the Peacekeepers' Oath—and even if it wasn't, I couldn't just leave you here."

The Oath bound the Peacekeepers—even those who'd left active service, like Moraghan—to intervene in situations that could be called class-one emergencies. It was up to an individual to choose the most effective form of intervention, as the Peacekeepers' Supreme Command quite reasonably held they couldn't dictate specific actions in such an emergency, and the actions prompted by that part of the Oath had varied widely. Jan Migisi, during the bloody uprising on Brigit, had assassinated the leaders of the three radical parties, and persuaded the survivors to call for mediation; Chang Loris, facing a similar situation on Cratos, had settled for rescuing the leaders of the old guard. Both actions had ultimately been sanctioned by the Supreme Command. The only consistent thing was the obligation to act when confronted with the possible destruction of a society.

"Do you really think things are that bad?" I asked.

Leith smiled, without humor. "Don't you?"

The thought was profoundly disturbing. I shied away from it, asking instead, "How dangerous is it really, taking off now?"

Leith shrugged. "Not dangerous at all, unless there's a tremor just when I'm trying to lift. The Port Authority has to take that chance into account, and they can't afford to run risks on a large scale, but—not really dangerous."

It took Trivally and Nezera less than an hour to get the lighter ready for liftoff, and most of that time was spent pumping fuel into the Koniko's immense tanks. Guil had the course plotted in about half that time—Orestes and Electra were almost in syzygy, an easy plot to make—and then we all stood around until at last Trivally signaled he was ready to let us aboard.

The Koniko was an old model, with worn padding on the walls of its cylindrical airlock. Nezera took us in, pointing Leith and Guil toward the tiny command capsule, then led Alkres and me into the empty passenger compartment. There were a dozen first-class couches to choose from—

the ones that folded back into truly comfortable bunks—
and two dozen of the less luxurious standard-class couches
beyond that. Nezera grinned.

"You might as well sit up front and be comfortable."
Her smile faded quickly, and she pointed to a pair of
closed compartments, one on each side of the passage
leading to the command capsule. "The head's on the left,
galley on the right. You'll have to serve yourselves, I'm
afraid, but it's fully stocked." She paused again, listening
to voices in her headset, then said, "Better strap in, now.
Trivally's ready to take her out."

Nezera helped me fasten Alkres into the first couch,
then showed him how to work the controls while I fastened myself into the couch directly across the aisle from
the ult'eir's. The technician gave me a quick, professional
glance, and then an approving nod.

"You're all set, then, Medium. Screen controls—"

"Under my left hand?" I asked.

"Right. Good luck." She glanced quickly at Alkres, very
pale against the dark-brown padding. "Come back soon
and safe, sor."

The boy whispered something in reply, but Nezera was
already gone. Alkres had never been off-world before, of
course, and the first time is always frightening, even in
normal circumstances. I wanted to lean across and take his
hand, but I was held back by the safety webbing. Instead,
I touched the screen controls, and fiddled with the buttons until I'd found the views from the outside cameras.
The wall and the retracted umbilicals were slowly reced-
ing: I hadn't even realized we'd begun to move.

The intercom crackled overhead, and Guil's voice said,
over the mutter of Leith's checklist, "We're starting the
fans."

The ship shuddered deeply as she spoke, and I was
grateful for the warning. Alkres took a deep breath, his
hands closed tight on the ends of the armrests, but said
nothing. In the screen, the side wall swung away as the
pilots turned to face the hangar doors. They were sliding
back already, and clicked into place as the ship steadied
into the taxiway. A distant voice spoke in the intercom.

"You're heading directly onto strip three. Pass the yellow line before you start main engines." It was Trivally.

He sounded more than a little nervous, usurping Traffic Control's job, but at least there was no other traffic to worry about.

"Affirmative," Guil answered. Her voice was much louder, and I guessed she'd forgotten to switch off the passenger intercom. I could still hear the sexless voice of the computer, running through the last bit of the pilot's checklist, and Leith's monosyllabic responses.

"Shouldn't there be another crewman?" Alkres asked suddenly. "An engineer, or something?"

He looked genuinely frightened again, and I said quickly, "The computer does that on this ship, I think—I'm sure of it."

"Oh." Alkres leaned back in his couch, trying very hard to relax.

"It'll be all right," I said. "Remember, this is a low-G planet, so the lift's nothing to worry about. You'll feel the pressure, but the couch will take a lot of it."

He hunched his shoulders a little under the webbing, and didn't answer. I wondered if it wouldn't be better to leave him alone, and looked back at the screen.

The Koniko was just passing through the hangar entrance, ground fans whining very softly. Ahead stretched the vast expanse of the taxiway, and then the runway itself, both still outlined with lights, even though the port was officially closed. A yellow band, gleaming in the Koniko's headlights, marked the end of the taxiway and the beginning of the runway.

Leith's voice said, "Oh, they're getting nervy, aren't they?" Guil laughed, and the captain said, more sharply, "No, don't answer. Let them sweat."

I guessed she was talking about the control tower. Leith's voice sounded again, once more smoothly professional. "Give me full power on the ground fans, please."

"Ground fans at full power," Guil answered instantly. The noise in the well-shielded passenger cabin didn't seem to increase, but in the screen, the marker lights began to move past more quickly.

"I don't like the looks of those vans, Leith," the *para'an* went on.

"Let them play chicken if they want," Leith answered promptly. "I'll overrun them if I have to."

"If you can," Guil said.

Leith laughed. "I can."

The Koniko's cameras were fixed, pointing straight ahead. I would've given anything to be able to adjust them, to see what the two pilots were talking about—or to be able to ask them directly, for that matter—but the intercom was a one-way instrument. The control tower must've sent out its emergency equipment to try to block the runway, I thought. At least I know the Destiny field doesn't have gunboxes—unless the Brandr brought some with them? That was an appalling thought, and I could feel the sweat pearling on my forehead. I could picture the results only too easily: one missile among the Koniko's fuel tanks, and there would be even less left of us than there was of the people at the Tower. I brought myself under control with an effort. Even if the Brandr had equipment to spare for the supposedly closed spaceport—and there had been no word of missile launchers or gunboxes of any kind in the rumors we had heard before the attack—there were still Halex in the control tower who could, and would, stop them from attacking too quickly.

In the screen, the yellow line had just vanished beneath the Koniko's nose. Guil gave a grunt of satisfaction. "They're dropping back."

"I thought they would," Leith answered absently. "Computer, commence checklist for main engine start."

At that moment, the ship shuddered, the entire world staggering drunkenly sideways. Alkres gave a little yelp of fright, and Guil swore viciously. In the background, I could hear the computer droning through its routine. It asked a question, and, getting no answer, repeated it. Leith said, unnecessarily, "Tremor." Her voice was not quite steady.

"Do we scrub?" Guil asked.

There was a long silence, broken only by the computer's monotonous voice. Then Leith said, "No."

"Aftershocks," Guil said, warningly, and Leith interrupted.

"There haven't been any before. I'll chance it." Her voice faded, as though she'd turned away again. "Feed cock open."

The computer continued its list as though there had

been no pause. At last, I heard its voice announce, "Ready for main engine start. All systems at standby. Brakes full on."

"Brakes full on," Leith echoed. "Beginning main engine start."

Guil said, pitching her voice to reach the intercom microphone, "We're beginning the count, people. Main engines're starting—now."

Her words were drowned in the sudden burst of noise from the tail of the ship. The Koniko shook under the sudden rush of power, and I saw—I could barely hear anything, over the roar of the engines—Alkres's mouth open in another frightened cry. I shouted, not knowing if he would hear, "It's a normal start. Don't worry!"

Then, quite suddenly, the engines hit their takeoff point, and one of the pilots snapped off the brakes. The Koniko bounded forward, the runway lights blurring almost instantly into a single line. We bounced, and then the Koniko's nose rose steeply, and we were gone. The cameras showed only featureless sky, the stars drowned in Agamemnon's light, but I could imagine the starport dropping away beneath us. The acceleration increased steadily, pressing me back into my couch. The cushions molded themselves around me, taking some of the strain. Still, it wasn't pleasant, and I turned my head with an effort, trying to see how Alkres was handling it. The Patriarch was flattened in his couch, hands still locked on the armrests, face white but set in a stern mask. He was coping in his own way, and I turned my head back toward the featureless screen.

The pressure and the engine noise stopped together. In the sudden silence, Leith said, "In the groove."

"Confirmed," Guil answered. "Everything all right back there, Trey?"

I glanced at Alkres, who nodded. His movements were cautious in the lack of gravity—wisely so, I thought, remembering my own first bout with spacesickness. "So far, so good," I said, and then remembered that the intercom was one-way. Carefully, I unfastened my webbing and let myself drift up off the couch, feeling my way toward the galley where I knew there would be a crew intercom. It took me a few minutes to get there—I hadn't been in a spaceship that lacked internal gravity in some time, and I had lost my space legs—and another few minutes to find and figure out the intercom system. At last, I pushed the answer bar, and said, "We're all right, thanks. How're things up front?"

"Pretty good," Leith answered. She still sounded excited, exhilarated by the liftoff. "We're on course, and should reach Electra in about thirty-six hours, give or take thirty minutes—I'll know for sure when we hit the correction point. Nobody's following us—"

"I'm not surprised," I said, and Leith laughed.

"No, that tremor would tend to discourage them. And even if someone does decide to risk the lift, we'll have about an hour's head start."

That head start would increase the longer any pursuers waited, too. I said, "Sounds good to me. Let me know if you want anything from the galley, or if I can spell somebody. If not, I'm going back to the kid."

"Good idea," Leith said. "I'll let you know if we need anything."

I took my hand off the answer bar, and started toward the galley door. I had my hand on its latch when a thought struck me, and I turned back toward the row of storage cells. It wasn't hard to find the Koniko's aidkit—the cell was marked with the red cross, star, and crescent—and I pawed through the sterile packets until I found the one I wanted. I tucked it into my tunic pocket, and headed back to the cabin.

Alkres was very pale, his forehead damp with clammy sweat, but he managed a ghastly smile as I pulled myself back down the corridor. Already, it was getting easier to move in the lack of gravity, and I swung myself into position beside Alkres's couch with a sort of grace.

"I'm glad everything's going right," the patriarch said faintly.

"You look awful," I said. "Are you feeling spacesick?"

Alkres started to nod, and thought better of it. "Yes."

"Right." I took the packet out of my pocket, and hooked my foot under the grab bar at the base of his couch to steady myself before ripping open the sterile paper. The injection cylinder started to float away, and I caught it awkwardly. "By rights, you should've gotten a time-patch before we left, but this was hardly a well-planned trip. We're lucky the stewards keep these aboard, just in case." Alkres was watching me warily, and I plunged on, hoping to distract him. "The injection will make you feel better almost at once, and by the time it wears off, the patch will have taken over. All right?"

"All right," Alkres said, and turned his head very carefully away as I pressed the head of the cylinder against his skin. The check-bead at the end of the cylinder went from red to clear as the cylinder emptied, and I pulled it away, tucking it into a pocket.

"I do feel better," Alkres said, sounding very surprised. His color wasn't much better, but he was moving his head a little less gingerly. I smiled, and took the square adhesive pouch out of the aid pack.

"I'm going to put this on your wrist, over the surface veins," I said, suiting my actions to my words. "You may feel a little itching, or maybe not; it's nothing to worry about either way." I finished wrapping the security tabs around the boy's wrist, and let myself float away again. "That should last you for the trip. Now, if you can sleep, that's the best thing. It'll give the medicines a chance to work."

"Thanks, Trey," Alkres said. "I'll try." He leaned back in the couch, closing his eyes.

I pulled myself back to my couch, and fastened the webbing around me again. I was exhausted, and there was nothing I could do to help, at least for the next few hours. I would follow my own advice.

Chapter 11: Trey Marturin

The flight itself went smoothly. By the time I woke, we were well into the rings, on a well-buoyed track that Guil assured me she could fly in her sleep. The *para'an* had chosen a somewhat roundabout course in order to make use of that partial gap, adding an extra five hours to the journey as we passed the rings, and then turned to chase Electra along her orbit. Even I knew that this was the sort of maneuver that ate into the fuel reserves, but when I voiced that worry, Leith only laughed and reminded me that the Koniko was running virtually empty. There was plenty of fuel to spare.

I did my best to make myself useful, preparing meals from the galley's limited stock—not much of a chore, just adding hot water to pouches of freeze-dried foods—and sitting in while one or the other of the pilots snatched a few hours' sleep. That wasn't a particularly difficult job, either, and Alkres took his turn at it as well once he adjusted to weightlessness. Electra swelled slowly in the forward screens, first a blue-white point small enough to be eclipsed by any piece of ring debris, then a disk the size of my thumbnail with distinct blue-and-white markings, and finally, as we left the rings, a world the size of

253

my palm, with distinct seas and a single snowy continent beneath the swirling clouds.

Six hours out of Glittermark, the first-approach buoy hailed us. The signal, coming in over the open intercom, woke me instantly. I struggled free of the safety webbing and was halfway to the command capsule before I had fully realized what I was doing. Alkres wasn't far behind. We had discussed what to do—when to ask the Orillon Patriarch for sanctuary—a dozen times before this, but we hadn't come to any firm decision. Now the decison point was at hand.

The pilots exchanged glances as I swung to a stop, floating just inside the hatchway. Alkres, who fitted more neatly into the command capsule's limited space, pushed past me to catch the nearest grab bar. Guil's hand was on the abort button of the registry transponder, preventing its automatic answer.

Leith said, "Well, Trey?"

I took a deep breath, the previous days' arguments flashing through my mind. It would probably be to our advantage to present the Orillon Patriarch with a fait accompli—under the code, he could not refuse to shelter Alkres—but at the same time, I didn't want to insult him by forcing his hand. Still, we were only six hours out of Electra's only city. That would give him sufficient notification, but wouldn't give him much time to think up an excuse to refuse us. We could always broadcast later requests, if we had to appeal to public opinion—and that seemed unlikely. After all, the Orillon Patriarch had been the only genarch to protest the Brandr action. I nodded to Guil.

"Go ahead and answer. Tell them you want a line to the Tower, but see if you can go through check-down first."

"That's standard," the *para'an* answered, and took her hand off the abort button. Immediately, lights rippled across the transponder's checkplate, recording both the buoy's inquiry and our answer in the Koniko's automatic log. Leith watched the main communications board. We waited while the buoy digested our registry codes, discovered no incoming flight that matched those numbers, and passed its dilemma on to the Glittermark field. Ten minutes clicked by on the capsule's chronograph before the signal panel lit: it seemed Glittermark had been taken by surprise.

Leith touched keys, matching frequencies, and the pinlight went from orange to green. "Open channel," she said softly, warningly, and hit a second button.

A light changed color, and after a moment, a soft female voice said, "Koniko 573, we don't show a scheduled landing. What's up?"

Glittermark field was obviously an informal operation. Guil gestured rapidly at the communications board. Leith shrugged, and touched another key sequence. The *para'an* adjusted her headset microphone, and said, "Kame, is that you?"

"Guil?" The field operator controlled her response instantly. "This is Kame Orillon."

"It's Guil," the *para'an* said. "I didn't think we'd be this lucky. I'm bringing in an unscheduled launch. Can you give me field space?"

There was a silence, and Guil took advantage of the moment to cover her microphone with one hand. "Kame's a cross-cousin of mine," she said, softly. "That's a break."

"That's an affirmative on field space, and on a first-approach landing," Kame said. "Are you in trouble, Guil?"

"Not me, exactly," Guil began, and the field operator broke in.

"Are you messing in the troubles on the big world?"

I bit back a laugh. Electra was supposed to be under the same code that stifled Orestes, yet here was a field operator—a Family member, neither *para'an* nor ghost—treating the whole thing as a matter of mere "trouble on the big world." Maybe it was just because Electra was held by a single Family, but I felt my spirits rise for the first time since leaving Orestes.

"In a manner of speaking," Guil said, and looked almost embarrassed. "I want to contact the Tower, after we've matched coordinates."

There was another brief silence. When Kame spoke again, the teasing note was gone from her voice. "And who will I say's calling, then?"

Guil glanced at me. I touched my chest, then pointed at Alkres. The *para'an* nodded, and said, "Trey Maturin,

Medium for the Halex Family, for Alkres Halex, of Halex, in Halex."

The speaker whistled painfully, and I waited for Leith to adjust the frequency, before I realized the noise had come from Glittermark. "When you play, you play big, I'll give you that," Kame said at last. Her voice sharpened again. "I'll pass that message at once, Koniko 573, but we'll match coordinates first."

"I confirm," Guil answered.

"Baseline course?" Glittermark said, and I let myself drift back through the command capsule's hatch. Leith detached herself from her couch and followed, pointing for Alkres to take her place in front of the consoles. The patriarch did as he was told, his expression at once determined and uncertain.

Leith caught herself outside the galley entrance, and hooked one foot through a floor bar so that she could stretch a little. I waited. At last, the captain said, not looking at me, "Exactly what are you going to ask him for, Trey?"

I had been asking myself the same question for the past thirty-six hours without finding any good answers, and that frustration sharpened my voice. "For sanctuary, first, and then for his support at the next Ship's Council." Whenever that may be, I added silently. The date had not been set for the emergency meeting requested by Yslin Rhawn, or at least it hadn't been set when we left Orestes. I only hoped they hadn't met already—but that seemed unlikely. It took time to set up these things, even if the Orillon Patriarch was only planning to attend by holo-link.

"And if he says no?" Leith asked. I pulled my mind back to her questions, angry that she kept harping on the uncertainties.

"He won't."

"He could," Leith persisted. "What then?"

I took another deep breath. "Grant me I know my business, Leith. Landret Orillon will give us sanctuary, I'm sure of it." Leith nodded, lifting a placating hand, and I wished I really were as certain as I'd sounded.

"Do you think he'll back Alkres in front of the Council, too?"

I shrugged. "That's less certain, yes, but I think there's a good chance he might. No one else filed a protest."

"It's a long way from a protest to open support," Leith began, and I glared at her. This time, she raised both hands in submission. "All right, I trust you. I'm just worried, that's all."

I sighed, my anger easing. "Me, too. Call me when you get through to the Tower?"

Leith nodded, and I pulled myself into the passenger compartment. The empty chairs stretched back into eerie shadow—the two spacers had turned out the lights in the rear compartment, a power-saving reflex—and I was suddenly very lonely. I didn't know for certain if Landret would give us sanctuary, though I was almost certain the code would give him no way of refusing us. But if he did. . . . I could either take the boy out of the system altogether, or I could take him back to Orestes. The former would not appeal to him at all, and I was not happy contemplating the latter. It would probably come to that—going back to Orestes—because I wasn't sure that I could, in good conscience, bully the boy into running out on both the only life he'd ever known, and his responsibilities to his people. The one thing Urban morality and the Oresteian code have in common is the concept of responsibility.

I turned my back deliberately on those empty, accusing couches, and drew myself down into my own seat, pulling the webbing around me. It was my responsibility to persuade Landret to shelter us. I would not fail in it.

An hour passed, then another, and a third. We were well into our second-stage approach before Leith signaled from the command capsule that the Orillon Tower was on the line. I launched myself out of the couch, and was in the capsule almost before she had finished speaking. Alkres still clung to the strap beside the unused engineer's panel.

Guil said, her hand over her microphone again, "They'll be on in a few seconds. There's a headset over there."

I looked around for it, and Alkres handed it to me. I was still adjusting the boom when the light flashed on the communications board.

"Good luck," Leith whispered, and hit the button.

"Koniko 573, this is Edlin Tam'ne, Orillon Medium,"

the speaker answered at once. "I wish to speak to the Halex Medium."

"This is Trey Maturin," I answered. "I appreciate your responding so promptly."

The woman's voice lost none of its wariness. "I regret that Himself is in conference at the moment, or I'm sure he would attend to your business personally. In the meantime, may I be of assistance?"

"I trust so." I kept my own voice steely calm, not allowing anything except an academic courtesy to color the words. "My request is not of a particularly private nature. I take it you are aware of the recent—troubles on Orestes?" She couldn't be anything but aware of them, but I made her answer anyway.

"I have heard some news, yes," Edlin said. "Himself is much concerned."

"Yes, to the extent of announcing his intention of filing a protest," I said. "My employer has asked me to convey his thanks for that courtesy."

"A matter of duty," Edlin murmured, even more warily. She stopped there, wisely, leaving the next move to me. I took a deep breath.

"My other business is related. I speak for the ult'eir Alkres Halex, of Halex, in Halex, whom we believe presently to be the Halex Patriarch, in lieu of other known survivors from the mainline Family."

That brought a soft gasp from Edlin, as I'd hoped it would: nothing showed better how far outside the normal bounds of feud and raid the Brandr had stepped. I went on as though I hadn't heard. "We ask Landret, as Patriarch of a Kinship not party to this feud, for asylum, one genarch to another. I also ask, as a favor to Himself, if you or yours have any word of the other children who were at the Tower. They were taken to the Ansson Hold, but we've had no chance to hear more of them."

Alkres shot me a grateful look. It had not been safe, in Destiny, to query the comnet, and the newscasts had said nothing. Once we had left Orestes, we had lost access to the 'net.

Edlin said, "For the latter, I can set the Patriarch's mind at rest at once. We had word some twenty hours ago—on the main newscast out of Destiny, which would be reliable—that those children have been restored to their closest kin."

"Those who have any left," Alkres muttered. I half hoped the other medium had heard him.

"As for the first matter," Edlin continued, "that is, of course, for Himself to decide. I will place the question before him at once, as genarch to genarch, and will return with his answer as soon as I may. For the time being, of course, I bid you welcome to Glittermark, and to Electra."

"Thank you for your courtesy and for your gracious assistance," I answered. "We are most grateful."

Edlin broke the connection then. I sighed, working my shoulders. I hadn't realized until then how tense I was.

"What's all that mean?" Leith asked.

"I don't know for sure," I answered. "She's made no promises, though she did give us the run of the city, unofficially. We'll have to wait for Landret's decision."

"He'll take us," Alkres said. "You'll see."

"I hope so," Leith said, but not loudly enough to be heard.

In the end, Alkres was right. Edlin barely waited long enough to keep up the pretense of Landret's being "in conference" before she came back on line. She brought us the formal offer of sanctuary, and, quite fortuitously, Landret's promise of further—if unspecified—support. The others were so delighted by that that I didn't have the heart to mention my doubts that it would automatically extend to supporting a Halex claim against a Rhawn upstart in the Ship's Council. The Orillon Heir, Edlin finished, was by a lucky chance still in Glittermark. Her people would meet us at the starport, and she would personally bring us to the Tower.

"That's good news," Guil remarked, after the medium had signed off.

"Oh?" I didn't know the Orillion Heir, and said as much.

Guil smiled. "Signe Orillon is good people—she's been Portreeve for a few years now. I think she'll back you, just because this kind of trouble is bad for trade."

Unless, I thought, she'd rather see the Rhawn into power just to keep things quiet. I didn't say anything, and

Alkres said, "I met her, once, when I was a kid. She runs an iceboat."

I couldn't tell from his tone whether that was supposed to be a recommendation or not.

Leith looked up from her multiple screens. "You two had better go back and strap down. We'll be beginning descent in about forty minutes."

We did as we were told, and waited out first the forty minutes to entry, and then the interminable descent through Electra's atmosphere. The viewscreen fuzzed orange almost at once, and did not clear until we were in the final leg, flattening out for the conventional landing at the Glittermark field. Electra was a cold world, colder even than Orestes. The land beneath us was solidly white, a permanent snowfield; only the heated runways showed dark against the glaring brilliance. I made some hasty calculations: it was Day on Electra, just after Sunrise, with about forty-eight hours to go to their Eclipse.

And then we were down. Guil—or Leith; I didn't know for certain who was flying the Koniko—applied the brakes and the ship shuddered, slowing reluctantly to a jolting crawl across the runways. We turned, lining up on the indicated taxiway, and I caught my first sight of Glittermark.

The city lived up to its name. The buildings were short and squat—Electra may be less seismically active than Orestes, but there's still a serious danger—with steeply pitched roofs that bore permanent crowns of snow. The weak sunlight sparked from the ice that had formed beneath those caps of snow, casting bright reflections across the rows of buildings. They stretched for kilometers in either direction: Glittermark's residents could not build up, but they could build out.

"Oh, it's pretty," Alkres said, involuntarily, and I had to agree.

The Koniko swung again, and a series of outbuildings, hangars and machinists' shops, swam into view. Beyond them, I saw what seemed to be a rough-ridged sheet of pure ice, patched here and there with duller spots that must be snow. Agamemnon's thin crescent hung just above the horizon, but I knew it only by the familiar colors, bright against the dark sky. Its bow was only a third as big as it appeared from Orestes. Then the main port building slid into the picture, cutting off my view. We steadied on a dock marked with a blinking light, and the pilots brought us sedately to a halt beside it.

Leith's voice sounded in the intercom. "Attention, passengers, we have arrived at the gate in Glittermark. Thank you for flying the Escape Line."

Alkres gave a dutiful smile, struggling with his safety webbing. After thirty-six hours of zero gravity, the returned weight was obviously something of a shock. I couldn't really feel the difference between Electra and Orestes, though I knew there was one, and pulled myself slowly out of my couch. For the first time since I'd come to Orestes, the gravity actually seemed to have *pull*. It was not a pleasant sensation, after I had gotten used to trading on my off-world strength. I made a silent promise to find a recreation suite as soon as I had the chance, and moved to help Alkres. He wobbled a little when I pulled him to his feet. I supported him as I helped him unfasten the wrist pouch, and he steadied slowly. In the background, I could hear the pilots' voices, and the computer's sexless tones, finishing the docking check. Then, over that background murmur, I heard the chime of the main communications board. The voices stopped, and someone pressed the respond button. A new voice filled the cabins.

"Sor Alkres. On behalf of my father, and on my own, I welcome you to Glittermark, and to Electra." The voice was a woman's, rather deep, with less of the Oresteian accent than I had expected: Signe, Orillon's Heir.

There was a moment of silence after she'd finished speaking. Then Leith said hastily, "There's an outside intercom by the hatch."

"Thank you," Alkres said, though he knew she couldn't hear him, and moved forward cautiously to the hatch. He found the broadcast button after a moment's study, and pressed it. "Thank you for your welcome, ama, and for all the kindness your Family's shown to me. To me and mine," he amended hurriedly, an anxious frown on his face. I nodded, I hoped encouragingly, and after a moment's thought, he took his finger off the button. "I think I said everything."

"I think so," I said, and reached for my cloak, which I had stowed in the cell set into the bulkhead beside the couch. My clothes were looking ragged, despite Leith's having shown me how to wash the shirt in the zero-g shower; the magnificent cloak would cover a multitude of sins. Alkres hauled his bag out from the cell just as the two pilots came into the passenger compartment. Both women had on their best to neaten their appearance, but Leith looked acutely grateful for her leather coat. I was glad to see she'd returned her blaster to its place in her campaign bag.

"The tube's in place," she said. "We can pop the hatch whenever you're ready."

Alkres took a deep breath, and slung the borrowed bag over his shoulder. "I'm ready." His voice quavered a little, but we all ignored it.

"Seals are green," Leith said, automatically. Peacekeeper routines are drilled very deep into the psyche.

Guil gave her a rather amused look, but answered, "I confirm, seals are green."

"Opening the hatch," Leith continued, making a face at her own unnecessary caution, and swung the wheel. The tri-leaved hatch irised, opening onto the docking tube. The pilots had positioned the Koniko perfectly: the tube segments were at minimum extension, pointing straight into the port building. A knot of people in bright clothing waited just beyond the blued steel ring of the tube's base.

Alkres squared his shoulders, and stepped out onto the tube's padded surface. I positioned myself carefully at his left shoulder, and followed. The spacers lagged behind, and I heard Leith murmur something that might have been a curse.

As we crossed the ring at the end of the tube, a woman stepped out from among the waiting group, and took a few steps forward to meet us. Seeing Alkres's stiff figure, she checked what might have been an embrace, and instead offered both hands in sober, adult greeting.

"Sor, welcome," she said, and Alkres answered, "Many thanks for your hospitality."

The woman smiled, including all of us in its warmth. "I think we won't stand on ceremony, under the circumstances. I'm Signe Orillon."

"Trey Maturin," I answered. "Halex Medium." The others introduced themselves, too, but I wasn't really listening. The Orillon Heir was a striking woman—not particularly tall, but with a beautifully regal carriage. She had a rather long face, with a starkly defined cheek and jaw, and the Orillon slanted eyes. Her brows tilted upwards, too, following the line of her eyes. Her lips were a fraction too long and thin to be conventionally beautiful, but they gave strength to an otherwise delicate face. Her jet-black hair was drawn up in a heavy topknot, bound with a strip of purple cloth patterned with the Orillon seaflower, that served to emphasize the lurking delicacy. Then she smiled again, and that image vanished, to be replaced with the woman—the Heir—who managed a world's spaceport. She was not that much younger than I was, I realized with surprise.

"My husband, Berild," she was saying, almost parenthetically, and I felt a moment's pang. That was absurd enough to sober me; I returned the man's friendly greeting, studying him curiously. He was no taller than the Heir, but broad-shouldered, with a mane of chestnut hair only partly controlled by the purple ribbons woven through it. He was handsome enough, in a quirky, good-humored way, but he lacked Signe's striking beauty.

Signe introduced the rest of her party as well, but so quickly I was unable to put names to faces. I identified the medium, Edlin, from the badge pinned to her collar, but that was all. Signe went on, oblivious. "My father wants to welcome you as soon as possible, so I thought we'd return to the Tower in my iceboat. It's as fast as anything else, and a good deal more private."

Alkres nodded gratefully at that, and I was again impressed by the Heir's courtesy—and by her political sense. It was only sensible for the Orillon not to advertise their support of the awkward Halex claimant until Landret had decided exactly how far he was willing to go on our behalf. It was their good luck that politics coincided with politeness.

The Heir's boat was docked at the iceport itself. A snow car was waiting at a service door, and the Heir bundled us to it and aboard before we could think of protesting. The car was crowded, and the nose ski grated unpleasantly on the half-melted ice of the access road before the driver got the weight distributed properly and fed power to the tracks.

Iceport and spaceport shared the same strip of flatland that ran between the low hills of the town and the ridged ice of the perpetually frozen Closed Sea. At first, it was hard to tell which buildings belonged to which complex, but then we swung past the last of the massive hangars and turned down a row of low-roofed, thick-walled, hired-storage blockhouses, and I caught my first glimpse of the iceport.

I had forgotten that many of the transports that crossed the Closed Sea carried sails as well as fans. The road we were travelling seemed to end in a forest of masts, each webbed with a complex network of multi-colored lines. Ice glittered here and there, and beyond those masts lay the dulled ice of the Closed Sea.

"Sailing ships?" Leith said, from behind me.

"Cheaper than fossil fuels," Signe answered cheerfully, "and a lot more reliable than electrics. Our settlements lie mostly on the solid land ringing the Sea—there're one or two fish towns on the ice, but nothing that really counts—so the boats tend to be the fastest way to get around."

"How much actual land do you have?" Leith asked idly. "The two continents looked pretty small from orbit."

"The continents, and a scattering of volcanic islands in the southern hemisphere," Signe answered. She seemed glad of the innocuous topic. "But those are mostly uninhabited—there isn't anything on them, really."

"Of course, what looks like the biggest landmass is mostly ice," Berild interjected. He grinned. "They say the Closed Sea's the caldera of the biggest volcano this world's ever seen. We'll all be in for a surprise if it ever comes to life again."

"You know that theory's been discredited," Signe murmured, but she was smiling.

The car turned again, this time onto a broad boulevard that ran along the head of the wharves. Most of the berthing spaces were full, and lines snaked from hulls and masts to a grid that formed a sort of ceiling for the length of each wharf. Power lines, I guessed, and communications hook-ups. The iceboats came in all sizes, from the sleek, brilliantly painted needles that had to be sport boats, to broader-beamed craft that sat squarely on their triple runners, to squat fishing boats that carried four or five net-booms to their single mast. Almost all of them had fans as well, set into the sterncastle in the channel between the runners: working ships that could not afford to be becalmed.

Alkres nudged me then, and I could see the effort he made not to point. "What is that, that ship?"

I looked, and shook my head. "I have no idea." It was a massive thing, three times as big as any other ship in sight, so large that it took up two of the dock spaces. It was painted from runners to deck rail in a crimson that gleamed dully, like enamel. Smaller, drabber ships were snugged up against its outer side like nursing children.

"Ama?" Alkres leaned forward to touch the Heir's sleeve. "What's that, please?"

Signe glanced over her shoulder. "Oh, that's a factory ship—a fleet mother-ship." She raised her voice a little, to carry over the hiss and clank of the car's tracks. "Agnar, what's the *Chijo* doing in port so early?"

The blondish, bearded man sitting beside the driver turned awkwardly to face her. "Cracked strut. Didn't you get my memo?"

Signe shook her head. "Give me a report later."

We were almost at the end of the icefront now, the long lines of the commercial wharves giving way to smaller berths that housed more of the slim, brightly painted private yachts. The car slowed, then swung into the bay at the entrance to the final dock. The driver lowered the door, and we climbed out onto the heated surface of the dock. The grid running the length of this wharf was decorated with painted bosses in the shape of the Orillon seaflower: clearly, this was the mainline Family's private dock.

"This way, sor, if you please," Signe said, and offered her arm. Alkres rested his hand on her gloved wrist, an unhappy parody of the adult gesture, and they started together toward the iceboat that waited at the end of the wharf. The rest of us followed.

The Heir's boat was as brightly painted as any of the needle-yachts—I guessed visibility was a highly desirable quality, in the event of a malfunction somewhere in the emptiness of the Closed Sea—but much broader in the beam. The carbon-compound masts were already set, and a couple of sailors were busily threading the last control lines into their winches. At the Heir's approach, the young man who had been supervising the sailors stepped from the rounded deck to meet her, touching his forehead in salute.

"Everything's in order, ama."

Signe nodded, not quite returning the salute. "We'll come aboard, then, Hildur."

The young man—I assumed he was the actual captain, though Signe would hold that title—whistled sharply, and caught hold of one of the stays supporting the mast. He swung himself back aboard just in time to catch the main hatch as it popped from its seat, and keep it from crashing against the polished decking. A segmented gangway of fleximesh unfolded itself and locked into place against the edge of the dock. Signe crossed without waiting for a handrail to appear, and Alkres had to follow. I was glad to see that Hildur had moved to stand by the hatch. It was a good three meters to the ice from the gangway.

The handrails clicked into place as Signe vanished into the hull, and I was glad of their protection as I made my way across the unstable mesh. The interior of the iceboat was comfortable but not lavish, with a single row of armorglass ports along each side of the hull. A passenger pit was tucked into the widening stern just ahead of the helmsman's position. A single ladder led to a lower level: sleeping quarters rather than cargo space, I guessed, but there was no time to ask questions. Already, the rest of the iceboat's crew had taken up their positions by the interior winches, and a frail-looking woman who appeared to be in her early twenties stood by the tiller bars. For a moment, I wondered how she could see to steer, and then I saw the weirdly angled mirrors suspended from the ceiling.

"Clear below?" Hildur called from the deck, and Berild answered, "All clear."

The main hatch closed over us. The nearest sailor dogged it shut, and darted back to her place. Signe waved us to the seats in the passenger pit, but her polite invitation was drowned out by the coughing roar of the fan. There was a shrill whistle, barely audible over the noise, and sailors at bow and stern bent rapidly to their winches. The iceboat shuddered and then, very slowly, slid away from the dock. Despite the noise of the fan, we weren't moving very fast. The ships tied up at the neighboring dock formed a stately procession in the ports.

Then we had passed the end of the docks, and the boat turned slowly, as deliberately as a starship lining up for takeoff. The ice beneath the runners was surprisingly smooth. Far ahead on the ice, I could see a line of emergency-red pennants, their staffs bending almost double in the freshening wind. The boat swung further, and I realized we were heading for an opening in that line of flags.

There was another whistle from the deck, and the woman at the helm flung her weight against the tiller bars. The boat slowed, the scree of brakes against ice clearly audible above the fan's sound. It was very like the sound of a sledge's brakes, and I shivered. Leith, sitting next to me, felt it and gave me a sympathetic glance. I looked away, feeling unreasonably annoyed. On the opposite bench, Guil craned her body sideways to see out the nearest port, and I wondered just what she was looking for—the spaceport, Glittermark, her home? I wanted to ask, but conversation was impossible—a further annoyance, I thought, if the fan's going to be on the entire trip. I didn't even know how long it would take us to reach the Orillon Tower.

Abruptly, the fan cut out, leaving us in a silence that was broken an instant later by a series of flat, explosive cracks like the discharge of an electric carbine. I jumped, and I felt Leith's hand move toward her hip where her blaster had hung.

Signe said hastily, "Hildur's set the sails, people. We should reach the Tower in an hour or two."

I breathed a sigh of relief, and heard it echoed by Leith. Alkres's face was a study in affronted dignity, and I was glad the Electrans were too polite to laugh. The line of flags slipped by in the ports, and one of the Electrans— Tirzen, I thought his name was—called, "Time, please?"

"Marked, sor," the helmsman answered.

In the same moment, a hatch opened toward the boat's bow, and Hildur and the two crewmen who'd been on deck with him dropped back into the body of the boat. The crewmen took their places at the winches set along the hull, while Hildur came aft, touching his forehead again. The boat jumped and skidded—the ice was much rougher now—but he kept his balance easily, one hand on the grab bars running overhead.

"On open ice, ama, and all sails set. Any orders?"

Signe shook her head. "Carry on, as usual."

"Very good, ama," Hildur said, and moved aft to join the helmsman.

The rest of the trip passed quickly enough. Berild brought out a deck of cards and he and three others began a desultory game of Chance. Signe did her best to engage Alkres in conversation, but neither one was really interested in talking. Leith dozed. The rest of the Electrans watched the card game, now and then muttering a comment on the play. Guil stared into space, her expression betraying nothing of her thoughts. I was just as glad of the quiet. I had no idea what I would say to Landret Orillon, or how I could persuade him to help us; the only weapon I had was the code, which had proved unexpectedly weak on Orestes. And Electra was said to be far more lax than Orestes.

After about an hour's sailing, the first shadow of headland appeared on the horizon. It was an impressive sight, the dark, reddish-black rock in stark contrast to the grey ice of the bay, and to the masses of snow clinging to the higher ledges. Behind me, I heard Signe pointing out the tip of the Orillon Tower, but I barely caught a glimpse of the steeply raked roof before the iceboat slid under the lee of the cliff. Atreus's direct light vanished, to be replaced by a green, uncertain light, as though we'd slipped underwater. I leaned forward curiously, craning to see out the boat's narrow portals, and caught my breath sharply. The cliff above was not as steep as I'd thought at first. It rose in crumbling ledges, and each ledge was piled high with snow that had melted and refrozen into caps and falls of blue-green ice, banded here and there with fresh snow. The distant sunlight was reflected from it, throwing the strange light. It was almost as though a miniature Agamemnon had been spread out along the cliffside.

At my back, Berild gave a crow of laughter. "Impressive, isn't it? We lose a couple of boats every year, when somebody sails too close during a warm spell."

The comment made me look up a little uneasily, but I couldn't think there was much danger of the ice melting, even in Electra's Day. Still, the helmsman kept us meters away from the base of the cliffs—not just because of falling ice and rock, I realized suddenly. Close to the wall of rock, the ice was ridged and distorted, and there were dark shadows buried beneath the uneven surface: rocks that had fallen during the warm spells, and been swallowed by the subsequent freezing.

"It's beautiful," Leith said, and sounded almost surprised.

Guil gave her a lopsided smile, but said nothing.

Berild's grin widened, but his words were cut off as the boat's fan roared to life. Hildur and most of the crew had vanished through the forward hatch while we watched the ice, I realized, and I guessed they had taken in the boat's sails. We slowed, brakes biting into the ice to supplement the fan, and swung to face the cliff. There was an opening at its base, set so to be almost invisible until you were directly opposite it. Then lights flared in the cave's depths, and the boat slid neatly into its protected dock, bumping gently against the wharf before the gloved dockhands had it under control. The fan's noise died away to nothing.

"Very nice," Signe said, with a nod to the helmsman. The hatch rose then, and she stepped easily across onto the dock without bothering to trigger the gangway. The rest of us followed, Hildur waiting to help the uncertain. As I stepped onto the dock, Signe turned away from an older man and came back to join Alkres.

"Sor," she began, and raised a hand in my direction, "and you, Medium, you'll want to hear this."

I joined them obediently, wrapping my cloak more tightly around my body. It was very cold in the cave, despite the heaters that glowed at either end of the dock.

"My father's sent word that he's willing to see you now, or after dinner, if you're too tired," Signe went on. "He puts himself at your disposal."

Alkres darted a quick glance in my direction, but I could feel Signe's eyes on me, and was careful to keep my face expressionless. It would not help us for the Orillon to think that I was acting as puppetmaster. The boy looked away again, and said, "Since he offered, ama, I think it'd be better to see him now. That way we can maybe enjoy dinner."

The older man, some sort of Family steward, I guessed,

looked a little shocked at Alkres's comment, but Signe laughed. "Wise move, sor. I'll take you up, then."

Alkres started to follow, but I touched his arm. "Leith and Guil?"

Alkres gave a guilty start. "I forgot. Ama, what about Guil and Captain Moraghan? Will you see to them, too, please?"

"Berild has the matter in hand," Signe answered, carefully repressing a smile. "We wouldn't be such bad hosts, sor, I promise."

Alkres blushed at that, but realized there was no real answer. "Thank you, ama."

A tiny lift-tube carried us up through the cliff to the Tower complex. Unlike the Halex Tower, the Orillon Tower had no single focus; instead, square, three-story buildings formed three corners of the pentagonal compound, while long, barn-like structures made up the sides. Flat sheets of mirror-glass glittered from roof-tree to the first-floor ceiling, and I guessed that, like the Halex, the Orillon kept greenhouses tucked beneath the steep roofs. I doubted, though, that they'd have much success in Electra's colder climate.

Signe led us directly across the courtyard toward the nearest of the three-story buildings, disdaining the shelter of the compound's other buildings. The unfamiliar cold struck through my boots—city boots, not the thick felt Oresteians wore against real cold—and set me shivering even beneath my cloak. I glanced at Alkres, and saw that he was shivering, too, gloved hands tucked deep into his tunic pockets. Not for the first time, I wished we'd had time to get him a coat, and a bashlyk for his head and face. But we could get those here, I told myself sternly—if Landret consented to help us.

It was much warmer inside the buildings, almost startlingly so, or at least it seemed warmer, after the frigid air outside. It was also a much brighter place than the Halex Tower had been. Lights were hung in every shadowed corner—lamps with fretted, gaily colored globes, as well as more practical plain ones—and the walls were painted with fanciful scenes of a city that floated on the surface of an unfrozen sea. Panels of striped silk in warm colors, reds and yellows and creamy whites, hung from the main staircase. Some of the panels had been sewn with thin strips of reflector cloth, I saw as we came closer, and a mobile, its pendants made of some highly polished metal, was hung directly beneath the skylight that dominated the stairwell. More mirrors lined the walls, reflecting and redoubling Atreus's feeble light.

"Father claimed it would cost more money than it was worth, when my Uncle Belen showed him the design," Signe said. "Now he's talking about adding a skylight to the other towers."

"It's wonderful," Alkres said. He kept his head tipped back as we made our way up the staircase. I had to steady him twice before we reached the first landing.

The Orillon Patriarch was waiting for us in his private study. This was a double-edged compliment, and I had to admire him for it even while it annoyed me. The room was small—I hadn't seen any really large rooms in our passage through the Tower, and assumed it was for warmth—and the walls were paneled with strips of goldenwood, rather than painted. There were half a dozen tape-carousels scattered about the room, each almost as tall as I, with very few empty slots: not merely a working office, I thought, but a library. Landret Orillon was sitting behind a rather battered executive's desk, but he had shut down his console as soon as the door opened, and now looked up in greeting. I had only seen him in hologram before; up close, his thin face looked almost haggard, and there were puffy circles under his eyes. His hair, pulled up and back into the traditional topknot, was grey, streaked with white.

"Welcome to my house, Alkres," he said, adult to adult, without the condescension Alkres had been braced to meet, and hauled himself to his feet. I heard Signe's quick intake of breath, and saw Landret fumble with something out of sight behind the screen, bracing himself bodily against the desk. Then the Orillon Patriarch had himself under control, and pulled himself awkwardly out into the main part of the room, leaning heavily on a pair of crutches. It had to be the arthritis that was endemic here, I thought blankly. Herself had suffered from it. . . . I had never seen Landret standing, of course, but I had never heard any gossip, either: he had to be quite a leader to achieve that sort of silence.

Landret stopped when he reached the cluster of chairs that stood near the middle of the long room, and freed one hand long enough to gesture toward them. "Please, be seated. Signe, will you do the honors?"

"Of course," the Heir murmured, her face unreadable, and turned away toward a standing cabinet. She returned a moment later with a tray of drinks, and coffee with its trimmings.

Landret lowered himself into a chair that had obviously been built specially for him, and freed his forearms from the crutch-rings with a sigh. Alkres started, and sat quickly in the closest chair. I seated myself on a tambour at his side.

"Will you take coffee, sor, Medium?" Signe asked, and I resigned myself to the polite small talk of the coffee service.

When at last we each had a glass, and had commented at some length on the spices and the savor, Landret leaned back in his chair, darting a mischievous glance in my direction. When he spoke, however, it was to Alkres. "Well, sor, we are in private here. May I suggest that we dispense with the formalities for now, and discuss this like the kin we are?"

"Kin?" Even Alkres looked a little blank at that.

"Distantly," Landret said.

Signe said, "If we're being informal, Father, I'll bite. How are we related?"

"Come now, daughter, what good are history lessons if you don't pay attention? Andres Orillon married and divorced—or was divorced by—Jessa Halex before *Home Rule* ever reached Orestes. Their child was Engineer at the Landing."

He was talking about events that had happened fifteen hundred years ago. It was hardly much of a claim to kinship—and if we couldn't do any better, after generations of intermarriage, Alkres could be in trouble. Quite possibly that was what Landret had meant to emphasize, I thought, and a chill went down my spine. I had known Landret was a formidable man—how could he be anything else, Patriarch of the one Kinship that stood outside the immediate tangles of Oresteian politics?—but I hadn't realized just how formidable he could be. I just hoped the revelation hadn't come too late.

"If we're being informal," Alkres said, "I don't think we ought to count that. It doesn't seem to be anything more than formality."

It wasn't a bad riposte, from a fifteen-year-old to a man four times his age. Landret smiled. "I suppose that's true. Now—" His voice sharpened suddenly, flicking from banter to cold question. "Just what is it you want from me, Alkres Halex?"

I stiffened, but knew I could not answer the old man's question. He was testing Alkres, I recognized that much, but I couldn't quite see the answer he wanted. Silently, I willed the boy to answer carefully.

Alkres shot a glance in my direction, but looked away as quickly, and I knew he'd recognized the test as well. The shadow of a frown showed on his face, but his voice was perfectly polite. "Sor, I've come to appeal to you, under the code, as Patriarch of a Kinship to another. I'm being cheated of the rights we all swear to protect when we promise to follow code, and I ask you to help me—I ask for sanctuary, and for your sanction."

Landret didn't answer for a long moment. At last, he said, "But what exactly do you want?"

Alkres's frown deepened. "I told you—" He broke off, and said, with creditable steadiness, "Perhaps I didn't make myself clear; I'm not quite used to being Patriarch. Perhaps Trey could make it clearer."

"Serves you right," Signe murmured, and Landret's mouth twitched once. He controlled himself, however, and said, "Very well, Medium, let's hear your explanation."

"I don't see quite what I can add to Himself's appeal," I said, keeping my expression as open and innocent as possible. It is not a look I do particularly well, but it would serve, for this. "He—all of us—ask for sanctuary here, for shelter, and Himself wishes your sanction to speak before the Ship's Council. I think this is unquestionably a matter for the Council, sor."

"Why should I sanction you?" Landret leaned back in his chair, dismissing me as if I no longer existed. I felt sure he was doing it deliberately, to goad me into—what?

I didn't know what he was pushing for, and that uncertainty helped me keep my anger under firm control.

Alkres lowered his eyes, looking out from under his lashes. It was a trick I'd seen him use before, to hide annoyance at his cousins, and I doubted he knew how demure it made him look. After a moment, he said, "Because I've been wronged."

There was a long silence, and then Landret said, "Trumped, by God. How old are you, Alkres?"

"Fifteen," the boy answered defiantly.

Landret nodded. I kept my face straight with an effort. Whether he'd fully intended it or not, Alkres had picked exactly the right words to sway the Orillon Patriarch. Under the code, of course, Landret was obliged to help him, and Alkres would have been within his rights to invoke that openly—but then Landret could have pretended to accept the Brandr justification of the attack, which ruled out any argument that any Halex had been wronged. This way, by simply assuming that Landret would follow the code, Alkres had put the older man under an obligation he could not refuse.

"Very well," Landret said. "You and yours are welcome here, as my honored guests, and I will sponsor you to speak to the Council—though I cannot promise more than that." He did not bother qualifying the statement, and Alkres's eyes widened briefly at that assumption of equality.

"I beg your pardon, sor," I said, "but when does the Council meet?"

"At Sunset," Landret answered. "Our Sunset." He reached for his crutches again, fitting his arms into the rings without seeming to look at them. "Until then, consider my household to be yours."

It was obvious dismissal, and we stood. Alkres said, with unexpected dignity, "It's been so long since people have behaved properly, I hardly know what I'm supposed to do. Thank you, sor."

Landret smiled. "Very prettily spoken, but it's only right. Signe, see them to their rooms."

As I'd expected, Signe turned us over to one of the house-stewards as soon as we'd reached the bottom of the great stairway, but as a courtesy, she walked with us to the neighboring Tower, where most of the Family was lodged.

We were housed on the second floor, Alkres in a two-room suite usually reserved for Signe's child, the rest of us in the rooms to either side. Guil and Leith had chosen to share the larger room, and I wished with all my heart I had someone to share mine with. If Rehur had chosen to come with us. . . . But he had been right, it would have been impossible to keep to the code on the long flight.

"If you'd like, Medium, I can have your dinner sent up," the house-steward said, tentatively. "Don't worry about the Patriarch, I can see to him."

I hesitated, and she nodded toward the closed door of Leith and Guil's room. "They'll be eating informally tonight, Medium. It's no trouble."

I glanced at Alkres's door, knowing I should go down to dinner with him, but the temptation of a few hours' peace and quiet, away from all my responsibilities, was overwhelming. "Thank you, I'll accept the offer."

The house-steward nodded. "I'll send the tray in just about two hours."

"Thank you," I said again, but she was already out of earshot.

This room was not as luxurious as my quarters in the Halex Tower—just a single room, with a stove-bed set into the near wall, and a tiny, palm-sized window—but it was perfectly comfortable. The painted walls were more muted here—abstract geometrics done in subtle, pleasing colors—and the furniture was the heavy, practical stuff I'd gotten used to on Orestes. More important, the wall heater, set in a carved frame of the charcoal-colored holdstone, had its own control. I hesitated only for an instant before turning it to its highest setting, telling myself I would be more conservative tomorrow. When the coils were glowing orange, I unfastened my cloak and set it aside, newly aware of my filthy clothes. There would be a communal bath somewhere nearby, of course, but there wasn't much point in washing if I had nothing clean to put on afterwards. Without much hope, I pulled open the storage drawers set into the wall beneath the bed. No clothes, as I'd expected, but there was a light quilted robe. I could ask the house-steward to find me some better clothes when she brought the tray. I stripped, wrapped the robe around me, and went looking for the baths.

It was crowded, of course, just before the dinner hours, but most of Oresteian etiquette evolved to deal with crowding. I managed to find a free cubicle, and spent a luxurious half hour washing away the last of the grime. Then, winding the robe tightly around me, I hurried back through the cold corridors to my room. The steward had been there before me, but my curse died away when I saw that she had left me not just the dinner tray but a complete change of clothing. A pile of ceramin laundry tags lay on the desk beside the tray. I dressed—the steward had made an accurate guess of the correct sizes, though the undershirt was a little short in the sleeves—then scrawled my mark on each of the tags. It was the work of a minute to fasten the cords to my filthy clothes, and I shoved them outside for the launderers to collect. It was only after I'd finished eating that I remembered I still didn't know precisely when Electra's Sunset was.

I'd never been anywhere on Orestes without finding an almanac close at hand, but it took me some minutes to find the slim pamphlet, tucked almost out of sight beneath the reader. I flipped through the flimsy pages until I found the current date—just past Electra's Sunrise, I discovered—and began counting diagrams. The concentric circles showed the moons' relative positions every twelve hours; Electra would cross the line into Sunset in about six calendar-days. That meant I had a little time before the Ship's Council met, and I didn't intend to waste it.

Neither did some others. Over the next three calendar-days, Guil managed to discover an old friend who worked on the tower switchboard, and persuaded him to keep us informed of events on Orestes. The news was mixed: the Brandr, aided and abetted by Yslin Rhawn, still managed to keep control of Destiny proper and the more settled parts of the Mandate, but they were unable to subdue the small-hold miners who had benefited so much from Herself's efforts, or the Destiny Necropolis. This was somewhat encouraging, especially when we began hearing rumors of perfectly respectable Family members—not merely of the mainline Family, but of the Branches as well—vanishing for calendar-days in the Necropolis, to reemerge as ghosts or *para'anin*, or simply as themselves, newly committed to Alkres's cause. The Brandr, it was said, were looking for any excuse to close the Necropolis, but every attempt had brought renewed threats of rioting. Rehur and his friends were doing their job well, as the script demanded. I only hoped he would have the sense to stop short of the usual denouement.

And then the ships began to arrive from Orestes. There weren't many, of course—the Brandr held both space-ports now, and the moons were moving apart, so that it took almost seventy hours to make the crossing—but the ships that did manage to lift brought Family members to show their support for their new Patriarch. Most had thought to bring money, thank God, since we could never have paid for their keep in Glittermark, and Landret Orillon agreed to support the rest. Alkres asked for and received a daily account of the costs, an adult gesture that pleased the Orillon Elders, and deceived no one. By ones and twos, the new arrivals made their way to the Orillon Tower to pay their respects to Alkres, and each one brought more news of resistance that stopped just short of open rebellion. Many of them were Rhawn, outraged by the Holder's behavior, and for the first time, I began to think that we might be able to win outright in the Ship's Council. The newcomers, some of whom I'd known slightly at the Tower, were less sanguine, but I couldn't help hoping.

Two days before the Council was to meet, the Donar landed at Glittermark, diverted from Orestes. I was sitting with Leith in one of the Tower's common rooms, staring out the low window at the thin snow blowing across the headland, when Guil arrived with the news. It meant nothing to me, and I frowned, but Leith's slow grin warned me that something important had happened.

"You know Petrovich, too, don't you?" she asked, still with her catlike smile.

Guil nodded. "Well enough, yes."

"Go talk to Colgar, see if he can give you a clear line to the Donar, and see what Petrovich is carrying. If it's right, get him to hold off doing anything about it until he's talked to me—or to Trey," she added, with a quick glance in my direction. "Just don't let him talk to anyone from off-world first."

Guil nodded again, unresentful of the order, and vanished. I said, "What's this all about, Leith?"

Moraghan's grin widened again, irresistibly. "*Donar* works under contract to Fenris and Sons, usually—that's who your Halex were dealing with, right? If we're lucky, we've got your boy's arms shipment."

"That would be too lucky a coincidence," I said.

"Would you want to put money on it?" Leith asked, and I shook my head.

"I don't bet on a sure thing. There's no sport in it."

As it turned out, though, I had to eat my words. Before Guil had time to contact her friend, a runner arrived from the switchboard to announce that a Captain Petrovich was looking for either a Captain Moraghan or a Mediator named Trey Maturin. We went down to the switchboard together, Leith crowing her victory.

The *Donar* had brought the Halex arms, but it had also brought complications. Leith's friend on the Trade Board had been unable to stop the first—Brandr—shipment, but on hearing of the unrest on Orestes, he had ordered Fenris and Sons either to stop or divert the second shipment. Evgen Petrovich had received the message just as he made the last jump to the system buoy. Fuel requirements left him no choice: he had to come into the system to refuel, so he had requested emergency berthing on Electra. That brought the weapons directly into the hands of the intended recipient, or at least it should have done so. Petrovich cited his orders from Fenris and Sons, and refused to consider delivery until he'd talked to his employers. I did my best to persuade him, but he remained adamant: only Fenris herself could authorize the release. He did agree to contact her, and I ended the conversation with the request that Fenris contact me if she had any questions.

Apparently, she didn't: within fourteen hours of my conversation with Petrovich, the captain was back on the 'net with apologies. Fenris took the position that the goods had been bought and paid for legally, and that she could not and would not stand in the way of their delivery to their rightful owner. That Alkres was that rightful owner, she had no doubt, and we made a brief foray into Glittermark to sign the appropriate papers. Signe, as Portreeve, waived the storage and import fees, and Alkres was left in possession of a blockhouse full of expensive weaponry.

On the way back to the Orillon Tower, I couldn't help wondering if I'd done the right thing in persuading Petrovich to release the cargo. After all, I knew precisely what Leith's Trade contact had been trying to do—prevent further killing—and, as a Mediator, I was supposed to be working toward the same end. Putting blasters in the hands of the Halex was not likely to stop the fighting—but it might give Alkres what was rightfully his. And yet, Alkres was still a fifteen-year-old boy. Even if he did win back the genarchy, wouldn't that just guarantee more fighting, as people fought to control him? Maybe not—probably not, I told myself. There are mechanisms for choosing guardians . . . all of which involve the Branch Holders. I couldn't help remembering what I'd told Alkres, back on Orestes: neither law nor justice was everything, and sometimes keeping worlds intact was more important than either. Was I just making things worse by fighting for Alkres's rights? There never were any easy answers to questions like that, and in the end, I fell back on the only justification I could give. What was happening was wrong, and should be stopped; I would do what I could to end it. Besides, if I hadn't acted, Leith would have, or Guil. And maybe, I told myself, just maybe, the Ship's Council would decide in Alkres's favor.

Sunset was cloudy, the distant sunlight glowing through a break in the clouds just above the horizon, Agamemnon's ghostly shape barely visible behind the milky screen. It had stopped snowing the day before, but the Closed Sea shone eerily white under the new coating. It had been an unusually cold calendar-year, Signe had said; the green-houses were hard put to keep up with the demands. . . .

I shook myself then, and reached for my overtunic. I was to attend the Council this time—Landret had found an obscure point of the law relating to minor heirs, and was certain he could convince the other genarchs that it applied in my case—and I had chosen my clothes with care. I could not hide my off-world origin easily, nor did I particularly want to, just in case I could use my Mediator's status to advantage, but at the same time, I couldn't afford to look too outlandish. There were some very conservative

Holders among the Council members, and I didn't want to antagonize anyone. The house-steward had found me clothes of good material, but of sober cut and color, plain felty trousers and a knitted tunic whose only decoration was a band of fancier stitches across the shoulders. The dull reddish-brown—one of the colors of undyed hoobey fleece— was not particularly flattering, but it was at least unexceptionable. I leaned forward to study my reflection in the mirror for a final time, then adjusted the medium's gorget I had borrowed from Edlin around my neck. It was time to go.

The Orillon Patriarch attended most Councils by D-com link. The auditorium was in the lower levels of the Tower, as close as possible to the great generators that drove its projectors. It was a cold, rather unpleasant room, the harsh lights of the cameras seeming only to add to the chill, though I knew they would be hot enough before long. The technicians were there already, and had been for at least an hour, seated behind their horseshoe-shaped console in the far corner of the room. The attendees' bench—actually, chairs behind an elaborately carved table, draped with a bright cloth to hide Landret's legs—was at their right, facing the display tank. It was alive, light swirling like fog behind the glass, the technicians waiting for Landret's command to bring out the latent images.

The Orillon Patriarch was already in his place, leaning back in a chair that was almost as elaborate as a throne. Alkres, wearing clothes borrowed from Signe's child, sat at his right, his mouth set in a hard line that only just disguised his nervousness. Signe sat at her father's left, and there was an empty chair beyond her for the Tam'ne Holder. I took my place behind Alkres's chair just as the Tam'ne entered the room. I had not met Galar Tam'ne before, and I took advantage of the moment to study him discreetly. He was young to be a Branch Holder, perhaps even younger than Signe, but his good-natured face didn't show any awareness of that as a disadvantage. The Tam'ne symbol of three seaflowers arranged in a triangle was tattooed on his broad cheek—the first such tattoo I'd seen on Electra—but his thinning hair was cut quite short, rather than pulled into the usual topknot.

"I'm sorry to be late, sor," he said. "It's a long flight from the Base."

"You're not late, yet," Landret answered, and nodded to the technicians. "Let's begin."

The technicians adjusted their machines, and the fog in the display tank greyed slightly, taking on new depth. As we watched, ghostly shapes began to form—first the hard, dark lines of the genarchs' table, then the tier of seats where the Branch Holders sat. The Holders themselves were little more than shadows, but even as I thought that, the images hardened and became real. I saw a technician give a discreet thumbs-up.

Landret cleared his throat. "Compatriots, we are met."

Shemer Axtell, who sat in the Arbiter's seat at the center of the long table, gave him a distinctly unhappy look. "We are met," he agreed.

"I protest." That was Halfrid Brandr, leaning forward in his place at the very end of the genarchs' table. "A point of order."

"State it," Shemer answered. I felt cold. I hadn't expected the Brandr to attack so promptly, or so completely without finesse. It did not bode well for the rest of the meeting.

"There is an off-worlder present," Halfrid answered, and tried unsuccessfully to hide a smirk. "This is strictly against accepted procedure, as Landret Orillon well knows."

Landret lifted a hand. "A point to the point of order, Shemer. The Halex Patriarch is still a minor, and as such is entitled to the presence of the advisors of his choice."

"Alkres Halex—who is not by any stretch of the imagination a Patriarch—" Halfrid broke off abruptly as a woman—the Jan Holder, by her tattoo—leaned forward to murmur something in his ear.

"Alkres Halex, whatever his status, is old enough to have accepted the code," the Brandr Patriarch continued. "He is therefore considered an adult."

"You can take the oath at twelve," Landret answered. "No one ever said twelve was adult, Halfrid."

The Brandr started to say something else, but Shemer laid his right hand flat on the table. "The point has been called," he said. "I put it to the vote: may the medium stay? Do you have objections, Halfrid?"

The Jan Holder leaned forward again, and the Brandr shook his head, scowling.

"Then I call the vote," Shemer continued. "I vote, for Axtell, aye. Brandr?"

"Nay."

"Fyfe?"

"Nay."

"Orillon?"

He had left out the Halex, I thought. Araxie Fyfe slammed her hand on the table, even as Landret said, "Aye."

"You haven't completed the call," the Fyfe Matriarch snapped. "What about the Halex?"

Shemer looked down his nose at her. "Ama, we're meeting to decide who holds that Mandate. You can hardly expect me to let either party vote."

Araxie subsided, scowling. Shemer glanced deliberately at the Brandr, but Halfrid had schooled his face into an approximation of unconcern. "Very well," Shemer said. "The vote is tied—two votes for, two votes against. As Arbiter, my vote decides. The medium may stay."

Halfrid leaned back in his chair, frowning, and Araxie muttered something under her breath. Landret folded his hands carefully in front of him, trying not to betray any satisfaction. I realized I had been holding my breath, and let it out slowly. It wasn't much of a victory, I knew that, but at least it was something. Certainly it was proof that Shemer Axtell wasn't going to let the Brandr have everything their way.

"To business," Shemer went on. "It has been charged before the Ship's Council that Eldrede Halex, late Matriarch of Halex Kinship, acted against code, breaking it grossly and in so many ways that the only possible remedy is their expulsion and the reversion of genarchy and Mandate to the Kinship's senior Branch, the Rhawn. In response, it is charged that the Brandr have acted outside code in their attack on the Halex Tower, which resulted in its destruction and excessive loss of life. Who will speak to the first charge?"

"I will," Halfrid said. My heart sank. It was bad that the Brandr were geting to press their charges first, and worse that his accusation was phrased in such a damaging way. We—Alkres—had to prove not only that Herself had not broken the code, but also that the Brandr had stepped over the line themselves, and there had never been much of a prohibition on bloodshed in the code.

Halfrid spoke well, repeating and elaborating on the statement he had made over the Destiny comnet immediately after the attack. Eldrede Halex had constantly tried to destroy the code, first by winking at infractions within her own Kinship, and then by preferring the services of off-worlders to the work of Oresteians, or even of her own kindred. Alkres stirred at that, but said nothing.

"I attempted to check this behavior by the sanctioned means," Halfrid continued, "both in the Ship's Council and in the Kinship Councils, but without effect. Eldrede, backed by her closest kin and indeed by most of the mainline Family, persisted in her efforts to avoid the code." He paused, and nodded in Araxie's direction. "This is most evident in the incident which led to feud between our Kinships and the Halex. The Halex behaved in such a manner as to prove their disregard for the code."

Alkres made a choked noise at that, quickly bitten off, but Halfrid stopped, staring at him. Shemer said, after a moment, "Did you speak, sor?"

Alkres shook his head slowly, saying in his most innocent voice, "No, sor."

It was well done. I saw Asbera Ingvarr, sitting with the other Holders in the tier of seats behind the genarchs' bench, grin openly. Shemer passed a hand across his mouth as if to wipe away a smile, and said, "Continue, please."

Halfrid took a deep breath, but the rolling momentum of his speech was gone. "In our attack, we acted not merely to prosecute our feud, but to destroy a danger to our way of life. This is why I ask the Council to declare all surviving members of the mainline Halex to be codebreakers and as dead, and to confirm the senior Branch Holder as the rightful genarch."

"You can't do that," Landret said. "Wholesale death, for every living Halex? It's hardly reasonable—your own people up in the Tolands don't have anything to say about what you do, Halfrid, and you can't demand the same accountability from another Family."

"It's everyone's duty to uphold the code," Halfrid answered frostily. "It was their duty to stop her."

Shemer laid his hand on the table again, cutting off Landret's retort. "Guilt and punishment are two separate issues. We'll decide on guilt first, if you please."

Halfrid subsided, looking pleased enough at having been able to air the suggestion. Shemer stared sternly into the cameras, so that it seemed he was looking directly at Alkres.

"Alkres Halex, as ult'eir and claimant to the genarchy, do you wish to answer these charges?"

I could see the boy's shoulders tense, but his voice was steady enough when he answered. "Yes, I want to answer them—though I hardly know how. They don't seem to make any sense."

I had to agree with him there, but I touched his shoulder discreetly in warning. He couldn't afford to lose his temper, especially not so early in the proceedings. His left hand closed into a tight fist, and I knew he'd understood.

"To begin at what I think is the first issue," Alkres began again, "it's true that Halfrid Brandr complained, oh, a dozen times, to the Ship's Council about breach of code, but in all but two cases, the Council said we were right. In those two cases, Herself—my grandmother—obeyed the decree of the Council, and was only assessed a fine."

We were on firm ground there, I knew. I had spent the past few days hunting out those statistics, and then making sure that Alkres memorized them. He was word perfect, but still he gave a quick glance over his shoulder. I nodded slightly, just as Halfrid said, "Even if those numbers are right, the actions of a truly law-abiding genarch would not have been questioned so often. And I think there were other instances."

Alkres hesitated, taken aback by the direct challenge, even though he knew the Brandr was in the wrong. I leaned forward a little and whispered, "You can ask the recorder for a ruling."

Alkres nodded. "Sor, Arbiter, I think that question could be settled better by the Recorder."

Shemer nodded, and gestured to the oldest of his Holders. The man touched a series of keys on his lapboard, then leaned back a little to study the results. After a moment, he said, "The boy is substantially correct. Fourteen accusations were filed over the last fifteen calendar-months, all by Halfrid Brandr, and all but two were disallowed. Those two were considered to be minor, and were settled by fine."

Halfrid frowned, and Shemer said mildly, "That is the official record of the Council. You may continued, Alkres."

The boy nodded. "Thank you. So, my answer to the charge is that, if the Ship's Council didn't say we were code-breakers, it's not the Brandr's place to accuse us. Their attack was without justification."

Halfrid smiled slowly, and Araxie Fyfe said, "We were at feud."

"The question of off-world interference was never brought before the Council," Halfrid added.

"But you called in off-worlders, too, or you wouldn't've been able to take the Tower," Alkres retorted. "That makes you no better than you say we are."

Halfrid's smile widened unpleasantly. "We did not call in off-worlders," he said, with the air of a schoolteacher correcting a student's mistake. "We purchased some weapons from an off-world firm, purely in order to counteract Eldrede's riches—riches earned by prostituting her Kinship to off-world demands—"

"That's not true," Alkres cried, and the Halex Branch Holders muttered to each other. Even Yslin Rhawn looked annoyed.

Halfrid said strongly, riding over the protests, "We did not seek or receive any off-world assistance. There is no comparison."

I winced, recognizing too late the trap he'd set for us. By emphasizing the question of code-breakings, and insisting that it be settled first, he'd robbed us of our best weapon—the Brandr demand that the Rhawn be promoted to head of the Kinship. If the Brandr accusations were justified, there could be no question of Alkres's being wronged; Yslin Rhawn would logically and correctly be the new genarch. I had been counting on the sheer outrageousness of the demand to sway the other genarchs and Holders, but I had miscalculated. Now the whole thing turned on the legitimacy of Eldrede's off-world connections, and I knew how jealous the other genarchs had been of the wealth and foresight that let her form them.

"As for the attack," Halfrid went on, "we are at feud, and will be until the matter is settled."

Shemer laid his hand on the table. "The propriety of your attack is not at issue now. The question is, I believe, that of the activities of the Halex Matriarch."

Halfrid nodded, still smiling, and Alkres said desperately, "Sor, I'm not finished with my defense."

Araxie sighed audibly, and even Shemer frowned. Landret's face was frozen in a bored mask that I knew hid his concern.

"It's my right to call witnesses, isn't it?" Alkres went on. "And I have witnesses who can prove my grandmother just employed off-worlders—employed them just the way you employed off-world weapons, Halfrid Brandr. There's no difference."

It was a good try, I thought, detachedly, but I doubted it would work. I would say what Alkres wanted, of course—it was no more than the truth—but I was the only witness available. I wasn't even sure they'd let me speak.

"What witnesses?" Shemer asked.

"Our medium, Trey Maturin," Alkres answered, and Halfrid gave a cry of protest.

"An off-worlder, and a prime example of what I've been talking about. Shemer, you can't allow it."

"And others," Alkres said, but Araxie cut him off.

"Halfrid's right, the medium has no right to speak—no right to attend, for that matter!"

"That question has already been decided," Shemer said, with glacial dignity. "The medium may speak."

"I have other witnesses," Alkres said again.

I frowned, not knowing who he meant, and murmured, "Be careful, Alkres."

The boy didn't seem to hear. "I have more witnesses," he said, more insistently.

Shemer said, "Name them."

Alkres took a deep breath, his thin shoulders moving visibly under his tunic. "The Branch Holders, my Branch Holders, who were there when the decisions were made, and know exactly what went on. You'll have to listen to them—and I charge you Holders, as Patriarch, to answer truthfully or face the code."

"Oh, Alkres," I whispered, almost to myself. If Yslin Rhawn were honest, it would have been a brilliant move—but the Rhawn Holder wanted the genarchy. He wouldn't even have to lie, either; he had always opposed Herself's plans. . . . I pulled myself together, aware that Alkres was speaking to me.

"Trey, will you explain to the Council just what your duties were with the Family?"

Halfrid smirked, not needing to say anything.

That did it. I threw away all caution and drew myself up to my full height, deliberately stressing the clipped off-world accent. "Sirs, I am a Conglomerate Mediator by training, employed by the Halex Kinship both as a mediator and as a medium, accepting the local definition of the latter's duties. By a mediator's standard contract, I am an employee of the Kinship—the Kinship considered as a corporate entity—and am bound by that contract to consider the Kinship's best interest at all times. You would know better than I what a medium's business entails; I've done my best to adhere to the model laid out for me in my contract." I took a grip on myself then, and went on, trying to chose neutral language. "My contract states quite clearly that I'm an employee of the Kinship—of the genarch." I started to add something else, but saw, out of the corner of my eye, Signe shake her head almost imperceptibly. I stopped, waiting.

Araxie said, "The testimony's meaningless, coming from an interested party."

"That's very bad logic, Araxie," Landret said.

"That's a matter for each of us to decide," Shemer said, sharply. He glared at Alkres. "And your other witnesses?"

"I ask each of you," Alkres began, "Barthel, Asbera, Yslin: you were there in the Kinship council each time my grandmother had dealings with off-world. Was she really 'prostituting the Kinship,' or was she just doing our business the only way she could?"

There was a long silence, the Holders looking acutely uncomfortable. Yslin, I thought, was faking it, panting for his chance to stab Alkres in the back. After a moment, Shemer cleared his throat. "Sors, and ama, you must enter."

Asbera Ingvarr looked up sharply. "I will, then," she

said, and turned a hostile glance on Yslin, daring him to interrupt. "I was at the meetings, yes, and I say, with the Patriarch, that there was no breach of code, no more than there was any of the times Halfrid Brandr charged it. And that's the exact truth, under the code, no matter what anyone else tells you."

Halfrid sneered openly. Shemer said, "Ansson?"

Barthel Ansson licked his lips, then made an odd, shrugging motion. "I saw no breach of code when I was there," he said. "I ask the Council to excuse me from any further questions."

Damn him, I thought, he's ruined us. I kept my face steady, bracing myself to hear what Yslin Rhawn would say. The Holder did not speak, and finally Shemer said, "Rhawn."

Yslin faced the cameras, eyes tragic. Only the slight twitching at the corners of his mouth betrayed his real feelings. "Sor, ama, this isn't easy," he said, and sighed tragically. He made a great show of choosing his next words, and it was all I could do to keep my lip from curling in contempt. Surely no one was being taken in by this incompetent, I thought, knowing perfectly well it was to their advantage to pretend to believe. They can't believe him.

Yslin sighed again, and spread his hands to indicate he was abandoning some position. It was more like a dancer's mime than any human gesture, and I sneered, knowing Yslin would see. His eyes flashed angrily, but he kept his voice under control. "As many—most—of you know, I have often opposed Herself's dealings with off-world. As for code-breach, I—I'll just repeat what's already been said," he said, with the air of a man who's just found a way out of a difficult situation. "There were accusations made before the Ship's Council, but they weren't proved."

"Two of them were," Halfrid murmured, and Yslin bowed his head

"That's true."

After that, the issue wasn't in doubt. With only one Holder willing to stand up for him, Alkres had no chance of winning; Shemer's poll was barely a formality. The mainline Halex were found guilty of breaking the code, and the Brandr attack was accepted as justified. Only

Landret voted for us, and he had the stiff, blank look of a gambler who knows he holds the losing cards.

"That brings us to the second question," the Brandr Patriarch said loudly, flushed with victory. "What's to be done about the mainline Family?"

"You have no proof that all the mainline kin conspired to break the code," Landret said wearily. "That's not a reasonable assumption."

"They must be punished," Araxie said. "It was their duty to oppose breach of code—with their lives, if necessary."

"How many of them had the opportunity to oppose Eldrede?" Landret asked. "I repeat, what Halfrid proposes is not a reasonable punishment." He hesitated, then added, under his breath, "It's an act of malice."

Halfrid bridled at that, but Shemer pretended not to have heard. "What do you suggest as a reasonable punishment, Landret? They have been found guilty—something has to be done."

"It seems to me that the guilty have already been punished," Landret said, "and more severely than the law requires. Levy a fine, if you feel something else is needed, but nothing more."

"Not nearly enough!" Araxie snapped.

Halfrid said, "Fines are all right for minor offenses. This is a major crime—we've never dealt with anything so serious, not since before the Landing."

Alkres had controlled his anger until then, but the comparison with the semi-legendary generation-ship mutiny, the original sin that brought the colonists to Orestes instead of warm, fertile Agni, was too much for him. "How dare you? You're acting more like the Mutineers; we never did."

"Alkres!" I put both hands on his shoulders, forcing him back into his chair. That was the one insult never spoken on Orestes: one could skirt it, as Halfrid had done, but Alkres had stepped over the line. Distaste and disapproval warred in Shemer's face, and in the faces of the Holders. Out of the corner of my eye, I saw Landret slowly shake his head. Alkres subsided, his shoulders rigid under my hands.

"Enough!" Shemer glared into the cameras. "It has been

proposed that the mainline Halex be punished for breaking the code by their disenfranchisement, and that the Kinship be given over to the senior Branch Holder; or that, the senior members of the mainline kindred being true-dead, the remainder of that kin be punished by fine and/or forfeit. Is there any other proposal?"

There was a movement among the Brandr Holders, and a rat-faced man, the youngest of the Holders, leaned forward, clearing his throat. "If I might speak, sor, and Arbiter?"

Shemer glanced at Halfrid, who shrugged, frowning. The Axtell Patriarch said, "Very well. Permission being granted, I recognize the Holder Stennet Fira."

"Thank you," Stennet said, with another wary glance at his genarch. "I don't have another proposal, but I do offer an amendment to Himself's. With all respect, Landret Orillon's right, you can't punish all the mainline for the matriarch's doings. I propose that the surviving members of the mainline kin be allowed to accept membership in whatever other Branch they're closest kin to, and that they be declared dead only if they refuse that offer."

I sighed, and saw Landret lean back in his chair. Stennet had just killed our last chance to stave off disaster, and we both knew it. Signe was whispering to the Tam'ne Holder, and Galar appeared to be listening intently, but then Shemer called the vote, and I turned my attention back to the display tank.

"Brandr?"

The Jan Holder was still murmuring at Halfrid, who made a face, and waved his hand impatiently at Shemer. "All right, aye. I accept the amendment."

"Fyfe?"

Araxie nodded. "Aye."

"Orillon?"

Landret sighed deeply. "I oppose the entire suggestion."

"Do you abstain?" Shemer asked.

Landret's lips tightened—the first signs of anger I'd seen him show—but then he mastered himself, and said, gravely, "No. I believe both versions of this proposal to be pernicious. However, this is the lesser of the two evils. I vote aye."

"Axtell votes aye as well," Shemer said. "The amendment is accepted."

Alkres leaned back in his chair. "We've lost, haven't we?" he whispered.

"Maybe not," I said. I heard the doubt in my own voice, and made myself speak the truth. "But it doesn't look good."

"I shouldn't've said anything," the boy murmured, half to himself, and I shook my head.

"It's not your fault," I began, but then Shemer had laid his hand on the table again.

"Are there any other proposals, or further amendments?"

Landret lifted his hand. "I ask that the Holders be polled as well. This is, after all, a matter that concerns them deeply—more so than most things that come before the Ship's Council."

"Some it concerns more deeply than others," Signe said, with a meaningful glance at Yslin Rhawn. The Tam'ne Holder laughed, and Stennet Fira put his hand over his mouth.

Shemer ignored the byplay. "That seems reasonable. Is there any objection?"

"I don't have any objection," Halfrid said abruptly, "but there's something I'd like to say. My honor has been called into question and under code I'm entitled to answer that."

"That question hasn't come before the Council, and won't come before it now," Shemer said, sounding almost startled.

"Nevertheless," Halfrid said. The two genarchs locked eyes, and it was Shemer who looked away.

"All right," he muttered, "speak your piece."

"I'll say this, then," Halfrid began. "I hold the judgment of the Ship's Council to be an admission that our feud against the Halex, and each action of that feud, was justified. I further state that opposition to this decision is grounds for feud, and will be treated as such."

"You can't do that," one of the Fyfe Holders said, involuntarily, and the Matriarch hushed him.

I held my breath. Surely, this would be the final straw; surely, they wouldn't give in to such a blatant threat. Maybe we had a chance after all. . . . Then I looked at the

wary, frightened faces around the table, and knew that last
hope was gone. Neither Holders nor genarchs looked ready
to lead an opposition movement—not even Landret, though
Signe and the Tam'ne Holder were whispering together
again. Araxie was smiling, openly enjoying her vicarious
triumph, and I felt a chill go up my spine. What would we
do, if—when—this effort failed?

"Your statement is noted for the record," Shemer said
flatly, not looking at Alkres. "Very well. I will poll the
Holders of each Kinship, and then the genarchs, in the
usual order. Berngard of Axtell?"

"Death," the elderly Holder answered promptly. I supposed I couldn't blame him for being afraid to oppose the
Brandr—how could he, when his Patriarch had backed
down first?—but I despised him for answering so quickly.
The same disgust was reflected in Galar Tam'ne's face, and
he whispered something more to Signe.

"Why bother polling them?" Alkres whispered. "Let's
just get it over with."

"Emelon of Axtell?" Shemer continued.

"Death." The Emelon Holder looked at her hands, unable to meet Alkres's accusing stare.

"I don't know," I said. "Maybe to get them on record, if
we can ever appeal?"

"There isn't any appeal from the Ship's Council," Alkres
said bitterly.

"Hadulin of Axtell?" Shemer asked.

Hadulin made a face, distorting the axes tattooed on his
forehead, but nodded. "Death."

"As Arbiter, I reserve my vote," Shemer said. "Elgeve
of Brandr?"

There were no surprises from the Brandr Holders, though
neither the Jan Holder nor Stennet Fira looked particularly pleased with their Patriarch's statement. Alkres shivered convulsively as Halfrid cast his vote, but said nothing.

"Charlot of Fyfe?" Shemer asked.

The two Fyfe Holders voted with their Matriarch. Araxie's
voice, when she cast her vote, was almost indecently
pleased with herself, and even her Holders looked a little
embarrassed by her attitude.

"Ansson of Halex?" Shemer asked, and by some tremendous effort of will kept his voice completely neutral.

Alkres tensed, staring at Barthel as though he could influence the Holder by sheer strength of will. Barthel looked away, glancing at the other Halex Branch Holders, then leaned his face in his hands. "A moment, please," he said, in a muffled voice.

Halfrid Brandr started to say something, but the Jan Holder forestalled it. There was a long silence, broken at last by Shemer clearing his throat. Barthel looked up, eyes wild.

"I cannot vote, I won't vote. Let me be."

"Ansson of Halex abstains," Shemer repeated, after a moment. "Ingvarr of Halex?"

Asbera shot a contemptuous glance at Barthel, then faced the cameras squarely. "I can vote, and I will. I vote for a fine, if anything, and the hell with you, Halfrid Brandr."

Bravely spoken, I thought, but not much use at this late date. If she'd only declared herself so unambiguously earlier, we might not be in this position.

Halfrid said, ominously, "I won't forget this, Ingvarr."

"Be quiet!" Shemer seemed to have recovered some of his confidence. "There will be no threats in the Council."

"He might've said that earlier," Alkres muttered.

Shemer looked up and down the table again, compelling quiet. "Rhawn of Halex?"

Yslin looked down at his hands—less from reluctance, I thought, then to hide his smile. Still looking down, he said, "Death."

Someone among the Holders hissed softly, but the sound was cut off before I could see who had made it. Alkres said, very quietly, "Yslin never did like me."

"It doesn't have anything to do with you," I murmured. "Never think it does."

"By the decision of the Council, the Halex genarchy is considered disputed and casts no vote," Shemer continued. "Tam'ne of Orillon?"

Galar hesitated, his long mouth drawn into a pained scowl, and Landret said, "One moment, please." He fixed his eyes on Halfrid. "This statement of yours, Brandr. Essentially, you said you consider opposition to you grounds for feud. Is that correct?"

Halfrid hesitated, and I found myself hoping the Brandr

Patriarch had finally miscalculated. Surely he couldn't afford to admit openly that that was what he'd said—though everyone knew that was what he'd meant—but if he backed down, softened the threat, maybe it would put heart into the other genarchs and their Holders, give them a chance to recast their vote. . . . Then Halfrid smiled, and I knew we'd lost.

"Yes, that's correct," the Brandr Patriarch said. "I stand behind it."

Landret sighed, suddenly looking very old. Galar and Signe exchanged nervous glances, and at last I understood what I should have realized from the beginning. Electra was a land-poor world, and what they had was good only for mining. Signe had said the greenhouses had been having difficulties because of the cold—and where else would Electra, the Orillon Mandate, go for food but to Orestes? The Brandr had held the winning card all along.

"Tam'ne of Orillon?" Shemer said again.

Galar sighed. "Death," he said, reluctantly.

"Orillon?" Shemer asked.

Landret closed his eyes. "Death."

Alkres's mouth trembled as though he were about to cry, but he controlled himself in time, staring at Landret as though he'd never seen him before.

"And Axtell votes for death," Shemer said softly. He looked away from the cameras, not meeting Alkres's eyes. "The decision of the Council is, then, that the mainline Halex are as dead, but that they may for the time of one calendar-month function as living in order that they may, if they so choose, become part of the closest Branch. At the end of the calender-month, any Halex of Halex still claiming that Family will be as dead. This is the decision of the Council."

"I protest that," Galar said suddenly. "I protest all today's decisions."

"You can't do that," Araxie said.

"On what ground?" Shemer demanded.

"Undue influence and wrongful action," Galar shot back. Unbelievably, he was grinning—nerves, I thought, as much as anything, but then I saw that Signe was smiling, too. Landret was watching both his Heir and his Holder, gambler's eyes narrowed, waiting to see what they were doing.

"I do not accept the judgment," Galar said again, and folded his arms across his chest.

"You have no choice," Halfrid said.

Galar ignored him. Shemer frowned, the recorder whispering in his ear and then leaned forward again. "Tam'ne, you must accept the judgment of the Ship's Council. The vote has been taken and the judgment stands."

"I don't accept it," Galar said stubbornly.

"Then by God we'll make you accept it," Halfrid growled.

Landret lifted a hand, and I realized that this was what he'd been waiting for. "That's a matter for my concern, Halfrid, not yours."

"You must compel him to accept," Shemer said.

Landret bowed. "I will speak to him, certainly, you have my word on it. But this remains a matter for the Orillon Kinship—and no concern of the Ship's Council." He snapped his fingers at the technicians, and said, "I withdraw from the meeting."

On his signal, the technicians cut power, and the images in the tank faded. The last thing we saw was Halfrid Brandr leaning forward as though he could force the camera link to remain open, his face contorted into a mask of rage. Landret laughed softly, and I turned to face him. The Orillon Patriarch was looking at his Heir with a mixture of exasperation and affection.

"That was nicely done, daughter," he said, "but risky, very risky."

"It was the only thing to do," Signe answered, but she looked pleased by the old man's praise. "We've got a little time, now."

"I don't understand," Alkres said. He gave Landret a bitter glance. "Why bother, when you didn't stand up for me in the first place, when it might've made a difference?"

Signe flushed, but Landret said, quite calmly, "I apologize to you, Alkres, for not being able to do more. My people are fed from Orestes—from the Brandr Mandate, for the most part. I won't ask them to go hungry for you. I can't."

It was a statement familiar from a dozen holoplays, the proper—the only possible—response. Alkres looked away. "I know," he said, and turned to me. "What do we do now, Trey?"

I shook my head. "I don't know. At least we've got a calendar-month to work in—and at least the Kinship isn't completely bound."

I hadn't meant as a reminder, but Alkres nodded. "Yes. Thank you, ama, and sor, for arranging that."

Galar, flushing, shrugged one shoulder. "My girl's your age," he said. "I wouldn't want her left friendless."

Signe smiled. "As I—as Father—said, it's a matter of duty."

Alkres looked at the floor. "I'm sorry about what I said, sors, and ama. I wasn't thinking."

I held my breath, hoping the others would understand what that speech had cost the boy, and not laugh at him. Signe's lips twitched—she had children of her own—but she said nothing. Landret said, with admirable gravity, "I accept your apology, sor, as you accepted mine."

Alkres nodded.

"Well, Medium," Landret went on, "you'd better start thinking what you're going to do. I have some people who might be of use to you in that—shall we meet for dinner, you and Himself?"

I nodded, wondering just what we could do, short of armed conflict, but Alkres shook his head. "Please, sor, could we do that tomorrow? I—I'd like to be by myself for a while." In spite of himself, his voice trembled a little.

Landret's face softened. "Of course, forgive me. Tomorrow, then."

"I'll have your dinner sent up to your rooms?" Signe asked, the practical words belied by the concern in her voice. Alkres nodded.

"Shall I walk back with you?" I asked. The boy nodded again, and I gave Landret a quick look. "If you'll excuse us, sor?"

Landret nodded. "Of course. I'll see you tomorrow at dinner, then, if not before."

I put my arm around Alkres's shoulder, drawing him away. The tunnel that led back to our tower was empty—I doubted it was ever much used—and, after a moment, I heard him sniffle softly.

"Alkres?"

He turned violently away, but not before I'd seen that he was crying. Not quite knowing what I should do, I held out my arms and said his name again. He turned a scowling, tear-marked face in my direction, then, with a silent wail, flung himself against me. I held him, feeling completely helpless, while his body jerked and shook against me. He made no noise, except for his gasping breaths, and somehow that seemed most pitiful of all. At last the sobs slowed, then stopped altogether, but he clung to me for a moment longer before finally pushing me away.

"I'm all right," he said.

I nodded, not daring to say anything, and we walked in silence the rest of the way back to our rooms. Alkres stopped outside his own door, one hand on the latch.

"I'm all right," he said again. "Thank you, Trey."

"Are you sure you don't want some company for a bit?" I asked.

He shook his head. "No, thank you. I'm fine."

I wasn't at all sure that I believed him, but I couldn't question him without questioning his precarious adulthood. I nodded instead, and went on into my own room.

I settled myself in the chair I'd drawn up close to the heating unit, and reached across to turn the dial to a higher setting. The machinery whined faintly, and the coils slowly brightened, but it did nothing for the inner chill. As I'd said to Alkres, I had no idea what we were going to do, and the only alternative to taking him off-world—out of the system—seemed to be to lead an attack on Orestes. The idea of smashing Halfrid Brandr was an appealing one, to say the least. I closed my eyes, remembering the ruin of the Halex Tower, picturing the Brandr Tower reduced to the same pile of smoking rubble. At that moment, there were few things I wanted more, and I brought myself back under control with an effort.

While it would provide me with a great deal of personal pleasure to kick Halfrid's teeth in, as a mediator, I couldn't sanction an attack on the entire Brandr Kinship. If the Halex were not responsible for their genarch's actions, then neither were the Brandr. . . . But the Brandr had taken an active part in the attack, a voice whispered in the back of my mind. They were the main assault force. You can't really equate the two. A mediator's responsibility is to try to keep the peace, but it's also to see that justice gets done, because in the long run that's the only way peace can be maintained. And that's doubly true in this case. The system—the code—is beginning to fall apart. In fact, it's been failing for some time now: the increasing severity is just one sign that it isn't working the way it's supposed to. If you help patch it together this time, you're just setting the stage for an even nastier blow-up later on. In this case, the best thing may be to end it now, and see that something better is built after it.

It was dangerous reasoning, and I knew it, but I didn't see what else I could do, in good conscience. I was just grateful that a mediator's oath allows a certain flexibility. I pulled myself out of the chair, grimacing as I stepped out of the circle warmed by the wall heater. I wasn't competent to make any of the other decisions that would be necessary, or to assess the risks involved—or, for that matter, to know if an attack was at all practicable—but Leith was. I picked up the light throw that lay across the edge of my bed, and went to find her.

She opened her door at once to my knock, the worried frown on her face changing to a smile. "Trey. I'd hoped to see you."

"Is something wrong?" I asked.

"More than your Council's decision? No."

"It's not my Council," I said, and stepped inside. Her room was very warm, and I let the throw slip off my shoulders. Guil was nowhere in sight, which, I thought, probably explained the unusual warmth. "Guil's out?"

"Talking to her friend from the port," Leith answered, and shut the door behind us. "I hope you don't mind."

I shook my head. "I'm just as glad."

"Ah." Leith settled herself cross-legged on a square tambour, gloved arm drawn into her lap, and waved for me to seat myself. I chose the armchair, a duplicate of the one in my own room, and waited.

"I thought you might be," Leith went on. "What can I do for you?"

I hesitated, suddenly unsure of myself and of my motives, aware, too, that Leith was—had been—a Peacekeeper, and that her training in these things was ten times better than my own. She stared back at me, face inscrutable, and I knew I'd have to speak first.

"It's about Alkres," I said at last. Leith nodded, but said

nothing. I took a deep breath, and tried again. "The Council's decision is utterly unfair, and, I'm convinced, will only lead to more trouble if Halfrid Brandr keeps trying to bully the other genarchs. We've tried all the legal alternatives. We've got a warehouse full of arms: can we do anything with it?"

"The other genarchs seem perfectly happy to let this Brandr bully them," Leith said. "Why should that change? You'll just get him running the show."

"I don't think so," I said. "He's—he's a pushing man, I think. He'll just keep pushing, until they can't accept it. And then there'll be real trouble."

"Things're pretty bad now," Leith murmured, an odd almost-smile on her lips.

"They could be a lot worse," I retorted, stung. "Think about it, Leith, all the Kinships at feud with each other at once. And there's Asbera Ingvarr to think about—she's under the Brandr gun right now, and there's nobody to support her."

Leith grimaced. "I'm sorry, Trey, I'm just playing dev-il's advocate, I don't know why." She sighed. "I agree, I don't see what else you can do, except take the kid out-system."

"He wouldn't go," I said.

"I didn't think so," Leith agreed. "So what exactly are you asking me?"

"Two things." I held up two fingers, ticking off each point as I made it. "First, can we do anything effective with the materials at hand, and, second, will you help us?"

"Help how?" Leith demanded.

I stared, a little annoyed by her insistence on the strict routine. "In lieu of a more experienced commander, will you take command?" The moment the words were out of my mouth, I could see the problems that would cause. She was an off-worlder; to give her command of the attack force would only exacerbate the Halex problem. Then again, that was what we were fighting to overcome. More important, I doubted the Brandr had anyone who could match her.

"Do you have the kid's permission to make that offer?" Leith asked. She was grinning again, though for the life of me, I couldn't think why.

"No, not yet, but I think he'd give it."

Leith shook her head, the smile fading. "To answer the second question first: one, I was a drone-squad captain, not infantry. I only know theory, not practice. Two, I'd think my running the show would cause you more trouble than it's worth."

"Maybe," I said, "maybe not. I think it'd be worth the risk, but we can decide that later. What about my first question?"

Leith was silent for a long time. "Yes," she said at last, very quietly, "there's something we could do with the resources available—something that should be extremely effective—but you're not going to like it."

When she didn't continue, I raised my eyebrows. "Well?"

"The Brandr hold Destiny, right? We attack Madelgar."

I didn't say anything for a moment, and Leith hurried on. "Look, I know there'll be problems with their code, but think about it as a strategic problem for a minute. Most of their troops must be concentrated in Destiny—or elsewhere in the Halex Mandate—leaving Madelgar virtually undefended. If we take their capital in a coup de main, they're forestalled from using a threat to Destiny to stop us from doing anything." She paused, frowning. "It'd have to be a two-pronged attack, of course—a small force leaving from here with the heavy arms to rendezvous with, say, troops from this Ingvarr woman's territory, and anybody else who doesn't like what's going on." She pursed her lips thoughtfully. "I bet we could get some troops here—Signe should help."

I couldn't sit still any longer. I rose and crossed to the tiny window, resting my hand against the cold metal of its frame. Outside, the now-cloudless sky was red and gold, charged with the deceptive light of Sunset. The snow-covered surface of the Closed Sea seemed to glow with a blue light of its own. Agamemnon and Orestes were out of sight overhead. I stared until my breath misted on the the cold glass. Leith's proposal was appealing—more than that, I thought it would work. The code wouldn't matter: if the Brandr attack on the Halex Tower was legitimate, then so was any Halex retaliation.

"The problem," I said aloud, "will be getting other troops to rendezvous with us. How can we let the rest of the Halex know what's being planned, without compromising the plot?"

Leith smiled. "I think it can be done. We've got enough committed Halex waiting in Glittermark; let a few of them go back to Orestes, carrying the word. Guil's friend down on the switchboard should be able to set up secure communications."

It all made sense. I broached the idea to Alkres the next morning, and we put it before Landret and Signe at dinner. Patriarch and Heir made only token protests before agreeing, and Signe, in her capacity as Portreeve, offered us the use of ships from the Kinship's commercial fleet. Galar, informed of the plan, offered to recruit troops: there were plenty of Electrans who objected to the Council's decision.

Over the next few days, we brought the most reliable of the refugees in Glittermark into the plan, and found three who agreed to return to Orestes to recruit support among the dissatisfied members of the Kinship. All three thought they could promise a sizable response, and their first reports, made over the private circuit set up by Guil's friend within twenty-four hours of landing, proved that, if anything, they'd underestimated the response. A fourth refugee, a *para'an* of Ingvarr, volunteered to contact Asbera, and, once again, the response was better than we'd anticipated. Asbera herself was more than willing, and the Branch volunteered almost to a man.

Our only failure came in trying to reach the groups of ghosts and *para'anin* still holed up in the Necropolis. Our first messenger failed to make contact with us; the second was unable even to enter the closed Necropolis, turned back by Brandr guards on all three attempts. She reported this from the Ingvarr Hold, where she'd taken refuge, and we decided to leave things as they were. Destiny and its Necropolis would find out soon enough what we were planning. We could rely on them—I could rely on Rehur— to act appropriately.

Leith assumed the direction of the attack, and, somewhat to my surprise, no one either protested or asked for a clarification of the situation. Guil consulted with the port computers, and came up with a course through the rings. It would be a long flight, almost seventy hours, but if we moved quickly enough, we could reach Orestes during the Eclipse. More rapidly than anyone had expected, the pieces of the plan came together, and on the fifth day of the new month, we sent the final signal to our contacts waiting on Orestes. We would land at Madelgar at noon on the tenth day—a time and place known only to our contacts—and rendezvous with Asbera and her troops then. Six hours before midnight of the eighth day, we lifted for Orestes.

Chapter 12: Guil ex-Tam'ne

The last of the tugs lifted to orbit, a flare of white light
on the long-range screen, and Guil checked her coordinates for the tenth time, fitting her own ship into its slot in
the line. She was third, behind two class-four freighters,
and had been telling herself for days that she was just as
glad to trade the prestige of leading the attack for the
relief of flying the smaller, more maneuverable Virago.
Moraghan was on the lead freighter, of course, with Maturin
and the boy patriarch, though Glittermark's senior pilot
would be doing most of the work. Briefly, Guil envied the
other pilot—envied him the chance to see Moraghan fly,
something she herself had never seen—but pushed the
thought away as chimes sounded along the board.

"Toshiba's in line," the copilot reported, unnecessarily.
He was a *para'an* of Rhawn, half of a brother-and-sister
piloting team that Guil knew only by reputation.

"Thanks, Corrie," she said, and turned her attention to
the main sensor screen. The image was split, the biggest
window showing the enhanced picture from the forward
cameras—steering jets flared along the second freighter's
side even as she watched, edging its stubby wing in blue
flame—the two smaller windows displaying schematics.

The left-hand window was just the alignment display, the pale red cross lined up neatly on the freighter's sternbox. The right-hand window showed the radar view of the entire formation, six ships spread out in a ragged line, the curve of the moon just visible beneath them. At the top of the screen, the radar was just picking out the first echoes of the rings. It wasn't much of a formation, Guil thought, at least not compared to the great armadas that had set out to conquer other worlds in the Conglomerate. Six ships, the two biggest a pair of freighters that weren't even rated for interstellar travel, the rest a scattering of tugs and transports that were too small to carry more than a hundred people among them—too small even to carry weapons as well as passengers. . . . It was still the biggest fleet that the Oresteian system had ever seen, and Guil felt a half-guilty excitement at being a part of it.

"From *Andrasteia*," Corrie announced. "It's the go-ahead."

Andrasteia was the lead freighter, Leith's ship—Leith's flagship. Guil nodded, momentarily afraid to speak for fear she'd betray her leaping pleasure. She swallowed hard, and said, "I'm unlocking the board."

"I observe you," Corrie said, formally. Then some movement near the rear of the control cabin caught his eye, and he turned, frowning. "I thought you were going to get some sleep, Costa. You need to be fresh for the rings."

The third pilot flushed guiltily. "I couldn't sleep," she said. "I wanted to watch."

"There's not that much to see," Guil said, and smiled, recognizing an echo of her own excitement. "Have a seat, if you want."

"Thanks." Costa hooked an arm through the strap bolted to the rear bulkhead, and swung there, floating comfortably in the lack of gravity.

Guil turned back to her console, giving the control layout one last glance. It was a standard Conglomerate small-ships board, of Urban manufacture, familiar from years of working out of Destiny port. She reached for her tape case, pulling it free of the couch arm, and stuck it to the edge of the board. "I'm unlocking the board," she said again, and reached overhead to flip the master switch.

"I observe you," Corrie said again.

Guil nodded absently, and unlatched the thin case, pulling out the first tape. It wasn't really a tape, of course—the name had outlasted the original technology by centuries—but a palm-sized square of apparently solid plastic, its edge serrated in a complicated pattern.

"Starting main navigation loading sequence." Guil flipped the series of switches, watching the lights fade from blue to orange to green. One light, set beneath a data port, blinked insistently, and she slipped the first tape into the slot. The navigator's workscreen flashed once, and went dark again, a cursor now blinking in its lower corner. After a moment, the cursor vanished, to reappear in the correct position at the upper left corner of the screen.

"Main loading sequence completed and confirmed," Corrie said. He touched a set of keys on his own board, and nodded at the results. "And double-checked."

"All right," Guil said, and pressed a red button set well away from the rest of her keyboard. A two-toned chime sounded, and the computer's flat voice intoned, "Warning. Input will override current data. Warning."

Guil ignored the voice, and pulled out the second data tape. She held it up, letting Corrie see the lettering on its label, and the other pilot nodded. Satisfied, Guil slipped it into the feeder port, and keyed the sequence. There was a soft whine, barely audible over the whistling of the air vents. After perhaps a minute, the tape popped back out of the port, and the screen flashed the words, "Primary data transfer complete."

Guil slid the second tape back into the case, and pulled out a third, this one bright blue. Again, she held it up so that Corrie could double-check the label—this was the most recent set of ring observations—before slipping it into the feeder port. The workscreen went blank again, and the familiar whine signaled data transfer. Then it stopped, the cursor reappeared at the top of the workscreen, and the tape was ejected. Guil removed it, and replaced it with the fourth and final tape, the beacon codes that allowed the computer to interpret the ring charts contained on the previous tapes. She reached for the black tape that was her personal log, and stopped abruptly. There were no other tapes in the slots above the logboard.

Corrie saw the direction of her gaze, and made a face. "I

know. It's hard to decide if you really want this flight on your union record, isn't it?" His voice changed, became formal again. "I confirm full check-in procedure. Test sequence?"

"I'm beginning the test sequence," Guil acknowledged, and pressed the button beneath the workscreen. The screen changed color—another safety device—and a tiny tape port, less than half the size of the main tape ports, slid open. Guil plugged in the five-centimeter test tape, saying, "I gather the two of you decided against it?" She nodded toward the logboard.

Corrie looked embarrassed. Costa said, from her place on the bulkhead, "Actually, we thought we'd talk it over with you, first."

"Oh." Guil typed in the phrase that switched her keyboard to the workscreen, and keyed in the first call-up codes, buying time. Did she really want this on her union record, especially when the personal logs couldn't be erased or modified? At least not easily, she corrected herself, and certainly not for a price she could manage. But that was only if they lost. If they won. . . . She smiled to herself, watching letters and numbers spraying across her screen. If they won, there would be hundreds of pilots trying to claim that they had flown in the invasion fleet; she would want the log tape to prove her claim. "I'll log it," she said, as much to herself as to the other pilots, and leaned across to slip the tape into the first-pilot's slot before she could change her mind. The cover slid closed across the port, locking it in place for the duration of the journey.

Corrie glanced over his shoulder at his sister. "Well?"

"I say we do it," Costa answered.

Corrie nodded, and pulled out his own log tape, sliding it into the second-pilot's place. Costa released her grip on the strap and floated forward, pulling her own tape from her pocket. She slipped it into the final port, and pushed off from the console, letting herself drift back toward the bulkhead.

"Isn't it nice to have a stake in things?" she murmured, with an ironic smile.

Corrie grunted something, and Guil hid a grin. *Para'anin* or not, the two Rhawns had had a stake in this from the beginning, far more than she herself had ever had. She turned her attention back to the workscreen, watching the course line snake across the upper window. It was the correct pattern, the computer matching the simulated beacon signals perfectly, but she called up a second, different pattern just to be sure. It, too, showed a perfect response, and she punched the end-test button as soon as the screen emptied again. The test tape popped back out of its slot, and she put it back in the case with the rest.

"Chart and data transfer is complete," she announced formally. "The check test is nominal—you can signal *Andrasteia* we're ready, Corrie."

"I confirm transfer and tests," Corrie murmured, swinging the communications board out from its place flat against the right-hand bulkhead. The plan called for all communications to be carried out by burst-code, rather than voice, to lessen the chance that the Brandr might pick up transmissions. Privately, Guil thought it was highly unlikely that the Brandr would bother monitoring communications in the ring, but Moraghan had insisted. She watched as Corrie typed in the proper code phrase—the card with the established signals was taped to the com board itself, just below the transmitter buttons—then checked it, and pressed the button that would send the message on its way. A moment later, a single number flashed on the screen. Corrie ran his finger down the list of signals and said, "*Andrasteia* acknowledges."

"Good enough," Guil said. "I have control." Without waiting for Corrie's answer, she pressed the log-in button and typed her union number and code word. The logboard chimed twice, and the red light came on beside the first-pilot's port.

Corrie unfastened the last of the safety webbing, and pushed himself gently out of his couch, executing a neat Immelman in the control cabin's central volume. "I'll check back in a couple of hours," he said. "Is there anything you want from the galley?"

Guil shook her head, and Costa said, "I'll relieve you in eight hours, Guil."

"Thanks," Guil said. "If I want anything, or need you to spell me, Corrie, I'll buzz you."

"Right," the Rhawn answered, and then they were gone, the hatch sealing itself automatically behind them.

Guil sighed, settling herself more comfortably in the couch's harness, and turned her attention to her screens. It wasn't exactly usual for the senior pilot to take the first flight stage—the stage that brought a ship up to the ring— but the course she'd helped choose took the little fleet through some of the ring's most dangerous sections. If she was to be fresh for that, she would have to take the first watch, and leave Costa to handle insertion.

Sighing again, she leaned across the board to press a button on the sensor console. Lights flashed briefly, and a new set of figures appeared on the workscreen. She hit the code sequence that dumped that data to the tracking computer, and pressed the button that displayed the resulting graphics on the main screen. The screen dimmed slightly, a band of individual lights spreading across the screen as the sensors picked up the asteroid beacons. Guil touched keys, defining parameters, and the picture shifted, sharpened, until the screen showed only the wedge of the ring lying between the fleet and the point Orestes would reach in sixty-five hours. Orestes itself was not yet visible on the screen; the only other lights were the red wedges that marked the positions of the two lead ships.

Guil watched the image form without really seeing it, wondering what they would find when they reached Orestes. She had landed at Madelgar before, and so was reasonably familiar with the spaceport there. It was smaller than the main field at Destiny, but large enough—just large enough, she amended, with a silent laugh—to take the entire fleet. The airfield was separate, of course, and more than adequate to accept the incoming flyers—always assuming, she added, that things went as planned. Still, even if they didn't all show up, some would, and the heavy arms in the freighters' holds should make all the difference. With some surprise, she recognized the knot in her stomach as fear.

She sighed, trying to shake off the feeling, and touched a second button on the sensor console. In the screen, the points of light shifted, became strings of characters, beacon codes as familiar to her as any Destiny landmark, but she stared past them, not really paying attention. Moraghan had been so calm during the planning sessions—too calm, Guil thought, almost cold. By almost imperceptible stages, the off-worlder had become a stranger, a woman Guil did not know, and did not particularly want to know. That, she finally admitted, was the real reason she had not protested Moraghan's choice of pilot: she had not wanted to spend seventy hours cooped up in a control cabin with the person Moraghan had become.

Well, that's what it means to be a soldier, Guil told herself, and pushed impatiently against the safety harness. Moraghan's a good one, by all accounts. Be glad she's leading you. Almost angrily, she punched figures into the workscreen, checking on the second stage of the course. Costa wouldn't have much to worry about; the opening leg was fairly clear, with only a few of the clustering rocks the pilots called shoals to avoid. The second leg was a little more complicated, with the big rock known as TTN-7 just impinging on the course. However, that shouldn't be a problem, she thought, unless we're running behind schedule.

With the third leg—her own next watch—things started getting tricky, and she punched for a more detailed outline of the course. The picture in the screen swam and reformed, but she was unable to concentrate on its details. Instead, the image of the field at Madelgar filled her brain. It wasn't the easiest approach, especially landing immediately after two other ships—she would have to be careful to leave room for the three tugs following her—and she would get no help from the Tower. Not that the Tower was much help in any case, she added bitterly. They always seemed to know when a Destiny pilot was diverting to their field, and took a positive and perverse pleasure in being as unhelpful as possible. And when the pilot was *para'an*, as well. . . . Unconsciously, her lips thinned, her mouth setting into an expression of masked anger so habitual she barely recognized it for what it was. There were one or two of the port employees she'd take personal pleasure in killing, especially after her last job out of Madelgar. She had been prepared to use that excuse—that she bore a measure of the guilt in having brought in the off-world guns for the Brandr—in order to get a chance at her own revenge. It was just as well that Alkres—or, more likely, Maturin and Moraghan together—had decided to welcome *para'anin* into their army; she would not have enjoyed reminding the Halex Patriarch of her part in the arms delivery. Still, she thought, it would have been worth it.

She shook herself then, and turned back to study the screen, forcing herself to concentrate on the course laid out before her. Here things began to get difficult—the linked patch of stones and debris known as the sandbars would come up about an hour into the watch, and there were almost always difficulties passing their position. The fine debris, though not really large enough to pose a direct threat to the ship, formed a sort of background clutter that could hide larger and more dangerous rocks from the ship's sensors. Guil was glad Moraghan had agreed to reduce speed until the fleet was well past the sandbanks. Less than thirty minutes beyond the sandbanks was the worst hazard of all, the rock labeled BRRH-56-J. It was a jagged, friable piece of rock moving in an eccentric orbit, trailing, as always, a tail of lesser debris. BRRH-56-J killed one or two people every year, usually prospectors who strayed too close in search of usable chunks of rock in its tail; over the years, it had been responsible for two of the three biggest accidents in Orestes' history. Guil, like most pilots, disliked and distrusted it, and under any other circumstances would go out of her way to avoid it.

The computer chimed, and the course projection on the main screen shifted slightly: another hour gone. Guil sighed, checking her second watch course a final time, then hit the keys that would return the present course to her workscreen. The computer was doing the actual flying right now; her job was merely to keep an eye on its functions. Unbidden, the image of Madelgar rose again in her mind, all stubby towers and bright-tiled roofs rising above the woven metal of the field fence. She wondered what it would feel like to carry one of the heavy assault guns, to feel the heat of its power pack against her ribs, to turn it on the fence and the buildings and the people who'd called her *para* once too often. It was a strange feeling, as heady as wine or the rising heat of desire, and she wasn't at all sure she liked it. Frowning, she switched functions on the workscreen, and began again to review the trouble spots in the course ahead.

Costa relieved her promptly, as scheduled, just before the Virago entered the ring. Guil stayed in the control cabin just long enough to acknowledge the "raise screens" signal from *Andrasteia*—the communications board was hard to reach from the first-pilot's chair—then swung herself aft to the galley for a hurried, tasteless meal. Through the compartment's open stern hatch, she could see the twenty-odd passengers sprawled in their couches, some asleep, some talking quietly, some playing cards or reading, and took a quick turn down the main aisle to make sure everything was in order. Right now, and for the next seven hours, she was the copilot; the passenger compartment was her responsibility.

There was nothing that needed doing for the passengers. Those who were subject to spacesickness had been dosed with various medications before liftoff, preventing the most common problem facing a tug's copilot; no one seemed to need instructions for using either the galley or the zero-G toilet, the second and third most common difficulties. Guil let herself drift back to the tiny pilot's cabin.

Corrie was asleep in his bag, light-blocking curtain pulled closed around his cubbyhole. Guil floated into her own compartment, deliberately shifting her frame of reference so that the sleeping bag, actually perpendicular to the ship's long axis, was now suspended horizontally, and stretched out against it, hooking her feet under a strap of the safety webbing. She glanced to her left, making sure the intercom was open if Costa needed her help, and reached for her book in its reader. In two hours, she would see if Costa wanted a meal, or just wanted to take a break, but for now, she would relax a little. She pressed the cue button, shooting the tape to the place she'd stopped the night before, and leaned back against the bag, losing herself in the fiction.

The watch cycle passed without incident. As was more or less traditional among the pilots, Corrie roused himself an hour before he was due on watch to shower and breakfast, and announced that he would handle the copilot's work for the last fifty minutes. Guil nodded and turned in: she would do the same for Costa at the end of the next watch.

The beep of the alarm woke her on schedule; she showered and grabbed a skimpy breakfast before warning Costa she could turn in. The other woman nodded, yawning, and vanished into her cubicle almost before Guil had finished talking. Instead of waiting in the pilot's cabin, however, Guil drifted forward, to kick the release at the edge of the control cabin's hatch. Corrie did not turn as the hatch slid open, eyes fastened on the screen.

"How're we doing?" Guil asked quietly, pulling herself into the copilot's couch.

"Not too bad," Corrie said, sounding a little doubtful. "The sandbanks are looking a little dense—a lot of midges cluttering up the screen. I'm concerned there might be something bigger broken loose."

Guil leaned sideways to study the radar display, though she did not touch the tuning knobs. The sandbanks did show a number of flashing orange blips, bodies large enough to pose a potential danger to the ship's sensor suite and outboard mountings, but not really big enough to be a danger to the hull—midges, in the pilot's jargon. The radar wasn't penetrating that screen of debris at all. She frowned, then jumped as the part of the screen displaying the picture from the main camera flashed white. The ship's defensive screens had just vaporized something a little larger than dust. She grimaced, annoyed that she had allowed herself to be startled by something so common in the rings, and Corrie nodded.

"There's been a lot of that, too," he said morosely.

"Wonderful," Guil muttered. "Any word from *Andrasteia?*"

"No." Corrie shook his head. "Nothing yet."

"Mmm." Guil studied the readings in the copilot's repeater, checking density and reflected mass against the readings stored in the computer's memory. Both were high, but still within normal limits. She chewed at her lower lip. Under normal circumstances, she'd signal the lead ship—or Glittermark, for that matter—and report her intention of changing course, but Moraghan had forbidden unnecessary transmissions. "We'll wait and see," she said at last.

"You're the boss." Corrie glanced at the chronometer stuck to his console, and reached for the harness buckles. "I'm just as glad it's your problem."

Guil smiled and pulled herself free of the copilot's couch.

They changed places with practiced efficiency, and Corrie said, "Do you want me to stick around for the first couple of hours?"

Guil hesitated for a moment, then nodded. "I'd appreciate it." The next two hours would see the most dangerous part of the ring passage; the copilot's help just might make all the difference.

Corrie nodded back, fumbling himself into the copilot's harness. He stopped with it half-fastened. "Damn, I didn't think. Do you want anything first?"

Guil shook her head. "Thanks, no, but get yourself something if you want it."

Corrie hesitated, then slipped back out of the harness. "I'll be back in a minute," he said, and vanished.

Guil stared at the screen, just as glad for the few moments of privacy. In the enhanced view projected across most of the big screen, the bigger rocks moved through a swarm of lesser debris, a ponderous dance of giants. The sandbanks were a blurred shape at the bottom of the picture, too complex even for the computer to sort out. Somewhere beyond lay BRRH-56-J. She put that thought from her mind, and concentrated on the sandbanks.

The computer chimed twice—the new-data signal—and flashed a string of numbers. She deciphered them quickly: the incidence of dust-sized debris was increasing, and the sensors were picking up more and more debris in the pebble range. Even as she read the final line of code, another, bigger piece of debris struck the Virago's screens, and vanished in a flash of light. Frowning, Guil punched for a readout on its size. The computer considered for a moment, checking the amount of power used to destroy it, and finally produced a number. A pebble the size of my thumb, Guil thought, and we're still—she touched keys— thirty minutes from the banks. That's not a good sign.

The hatch slid open, and Corrie floated back into the compartment, a liquid-meal pouch clutched in one hand. He maneuvered himself into his couch with the other, saying, "Anything yet?"

Guil shook her head. "We'll just have to wait," she said again.

The density reading steadied, hovering just below the level Guil considered dangerous. She watched it for a few

minutes, then turned her attention to the sensor board,
fiddling with the controls until the secondary suite was
scanning specifically for the larger chunks of debris Corrie
had suggested might be hidden behind the band of smaller
material. The two freighters ahead of the Virago blocked
the scan, but she kept on anyway, swinging the reflector
along its track. Nothing showed, as she'd more than half
expected, and she switched the suite back to its normal
operations.

The communications board chimed again, and Corrie
said, unnecessarily, "Incoming signal." He swung the board
across his lap, eyes flickering from the screen to the list of
codes. Finally, he said, "*Andrasteia*'s picking up a high
concentration of debris, maybe screening something. We're
to alter course."

Guil frowned. "Patch the coordinates through to me."

Corrie nodded, fingers moving on his keyboard. A moment later, figures appeared in Guil's workscreen. She
studied them, still frowning. "And how's this going to
affect passing BRRH?" she murmured, half to herself.
Corrie shrugged, but the senior pilot didn't notice, too
busy punching numbers into the screen. The tiny course
display swam and steadied, one section of the projected
line suddenly flashing yellow. Guil swore softly. The new
course would avoid the patch of debris *Andrasteia* had
picked up, but it would take them into the edge of the
"bow wave" preceding BRRH-56-J.

"Query that," she said.

Corrie punched keys on his board, and waited. A few
seconds later, he shook his head. "Exact repeat. That's the
line they want."

Guil hesitated, chewing gently on her lower lip. Most of
the time, the bow wave wasn't too dangerous, no particles the ship's screens couldn't handle. Every so often,
though, there was a bigger rock there, always obscured by
the rest of the dust and debris. But that really only happened at close approach, she told herself, annoyed at her
own concern, and Orestes and Electra were almost at their
greatest distance. It should be fairly clear.

"Do you want to try an alternate course?" Corrie asked,
craning his neck to see the pattern on Guil's screen.

Guil shook her head. "An alternate would waste time—acknowledge, and signal we'll comply."

"You're the boss," Corrie answered, not entirely happily, and bent over his keyboard. A moment later, he said, "*Andrasteia* says we're to commence firing in seven minutes, bursts at thirty."

Guil nodded, feeding the information into the workscreen. The numbers looked right, but she ran a quick verification on them anyway before dumping them to the main control board. Lights flashed as the machine checked its copy against the originals, and then the standby light came on. Numbers began flashing in the lower corner of the main screen, ticking away the countdown.

"All secure?" Guil asked automatically, and Corrie nodded.

"All secure."

"You might want to warn the passengers."

"I'll do that," Corrie said, and reached for the in-ships intercom.

Guil turned her attention back to the workscreen displays, not really hearing the other pilot's cool-voiced announcement. She couldn't help wondering if she'd done the right thing in agreeing to the course change. After all, Moraghan was an off-worlder; no matter how good a pilot she was, she didn't know the ring. It was never good policy to court trouble with BRRH-56-J; you almost always got it. Guil shook herself then, watching the seconds tick away on the main screen. Moraghan might not know the ring, but she had an Oresteian pilot aboard, a senior union member with dozens of years' experience. Moraghan has more sense than to override that kind of knowledge, Guil thought, which means Leith's pilot must've approved this.

The last seconds ticked away. In the main screen, Guil saw jets flare along *Andrasteia*'s hull, and then along the wings and hull of the next ship. A moment later, the steering alarm sounded, and the hull seemed to tremble slightly. A second set of numbers appeared on the screen, counting the duration of the firing.

"All jets fired," Corrie announced. "Everything's nominal."

The asteroids shifted slowly in the screen, the ships

seeming to remain motionless while the ringscape turned around them. For the first time, BRRH-56-J swam into view, warning beacons blinking at the ends of its long axis. Two or three people had been killed planting those beacons, Guil remembered, back before the remotes were put in service.

The second countdown reached zero, and the second set of jets cut in, checking the Virago's swing. Corrie checked his instruments, and said, "Stop-jets fired. Everything looks good here."

Guil consulted her own boards, and nodded. "We're on the new course. Pass that word to *Andrasteia.*"

"Right." Corrie typed in the proper numbers, and added, an instant later, "*Andrasteia* acknowledges. How far is it?"

He didn't have to define his pronoun. Guil checked the radar display, and said, "Nineteen minutes, on this course. You better make sure no one's floating loose in the back."

Corrie nodded, loosening his harness, and floated out of the control cabin. Guil leaned back into the couch, feeling her body rebound slightly against the padded harness. BRRH-56-J loomed in the screen, the beacons strobing at either end, casting an instant's light across the cratered rock. In each flash, a jagged ledge stood out in high relief, where the rock had ripped away in sheets. The radar showed almost a hundred smaller bodies surrounding the main stone, and Guil knew there would be more hidden in the clutter.

She looked away from the main screen, turning her attention to the workscreen and the numbers projected there. The density readings remained uncomfortably high, but there was still no sign of any dangerous concentrations of debris in the bow wave.

The hatch opened again, and Corrie drifted back in. "Everything's secure aft," he said, pulling himself into his couch. "I warned Costa, too, just in case."

"Thanks," Guil said. Not that there was much the third pilot could do, in case of trouble, but it was her duty to share at least the worrying.

"How's it looking?" Corrie asked.

Guil gave him a rather sour glance—he could see the screen, and she didn't feel much like talking—but suppressed her annoyance, saying, "Yellow all through."

"That's a relief—though I guess it doesn't really mean anything. I mean, after the stories you hear, how it can go from clear to red near the BRRH, especially in the bow wave. . . ." Corrie seemed to realize he was babbling and broke off, flushing.

Guil nodded, soothingly, not really listening. In the main screen, little lights appeared around the *Andrasteia*'s image, like tiny flashes of lightning: the freighter had entered the edge of the bow wave, and its screens were vaporizing the debris. So far, so good, Guil thought, as the same lights appeared around the second ship. Nothing really big, nothing the screens can't handle. . . .

"How long will we be in?" Corrie asked.

"About twenty minutes," Guil answered, and gave a humorless grin. "It won't seem that short, believe me."

Corrie mumbled something that the other didn't hear. Guil fixed her eyes on the screen, resting her hands lightly on the edge of the board. As always, the temptation to take control herself was almost overwhelming, even though she knew, rationally, that the computer would hold the course as well as—even better than—she could. The main screen flashed white, and she jumped: the *Virago* had entered the bow wave. The screen flashed again, two lights together, but she made herself count ten and then fifteen flashes before saying, "What's the reading?"

"Mostly dust," Corrie answered, eyes on his screen. "A couple of midges, nothing bigger."

"Good." Guil kept her eyes on the screen, watching the flashes of light that surrounded her own ship, and danced along the wings and hull of the freighter ahead of them. Once, when she was much younger, she had flown with friends across the Ice Bridge that linked the land around the Closed Sea to the Big Island. They had run into a storm, and before they could lift out of it, an electrical charge had built up on the wings, and discharged itself in a spectacularly strange display. That was what the two freighters looked like; she almost wished she could see the same fire surrounding the *Virago*.

Suddenly a brighter light flashed against *Andrasteia*'s port side, a blue-white flare with a core of flame. Guil swore, and more light blossomed against the second freighter's hull. "Emergency power to the screens," she snapped.

Corrie's hand was already moving the power lever, jamming it all the way forward in its slot. The cabin lights dimmed fractionally, and then the main screen turned white. The *Virago* shook under the impact, the sound transmitted through the hull as something too large to be completely vaporized by the screens crashed and tumbled the length of the ship. The intercom carried shouts and curses from the passenger compartment.

"Status?" Guil demanded, punching buttons on her own board. The screen was slowly fading back to normal, but she hardly noticed, concentrating on the numbers coming from the sensor suite. A couple of the smaller nodes had been carried away or crushed, and there were holes in the radar image.

"No hull damage," Corrie reported, shakily. "Environmental's all right, so's the power plant, and communications. Your side?"

Guil grunted, not wanting to speak until she was sure she could control her voice, and concentrated on the sensor board. By readjusting a couple of the larger pickups, she could compensate for the damaged nodes; the resulting picture would be a little less clear, but it would provide full coverage. She took a deep breath and said, "We lost a couple of sensor nodes, nothing serious. What about the other ships?"

Corrie shook his head. Then the communications board chimed, and he reached for it with a shaking hand. "*Andrasteia's* all right," he said, after a moment, "and *Topper* reports only minor hull damage. We're to report our status."

"We're fine, then," Guil said, trying to project more calm than she actually felt. "Pass that along, will you, Corrie?" Now she was talking more than was necessary. She stopped abruptly, scowling. Her heart was still racing; she took another deep breath, trying to relax, then bent forward again to adjust the sensor suite. Ironically, the density reading was already beginning to drop, as though BRRH-56-J had shot its bolt with that one spectacular encounter.

"*Andrasteia* acknowledges," Corrie said, "and it looks like the tugs are all right, too. They're not reporting any damage."

"Good," Guil said again. As she spoke, the screen flared again, but it was feeble compared to the earlier lights.

The rest of the ring passage was surprisingly quiet. Even the spot shoals that made up most of the ring's inner edge were passed without incident, and the fleet changed course for the final time, heading into Orestes on the Madelgar approach line. Guil settled herself into the pilot's couch again, scanning the radar window displayed on the main screen. There was no traffic to speak of—just a few high-flying aircraft almost lost in the ground clutter from the moon's surface—but a single light flashed red in the middle of the screen. That was the Madelgar approach buoy. Guil eyed it warily, glad that Orestes had never had a particularly complicated defense system. The few guard buoys and automated battle stations, put into orbit almost a hundred years earlier, during the Controller scare, were out on the edge of the system proper, not in planetary orbit. Still, she braced herself, waiting for the ID call.

It came at last, a light flashing on the communications board. Corrie, riding copilot again, jumped, even though he'd had his hand on the transponder's abort bar. The light kept flashing for perhaps two minutes as the buoy's computer tried to get a response from the approaching ships' transponders, and then winked out. The two pilots exchanged nervous grins.

"What's our screen rating?" Guil asked. She had asked that before, but could not seem to remember.

"Extra-heavy-duty," Corrie answered. "That should be enough."

Guil heard the note of doubt in his voice, and nodded agreement. Extra-heavy's good enough to keep out most of the ring debris, she reminded herself, as you saw on the way down. It's not as though the Brandr have any real fighters, just the standard ones with some guns mounted on the wings. The screens will handle that easily.

Another light flashed on the communications board, and a voice said, "Attention, unlisted flight, this is Madelgar Approach Control. Your transponder does not answer our buoy. I repeat, your transponder does not answer our buoy. Please respond with name and registry information."

"Kill it," Guil said.

Corrie twisted a knob, and the voice faded out.

Guil stared straight ahead, trying to exorcise the knot of fear in the pit of her stomach. She knew perfectly well that the Brandr didn't have sophisticated aircraft—certainly nothing capable of interfering with the Virago's approach—but in her mind's eye she could see the outline of a missile flowering on the radar window, growing despite her attempts at evasion, could see the explosion that would end everything. . . . She shook herself, hard, but could not completely banish that image. They were still a few minutes away from entering the atmosphere; if she acted now, she could pull out, and avoid the fighting. She closed her hands around each other, squeezing almost painfully hard, keeping them in her lap by sheer force of will.

"Screen status?" she said, in a mechanical voice she barely recognized as her own.

"Standard reentry," Corrie answered.

"Put them on full," Guil said.

"Full power," Corrie acknowledged. There was a note of relief in his voice, too.

The Virago struck atmosphere then, and Guil gave a sigh of relief. The decision was out of her hands now; they were committed to the descent, and to the battle. She rested her hands against the twitching manual controls, waiting for the Virago to shed enough speed so that she could take over.

"I have aircraft on radar," Corrie announced.

"ID?"

"Nothing, yet," Corrie answered, his voice under tight control.

Guil swore. An unidentified ship was probably hostile, Brandr, and she was still trapped in the speed-killing descent mode, an easy target. Then the warning chime sounded, and she seized the released controls, pulling the Virago up and away from her previous course, buying time to look around.

Below, caught by the left wing camera at its farthest downward extension, the Grand Shallows showed blue-violet in the fading light, only lightly obscured by thin wisps of cloud. The delta south of Madelgar, darker land seamed with multiple channels and the scars of old river-beds, was clearly visible; Madelgar itself was just out of sight to the north. Guil touched a button, adjusting the cameras, and caught a quick glimpse of the crowding buildings. The field lights were hard to pick out at this height, but the audio beacons were already chirping in the speakers.

She glanced again at the radar windows, checking the position of the other ships of the fleet, and rolled sideways, looking for the aircraft. At this altitude, the Virago handled fairly well, but that would change as they dropped deeper into the atmosphere.

"I see them," Corrie cried. "I see them. They're low-flying birds, they can't get up here."

Guil eased the Virago into a bank, turning wide to avoid the other ships spread out across the sky. As Moraghan had ordered, they were holding in a sandwich formation, three hundred meters between each "layer"; as long as no one was frightened into a sudden change of altitude, Guil thought, there shouldn't be any danger of collision. She swung the Virago in an easy circle, adjusting the cameras with her free hand. Sure enough, as Corrie had said, there was a cluster of aircraft hanging at the dividing line. As she watched, one peeled off, arrowing for the Madelgar field, but the others remained, circling. It was a clever tactic, she thought, grudgingly. For now, the ships were safe, but as soon as they committed themselves to a line of descent into the field, they would lose most of their maneuverability.

"More aircraft," Corrie announced. "No ID—no, wait, it's our people. They're moving in to engage."

Guil glanced at the radar display again. A second group of flyers, these picked out in blue light, were moving into range, the smaller ships breaking off from the rest to climb toward the hovering Brandr. The rest—larger craft; transports, almost certainly—continued toward the airfield.

The communications board beeped twice, and the ship-to-ship radio crackled to life for the first time since leaving Electra.

"All right, people," Moraghan said, conversationally. "We've got air cover now, so let's go in. Stay in your line, and follow the plan. Clear and out."

"Virago acknowledges," Corrie said, without waiting for orders. He glanced at Guil. "We're going in?"

"We're going in," Guil answered. "Better warn the passengers."

"They'll've heard," Corrie said, but reached for the intercom anyway. "Attention, people, we are beginning the run into Madelgar Field. Stand by to jump as soon as we land. Squad leader, report as ordered."

Guil swung the Virago in a final circle, eating up time and space as the two freighters swung themselves into the invisible approach line. She let *Topper* drop almost sixteen hundred meters before putting the Virago into the shallow dive that would bring her down onto Madelgar's main runways. The Virago fell quickly, controls trembling a little under the strain. Guil pulled back a little, flattening the dive even further, and felt the strain ease. Already, the increasing atmospheric drag was making itself felt. The Virago responded sluggishly to her touch.

"Trouble, Guil," Corrie said. "Couple of flyers."

"I see them." The craft were circling to intercept the Virago's path as soon as it reached their operating range. Guil studied her readouts, wondering if she dared pull out, but decided that would only foul up the pilots following her. "Emergency power to the screens," she snapped. Her mouth was dry, and tasted of metal; it seemed for an instant that there was a smell of ozone in the air.

"Emergency power on," Corrie answered, hoarsely. He drew a ragged breath. "Two minutes to intercept."

Guil tensed her shoulders against the harness. The Brandr shouldn't have anything that could penetrate a heavy-duty screen, she told herself; they shouldn't be able to hurt us. . . . But suppose they rammed us? The thought made her blood run cold, and she tightened her grip on the controls, leaning forward a little as though that would give her a better view of the screen. If they try it, I'll roll, take it on the hold, that's the least vulnerable part of the ship. . . . But they shouldn't try it—it'd be suicide.

Then a dark shape flashed across the screen, and was gone before she could properly identify it. A second later, the screen flashed white and the ship rocked to the multiple explosions.

"Status?" she said, moving the controls gingerly, feeling for damage.

"Hull's sound," Corrie answered. "So far— Wait, here they come again."

Guil swore. They were too far down in the atmosphere

to attempt evasive maneuvers, and the scanty cloud cover was no use at all. The approaching Eclipse was still too far away to provide them with any cover. She stared at the screen, wishing bitterly that the Virago were armed.

The ship bucked, little explosions marching forward along its belly. Guil swore again, clinging to her controls and then a dark shape filled the screen, pulling up from under the Virago's nose. Then it was gone, and the Virago slid through the space it had occupied only a few seconds before. Corrie leaned back in his couch, eyes closed, breathing hard.

"Oh, God, for a rack of missiles," Guil said, through clenched teeth. "God, I'd've had him."

She checked her radar again, still muttering to herself. The two freighters seemed unscathed, and the lighter Halex craft were at least keeping most of the Brandr flyers occupied. The two ships that had attacked her were nowhere in sight, and she couldn't spare a hand to adjust the sensor suite. "Any sign of those aircraft?"

Corrie adjusted the radar, shook his head. "I've lost them—no, wait, there they are." He looked across at the other pilot, grinning. "A couple of our people came to our rescue."

"Good for them," Guil said, rather sourly. "I hope they keep them off our backs."

"Looking good so far," Corrie answered.

"Are we still getting the port beacon?" Guil asked.

"So far," Corrie said, after a moment. "They're bound to cut it, though—unless their pilots need it?"

"Don't borrow trouble," Guil said. Privately, she hoped the Brandr flyers were dependent on the field's directional broadcast. Having it on would make all the difference in trying to land.

She scanned the main screen again, watching the port complex swell in the viewscreen. The cameras showed the delta-land rushing past, the channels like ribbons of tarnished silver in the rapidly fading light. Ahead, the blue lights of the runway beckoned, red lights flashing from the distant tower. The smaller digital display showed the proper approach as a pale blue line, ending at the runway's end. The yellow box was steady, indicating they were still on course. Then, abruptly, that box vanished. A heartbeat later, the rest of the picture winked out.

"They've cut the beam," Corrie said.

Guil swore, her hand stabbing for the switch that controlled the beam reader, flicking it off. Corrie leaned across to play with the sensor controls, twisting the enhancement switch to maximum and bringing everything to forward view.

"That's good," Guil said, not daring to take her eyes off the swelling image. "That's fine. What are the fighters doing?"

Corrie glanced at the radar screen. "Don't worry about them, they've got problems of their own. All right, *Andrasteia's* down."

"Good," Guil said again. The end of the runway was approaching quickly, but *Topper* was still ahead of her, sinking toward a heavy landing.

"And she's cleared the runway," Corrie said. "*Topper's* touched, and rolling. And she's clear."

Guil took a deep breath. That was one fewer thing to worry about; now there was only her own landing, without the beam to keep her lined up or Port Control to talk her down. She shifted her shoulders, feeling the tension there, and forced her muscles to relax. The end of the runway, marked with broad white stripes, swelled in the screen. She pointed the Virago's nose at what she hoped was the center of the stripe, and hit the switch that started the landing sequence. Lights flashed across the board, and the computer said, "Warning. Beacon reader is not functioning. Repeat, priority warning. Beacon reader is not functioning."

"Shut it off," Guil said. "Handle it, Corrie."

"I've got it," the copilot answered.

Then the Virago flashed across the line of lights that marked the edge of the field, and Guil turned all her attention to the ship. She cut speed at a reckless rate, pulling up the Virago's nose until they were almost stalling, easing the ship toward the metalled surface of the runway.

"My God, there are vehicles on the path," Corrie shouted.

Guil swore, but held the Virago steady, her mouth

setting into an angry line. "Fuck them," she said. "I'm coming in."

"They're not moving, Guil."

"Fuck them," Guil answered, and dropped the Virago onto the runway. She caught the briefest glimpse of a heavy service van pulled broadside across the runway before the Virago, tires squealing, then smashed into it, shoving it bodily off the runway. The collision threw her back and sideways, but the harness held her at the controls. The image had vanished from the main screen: the bow cameras had been ripped away. Corrie was hanging half out of his harness, punching buttons on the sensor board. A new picture formed, slightly out of register in the middle, but clear enough to see another van, and a disaster unit, drawn up across the runway.

"Oh, God, more of them," Corrie said.

Guil swore again, and stamped on the throttle.

"You can't do that," Corrie began, and broke off as Guil turned on him.

"Watch me," she said, through clenched teeth. The Virago picked up speed again, until it was almost flying. Guil held it steady, caught in a strange, exultant pleasure, pointing the damaged bow straight at the blocking vehicles. She smiled, seeing tiny figures leap from the cabs to dive for cover along the sides of the runways, and laughed aloud as the Virago smashed into the first van, throwing it aside. It moved the disaster truck, too, though less easily; Guil's foot moved convulsively on the throttle, but she controlled herself in time. They were almost at the turnoff. She pressed the rudder controls experimentally, and was almost surprised when they responded. The Virago slowed, swung heavily toward the marked taxiway, hampered by the disaster van still tucked under its nose.

"Christ, Guil," Corrie said.

"I cleared the runway, didn't I?" Guil snapped. "We're in position—tell the passengers to get a move on."

Corrie struggled free of his harness, and fought his way out of the control cabin. Guil concentrated on pulling the slowing Virago farther onto the taxiway, turning it so that a wing was between the main body and the field tower. She brought ship's systems to a quick shutdown, grudging every second she spent on it. Already she could hear the

faint whistle of blaster fire: the people from the freighters
and the aircraft had engaged the enemy.

As soon as the last check light showed blue, she flung
back her harness and bolted from the cabin. The main
hatch was open, giving onto the protected side of the ship.
The squad leader, another of the Rhawn refugees, waved
to her from the hatchway. "All clear. You're the last one
out!"

Guil waved in answer, biting back the unreasonable
anger that threatened to overwhelm her, and ducked into
the pilots' cabin, emerging an instant later with a military
handblaster slung around her waist. She paused in the
hatchway, getting her bearings, and the squad leader leaned
close, shouting in her ear.

"*Andrasteia*'s over there. You're to get your weapons
from her."

Guil nodded, not looking at him. The Virago was too
small to carry her share of weapons; the freighters had had
to carry the bulk of that cargo. The full dark of the Eclipse
had set in, and, tardily, the port authority had cut the field
lights, increasing the darkness. *Andrasteia* was little more
than a bulky shadow, only a thin wedge of light spilling
out from her open cargo bay. There were other shadows
beyond her, and two more to the Virago's stern: the rest of
the fleet had landed safely. She drew her blaster and
jumped, disdaining the stairs.

Someone fired at her as she darted across the runway, a
bolt of raw energy slashing across the fused earth ahead of
her. She dropped to her knees, spinning instinctively, but
saw no one. She fired twice anyway, enjoying the kick of
the blaster and the electric smell that lingered in the air
after the gun was fired. She stayed crouching a moment
longer, hoping for another excuse to shoot, but nothing
happened. She pushed herself to her feet and ran, zigzagging, the rest of the way to *Andrasteia*.

Moraghan was standing in the hatchway, face remote,
supervising a stranger as he handed out the weapons. She
nodded to Guil as the pilot entered the hold, but did not
speak. Guil nodded back, not knowing whether to be glad
or sorry, and turned to the man with the weapons. He
handed her a laser rifle and turned away, but Guil caught
his sleeve.

"Let me take one of the assault guns," she said.

The man hesitated, glancing at Moraghan.

"I can handle it," Guil said impatiently. "I've used commercial drills."

The man waited, still looking at Moraghan. Guil took a quick breath, and let it out slowly, controlling herself with an effort. "Leith, you know I can use one. Tell him."

Moraghan lifted an eyebrow. "Are you sure you want to?" Before Guil could answer, the other woman's face twisted, and she said roughly, "If she wants to take it, let her. She's good for it."

"Thanks, Leith," the pilot said, Moraghan's strange look already forgotten. The stranger lifted the powerpack harness for her, and Guil shrugged herself into it. She tugged the straps tight across ribs and shoulders, enjoying the new sensation, then waited while the stranger plugged in the connecting wires and flipped the power switch. There was a faint buzzing, more a vibration in her ribcage, and she felt a gentle warmth under her right arm. The stranger handed her the stubby projector, and she took it eagerly, cradling it against her body.

Moraghan was still eyeing her strangely, and Guil made herself meet the other woman's gaze. "Join up with second squad," Moraghan said after a moment, and turned away.

"Right," Guil said, and jumped down from the hatch. She landed heavily—she was not quite used to the assault gun's weight—but righted herself without injury. A whistle sounded in the distance—two quick blasts and a longer one. That was the second squad's form-up signal, she knew, and turned toward it, hugging the gun to herself. Today, finally, old scores would be settled.

Chapter 13: Trey Maturin

We landed at Madelgar in the teeth of the Eclipse, aircraft following the spaceships down onto the double field. Perhaps a dozen flyers landed before us, the rest hanging back to protect the more vulnerable fleet. As the last spaceship dropped onto the field, those aircraft wheeled to begin their landing. I had heard of swarms of aircraft so large that they darkened the sky. This was not so large— maybe a hundred craft in all, and some of those very small—but it was an impressive sight. The Brandr craft were nowhere to be seen, destroyed or driven off while the spaceships landed. Our aircraft landed in waves, two or three at once, the dark sky behind them barred with light. Then they were down, bringing far more than the thousand men Moraghan had said she would need to make the plan work. A few flyers remained airborne, circling the field, ready to drive off any remaining Brandr craft.

Moraghan had planned the action as a coup de main, and sent squads to take and hold the city's key points, gambling that the main Brandr forces would still be in the Halex Mandate. We took the port easily enough—it held only a skeleton staff, which surrendered almost as soon as the ships were down—and the stadthall and main power plant. The main part of the city, stripped of combatants, offered little resistance. The remaining Brandr fell back on the walled Necropolis as their last possible defense, and ran into the squad Moraghan had sent to secure that strong point. Outnumbered, the squad was slaughtered, and Moraghan turned her attention to the new danger.

That, at least, is the explanation after the fact. I remember chiefly the darkness over the city, broken here and there by the brilliant flash of a laser rifle, or the redder flash of an assault gun. We had taken most of our objectives by the fourth hour of the Eclipse, though the Brandr technicians had cut the city's power almost as soon as we attacked. I remember the incongruously soft lights in the freighters' holds, and the stark white circle of the doctors' sterile field. And, of course, I remember the bodies, piling up on the fused earth runway behind the freighter that was our field hospital and headquarters. Alkres remained there—we could not risk his death—and I stayed with him, dividing my time between Moraghan's improvised communications station and the field hospital. We had three doctors, two Orillons who had come with us from Electra, and a volunteer from the Ansson Branch who was trying hard to hide her disappointment at missing the fighting. Most of the time they were enough to handle things, but every so often an unskilled pair of hands came in useful.

The reports trickled in: first the field was secure, and the squad leader had locked the surviving Brandr into one of the windowless storage buildings. Then the stadthall was taken, and the fourth squad announced it was inside the power plant complex.

"Trey!" It was the Ansson doctor, supporting another woman whose left arm and part of that shoulder had been burned away. It was obvious she was dying—I didn't understand how she'd lived long enough to reach the hospital—but a dark-haired young man hovered behind the doctor, his eyes wide with hope.

"See to him, will you?" the Ansson went on, and jerked her head at the man. We locked eyes for an instant, and she shook her head fractionally. I went to him, averting my eyes from the woman's charred flesh and scored bone, and took his arm, using all my strength to turn him back toward the hatch.

"Come on, the doctors can't work with you in the way." I kept my voice gentle, knowing he didn't really hear my words. He gave a convulsive start, and let me draw him away.

"Will she die?" he asked, still with a faint note of hope.

I looked away, hating myself for what had to be said. "I'm sorry." I made myself meet his eyes. "She's kin?"

"My true-sib—my sister." He closed his eyes for a moment, tears glittering in long lashes. "And my partner. Oh, Costa."

"I'm sorry," I said again, knowing how useless it was.

He stood for a moment longer, eyes closed, tears staining his cheeks. Then he took a deep breath, dragging both hands across his eyes. "I'm all right," he said, almost to himself, and reached for the rifle he'd discarded at the hatchway. He checked the power, ejected the spent pack, and slammed a new one into place, nodding to himself all the while. "I'll be fine," he said again, to me this time, and jumped down from the hatch. I caught a last glimpse of him running back across the field, and then he disappeared among the buildings' shadows.

"She's gone," the Ansson said wearily. "Give me a hand, Trey?"

Together, we lifted the woman's body by head and heels, the doctor's hand digging into the burned shoulder, and carried it across the hold to the loading hatch. There was a pile of bodies already beneath it. We dropped hers onto it, and turned back toward the improvised tables.

"Not too bad," the Ansson said. Something of my revulsion must have shown in my face, because she laughed softly, bitterly. "Trey, I'm from mining country. This is nothing, compared to a big cave-in."

I turned away from her, unable to speak, sickened and ashamed to have had any part in this. Luckily, there was no one waiting for her attentions—we must have hit a lull in the fighting. I went forward, stepping carefully over the double row of wounded, lying in drugged sleep, aid packs taped to their bodies.

Moraghan was nowhere to be seen, and there was a new tension in the air around the communications board. Alkres started to his feet at my entrance, and I moved to join him, saying quietly, "What's happened?"

"We don't know," Alkres answered.

At the sound of our voices, one of the people gathered around the board looked up. Seeing me, he said something in a low voice to the greying woman at his left, and came to join us.

"We got a transmission from the third squad—the one sent to the Necropolis—reporting heavy fighting. They were cut off, and second squad, backing them up, reported that a fairly large party had broken into the Necropolis and was defending it strongly. Captain Moraghan took a squad and went to reinforce them, but now we're being jammed. We can't pick up anything useful, except a rough position fix."

"So Leith—Captain Moraghan's all right?" Alkres interjected.

The man looked at him, and then at me, and answered carefully, "Her people are transmitting, sor, which is a good sign." He looked back at me. "We don't have many people to spare, Medium. Would you go forward, see what's happening, and report back?"

I took a deep breath, wishing I could refuse.

Alkres said, passionately, "I wish I could go."

"You know that's impossible," I snapped, more angrily than I'd meant. I looked back at Moraghan's aide, and nodded. "Of course I'll go."

"Thank you, Medium," the man said. He glanced over his shoulder. "Corol!"

I gasped at the sight of the man who stepped out of the shadows, and Alkres gave a little crow of pleasure. "I knew you hadn't heard," he said.

"I thought you were dead," I said.

Corol Ingvarr gave me a lopsided grin, and came forward to touch hands. "I wasn't there," he said, simply. "That's all."

I shook myself, trying to suppress the shock of seeing Corol Ingvarr alive again, after I'd thought him dead in the Tower. He had been my first guide on Orestes—the first of the Halex kin to accept me as a medium; after the field hospital, this was like a little resurrection.

"I can't spare you an escort," the commander was saying to Corol. The grey-bearded man looked offended.

"I doubt we'll need one," he said, stiffly. He turned to me, giving a little nod to Alkres as he did so. "Sor. If you're ready, Medium?"

"I'm ready," I said. I wished we did have a bigger escort—competent fighter though Corol might be, it seemed self-evident to me that two people alone practically invited attack—but I knew better than to say anything. I checked the charge on the blaster Moraghan had insisted that I carry, made sure the needle was on "full." Not that I thought it would do me much good if we were attacked—I had fired a blaster years ago, in training, and that was all—but I couldn't bear the idea of being without some means of defense. Bracing myself, I followed Corol from the ship.

The Eclipse was ending now, the darkness slowly lifting, shadows reappearing in the blackest corners. The streets were utterly empty, lower-floor windows blankly shuttered, doors locked and barred, or shielded with metal screens. We met no one until we passed the stadthall. A group of Halex were crouched on its broad porch, sonic mortars trained on the square around them. Handlights burned inside the building, marking it as ours. Corol paused to confer with the mortar squad's leader, then started off again, turning left down a narrow alley. I bit back an instinctive protest, and followed.

The alley gave onto a broader street that ran along the base of the Necropolis wall. In the distance, we could hear the whistle of blaster fire and the steady thump of a mortar. Corol grunted.

"Not this way," he said, and led me back up the alley until he found an even narrower cross street. This led into another filthy alley, and another, until at last we emerged into a wider street running perpendicular to the Necropolis wall. The street ended in a typical greengate, but the usual drop bar had been reinforced with a miscellany of objects—metal packing crates, shutters ripped from windows, a wrecked groundcar. A similar improvised barrier had been thrown up across the end of the street, and there were shapes crouched behind it. Corol whistled sharply twice, and several of the shapes turned, showing pale faces in the gloom. One rose and ran toward us, keeping to the shelter of the buildings to either side of the street. We advanced to meet it, hugging the buildings ourselves.

"Trouble?" the figure asked sharply. It was a woman's voice, but I couldn't make out many details of her face.

Corol shook his head. "Headquarters sent me to find Moraghan," he said. "You're being jammed."

The woman snorted. "That we knew," she said. "The captain's this way."

She led us back to the barricade, still hugging the walls of the buildings. Moraghan was crouched in the angle of a door, conferring with a technician in the muted glare of a handlight. She looked up at our approach, and her grim expression eased a little. "Good, Terend figured out what was happening and sent runners." She edged further into the deepset doorway, beckoning us in afterward. "They've got a strong force holed up in the Necropolis, and we're going to have to dig them out before we can implement step two."

Step two was informing Halfrid Brandr that we controlled Madelgar, and suggesting that we renegotiate. I nodded. Corol showed his teeth in a wolfish grin.

"But that's going to take some time," Moraghan continued. "Trey, I want you to stay here, we may need a medium. Corol, you get back to headquarters—go with him, Elevy—and tell Terend what's happened. Are they picking up any of the transmission?"

"Enough to get a fix on you, nothing more," Corol answered.

"Then tell him we'll use pulse code from now on," Moraghan said. "Also, tell him to implement step two if he sees anything moving from Destiny. Is that clear?"

Corol nodded. "Use pulse code from now on, and implement step two as soon as he sees anything moving out of Destiny. I'll tell him."

"Good," Moraghan said, and gestured to the woman who'd escorted us. "Get going, then."

They vanished into the shadows. Moraghan sighed, rubbing her gloved wrist. "We're going to have to break through now," she said, as much to herself as to me. She shook herself, working her good right shoulder, and touched the technician lightly with her gloved hand. "Pass the word, squad leaders to me."

I didn't hear much of the discussion that followed. The squad's amateur medic, identifiable as such by the heavy first-aid kit slung on her back, touched me on the shoulder. "You're the off-worlder, the medium?" she asked. "Can you give us a hand?"

I nodded and followed her, dodging the desultory fire from the greengates, across the road. A young man lay pinned beneath a pile of rubble, all that remained of a pledge-store's exotic facade. Another man crouched beside him, holding his hand. I winced, but then I saw that a fallen drum column had taken most of the weight. The young man was alive—and would continue to live, if we could get him out and back to the field hospital. It was getting him out that would be the problem. I crouched beside the medic, sheltered by the piled rubble, and studied the situation.

"We can't move it," the woman said, simply. "I thought, you're an off-worlder, you might be able to do something."

The second young man, the one who held the trapped man's hand, looked up at me with doglike hope and trust. He looked like the man who had lost his sister, and I looked away, suddenly afraid I'd fail him, too. "Is there anything I can use for a lever?" I asked harshly.

The medic nodded, and swept her hand through the dirt until she came up with a thin steel rod. I ran my hand along it, wishing the light were better. It felt like structural steel; if it were, it would be exactly what we needed. Awkwardly, I braced the far end against the ground, not daring to stand, and pushed with all my strength. It held, then skidded away from me across the metalled street. I caught myself painfully on one hand, just short of falling on my face. I could feel myself blushing, and was glad the darkness still hid all color.

"All right," I said, studying the rubble for a final time. "One of you, cover me, the other get ready to pull as soon as the weight comes off."

"I'll cover you," the medic said, shrugging out of the aid kit's harness. She picked up one of the men's rifles and stationed herself in the angle of the doorway.

I looked down at the two men, and saw with a shock

that the trapped man's eyes were open, his upper body braced and ready.

"I'll shout as soon as I'm free," he whispered. The other man shushed him, hands on his shoulders, ready to pull.

"All right," I said, and fitted the end of the rod under what I hoped was the most vulnerable corner of the dented shutter that seemed to be holding him. The thin drum column had fallen providentially in more ways than one: it lay in a good position to make a fulcrum. I took a deep breath and stood up. I was a perfect target in the waxing light, a darker shadow against the greying light of the street, but I tried to forget that, and pressed on the lever with all my strength. A bolt whizzed past my head, but the shutter didn't move. I swore and tried again, using every gram of strength I possessed. The trapped man gave a hoarse cry, and his friend dragged him backward, scrabbling over the broken metalling. In the same instant, a second bolt seared past me, just singeing the edge of my cloak. I released the lever, swearing, and batted frantically at the sudden flame. I smothered it between the thick folds, hardly realizing I'd burned myself, stumbling against the settling rubble. The medic fired twice, three times, but I knew from her face she hadn't hit anyone. Then she flung the rifle aside, and dropped to her knees beside the injured man, pulling a probe from the kit.

"Thanks," the other man said, breathlessly, his eyes still on his friend. "We're in your debt—Medium, did she say?"

I nodded, but my answer was cut off by the sudden shrilling of whistles up and down the line. The injured man muttered something, and the other man looked up sharply.

"Call-up," the medic said.

"I've got to go," the second man said, as much to his friend as to the rest of us. The injured man nodded, and managed a sleepy smile: the medic's work was already taking effect.

"He'll be all right now," the medic said.

The second man nodded, and darted away.

"Will you be all right?" I asked.

The medic nodded, pointing to a button on her kit.

"Oh, yes, I've called for a pickup. It's a pulse code, so they'll find us, don't worry."

A tremendous roar drowned out anything else she might have said. I winced, instinctively putting my hands over my ears, and turned to face the greengate. Leith had ordered her people to haul a sonic mortar into position at the center of the street, aimed to batter down the Brandr barricade. Even as I realized what had happened, it spoke again, flat waves of sound that shattered one of the shutters making up the greengate barricade. The last whole window remaining on the groundcar shattered in a spectacular spray of glass. Thinly, through the ringing in my head, I thought I heard a cheer.

The mortar fired again and again. I fell to my knees, wrapping my arms around my head, afraid I'd be permanently deafened by the crashing roar. Then it stopped. I lifted my head cautiously, afraid it would fire again, and heard a faint cheering. I shook my head, trying to get rid of the cotton-wool that seemed to fill my ears, and thought I heard the sound of blasters. I peered cautiously over the lip of our barricade, and saw that the greengate barricade had been broken, its components strewn in shattered fragments across the metalled street. The stub of the drop bar pointed at the ground, its mechanism destroyed. Our people—more people than I had realized were here—were running forward, mouths open as though they were shouting. Without knowing quite why I did it, I pulled myself across the barricade and followed.

I don't remember much that is coherent about the next hours. At some point my hearing returned, because I remember Leith's squad encountering another squad of ours, dug in around a dirty basement cabaret theater where a Brandr troop had barricaded themselves. Leith shouted, "Bar the door and leave them. Damn you, listen to me!"

Her last words were drowned by a feral scream, a woman's voice. Guil ex-Tam'ne rose like a fury from the rubble, assault gun held lovingly before her. She stood, seemingly unaware of the blaster fire from inside, heedless of the bolt that clipped her shoulder, knocking her backward a step or two, and fired repeatedly into the door.

The steel rang and shattered. Guil shrieked again, word-lessly, and charged the stairs, the rest of the squad following.

"Guil, no!" Leith shouted, but the words were lost in the sudden roar of blaster fire from inside. She looked away, the soldier's mask cracking briefly into something alive and tragic. Then she had mastered herself, and turned her back on the theater, stalking away toward the next objective.

I remained for a moment, I don't know why, and saw Guil emerge, assault gun still cradled in her hands, followed by perhaps half of the people who'd followed her in. There was blood on her hands and on her vest, and more blood smeared in her white-blond hair, but I doubted much of it was her own. She was smiling fiercely, eyes oddly unseeing. I started toward her, but she turned away, pointing toward the center of the Necropolis.

"That way," she shouted. The people with her raised a cheer, and started after her.

I hesitated for an instant, then walked to the top of the stairway that led down into the basement. The light was growing stronger every minute, but the entrance and the first few feet of the hall were still in shadow. I paused again, then flicked on my handlight and went down two steps, shining the light ahead of me into the cabaret theater.

The sight sent me scrambling back up the stairway, retching convulsively. The floor was scorched with blaster marks, and patched here and there with great smears of blood, as though some giant insect had been crushed against it. Blackened bodies lay where they had fallen, limbs shriveled to bone. I leaned against the stair railing, vomiting. When I had finished, I stood there for a long moment, trying to steel myself to go down into that butcher's den. No one could possibly be alive down there, I thought, at the same time hating myself for my cowardice. That crew didn't leave anything living. I shuddered convulsively, too sore and empty to be sick again, and pulled myself away, hurrying after Leith's squad.

Some time later in that nightmare day, I fell in with another medic, and stayed with him well into the clock-evening. He was an older man, who wept constantly and silently for no cause I knew, but a good doctor. He treated Brandr and Halex indifferently, and the Brandr ghosts as well. Seeing that, I stayed with him, not wanting him to lose his life for treating them. There were plenty of wounded ghosts, too, and I did what little I could for them, treating their injuries and telling them to get out of the Necropolis if they could.

I doubt anyone left alive could tell you how the fire started. The power was off, though that hardly mattered to us as the Eclipse ended, but there were other fuel lines crisscrossing the Necropolis. Maybe a stray blaster shot hit a pile of vulnerable costumes and film somewhere in the backstage of one of the theaters. It could even have been set by angry *para'anin*. The first I remember is smelling smoke as I knelt beside a wounded girl, pinning her down until the anesthetics took effect. I looked up, startled, and saw a column of dirty smoke rising against the cloudy sky. The shock must have shown in my face, because the doctor looked up, too.

"Not good," he said, and sniffled, dragging a dirty hand across his stained face.

"How far away do you think it is?" I asked.

He shook his head, frowning. The wind, which had been blowing fitfully since the Eclipse ended, shifted then, bringing a sudden warmth and a smell of burning. "I don't know," the doctor said aloud, stuffing the probe back into the side of his kit, "but I don't think we should wait for a pickup." He nodded at the girl, soundly asleep now, her burns wrapped in layers of plastiskin. The drug pack taped to her chest moved slowly in time with her breathing. "You can move her, it's all right."

I hesitated—the burns under the bandages were deep and ugly—but the wind strengthened a little, bringing a wisp of smoke with it. I coughed, my eyes watering now, then bent and lifted the girl. She was very light, bones seemingly as hollow as a bird's. I had no idea whether she was Halex or Brandr, living or ghost.

"This way," the doctor said, and pointed.

I followed him through the twisting streets, trying to carry the girl as carefully as possible, until at last we reached Moraghan's temporary headquarters in one of the Necropolis's open squares. She had commandeered a couple of groundcars somewhere for the wounded, and I set the girl in one, glad to turn the responsibility over to someone who knew what he was doing.

Moraghan and a pair of squad leaders, one of whom carried his arm in a sling, were standing in the center of the square, looking up at the swelling pillar of smoke.

"We still can't raise the aid post," the unwounded one was saying nervously, his fingers tapping on the butt of his blaster.

"Surely they pulled out," the other one murmured, but his tone was less certain than his words.

Leith circled her left wrist with her unscarred fingers, turning and twisting it in their grasp. Her eyes met mine, and I nodded. She gave a sigh of relief, and beckoned. "Trey'll go and make sure."

The squad leaders gave me a rather dubious glance, and I nodded again. "That's right, I'll go."

"And I'll go with you." That was Corol, appearing suddenly at Moraghan's elbow. I guessed he had carried his message and returned, but I wouldn't've cared if he'd simply appeared out of thin air. I was very glad of the offer.

"Thanks," I said.

"Take one of the carts," Leith went on, and gestured toward them left-handed. "They're slow, but you may want them, if. . . ."

She let her voice trail off, mind already elsewhere, but she didn't have to complete the sentence. We would need something like the flat-bed carriers to transport the wounded, if the aid post hadn't been evacuated.

Corol nodded, and swung himself onto the driver's perch, hands and feet feeling for the controls. He checked the power indicators, and then released the main brake, hands flying immediately to the steering levers. "Come on, Medium!" he shouted.

I hauled myself up into the bed behind him, and a voice called, "Wait, I'll come, too." It was the old doctor, a tear still gleaming on his face.

I pulled him up, and Corol engaged the engine. We shuddered forward, gears clashing, and then he had the hang of it. He turned us neatly, and headed into the smoke. First it was just tendrils and the smell of burning. Then, backed by the fitful wind, it grew thicker, great gusts of it blowing across the street like fog. Corol coughed hoarsely, wiping at his streaming eyes. I leaned forward, trying to take shallow breaths, and steadied his hands on the controls. We slowed, the cart shuddering in protest.

"Here, take these." That was the doctor, scrambling toward the driver's perch, a surgical filter pulled tight across his nose and mouth. He held two more in his outstretched hand. I snatched them from him, and clamped one across Corol's face. He jerked his head, adjusting it, and I pulled the tabs tight around the back of his head. His coughing stopped, and he was able to lift a hand from the controls to settle it more comfortably.

"Thanks," he said, voice distorted by the filter.

I nodded, hastily fitting the second mask over my own nose and mouth. My eyes still watered, but at least I could breathe. "Where is this aid post?" I asked, and hardly recognized my own voice.

Corol shrugged, fighting the controls. "I thought you knew."

"About two more blocks, then down the street that angles off to the left," the doctor said, hitching himself still farther forward in the cart's bed, until he was braced against the low front wall. "It was a clinic to begin with." His voice trailed off unhappily, and Corol and I exchanged nervous glances. The smoke was growing thicker, though the fickle wind had changed again, blowing from behind us. Bits of charred material—paper, cloth, light things— drifted in the air around us, which was growing uncomfortably warm. I took off my cloak, wadding it securely into a corner of the cart, and saw Corol wrench open the neck of his tunic. I had been hearing a sort of rushing noise for some time now, I realized, and had dismissed it as wind or water. It was the sound of flames.

"I don't like this," Corol muttered. "I don't like this at all."

Neither do I, I thought, but said nothing, not wanting to seem less brave than they. The noise of the fire was growing steadily louder, and Corol throttled back, crashing the gears, until the cart was moving at little better than a walk. His thumb was poised awkwardly on the gear button, I saw, ready to throw the machine into reverse. Dense black smoke billowed from behind the buildings ahead of us, rolling in a dirty coil across the street, but as yet there was no sign of flames.

Then we'd reached an intersection, and the doctor was pounding on Corol's shoulder, pointing to our left. I swung around, startled, then realized we'd reached the turn. A street angled to the left, as the doctor had said, but instead of leading us farther into the fire, it made a sharp turn, leading off at about a sixty-degree angle from the street we'd been following.

"That's a break," Corol said, and gunned the engine, swinging us rapidly into the new street.

We needed one, I thought. On the far side of the intersection, the first rank of buildings was still untouched, but I could see a little way up the street before the smoke cut off my view. Flames danced behind the thermal windows. Even as I watched, the glass shivered along the highest row, and the fire burst through, tongues of flame licking eagerly at the roof.

"We'd better hurry," I said, and somehow managed to keep my voice even. Corol nodded, face set and grim. At my side, the old doctor shook his head, eyes fixed on the fire.

"There's never been anything like this," he said. "Never."

"Is this it?" Corol called, hand hovering on the brake. The doctor tore his eyes away from the fire and nodded, pointing to a building to our left.

"That's it."

It was a storefront clinic, the sort that you find in the poorer parts of every Conglomerate city, typical except for the heavy wood-and-metal shutters drawn tight across the doors. One of the shutters hung loose, its steel hinges shattered, and there was just enough room for a person to squeeze through the resulting gap.

"Look like they pulled out already," Corol said, but he throttled back even further until the cart was barely moving. He gave me an inquiring glance.

I looked back over my shoulder at the fire. It was coming closer, there was no question about it; already smoke was trickling from the roofs of buildings lining the intersection. We couldn't stay long—but I couldn't leave without being sure there was no one left inside. "I'll just take a quick look," I said, and swung down from the cart before I could change my mind.

"Wait," the doctor called. I turned, and he tossed me the handlight I'd left in the cart. I caught it, and ducked under the twisted shutter.

It was cooler inside, and the air was cleaner. I switched on the handlight and swung its beam across the room ahead of me. At first, I couldn't make sense of the lumps and shadowed shapes strewn across the floor, but then the beam caught and centered on something recognizable. It was a man's body, mostly intact, sprawled protectively across a second, heavily bandaged body. The plastiskin was brown with dried blood, but I couldn't be sure whose it was. I swallowed hard, tasting bile, and swung the beam back again, looking for whole bodies. There were a lot of fragments, and the floor and side wall were splashed with brown stains. I was about to back out, shaking and sick, when I heard a faint sound from the far end of the room.

I swung the handlight reluctantly in the direction of the sound. The beam flashed across a heavy counter, its polished face pitted and scarred from the explosion. The sound came again, a sort of mew that resolved itself into faint words.

"Help me . . ."

I took a quick step forward, then paused, trying to think. The fire was close behind; every second counted. "How many are there?"

There was a long silence. I had almost given up hope of an answer and was starting forward to see for myself when a second, stronger voice spoke. "Three—four alive, I think. Help us!"

"I'll be right back," I answered. "There's a doctor outside, I'm going for him."

There was a whisper of protest from behind the counter, but I ignored it. I stooped, setting the handlight on the floor, beam turned toward the ceiling, then backed hastily out of what was left of the aid post. Corol and the doctor stared at me, wild-eyed, and Corol jerked his chin toward the intersection where we'd turned.

"I sure hope there's nobody there," he growled.

I looked the way he'd pointed, and a shiver of fear ran down my spine. The buildings edging the intersection were fully engaged now, flames shooting from roof and windows. Huge particles of soot, mixed with sparks, rained down into the street, and the first buildings on our side were beginning to smolder.

"Something happened in there," I said, biting back my fear, "but there are at least three people still alive."

"God damn it," Corol said, but swung himself out of the cart. He left the motor running, and after a moment's search, found a broken stub of timber to jam under the driving wheel.

"Badly hurt?" The doctor ducked through the door ahead of me without waiting for an answer. He checked at the sight of the room, the wreckage made surreal by the upturned handlight.

"Behind the counter," I said, and stepped cautiously over the two intact bodies.

There were four people behind the counter, three heavily bandaged, eyes closed, medical packs taped to their bodies. The fourth crouched against the far wall, a blast rifle clutched in thickly bandaged hands. He—no, she— had worn a topknot; her hair fell now in matted strands, hiding her face. She swung the rifle in my direction as I stepped around the end of the counter, and I stopped dead, holding up my empty hands.

"My name's Maturin," I said. "I'm the Halex Medium." The doctor darted forward around me, heedless of the levelled rifle, and dropped to his knees by the nearest of the unconscious bodies.

The woman relaxed then, letting the rifle fall from her hands. "Thank God you came," she said, softly. "The grenade took out the transmitter."

"Grenade?" I asked, and bent to pull her gently to her feet. She stood, wincing, bandaged hands held well clear of my body. Beneath the straggling hair, I could see two deep parallel gashes along her cheekbone and jaw, completely obliterating a Family tattoo.

She nodded and said, in a voice breathless with pain, "Brandr—live, I think, not ghosts. Broke off the hinge and tossed a grenade in. We were just lucky the medics put us back here out of the way." She touched the counter gently, wonderingly, with one mittened paw.

"Those bastards." That was Corol, the cart secured to his satisfaction. "Medium, we've got to hurry."

The woman gave me a questioning glance as I helped her to the door, but I ignored it. She'd see soon enough, I thought grimly.

And then we were outside, in the sudden, stifling heat. The woman doubled over, coughing, as the smoke caught her. I lifted her bodily then, and put her into the cart. She retained enough control to draw her legs up after her, and waved me away. Still coughing, she curled herself up in the bottom of the cart. The buildings at the end of the street were fully ablaze now; even as I turned to go back inside, a piece of roof tile, one edge on fire, landed at my feet. I stepped on it, crushing the flame, but I could see more fiery fragments whirling through the air. I swore, and ducked back inside.

"You'll have to carry this one together," the doctor was saying, pointing to a person so heavily swathed in a mummy bag that it was impossible to tell if it were a man or a woman. The hooked nose and downturned mouth could have belonged to either. "The other two aren't as bad."

I nodded, and stepped around the counter so that I could take the stranger's shoulders. Corol stooped, laying careful hands on the stiffly wrapped feet. "On three," he said, and I could see the muscles tighten in his neck and hands. "One . . . two . . . three."

We lifted him together, as gently as we could, but even so I thought I heard a breathy moan as we carried him— her?—across the room. We stuck momentarily at the narrow door, but then Corol bent almost double, and we were able to slide out. The sleeve of my tunic caught on some piece of metal, then tore free before I could call for Corol to stop. We laid the mummy-wrapped body in the cart bed and ducked back inside, afraid to look at the sky.

The two remaining survivors were both small people, light-boned. I lifted the taller easily, and saw Corol lift the other, staggering slightly under the limp weight. As we crossed the room a final time, I saw the doctor kneeling beside the first bodies I'd seen, pulling the man's aside to examine the woman who lay beneath it. Her face was pale, somehow untouched by his blood or the force of the explosion, and I hoped for an instant she might still be alive. Then the doctor rose stiffly, shaking his head. I saw the ripped medical pack lying empty against her thigh, the anti-shock drugs that might have saved her life pooled on the floor beside her.

Then at last we were outside, battered by a scorching wind that drove burning scraps of buildings ahead of us along the street. Corol lifted his burden into the cart bed—the doctor, scurrying ahead, helped to steady the bandaged body—then swung himself up into the driver's seat. I lifted the person I was carrying over the tail of the cart and pulled myself in after him, hoping we hadn't left it too late. The buildings to either side of us were burning.

"The chock," Corol shouted, his voice barely audible over the noise of the flames.

I cursed, remembering too late how he'd wedged the wheel, and dropped back out of the cart to free the length of wood. The cart jerked forward, Corol's hand heavy on the controls, and I dodged back just in time. I caught the side of the cart as it rolled past me, pulling myself aboard, and lay panting in the bottom of the bed as Corol gunned the engine. It coughed—the bad air was affecting it at last—then caught with a roar. We rolled forward, picking up speed, running from the fire.

By the time we reached Leith's temporary headquarters, the fire following on our heels, she had decided to pull back to the Necropolis wall, and was calling on the force holding the stadthall to find the firefighters and get them working. We joined the retreat, mingling with a mass of Brandr ghosts fighting to get away from the flames, their few belongings carried on their backs. I saw a puppet theater group trying to save their projector, six or seven people hauling at the massive piece of machinery. They quickly fell behind, and were swallowed in the crowd. I never knew what happened to them.

By clock-midnight, the fire had jumped the Necropolis wall. That was enough to persuade the Brandr firefighters to cooperate, and fighting stopped across the city as Brandr and Halex fought side by side to halt the spreading flames. It did some good, but it wasn't enough. By the tenth hour, when the firefighters finally reported the fire under control, half the city had burned.

Leith withdrew to the field then, leaving a mop-up crew

to keep an eye on the firefighters. Sitting in the field hospital's hatch, I saw her arrive, at the head of a train of ragged and smokestained followers, the survivors of the attack. Somewhere, she had found a battered three-wheeled jigger, and steered it one-handed in a ragged arc across the field toward the grounded freighters. She was carrying something else in her other hand, the crippled hand—a pale brown bundle. As she came closer, I saw it was a baby.

She brought the jigger to a grinding halt at the foot of the stairs leading to the hatch, looking up at me with cold, empty eyes. I met her gaze, not knowing what to say, not looking at the baby that lay motionless in the circle of her gloved arm. Still silent, she swung herself off the jigger and started up the stairs into the field hospital. At her entrance, several doctors turned, and then the Ansson woman came forward, scooping the baby almost protectively into her own grasp. She held it easily, maternally, touching chest and stomach, then turned away, reaching for something on the instrument table. A moment later, the child's arms and legs wriggled, and it gave a feeble, crowing cry. For the second time, I saw Leith's mask crack, and she turned her back on them all, one hand hooding her eyes. I pulled myself to my feet and went to her, blocking the others' stares.

After a moment, she nodded and rubbed her good hand across her face as though reapplying her soldier's calm. "It's alive, Trey," she said softly. "The mother—I saw her die, but the kid's alive." She straightened her shoulders. "What's the word from Destiny?"

"Stalemate, up to now," I answered. "Terend's been doing what you said, just warning the Brandr not to interfere if they want to keep the city safe."

Leith made a face at that. "Such as we've left of it." She sighed, the mask slipping again. "I didn't count on a fire, Trey, I swear it. They always said at school, the thing you don't count on's the thing that's going to screw you." She looked down, pressing gloved palm to bare palm in an almost ritualistic gesture. "But it's happened," she said, more to herself than to me, "and at your choice. Accept it, and go on." She looked up, meeting my gaze, and actually managed something that might have been a smile. She looked dreadful—eyes smoke-reddened, sunk deep in their sockets, the red mark of a flying ember on her chin.

"Captain Moraghan!" For the first time since I'd met him, Terend Ingvarr sounded frightened. I turned, feeling ice along my own spine.

"Yes, Terend?" If Terend's voice had startled her, Leith gave no sign of it.

"Captain Moraghan, Halfrid Brandr is calling from Destiny, and he wants to talk to you and to Himself—he won't talk until you're there."

Moraghan gave an odd, twisted smile. "I was half expecting this," she said. "Trey, will you come with me?"

I nodded, and followed them back into the improvised communications room. Alkres was waiting there, as he had been all night, sitting bolt upright in an uncomfortable hanging chair. He was chewing on his lip as we came in, but as soon as he saw Leith, his tense expression eased a little.

"Oh, Captain Moraghan, I'm glad you're here," he said, with an attempt at adult calm.

Leith nodded. "Terend said Halfrid wants to talk to us?"

"Yes." Alkres shivered.

"Put us on, then," Leith said. As the technician made the adjustments, she glanced at me. "Make sure everything's done legally, will you, Trey?"

I nodded, just as the technician said, "Channel's open."

Leith squared her shoulders, facing the sound pickup as though it were another officer. "Halfrid Brandr? I'm Leith Moraghan."

The speaker crackled slightly—the ship's equipment wasn't really meant for this sort of work—and Halfrid said, "So you're the latest off-worlder the Halex have hired to do their dirty work. This just proves my point. The Ship's Council made the right decision."

"I'm not an employee," Leith said mildly. "I used to be a Peacekeeper, and I'm acting under the Oath."

I nodded approvingly. If the other genarchs were listening, that would make them think a bit.

Halfrid started to say something more, but Leith cut him off. "This can be gone into at a more appropriate moment. If you've got anything important to say, say it; otherwise, I have a proposal for you."

"And I've got one for you, Captain," Halfrid retorted. "You may hold my city—what's left of it, I heard what you did—but I've still got yours. I hold the power plant, and I tell you, if you withdraw now, I might—might—not blow it up, and half the city with it. Otherwise, it'll be city for city, Captain."

"I remind you we still hold Madelgar," Leith said.

"And I hold Destiny," Halfrid answered. "I'll destroy it, don't think I won't. I hold the power plant, remember that."

"I'd advise against any precipitous action," Leith said, still mildly, and made a chopping gesture to the technician. He cut the power instantly, and she took a step back, circling her gloved wrist with her fingers.

"Can he do that?" Alkres asked. There was a quaver in his voice, and Leith gave him an encouraging smile.

"Yes, he could do it," she said, "but so could we. He's just trying to scare us."

"That means stalemate," I said, unable to hold back the words any longer. "After everything we did, we're no better off than we were. It's all for nothing."

Leith glared at me. "We have Madelgar," she said, in a voice tinged with restrained anger. "That was the objective, Trey. We're exactly where we expected to be at this point."

I looked away, ashamed of myself for blaming her. She had never said this would be easy or without risk, had never promised more than she'd delivered. The things I'd seen in Madelgar were as much my responsibility as hers—more, perhaps, since I'd been the one to suggest an attack. She'd accepted her share of it; I couldn't—wouldn't—do any less. "You're right, of course, Leith. I'm sorry," I said. "What do we do now?"

Leith gave me a twisted grin, her anger gone as quickly as it had appeared. "We wait," she said, simply. "He'll talk, but we'll have to wait for it."

Chapter 14: Rehur

The basement room was cold, despite the camp-heater glowing in the center of the narrow space and the costume racks pulled into a circle for insulation. Rehur slipped his hands into the sleeves of his quilted coat—a gaudy thing, costume rather than clothing—and hugged his knitted tunic closer to his body. The Brandr had ordered *para'anin* to remove themselves to other precincts, and when that failed to restore order, had cut power into the Necropolis two weeks before, in an attempt to starve what remained of the population into submission. The ghosts, and those *para'anin* who'd chosen to ignore the order, knowing the city's byways better than any living person, had managed to smuggle in enough food and fuel to keep themselves alive and angry. The Brandr were forced to content themselves with barricading the greengates from the outside, only occasionally venturing inside the Necropolis wall. And when they did. . . .

Rehur smiled slowly, remembering triumphs as sweet as stage success. The Brandr soldier foolish enough to cross the wall might well meet a crossbow bolt in his belly—there were plenty of hunting bows and other light weapons in the Necropolis—or he might run into a bar-

349

rage of stones and taunting shouts, luring him into an ambush from which he would emerge bruised, humiliated, and, most important, weaponless. Rehur touched the blaster that hung at his own belt. He had taken it from a Brandr squad captain, a professional soldier grey-faced with fury at being beaten by a ragtag group of amateurs. That encounter had done much to erase Rehur's shame over his first meeting with Brandr soldiers.

The portable comunit squawked sharply, and he started, annoyed that he'd let his mind wander. Ume-Kai reached for the breadboarded control box, adjusting its knobs a millimeter at a time, then cautiously lifted the cup-speaker to his ear. He listened for a moment, then leaned forward until his lips almost touched the transmitter pickup. "Acknowledged," he said, very distinctly. "I acknowledge." Nothing seemed to happen for a moment, but then a light winked out among the sprouting wires. Ume-Kai leaned back on his heels, sighing.

"Well?" Rehur asked, after a moment.

"Nothing new," Ume-Kai answered. "We're still picking up that broadcast from Madelgar—I think it's a loop, myself. But that's all."

"Why didn't they warn us?" Rehur muttered. "We could've been of use."

The minne shrugged, reaching for the flask of tea. He poured two cups, sliding one across the floor to the younger actor, and wrapped his own hand around the other, trying in vain to warm his fingers. "They probably couldn't get through," he said. "The Brandr've had the gates sealed tight for weeks now."

"Even so," Rehur protested, but had to admit the other was right. A broadcast message obviously wouldn't've been of any use, and the Necropolis had been disconnected from the Destiny comnet when the area was sealed.

"Drink your tea before it gets cold," Ume-Kai said, "and be glad we've still got water."

Rehur made a face, but picked up the chipped cup. They were lucky that Destiny drew its water supply from a dozen different wells—the system had been set up to minimize the chance of earthquake damage—but less lucky in the quantity and quality of their other supplies. The tea was only palely green, and smelled faintly of seawater.

Then his mouth curved up into a wry smile. At least it was hot—in the middle of a siege, he could hardly ask for more. He sipped at the scalding liquid, watching Ume-Kai from under his lashes.

The minne had changed since he'd made himself one of the leaders of the Necropolis. His face had thinned—but then they were all thinner, living on short rations and hard exercise. The delicate line of cheek and jaw was blurred by a day's growth of beard, something that would have been unthinkable a calendar-month ago. His close-cropped hair had started to grow out, too, and stood up in an untidy brush. Self-consciously, Rehur ran his hand through his own hair. It was almost long enough to scrape together into a topknot; lately, he'd taken to binding it back with a short length of cord when he went out into the streets. Only Belit, asleep in one of the upstairs rooms, seemed unchanged by everything that had happened, though Rehur knew she carried a fresh scar along her ribs. The change in Ume-Kai was different, somehow, less a physical change than something more. The new authority sat well on him, brought out the strength a minne must hide or transmute into something more useful to his craft. . . . Or is it that I'm changing, too? Rehur wondered, still staring at the older man. He's taken command, all right, and that's made something new of him, but I've refused everyone who wants me to be a Halex. What's that doing to me?

He shied away from the thought, mouth contracting into a bitter line. I won't—I can't—play that role any more, he thought. I wasn't suited for it in the first place, and now, when it really matters, I'd only screw it up again. It's better, much better, to let Ume-Kai lead.

The comunit squawked again, and Ume-Kai reached for the controls. He adjusted them, wincing as he provoked a burst of static, then held the cup to his ear. Rehur watched his expression change from a look almost of boredom to one of surprise, and finally to anger.

"Meet me at the Rest," the minne said when the speaker had finished, leaning forward again to make sure the crude pickup transmitted his words clearly. "Tell the others, too. Meet at the Rest. Please repeat and acknowledge." He listened closely to the answer, then cut the connection.

"What's happened?" Rehur demanded.

Ume-Kai glared into space. "Halfrid Brandr's threatening to blow up the power plant, that's what."

"He can't do that," Rehur exclaimed. Ume-Kai managed an indulgent, distracted smile, and the younger actor hurried on. "He'll blow up the Gilbertine precinct with it, and probably burn down half the city—and we're holding Madelgar. He's crazy."

Ume-Kai shook his head, shrugging himself out of his fine wool wrap. "Apparently there was a fire in Madelgar, a lot of damage." He reached for his blast rifle, adding dryly, "It seems to have upset Halfrid."

Rehur made a face. He had learned to trust the minne over the past calendar-weeks, but he still found Ume-Kai's constant irony hard to take. The minne continued, sobering, "I've asked Lulan to get the others to meet us at the Rest. We can't just sit here and let it happen."

"What do you suggest?" Rehur asked, but loosened the cord that fastened the quilted coat.

"We have to stop them," Ume-Kai answered.

"How?" Rehur stopped, coat sliding down his back, arms still tangled in its wide sleeves.

"By force, if necessary," Ume-Kai answered, and, unbelievably, smiled. "Which it may not be. But I will need you, Rehur—especially your pretty Halex face."

Rehur froze, then slowly looked away, freeing himself from the coat. "I'll wake Belit."

"Wait." Ume-Kai caught the younger man's wrist in an unexpectedly strong grip. Rehur winced and tried to jerk free; failing, he stood his ground, watching the minne.

"You don't get out of this one so easily," Ume-Kai said, all mockery gone from his voice. "Lulan served your kin well. They'll listen to my idea a lot quicker if a Halex backs it than if it was just me. And you've got that face—hell, your twin was the Demi-heir, and for all I know you were Demi-heir before him—"

"No!"

"—so they'll listen to you," Ume-Kai finished, as though the other hadn't spoken. He shook the younger man lightly. "I need you."

"I—" Rehur faltered before the sudden contempt in the other's eyes. "What is this plan?"

"We're ghosts, aren't we? Or most of us are, anyway.

They can't acknowledge us," Ume-Kai said. "We can use that."

"It won't work," Rehur began, then hesitated, considering. Ume-Kai smiled.

"It will work," the minne said, "but no one'll believe it at first glance. That's why I need your support."

Rehur nodded, but said, "I'll screw it up, Ume."

"Think of it as another part," Ume-Kai answered. He smiled again, this time with malice. "Second-lead, not lead-villain. Don't worry, I'll prompt as necessary."

That's the second time someone's offered me second-lead, Rehur thought, remotely. Aloud, he said, "All right, I'll do it."

"Good." Ume-Kai released the younger actor's wrist, gave him a push toward the stairs. "Wake Belit, will you? Tell her what's up."

Rehur muttered a curse, angry and ashamed and afraid all in the same moment, and climbed the stairs to the main level, feeling his way in the half-light that filtered in through the distant skylight. At least we don't have to worry about finding batteries for the handlights for another day or two, he thought irrelevantly, trying to blot out the memory of Ume-Kai's face. At least not until the Dark—if we live so long.

Belit was asleep in what had been the company manager's office, curled on her side on the battered couch. The thick glass of the window was covered with an extra layer of batting, reducing the sunlight to a distant, milky glow, but the battery-powered heater in the corner of the room was barely able to keep the temperature at an acceptable level. Shivering, Rehur tapped gently on the doorframe. "Belit?"

The musician shot upright, reaching for the crossbow that lay on the floor beside the couch. Her hand was on the butt before she realized who had spoken, and relaxed. "Is anything wrong?" she asked.

Rehur nodded. "I'm afraid so. The Brandr's decided to counter by blowing up the main power plant—or at least that's what Halfrid's threatening," he amended quickly. There was no point in exaggeration. "Ume-Kai wants everyone to meet at the Rest."

Belit stood up, pulling on her gaudy tunic. She had not

been back to her own flat since the day after the first riots;
she had borrowed tunic and trousers from the costume
racks in the basement instead. The tunic was ordinary
enough, though brightly colored, but the only trousers
heavy enough to be practical were a pair of the exaggerated breeches worn in the most stylized plays. They hung
in heavy folds around her legs, caught at mid-calf with a
sort of tab, just barely practical. Too many people were
borrowing from the costume stocks these days, Rehur
thought, and realized he was quoting Rowan. The company manger was right, though, he thought. A lot of theater groups would be ruined before this was over, and not
just by borrowed costumes.

Belit wound a scarf around her red hair, and reached for
her crossbow. She had refused the offer of a more modern
weapon, saying she knew how to use her bow, and would
leave less demanding weapons to those who needed them.
"What does Ume-Kai think we can do about it?" she
asked.

Rehur shrugged.

"I'll tell you when we get to the Rest," Ume-Kai said,
from the stairs. "We're late. Are you ready?"

"I'm ready," Belit said quietly, slinging her bolt case
over her shoulder, bow balanced easily in her left hand.

Rehur sighed, pushing back his anger. "Coming."

They made their way toward Rita's Rest by the maze of
back streets, avoiding larger streets and squares for fear of
meeting a Brandr patrol that had slipped past the watchers
at the greengates. It had happened before, and now, of all
times, they couldn't afford the delay. The back door of
Rita's Rest opened into an alley that ran parallel to Broad
Street at that point. The door stood open a hand's-breadth,
then swung open farther at their approach.

"Hello, Ume-Kai." That was the Rest's regular doorkeeper, now managing the popular restaurant as a sort of
central meeting place for the ghosts and *para'anin* still in
the Necropolis. "Most everyone's here before you."

Ume-Kai gave her a quick grin as he ducked through
the door. "I know."

And I bet he planned it that way, too, Rehur thought.
He exchanged quick glances with Belit, who rolled her
eyes. Anything for an entrance.

The minne led them quickly through the Rest's empty, echoing kitchen, then through the backstage passage to the door leading onto the main floor. It was the only way into the main dining hall, where all the meetings were held, but Rehur had to bite his lip to suppress a grimace. They would make a grand entrance indeed, if he knew Ume-Kai.

Sure enough, the minne paused for a fraction of a second at the curtain separating the passage from the dining room, then, with a grand gesture, drew it up and back so that he could step through without ducking. The curtain rings rattled sharply, drawing all eyes. There was no need for the pointing spot he would have had at the Cockaigne, Rehur thought almost enviously. The minne paused just inside the door, forcing Rehur to step up beside him in order to come fully into the room, then swept forward to claim a table set conspicuously near the front of the room. Rehur followed demurely, knowing he would only look petty if he tried to spoil the scene, but seated himself on the edge of the low stage at Ume-Kai's shoulder. The minne gave the younger man a single swift, annoyed look, but said nothing. Belit joined Ume-Kai at the table.

The dining room was crowded, barred sunlight falling through the narrow front windows to light a sea of faces. Nearly everyone who'd stayed was there, Rehur thought, scanning the room. The main officers of the Streetwalkers' Tong were present, of course, and Lulan, with Shoba's daughter crouched beside her—the girl had been acting as a runner, Rehur remembered, passing on the information Lulan collected from her friends on the other side of the wall. It was rumored that Lulan had somehow managed to keep her comnet link, but the conciliatrix had resolutely refused to confirm or deny the rumor. Ash and Rowan should be here, too, Rehur thought, but scanned the crowd again without finding their familiar faces.

After Ume-Kai's spectacular entrance, there was a moment of silence, broken a few heartbeats later by a rising babble of questions. The minne lifted his hand in gentle rebuke, enjoying the sensation he'd created, and obviously prepared to wait it out. The president of the Streetwalkers' Tong made a face, put two fingers in her mouth, and whistled shrilly. There was instant silence.

"All right," she said, raising her voice to project to the corners of the room. "Ume-Kai, what's all this about?"

"Did you get my message, Amial?" the minne asked. Unlike the woman's, his voice carried effortlessly.

Amial nodded. "I gathered you had something further in mind." Her tone was challenging. Rehur saw the minne stiffen slightly, and relax again with an effort.

"That's right." His answer set off a renewed murmuring, and Ume-Kai raised his hands for silence. "I assume you've all heard that the Brandr are threatening to blow up the main power plant if the Halex don't give up Madelgar—and I thank you, Lulan, for passing on the information."

The conciliatrix bowed gracefully, still seated. With the corner of his mind that observed such things, Rehur noted the gesture for later use.

"Obviously, I think this is a bad thing," Ume-Kai continued, allowing a trace of humor to enter his voice. Then, abruptly, he became completely serious. "I propose we stop him."

There was another outburst, louder this time, and someone shouted, "How?"

The minne made a production of looking for the speaker, and a woman pushed her way to the front of the crowd, scowling. "How the hell do you propose we do it, minne?" she demanded.

She looked oddly familiar, Rehur thought, and frowned, trying to place the lined face. After a moment, he remembered. She was Gazel Ingvarr, manager of the Halex home farm—but Gazel was neither ghost nor *para'an*. Or rather, he amended, she had not been either before. Now, having gone beyond mere acknowledgement actually to speak to a ghost, she had put herself among the ranks of the dead. And there were a lot more like her, Rehur realized suddenly, even if they didn't all wear the ghostmark yet. There hadn't been time for most of the Family members to go through the *parachor* before joining the groups in the Necropolis, and there was, for once, a serious shortage of mediums, making keeping the code almost impossible.

"Just this, woman," Ume-Kai answered, and Rehur dragged his attention back to the scene in front of him. "We're all ghosts here, or nearly all—yourself included, ama. And Halfrid Brandr *says* he keeps the code. If we can reach the power plant. . . ." The minne let his voice trail off suggestively, then finished, "If we can reach the power plant, he can't touch us and keep code—he can't even see us, people. We can kill him."

"That's if he keeps code," another woman's voice, an actor's voice, said from the side. "What if he breaks it?"

"We'll still have helped the Patriarch," Gazel cried fiercely.

"We could all get killed in the process," someone else called, "killed true-dead."

"He'll keep the code." The husky voice came from the front of the crowd, and Rehur craned his neck to see the speaker. It was a blond woman sitting at one of the second-rank tables, he realized after a moment.

"Oh, he'll keep code," she said again, a thin smile on her lips.

"She knows what she's talking about," a man said, from somewhere behind her. "She's mainline kin."

"Good God," Rehur said, and heard his words echoed across the room. Still, the note of doubt was very strong in those voices; he could sense the crowd's uncertainty, could feel them wavering between action and inaction. Ume-Kai's head moved slightly, almost a nod, and Rehur shivered, despising himself for having to be prompted. He pushed himself reluctantly to his feet, knowing that even the stage's subdued day lighting would be enough to show off his Halex face. "Ume-Kai's right," he said loudly. "Halfrid won't have any choice."

"How the hell do you know?" someone shouted, and half a dozen voices answered from across the room.

"He's Rehur—Halex of Halex."

"Mainline kin."

"He was the Demi-heir."

Rehur looked away, not meeting Ume-Kai's quick, encouraging smile. The minne turned back to face the room, spreading his hands. "You see?" he said. "It'll work. Who's with us?"

There was a rumble of agreement, and the woman from the Tong said strongly, "All right, Ume-Kai, we'll do it your way."

Even then, it took time and debate to sort out exactly

who would take part in the attack—the Necropolis's existing organizations were informal in the extreme, and few ghosts or *para'anin* took authority well. It was agreed at last, after Ume-Kai insisted and Rehur backed him up, that only ghosts would go to the power plant, leaving the *para'anin* to open and hold one greengate for the attack party. Rehur took a quick look at the ghosts' faces, and made his way backstage to the Rest's tiny dressing room, rummaging in the drawers until he found half a dozen tubes of white makeup. Then he returned to the stage, and began daubing ghostmarks on the foreheads of those who didn't show them. After a few minutes, a line began to form.

He went on working, mechanically answering questions he barely heard, trying to suppress his sudden fear. Suppose Halfrid doesn't keep the code? he thought. We could all be killed, and we won't have helped poor Alkres one little bit. Or even if he does keep code, suppose there's some loophole we haven't thought of? You get the same result. But there aren't any loopholes, he told himself, trying to be firm. I know there aren't—and I know Halfrid will follow the code to the last letter. And even if I do get killed, it'll be worth it, to have had the chance to do him in.

He lifted the makeup stick again, and realized that it was Belit who stood in front of him. He paused, startled, and the musician said, "Look, Rehur, I want to go. Just mark me, will you?"

"You'll be dead if I do that," Rehur protested.

"I don't care." Belit's mouth set in a hard line, an expression Rehur had never seen on her face before. "I was in at the beginning; I want to be in at the kill." She shrugged then, trying to look nonchalant. "Besides, I may just go off-world when this is over. Rowan's been talking about it, and they'll need a synth-man."

"Have they, now?" Rehur said, then shook himself. "Are you sure, Belit?"

"I'm sure."

"All right," Rehur said dubiously, and drew the mark firmly across the musician's forehead before either of them could change their minds.

Belit smiled fiercely. "Thanks, Rehur," she said, and was gone.

"What's the world coming to?" the woman in line behind her said.

Rehur, busy tearing the wrapper back from the end of the makeup, looked up sharply. Gazel Ingvarr gave him a twisted smile.

"Never thought you'd see the day, did you, when people'd be begging to be marked as ghosts?"

Rehur shook his head mutely—he'd always been a little afraid of the sharp-tongued farm manager—and started to draw in the mark. Then his curiosity got the better of him. "Are you really *para'an*, too?"

Gazel snorted. "I'm as good a ghost as you are. Who was there to give *parachor*, with the medium gone? I doubt I could find three kinsmen for it, anyway."

"Oh," Rehur said. Not knowing what else to say, he added, "Good luck."

There weren't many ghosts to mark after that. Rehur finished with the last one, and tucked the last stick into his pocket automatically, smearing a blob of the stuff across the butt of his blaster as he did so. He swore and rubbed it off, then followed the others out into the light of Broad Street. It was growing late in the clock-evening, Agamemnon almost a quarter full overhead. Someone—probably a member of one of the transportation unions, Rehur thought—had commandeered a couple of the tramline's work cars. With much shouting and waving of arms, the *para'anin* were loaded aboard, and the two machines set off for the main greengate. The ghosts followed on foot.

By the time they reached the greengate, the fighting was over, and the surviving Brandr—most of the guard team; the *para'anin* had taken them completely by surprise—were trussed up in the display window of a nearby souvenir shop. Lulan and a young man from one of the cross-talk companies stood beside the raised barrier, waving cheerfully as the ghosts approached. The rest of the *para'anin* lined the gate itself, cheering. Rehur only caught a few words as Ume-Kai pulled him to the head of the line, all urging them on to destroy the Brandr. He shivered again, but with a pleasurable excitement, not from cold.

They led the ghosts down the High Street itself, the most direct route to the power plant. Windows opened as they passed, and closed again as the watchers realized what they were. Once, the leader of a Brandr patrol stepped from his station by a tram turntable, lifting his hand to stop them. He saw the white ghostmarks an instant later, and tried to turn the gesture into something else. His patrol hesitated; then, taking their cue from their leader, they turned their backs on the marching ghosts. Rehur gave a yelp of delight, but could not shake the sense that it was theater, not real. Farther down the line, a woman raised her voice in a mocking, cross-talk song.

And then they were at the power plant. There were two Brandr on duty at the compound gate, but they, too, fell back before the approaching ghosts. Ume-Kai struggled with the gate for a moment, and then Rehur and a tall woman threw their weight against it as well. The gate opened, reluctantly, and the ghosts streamed inside. As he turned toward the main building, Rehur could almost feel sorry for the two guards, who stood frozen in an agony of uncertainty. After all, even if they sacrificed themselves, admitted they'd seen the ghosts, and tried to warn Halfrid, it would take time to find a medium—more time than Halfrid had. Rehur shouted with the rest, trying to break through the wall of unreality, and hurried to catch up with Ume-Kai.

Two more Brandr flanked the building's entrance, but they, too, froze at the sight of the marchers. The ghosts jeered at them, emboldened by their successes, while Ume-Kai fiddled briefly with the latch. Rehur stooped to help, and the door swung open. The way inside was clear. The ghosts poured inside, catcalls turning to cheers and laughter.

They found the Brandr in the main control room, guarded by a final half dozen troopers. The squad leader froze, his leveled rifle wavering, as Ume-Kai appeared at the head of the stairs. The other soldiers did the same, eyes locking onto something in the far distance, and Ume-Kai bent to trigger the final lock, ghosts laughing and calling behind him. At that moment, one of the soldiers gave a strangled cry, and swung her rifle blindly. Without thinking, Rehur lunged forward, knocking her against the wall. The shot went wide, leaving a smoldering circle on the far wall. The rifle clattered to the floor, and another ghost grabbed it, leveling it at the rest of the desperately unseeing guards.

"Watch them," Rehur shouted, struggling to keep his hold. The sense of unreality was abruptly broken, and he was suddenly himself again. Another ghost lunged forward, pinning the soldier's arms, and Rehur allowed himself to relax his hold a little. "You're dead, woman," he said, almost conversationally. The soldier checked, startled, then went limp, her face contorted with silent, angry tears. The door opened.

The control room was already crowded, but more than a dozen ghosts forced their way in behind Ume-Kai. Rehur shoved his way to the minne's side, remembering at last to draw his blaster. Halfrid Brandr and perhaps half a dozen others stood at bay, trying not to see the ghosts that faced them. Ume-Kai was watching them, a cold smile on his face, drawing out the moment. He was waiting too long, Rehur thought; in another minute, they'll break the spell, someone'll move, and we'll all get killed. He stepped forward, momentarily displacing the minne.

"All right," Rehur said, pitching his voice to carry to the guards outside as well. "You're facing a metaphysical problem, sors and amas—one that may rapidly become a physical problem. We are ghosts, as you can plainly see—or rather, as you can plainly not see. But we can see you, and we are armed and extremely unhappy. If you don't back away from that control console, sors, you will die truedeath." He smiled maliciously, deliberately borrowing Ume-Kai's style of speech. "Of course, if you do, you'll be ghosts. As I said, a metaphysical problem."

There was a long silence. Halfrid's face writhed as he tried to suppress his anger, and Rehur felt the insane desire to giggle. The others—he recognized the Jan Holder, and the Fira Holder, and knew he'd seen some of the others when the Kinships met for the Ship's Council—stood very still, apparently oblivious to his speech. Then, very slowly, Halfrid turned on his heel until he'd turned his back on the waiting ghosts.

"Ramaht!" he said, voice hoarse with strain. "Trigger the charges!"

Rehur lifted the blaster and heard, from behind his

right shoulder, the harsh sound of a crossbow being drawn to full cock. The young man sitting at the control console hesitated, hands held well away from the keys.

"That's enough," an older man, blond and thin-faced, said sharply. "Ramaht, don't touch a thing."

Halfrid wheeled on him, face purpling. "How dare you interfere, Anath?"

"This has gone too far," the blond answered. "Stennet, Soem, Hesed, I put it to you that we've reached stalemate, and in honor the only thing left for us is to negotiate."

"I agree!" That was the Fira Holder, stepping quickly around the edge of a secondary console. "We've got to talk."

The Jan Holder hesitated, then nodded reluctantly. "I agree, too," she said.

"How can you do this to me?" Halfrid demanded. "Where's your loyalty to the Kinship?"

Soem Jan turned on him. "If you'd had any sense, this wouldn't've happened. Damn you, Halfrid!"

The third man—he had to be either the Erling or the Elgeve Holder, though Rehur was not sure which—nodded slowly. "All right, Anath, I agree."

Anath nodded. "Good. Olen, raise Madelgar. Tell them we want to talk." He paused, mouth twisting bitterly. "Tell them what's happened."

"You're dead now," Halfrid cried.

The communications technician bent to obey, ignoring the Patriarch's shout.

"You're all dead," Halfrid said again. Rehur took a step forward, the wild elation cracking into a monstrous anger, and seized the genarch by the collar.

"Oh, no, I'm not dead," he said softly, fiercely. "I'm very much alive. All of us are—and we're not going to play dead ever again." With a sudden effort, he threw Halfrid bodily away from him. The Patriarch stumbled against the nearest console, almost tripping over its chair. After a moment, he subsided into it, his expression almost childishly bewildered.

"Sor," the technician said. "Madelgar wants to know who's calling."

Anath sighed. "Tell them Anath Brandr," he said. "I speak for the Kinship now."

Rehur closed his eyes, not knowing, suddenly, if he should laugh or cry, wanting to do both. They'd won, they'd saved Destiny—but he'd changed everything. Nothing could be the same again, for better or for worse: the Necropolis, the world he'd loved best, had ended.

Chapter 15: Trey Maturin

The call from Destiny reached us just before the eighteenth hour. I started at the sound, almost dropping the glass of tea I'd been nursing for the past hour, and Alkres gave a little cry of alarm. Leith, who'd been asleep on a pile of cargo pads, sat up quickly, going from sleep to waking in one smooth movement. Before she could say anything, however, the technician whispered a curse, and turned the volume to full, his eyes wide.

The voice that boomed from the speaker was familiar— the same technician we'd been dealing with for the past six hours—but the words were not. "I am instructed to inform you that we are no longer in uncontested control of the power plant, and that we wish to discuss terms by which we may come to some peaceful settlement."

I drew a slow, shaken breath, wondering what had happened. At my side, Alkres gave a little bounce of sheer delight. Leith said, with startling calm, "Ask him to explain what he means by 'no longer in uncontested control.'"

Terend, who had ousted our technician from the seat in front of the console at the first words from Destiny, relayed the question. There was a brief silence, broken only by the whisper of static, and then the Brandr technician

364

said, with audible reluctance, "The power plant has been entered by ghosts acting on behalf of the Halex, who are currently holding the main control room."

Leith whistled softly, and Alkres said, "That means *they're* dead, too, all the Brandr." His smile faded slightly, and he looked up at me. "Doesn't it?"

"The hell with that," Leith said. "They're willing to negotiate." She turned back to Terend. "That doesn't sound like Halfrid to me. Who's speaking for them?"

Alkres was frowning now, looking puzzled. "Aren't they dead?" he asked again. "And aren't we dead if we talk to them?" I could see the same question on the faces of the Halex around me.

I took a deep breath, searching for the words that would convince them all that the world had already changed, and that nothing would be gained by fighting it. "Under the strictest code, I suppose they would be, and so would we," I said, calling back the tricks I'd learned as an actor to project my voice to the farthest corners of the hull. "But the strict code has been broken so many times already that I don't think we can ask anyone to follow it now. Besides, the whole purpose of the code is to make sure that right is done, isn't it? I think talking now—before more people are killed, more things destroyed, which will happen if we don't negotiate—is the only right thing to do." I was counting on my medium's status to add force to my words. I watched the faces as I talked. There was less whole-hearted acceptance than I'd hoped for, but there was a sort of agreement, the slightly shamefaced agreement of people who've been given a dubious excuse to do something they wanted to do anyway. But it was still agreement. Alkres nodded slowly.

"I see that."

"Trey!" Leith beckoned me over to the communications console. I muttered my excuses to Alkres, damning the woman for her bad timing, and moved to join her.

"Do you know anything about an Anath Brandr?" Leith asked. "He says he's speaking for the Brandr now."

I nodded. "That's maybe the best thing that could happen. He was a voice of reason at Ixora's trial, tried to stop the whole thing. We're in luck, Leith."

Leith nodded back, and said into the pickup, "All right, Anath, we're willing to talk with you."

It took us until mid-morning of the next calendar-day to work out the details of their surrender and all the safe-guards for our return to Destiny—and for their return to Madelgar—but by clock-noon, the first hour of Sunset, the first flyers lifted for Destiny.

There was still the larger question to settle—a question that had grown from a mere Halex/Brandr feud to some-thing that involved all five Kinships. Here, almost too late, I was able to act as a mediator, nudging the genarchs toward a workable solution, smoothing over the last rough spots created by the code. Even Araxie Fyfe came to terms at last. Only Halfrid resisted, unable really to un-derstand what was happening, and he was gently but firmly eased out of the Kinship government. The whole question was clearly too big for the Ship's Council, or for any existing governmental body. After weeks of talking, the genarchs agreed to create a new assembly, one that would represent ghosts and *para'anin* as well as the living. Ume-Kai, the minne who'd led the attack on the power plant, and the president of the Streetwalkers' Tong were the ghosts' rep-resentatives from the Halex Mandate. I looked for Rehur among their party—after all, he'd been a leader of their group, too, there at the last—but he was nowhere to be found. The other ghosts and *para'anin* were strangers, the latter drawn mostly from the various unions' upper echelons.

Once the assembly began to meet, there was little that I could do to influence its decisions. I was too closely associ-ated with the Halex to be accepted as an independent voice. I was forced to watch from the sidelines, unable to act, while the discussions went on without me. It was intensely frustrating, made worse by the fact that Leith had somehow managed to become an acknowledged part of the assembly—in effect, its mediator. I told myself that it was just the differences of training and situation, but I couldn't help being jealous of her position. I knew then it was time to leave Orestes.

Alkres, acting now under the advice of the Ingvarr and Ansson Holders, as well as the new Rhawn Holder, Yslin's sister, agreed to release me from my contract on the pro-viso that I find another mediator to replace me. I agreed, glad of the work, and threw myself into those negotiations. Then, quite suddenly, it was over. Anë Emilat, an old acquaintance from Baldur, agreed to take the job, and I was left with nothing to do for a calendar-week until she arrived.

I tried to stay away from the assembly and from the people I'd known at the Tower—they were doing effective, important things, and I was left impotent—but it was hard to find any substitute for politics. The Necropolis, open now in the Day as well as the Dark, was wholly changed. The theater still functioned, except for the cross-talk companies, which were slowly dying, deprived of the spice of the forbidden, but the plays had lost the context that gave them edge and meaning. It would come back—I hoped—when things were settled, but for now it was the ghost of its former self. I could not find Rehur, or any of the members of Witchwood.

In the end, I found myself back at the stadthall where the assembly met, watching the debates from the visitors' gallery. Viewed dispassionately, things were changing for the better: already, there was a commitment to a written constitution that would explicitly supersede any social code, and the class of "ghost" was to be outlawed. The greatest debate was over what should be done about the *para'anin*—and, the reverse of that question, how much of code and Kinship could be retained. And much would be retained, as custom if not as law, that much was clear.

At the midday break, I followed the crowd from the gallery, but instead of heading outside to the dozens of vendors' carts drawn up in the Stadthall Square or to any of the restaurants nearby, I made my way through the side corridors to the Stadthall Garden. I'd discovered it almost by accident during the negotiations that created the assembly—a small, almost pitlike room lit by a massive stained glass rosette that was either a skylight or a particularly sophisticated lamp. Nothing really grew in this garden; instead, the floor was spread with silver-white gravel, stones—crystal, faux-agate, goldstone, all the mineral wealth of Orestes and Electra—rising like islands from that severe sea, their colors changing in the glow of the rosette. It was a wonderfully serene place, and I felt the need of its calm.

I turned the last corner, pushing through the faded

curtain onto the little balcony that ran the length of one wall before leading into the twisted stair that brought one down into the garden proper. I started along the balcony, and was suddenly aware of rising voices. Someone was here before me. I hesitated, knowing myself hidden by the balcony columns, and glanced cautiously down onto the well-raked gravel.

Leith stood there, hands on hips, confronting a taller, fairer woman. I hadn't seen Guil since Madelgar; for a moment, that memory swam before me, chillingly real. Then I shook myself, forcing myself to see the *para'an* as she really was. She had somehow changed since our flight to Electra, though I could not quite define how she was different. Her mouth still held the same stern line, and her eyes were still unreadable beneath the halo of straw-blond hair. Then I realized what it was: the feral wariness—the sense of something coiled and waiting, balanced on the edge—was gone. She was not as dangerous as she once was, and perhaps more vulnerable.

The two women had been talking while I stood there, their voices too low to carry to me. I started to back away, leaving them to their discussion, when Guil's voice rose suddenly.

"I don't know! Hell, I don't like myself any more!"

Leith took a step forward, holding out her hand. Guil shook her head and turned away, starting up the staircase to the balcony. Before I could make my escape, she'd brushed past me and was gone. I took a step backward, wanting to get away, and Leith called, "Trey?"

Reluctantly, I stepped forward, and leaned over the balcony rail. "Leith, I'm sorry. I didn't mean to intrude."

Moraghan shook her head and motioned for me to join her in the garden. "You didn't, really," she said. "Anyway, I've been wanting to talk to you."

There was no polite way to refuse her. Unwillingly, I made my way down the stairs and stepped out onto the sand, marred now by two sets of footprints. Leith seated herself on the nearest of the rocks, legs crossed, gloved arm held close to her body. She was wearing Oresteian clothes now, knitted to her size, but she still wore the long glove, hiding the maimed arm.

"I hear you're leaving soon," she said, after a moment.

"That's right." I sat on the edge of a great chunk of faux-agate the size and shape of a small tambour, waiting to see what would happen. I was still jealous of her, of her position on the planet, and fiercely embarrassed that I'd been so inept as to witness the scene between her and Guil. I did my best to stay impassive, knowing I was being unreasonable, but I was certain she'd see.

Leith looked away, staring at her booted foot, and I realized abruptly that she was almost as uncomfortable as I was. "I won't be leaving," she said, after a moment.

"You're staying with Guil?" I asked, involuntarily.

"Yes." For a moment, Leith glared at me; then, with an effort, she relaxed a little. "If and when she'll have me. But I'd've stayed anyway. I think—I know I'm needed here. I haven't been needed in a long time."

"But with Guil?" I asked, more gently this time.

Leith stared at me, visibly fighting back anger. "I want to. As for what she did—I don't condone it, but good God, I can understand it. The way they've treated her, the way they've treated all *para'anin*—" She broke off, and went on, more calmly, "I saw this kind of thing before, when I was with the Peacekeepers—people who didn't know just how angry they were until it was too late and they'd done something crazy."

I looked away in my turn. Leith was right, I supposed, though the images of Madelgar still swam in my mind. Guil's exultant face as she left that blood-smeared cellar was too clear for comfort. It had been a dreadful revenge. Guil knew what she had done, too—*I don't like myself*, she had said—and that wouldn't make things any easier for Leith. But Leith was the Peacekeeper; as she'd said, she'd dealt with this sort of thing before. "What will you be doing?" I asked, trying to express an interest, a sympathy, I didn't entirely feel.

"I'll be a sort of grand arbiter," she answered, and gave a little, almost embarrassed shrug. "They understand the Oath, why I did what I did. And I understand the code."

I nodded, slowly, the envy draining away. She did understand the code, probably better than I ever could—she felt it, grasped instinctively the emotional nuances that had always defeated me—but she did so because she had been a Peacekeeper, and the Peacekeepers followed a

code as demanding and complex, if more flexible, as the
Oresteians'. I hadn't committed myself—couldn't commit
myself, not merely if I was to remain a mediator, but also
because it wasn't in me to give myself unreservedly to
anything. I had done everything I could for Alkres, and for
Orestes as a whole; the sad thing was, a mediator with
Leith's temperament could probably have done it better. I
sighed, recognizing a painful truth. "I wish you the best of
luck, Leith."

"Thank you." She nodded, gravely. "We'll manage, Trey,
I promise."

I saw Rehur a final time, the night before I was to leave.
He was ill at ease in the Family townhouse, and, I thought,
uneasy without the protection of the ghostmark. We made
love again, because it was easier than talking, and afterward things were a little better, raising the memory of that
first night in the Necropolis. He was going off-world himself, he said, as soon as Rowan and Ash could raise the
final freight payment. Witchwood was planning to compete in the Lesser Dramatists', the month-long open competition on Dionysus. If they won, he reminded me eagerly,
they would be allowed to enter the Greater Dramatists',
competing against groups with Conglomerate-wide reputa-
tions. I knew the dream perfectly well—I'd left Athene
myself in pursuit of it—and I'd learned the odds against it
since then, but I wished him luck all the same. He had the
potential to be a better actor than I had been, I suspected,
and I hoped he would fulfill it.

We said goodbye at the back gate of the townhouse, and
I let him out into the cool light of Sunrise. We stood for a
moment on opposite sides of the gate, staring up at waning
Agamemnon. A single strand of cloud bisected its arc,
turning it into a giant cabalistic symbol scrawled across the
sky. It was cold still—it was always cold—and I clutched
the cloak Rohin had given me even closer around my
shoulders. It had survived the attack on the Tower and the
fire of Madelgar almost untouched, only a few scorch
marks on its leather. I had decided weeks before that I
would keep it, regardless of the weight restrictions: there
were things about Orestes that were worth remembering,
and Rohin was one of them.

"You will look me up, if you get to Dionysus?" Rehur asked, for the third time.

"If it works out, sure." I knew better than to promise more—let him get settled in the Urban Worlds, first, prove to himself that he was no longer anyone's ghost, and only then could we even think of creating a relationship—but still it was hard to keep my voice casual. I touched his shoulder, pulled him into a final embrace, then set him gently away from me. "The best of luck, Rehur—to all of you."

The actor nodded, accepting the finality of my words. "I will see you again," he said, and stepped away, lifting a hand in farewell. I watched him walk down the narrow street, and did not step back into the house until he'd turned the corner out of sight. I also knew better than to rely too much on such promises; still, I couldn't stop myself from hoping just a little.

Eight hours later, under the clearing Morning sky, I left Orestes.

Excerpted from the CRO Planetary Survey Pamphlets, 3rd series: Orestes/Electra, *pub/protect date 1499.003 PoDr. Used by the kind permission of the Conglomerate Records Office, Baldur.*
Holidays observed system-wide:
. . . .Mediation Day:

  To encourage the resolution of public and private differences through mutual compromise. It is considered particularly appropriate to settle lawsuits, private quarrels, etc., on this day, or during the week preceding. Honors Trey Maturin, Conglomerate mediator responsible for the creation of the Grand Assembly (1428 PoDr). . . .

******

ROBERT A. HEINLEIN

"Heinlein knows more about blending provocative scientific thinking with strong human stories than any dozen other contemporary science fiction writers."
—*Chicago Sun-Times*

"Robert A. Heinlein wears imagination as though it were his private suit of clothes. What makes his work so rich is that he combines his lively, creative sense with an approach that is at once literate, informed, and exciting." —*New York Times*

Seven of Robert A. Heinlein's best-loved titles are now available in superbly packaged new Baen editions, with embossed series-look covers by artist John Melo. Collect them all by sending in the order form below:

REVOLT IN 2100, 65589-2, $3.50		☐
METHUSELAH'S CHILDREN, 65597-3, $3.50		☐
THE GREEN HILLS OF EARTH, 65608-2, $3.50		☐
THE MAN WHO SOLD THE MOON, 65623-6, $3.50		☐
THE MENACE FROM EARTH*, 65636-8, $3.50		☐
ASSIGNMENT IN ETERNITY**, 65637-6, $3.50		☐
SIXTH COLUMN***, 65638-4, $3.50		☐

*To be published May 1987. **To be published July 1987. ***To be published October 1987. Any books ordered prior to publication date will be shipped at no extra charge as soon as they are available.

Please send me the books I have checked above. I enclose a check or money order for the combined cover price for the titles I have ordered, plus 75 cents for first-class postage and handling (for any number of titles) made out to Baen Books, Dept. B, 260 Fifth Avenue, New York, N.Y. 10001.